SWEET CAROLINE

Noah hated to see Caroline in such distress. "Do you want me to talk to this Tim? Ask him to stop bothering you?"

Caroline whirled around, her expression an odd mixture of shame and gratitude. "*Neh*, that's not necessary. It's just that—" She took a deep breath and then blurted, "Tim wants me to bring my boyfriend to the game."

Boyfriend? The word punched Noah in the gut.

"Except I don't have one, so Tim meant you. I guess he believed us the other day. And I came here to ask you to pretend again, but I realize it isn't right. I was letting my pride get in the way, but I deserve to be embarrassed."

Her sentences whizzed out like a train whooshing down the tracks at full speed. Noah tried to follow her reasoning, but she'd jumped from one subject to the next.

"Whoa, slow down. I'm trying to understand. Tim wants you to bring your boyfriend?"

The rest of her nattering was slowly sinking in. *Ach*, Tim believed Noah was Caroline's boyfriend after their pretense. But he didn't see how that connected to her embarrassment. Unless she was ashamed she didn't have a boyfriend?

Then it hit him. The lunch. A favor. Caroline wanted him to be that boyfriend . . .

Books by Rachel J. Good

HIS UNEXPECTED AMISH TWINS

HIS PRETEND AMISH BRIDE

HIS ACCIDENTAL AMISH FAMILY

AN UNEXPECTED AMISH PROPOSAL

AN UNEXPECTED AMISH COURTSHIP

AN UNEXPECTED AMISH CHRISTMAS

AN AMISH MARRIAGE OF CONVENIENCE

HER PRETEND AMISH BOYFRIEND

Published by Kensington Publishing Corp.

HER PRETEND
AMISH
BOYFRIEND

SURPRISED BY LOVE

RACHEL J. GOOD

ZEBRA BOOKS
Kensington Publishing Corp.
www.kensingtonbooks.com

ZEBRA BOOKS are published by

Kensington Publishing Corp.
119 West 40th Street
New York, NY 10018

All Kensington titles, imprints, and distributed lines are available at special quantity discounts for bulk purchases for sales promotion, premiums, fund-raising, and educational or institutional use.

Special book excerpts or customized printings can also be created to fit specific needs. For details, write or phone the office of the Kensington Sales Manager: Kensington Publishing Corp., 119 West 40th Street, New York, NY 10018. Attn. Sales Department. Phone: 1-800-221-2647.

Zebra and the Z logo Reg. U.S. Pat. & TM Off.
BOUQUET Reg. U.S. Pat. & TM Off.

First Printing: July 2023
ISBN-13: 978-1-4201-5464-1
ISBN-13: 978-1-4201-5465-8 (eBook)

10 9 8 7 6 5 4 3 2 1

Printed in the United States of America

CHAPTER 1

As the spiked volleyball whizzed to the ground on the other side of the net, Caroline Hartzler whooped. They'd done it! They'd beaten the other team after tying the score twice. She high-fived the boy next to her, who'd made the final point.

"We did it!" She jumped into the air, arms spread overhead in victory.

"Caroline?" Anna Mary tugged at Caroline's elbow and whispered, "Calm down. You're the loudest one here."

Her best friend's words sloshed over Caroline like a pitcher of ice-cold lemonade. Once again, Caroline had let loose in her exuberance. She wilted and followed Anna Mary off the court.

"That's better," her friend said. "The whooping was a bit much."

"But we won the whole tournament." Caroline wiped the sweat trickling down her face. "Aren't you excited?" They'd been playing all day under the hot sun against fierce competition from youth groups from other *g'mays*.

"I'd be more excited if you hadn't done that pancake."

Caroline reached for a cup of water. "If I hadn't, we'd have lost the game." Her dive and slide had kept the ball from hitting the ground. And it allowed her teammate to make the final spike. Too bad the pancake had dirtied the whole front of her apron. Mamm wouldn't be happy. She'd warned Caroline to be careful before she left this morning.

Anna Mary sighed and shook her head. "I thought we agreed that you'd be quieter and less . . . less—"

"Of a show-off," Caroline finished for her.

"That wasn't what I planned to say," Anna Mary protested.

"But it was what you meant."

All around them players were shaking hands and congratulating each other. Caroline needed to get over there and tell the other team they'd played a good game. She gulped her water so fast she choked.

"Can't you do anything slowly?" Anna Mary tucked a few loose strands of Caroline's hair under her *kapp*.

Caroline drew in a long, deep breath. She loved her friend, but Anna Mary was starting to sound like Mamm. *Be more ladylike*, her mother warned all the time. *Slow down. Be quiet, be gentle, be calm.* Now Anna Mary was echoing all of Mamm's warnings.

Nobody seemed to understand how hard that was for Caroline. To be fair, though, she had asked Anna Mary for reminders. Caroline tamped down her irritation. She shouldn't complain—not even internally—about Anna Mary's advice.

"I'll try." Caroline forced herself to stroll toward the other players rather than sprint. As usual, she complimented each opposing player for at least one or two of their best moves.

"Great shoulder roll," she said to one.

He grinned. "Are you going to try it next time? If so, you're welcome to play on my team."

Two of his teammates smirked.

Caroline's cheeks heated, and tears stung the back of her eyes. She couldn't do that somersaulting move, not in a dress, and he knew it. He'd been trying to humiliate her, but she wouldn't let him know he'd succeeded. She acted as if he'd been serious. "*Danke* so much for inviting me," she said graciously, "but I'd prefer to play on a winning team."

As they passed her, one of the boys dug an elbow into the cheeky one's side. "She sure put you in your place."

His other friend laughed. "Guess it's not a good idea to tease a girl who's willing to pancake. She'll win every time."

The sour expression on the young man's face told Caroline she'd made an enemy. Someone like that didn't take kindly to being bested. And she'd not only won their verbal exchange, she'd also spiked the next-to-the-last point right at his feet.

"Looks like you upset him." Anna Mary came up beside her and tilted her chin toward the grumbling boy.

"I didn't mean to." Caroline never wanted to hurt anyone. Sometimes her outspokenness got her in trouble. She dashed after him, ignoring Anna Mary calling her name. "I'm sorry. I didn't mean to hurt your feelings. Will you forgive me?"

From the tight line of his mouth, she'd only made things worse. And she'd put him on the spot. Now he'd have to agree.

His curt *jah* revealed his reluctance.

She waited a moment in case he wanted to apologize to

her, but he didn't reciprocate. She turned to go but couldn't help overhearing his friends chuckling.

"Hurt your feelings? She thinks she hurt your feelings?"

Ach, why didn't she think before she spoke? She should have just apologized, not let her tongue run away with her.

Anna Mary caught up with her. "I guess we'll have to cross those three off the list of your dating possibilities."

Did her friend need to rub it in? Anna Mary, who'd recently started courting, despaired of Caroline ever finding a boyfriend. All the boys at church picked Caroline first for volleyball and baseball teams, and they enjoyed the fun ideas she came up with for group activities, but none of them had ever asked her to ride home after a singing.

And the one time she'd thought she'd found the perfect man for her, it had ended in disaster. Nobody, not even her own family or Anna Mary, knew the truth about that. Caroline usually blabbed about every detail of her life, but she'd kept most of that a secret. And she always would.

According to Anna Mary, Caroline's personality scared off possible dates. She was too outgoing, too open, too exuberant. Caroline understood her friend's point, but changing herself seemed impossible. It wouldn't be easy, but maybe she could find someone who'd appreciate her the way God made her.

Lord, I know that's a huge request, but can You help me find the right man for me?

"Caroline?" Anna Mary jostled her elbow. "Don't you have to get to work?"

Ach, she'd forgotten all about that. She'd promised her brother she'd be there as soon as the game ended. The Green Valley Farmer's Market stayed open until seven on Fridays. If she hurried, she might make it before the after-school and after-work crowds arrived. "But what am I going to do about my apron?" She couldn't work at the chicken barbecue stand with a dirt-smeared apron.

"Here." Anna Mary unpinned her apron. "Trade with me. I'll wash yours and give it back at church on Sunday."

"I can't let you do that."

"You don't have much choice, do you? Your brother needs you." Anna Mary thrust her apron into Caroline's hands. "That's what friends are for. You'd do the same for me."

"Of course I would, but you'd never slide across the ground."

"Just give me your apron. I'm standing here without one."

"I'm sorry." Caroline rushed to remove her apron and give it to her friend. "I'll make it up to you. And you don't have to wash it."

"Let's get going. I need to get home to help Mamm with supper."

Twenty minutes later, Anna Mary pulled her buggy into the auction parking lot. "Sorry for parking so far away from the market entrance, but I think it'll be faster for you to get out here."

"You're right."

A long line of cars waited to turn into the market parking lot. From this back parking lot, Caroline could cut through the auction storeroom and go through the side doors into the market. This heavy traffic meant the Friday rush had begun already. A lot of people picked up chicken for dinner on their way home. Her brother needed her. He'd be worried about her being so late.

She hopped out and waved. "*Danke* for dropping me

off." Then she barreled toward the nearest doors. Banged through them. And smacked into a hard chest.

Crash! Two crates hit the floor, sending little wooden pieces flying everywhere.

A man grasped her arms to keep her from falling. "Are you all right?"

"*Ach*, I'm fine." Or she would be. The collision had knocked her dizzy. Or maybe being so close to a man, inhaling the laundry-fresh scent of his shirt . . . Caroline took two unsteady steps back.

He didn't release his grip. "Are you sure? You look shaky."

Caroline turned her attention away from his piercing blue eyes. All around them, small colored bits of wood lay scattered. Still breathless, she nodded toward the pieces with her chin. "Let me, um, help you clean up." It would make her extra late for helping her brother, but she couldn't leave this mess. Not when it had been her fault.

Noah stared down at the pretty blonde in his arms. He should let go, but she'd gut-punched him in more ways than one.

"I'm so sorry." She bit her lip. "I seem to do nothing but cause problems today."

The tears shining in her green eyes made him want to comfort her. He couldn't decide if he'd like the teardrops to keep shimmering on her lashes or if he'd rather they'd slide down her soft cheeks so he could wipe them away with his fingertips. His heart urged him to pull her closer. But his head won.

He dropped his hands to his sides and forced his gaze

from hers. "Don't worry about it. You're in a hurry. I'll clean up." All he wanted to do was shoo her through the opposite door to wherever she'd been going.

"That's not fair. I can't leave you with all the work." She squatted. "What are these?"

"Pieces to jigsaw puzzles."

"But they're wood. I've only ever seen cardboard ones this small." Many Amish woodworkers made wooden children's puzzles, but these seemed much too tiny for children.

"They're from the early nineteen-hundreds."

She scooped up a handful and dumped them into the closest crate. "They all have smooth or bumpy sides. Where are the little tabs to hook them together?"

"They don't have any. The pieces just slide next to each other." Although Noah should appreciate her help, she was sweeping all the pieces together. "Listen, it would be better if I do this to keep them from getting too mixed up. They each need to go back into a certain box." Although they'd gotten jumbled, he could gather the ones closest to each box. That would make them easier to sort.

"And I'm only making it worse for you. I'm so sorry."

The wetness shining in her eyes touched him. "It's all right. I'll just take these off the auction list for tonight. It'll give me plenty of time to sort them later. Besides, you should go. Aren't you late?" Noah fervently hoped her answer would be *jah*.

She sucked in a breath. "I forgot all about my brother. He'll be swamped with customers." Jumping to her feet, she said, "I'll come back after closing and sort them into the correct boxes."

"Don't worry about it. I can do it." He didn't have

anything else to do tonight except return to his lonely home—if you could call a rented RV a home. And he certainly didn't need her around disturbing his peace of mind.

But as she rushed away, Noah couldn't keep his eyes off her. The only sane thought he had was that he needed to stay as far away from her as he could. If he didn't, she'd knock down all his carefully constructed defenses.

CHAPTER 2

Caroline zigzagged through the crowds and skidded to a halt near her family's stand. The line stretched from the center of the market around the aisle and out the door. Most of the people who'd been blocking her entrance stood waiting for chicken.

Her brother, Gideon, and their sister-in-law Nettie, were racing around trying to wait on people while Aidan lifted two French fry baskets from the oil at once. Caroline scurried in to help.

Gideon slid a whole chicken into a foil-lined bag. "Thank heavens you're here. We really need you."

"I'll wash my hands and be right there." She squeezed past Nettie, who was dipping out potato salad, and turned on the water at the sink.

As she soaped her hands, Caroline winced at her fingernails. After diving onto the ground and making that final volleyball save, she'd slid another few feet and dug her hands in the dirt to stop.

What had that auctioneer thought when she'd scooped up the puzzle pieces? Not only had she been mixing them up, making his work harder, but he must have been cringing at her filthy hands fingering the antiques. She scrubbed extra hard at her nails. Customers here at the stand wouldn't appreciate someone waiting on them like that either. When she went back to help the auctioneer, she'd make sure her fingers and nails were spotless.

"What took you so long?" Gideon asked as she slipped into place at the cash register. He lowered the customer's tray so she could see the items and ring them up.

"The tournament ran longer than usual. But we won!" Caroline reached for the cash the customer handed her and made change.

"Hey, that's great." Her brother flashed her a congratulatory grin.

"And then—" Caroline hesitated a second. Maybe she shouldn't tell him about the puzzle accident.

Before she could decide, Gideon held up a hand. "I want to hear all about it, but let's save it for after the rush."

Once again, she'd been thinking only of herself. She wished she'd learn to think of others before she did things to bother them.

After that, she stuck to food-related conversations and moved customers through the line swiftly, but did it with a genuine smile and caring attitude. The remaining hours passed quickly in a blur of to-go orders and trays for customers who chose to eat at the small café tables near their stand. They ran out of chicken ten minutes before closing, disappointing several customers, who turned away. Others ordered salads to take home.

Caroline breathed a sigh of relief when Gideon slipped out to lock the market doors at seven. "Wait," she called after him. She dashed to catch up. "I want to get out the side door to the auction."

"I'll open it for you later if you can't go around to the employee exit. Nettie needs help cleaning up."

"I can't." She darted past her brother. "I have to fix a mess I made at the auction. Besides, I covered for Nettie yesterday."

"Caroline!" Gideon's voice trailed after her, but she ignored his call and rushed through the door. Outside, people packed the auction tent, waiting in breathless anticipation for the next item. The auctioneer's patter began, one word sliding into the next in an unbroken rhythm of beautiful up-and-down trills. Caroline always admired the way they spoke so rapidly, yet they managed to make themselves understood. And they built the crowd's eagerness into a frenzy. A frenzy that raised bids, again and again, convincing even reluctant tightwads to go higher and higher.

She stopped in her tracks. This auctioneer not only had the best patter she'd ever heard, he also held the audience spellbound. And while he mesmerized those inside the tent, he also attracted Caroline's full attention. The man she'd run into earlier had been attractive up close, and he didn't lose any of that appeal on the stage.

Even as her pulse pitter-pattered, her brain sent out a warning. She'd made a fool of herself before over an auctioneer. Never again would she make that mistake.

To avoid him, she'd sneak into the building, sort the puzzle pieces, and leave before he finished. He still had quite a few goods lined up to auction, so he'd probably be occupied for a while. She'd finish as much as possible and slip out the far door before he returned.

Caroline hurried past the tent and eased open the storeroom door so she didn't bump into anyone. But the room appeared empty. She had no idea where to find the puzzles. She checked row after row of shelves filled with crates

Rachel J. Good

like the ones she'd spilled, but none held loose puzzle pieces.

"What are you doing in here?" a loud voice barked behind her.

She whirled around. Fred Evans, the assistant manager of the auction, stood, hands planted on his hips, glaring at her.

"I, um—" Would the auctioneer get in trouble if she mentioned the spilled crates? Like Fred's older brother, Russell, who used to manage the market before he got hauled off to jail, Fred had an explosive temper.

"Don't tell me." His mocking tone matched his sarcastic expression. "You're here to chase after another auctioneer."

Caroline bit her lip and tried not to show how much his words hurt. That relationship had humiliated her enough. And Fred knew it. He didn't have to be cruel and rub it in. "No, I'm not."

"Somehow, I don't quite believe you." A calculating look lit his eyes. "Oh-ho, just so happens we have a brand-new auctioneer. You're here to see Noah Riehl, aren't you?"

"Nooo." Her hesitant answer didn't sound convincing. But it was true. She wasn't planning to see Noah.

Fred laughed. "You're not a very good liar. I want you out of here before he gets done."

That wouldn't be a problem. She intended to avoid Noah.

"And stay away from my building. If I catch you in here again, I won't hesitate to call the police to report an intruder."

Straightening her back, Caroline added tartness to her

voice. "I'm not an intruder, and you know it. I work at the market." Her brother Gideon managed the market now, and he'd vouch for her. "I only came in here to fix something."

"Fix something? What would you be fixing in here?" He loomed over her and leaned in close.

Caroline shivered inside. His brother had gone to jail. For all she knew, Fred might be a criminal too.

The door banged open. Noah stopped in the doorway, his attention fixed on her. "What are you doing here?" His question didn't sound as mean as Fred's had. He just seemed confused.

"That's what I asked her," Fred said.

"I told you I'd take care of it." Noah met her eyes, and Caroline's heart bumped against her ribs.

She averted her gaze and hoped Fred couldn't hear the thumping. Fred stepped back a little as Noah approached.

"That's not fair." Caroline didn't feel right making Noah sort out the spill. "It was my fault."

"But—" He shot a wary glance at Fred, whose attention ping-ponged between them.

"And just what does she think you need her for?"

Noah, who stood more than a head taller than Fred, glanced down at him. "A project she offered to help with."

Fred turned to Caroline. "Well, he's made it clear he doesn't need you, and I've already told you to get out, so what are you waiting for?"

Shocked, Noah stared at Fred. "I didn't say that. And there's no need to be rude." Noah sent an apologetic glance to Caroline.

Fury blazing in his eyes, Fred turned on Noah. "I don't

want you fraternizing with other employees. Women employees."

"I have no intention of doing that." Noah frosted his words with ice.

"Good thing. Because it can get messy. If you don't believe me, ask Caroline here." Fred gestured toward her. "I lost a good employee, and it's all her fault."

Her stomach clenched. Why did he have to embarrass her like this? At least she'd already decided to stay away from Noah. Fred exposing her painful secret made it even more important to avoid Noah.

Caroline lifted her chin and did her best to maintain her dignity. "As long as you don't need me, I'll be going. I have plenty of work back at the stand."

Surprise flashed in Noah's eyes along with a hint of admiration. Then she flounced toward the door. She wouldn't let Fred get the better of her.

Noah couldn't let her walk off like that without an apology. If Fred wouldn't do it, Noah would do it for both of them.

"Wait," he called, and hurried to catch up to her. "Sorry. I don't want you to think—" He lifted his hands and shoulders in a shrug. "You know." He tilted his head slightly in Fred's direction. "*Danke* for coming to help. That was kind of you."

"You're welcome. I'd still like to fix the, um, problem."

He shook his head. "No need."

"If you're sure?"

Jah, he was sure. Very sure. Having her around would be too much of a distraction. "I have it all under control."

Cleaning up puzzle pieces, that is. He couldn't say the same about his emotions.

"Very touching." Fred sneered. "What are you doing back here anyway? You should be out there working. I'll be docking your pay for this time."

"I'm on my fifteen-minute break, and Butch wanted a turn with the mic. I came back here to see what I could prep for tomorrow."

Butch, Fred's spoiled eighteen-year-old son, loved to be in the spotlight even though he'd never really gotten the hang of the patter or coaxing an audience to buy, so they didn't make nearly as much money when he sold the goods.

Fred looked apoplectic. "Get out there now and take that mic away from him."

"If you say so."

"I do. Butch is not supposed to be onstage on Friday nights or Saturdays when we have our largest audiences. Go tell him I have an appointment, so he needs to lock up tonight." Fred fired a nasty look past Noah. "And you get out of here before I call the police."

Noah froze. *The police?* But Fred had focused on Caroline. What had she done?

"I didn't do anything, and you know it," she shot back.

Impressed by her spunk, Noah smiled at her. Fred intimidated most of the workers here at the auction. It was nice to see someone stand up to his bullying.

When her wide, generous mouth curved upward, sickness curled in his stomach. He'd let his admiration show, and she'd responded in kind. He'd made a terrible mistake.

"Don't tell me you didn't come in here to chase another auctioneer, Caroline Hartzler. That was an outright lie."

Her cheeks turned a lovely shade of pink. "It was not."

Fred snickered. "Then why are the two of you standing there staring at each other like a pair of lovesick teenagers?"

That sobered Noah. He'd let down his guard. Much too dangerous.

Caroline stood there with a stricken look on her face, and Noah's heart went out to her.

"Just ignore him," Noah whispered. "Come on. Let's go. I'll walk you out."

She glanced up at him, gratitude in her eyes. That look could easily melt a man's resolve. Noah steeled himself.

Caroline had the most expressive face he'd ever seen. A real contrast to him. He tried never to let his emotions show. Openness like that made her appealing. And spelled trouble. Big trouble.

CHAPTER 3

As Noah opened the door and ushered Caroline toward the market, Fred banged out the exit on the opposite side.

Caroline slowed her steps. "Once Fred's gone, I can work on sorting out the puzzles."

"*Neh*." The word exploded from Noah's lips. "You can't take that chance. He threatened to call the police."

She tossed her head. "I'm not afraid of the police. I wouldn't be doing anything wrong."

A strange expression crossed Noah's face, and his lips twisted into a wry smile. "Sometimes that doesn't matter. Besides, Fred told you to stay out, so you'd be trespassing."

"I have as much right to be in there as Fred does. My brother is in charge of Green Valley Market, so he has some say. And Mrs. Vandenberg's the real owner. She'll put Fred in his place." After she blurted out the words, Caroline wished she could take back her gloating tone. She'd only meant to defend herself, not to brag.

"You may have plenty of people to protect you, but you never know what the police might do." Noah stared off into the distance. "They might arrest you."

"I doubt it." Caroline was certain about that. "Fred

will never call the cops. They hauled his brother off to jail several months ago. I wouldn't be surprised to find out Fred's a criminal too."

Noah stiffened and turned away from her to concentrate on Butch. "*Ach*, he cut that off way too soon. He could have kept that bidding going. Both of those women would have gone higher, and that man over there had been considering a bid. You can see his disappointment."

Caroline followed Noah's gesture toward the rear of the tent, where the man was muttering something to the person next to him. "You're really good at this."

"I should be. It's my job. And I'd better get over there and do it before Butch loses any more money."

The man who'd hesitated to bid wasn't the only one facing disappointment. Caroline wished Noah could stay and talk, but he waved a quick goodbye.

"I have to go. Please don't take any chances."

"I won't," Caroline promised. He had nothing to worry about. Going back into the building wasn't risky.

She waited until Noah reached the stage and took the microphone from Butch, though. Then she couldn't resist watching him sell the next few items. He had a good instinct for people who wanted to buy but weren't bidding. As the competition heated up, he'd encourage the hesitators.

Noah directed his question directly to them. "You don't want to miss out on this one-of-a-kind armoire, do you? Look at all this detailed carving. You'll go home regretting it."

Most of the time, they responded. Once they got caught up in the bidding war, the price soared.

Butch, his jaw clenched, stood off to one side near the

back of the tent. Jealousy burned in his eyes. Caroline sucked in a breath. Noah had better watch his back.

The scowl on Butch's face reminded Caroline of his uncle Russell's vendetta against Aidan. Russell had set up an elaborate scheme, hoping to get the young teen who worked in their chicken barbecue stand arrested. Luckily, Russell had gotten caught in his own trap.

Caroline would hate for something like that to happen to Noah. She doubted Butch could get Noah sent to jail, but she wouldn't put it past Butch to get his rival fired.

She shook her head. Fred would never get rid of someone who was making him a lot of money. But she could help Noah by sorting out those puzzle pieces. Now would be a good time with the building empty and both Butch and Noah occupied.

It took all of Caroline's willpower to pull her attention away from Noah's riveting performance. If he'd glanced at her the way he focused on audience members, her hand would be in the air even if she didn't want the item being sold. Good thing she didn't have a bidding paddle.

As she forced herself back to the auction storehouse door, Noah's smooth, deep voice slid over her like warm honey. After she let the door slam shut behind her, his words still penetrated the cement block walls, but only faintly. She could enjoy them while she worked.

Caroline moved back to the spot where she'd stopped searching earlier. And following a few more forays up and down new aisles of shelving, she found the crates she'd been looking for. In the far back corner, she headed for an empty table, almost hidden by full storage units, to spread out the pieces.

Unlike the jigsaw puzzles her family enjoyed doing

together, these had no pictures on the boxes, so she could only guess at the designs. She sorted similar colors together and created a pile of creams and sepia tones that seemed to belong together. Then came the difficult part—fitting them into a completed puzzle. None of the pieces interlocked. She had to push them up against each other. A few shapes made an obvious match. But most could go anywhere. She found only a few edge pieces.

After a while, the central picture emerged of a baby. Once she figured out the puzzle followed the outline of a high chair rather than being a square or rectangle, it made it easier to add the remaining pieces. Caroline stayed so engrossed in her task, she didn't realize someone had entered the building until a shadow fell over the almost completed puzzle. She lifted her head.

Butch leaned against the nearby shelf, blocking her way out. His smarmy smile made her shiver. He'd tried to corner her several times when she'd come to see Zach, the previous auctioneer. She'd always managed to evade him.

"What are you doing back here all by your lonesome?" He waggled his eyebrows in a way that made her sick to her stomach.

But Caroline refused to let him know he frightened her. She kept her voice steady and waved a casual hand to the piles scattered on the table. "Sorting puzzle pieces."

"Looks more like you're *playing* with them."

His leer grated on her.

"Putting them together is the only way I can tell what box the pieces belong in."

"What are you doing that for?"

"I knocked these over earlier today, so I wanted to fix them." She feigned disinterest in him and reached for the final pieces. "There. This one is ready." She scooped the pieces into the box labeled "Baby in High Chair."

Butch took a step toward her. "We could find something more interesting to do."

"Puzzles are interesting." She dumped another pile of pieces onto the table. "Look, these cream-colored pieces seem to be edges. I bet they go together." She scooped up several of them. "Why don't you see if you can find more?"

"That wasn't what I had in mind." Butch's sarcastic tone warned her not to push him too far.

Sending up a quick prayer for protection, she reached for three wooden shapes with words on them. She squealed like a schoolgirl. "This says *Cat*!" She fitted a *T* and a *he* in front of it. "There. Now we know what this puzzle is. *The Cat*."

Butch stalked toward her. Caroline shifted in her chair. If he came any closer, he'd leave a large enough gap for her to escape. She was one of the fastest runners when the youth group played baseball, but could she outrun Butch?

"You always avoided me when you came to see Zach. But now we're finally alone together."

"Ooo, do you think those striped ones are cat fur?" Caroline pointed to wooden pieces on the far side of the table.

Momentarily distracted, Butch turned to look.

She jumped up, sending the chair crashing to the floor. She darted around him and dashed toward the market door.

"You little—" Butch whirled around and pounded after her, but she'd gotten a head start.

Just before she reached the door, it swung open.

"Look out," she yelled.

Noah stepped aside, still holding the door wide, and

Caroline raced through. Behind her, Butch skidded to a stop.

"What in the world?" Noah stared from one to the other.

"I need to go. I'm late meeting my brother. He's probably wondering where I am." Caroline couldn't stop her breathless babbling. If she did, she'd probably want to kiss Noah for coming to her rescue. Which wouldn't do at all.

But she could at least thank him. "*Danke*." *And thank the Lord!*

His forehead creased in a puzzled frown. "I hope I'm not interrupting anything."

"Actually, you did." Butch strolled toward the exit. "Caroline's quite an athlete. We were racing, and she beat me. But now I'll take her to the employee entrance to meet her brother."

No way! She'd never go anywhere with Butch. Especially not alone. And from now on, she'd keep an eye out for him.

"Don't worry about it, Butch," she said airily. "Earlier today, Noah offered to walk me over. He can do it now instead." She sent a pleading glance his way, praying he'd say *jah*.

What was going on here? Noah's head was spinning. And not just from trying to figure out the situation. The way Caroline gazed up at him so trustingly turned him inside out.

"Stop making eyes at him, Caroline. You know what happened with Zach."

Only Noah was close enough to see the hurt flare on her face. This might be a big mistake, but he had to come to her rescue. "I know you have to lock up, Butch, so I'll walk her back."

"Just don't go falling for her." Butch made his disgust obvious. "That girl's a tease. She's always throwing herself at men."

Noah ignored him. Something was off here, but he couldn't put his finger on it. When she first dashed through the door, he suspected Caroline had been running away from Butch, yet she stood here so calmly, so unperturbed. She didn't look the least bit afraid.

"Let's go, shall we?" Noah let the door swing shut and moved to her side.

People rushed past them to return their numbers and pay for their auction items. Others struggled under armloads of goods they'd bought. Caroline wove through the crowds at such a fast clip, he lengthened his stride to keep up.

"You're in a hurry?" When wasn't she? She'd flown through the door earlier today and slammed into him. Then she'd done the same a few minutes ago. And now, she seemed to be racewalking. Did she ever slow down?

"I want to get as far away from Butch as I can."

"I see." Noah's hands clenched into fists. So his first impression had been right. "Did he hurt you?"

"*Neh*, but only because I'm faster. If you hadn't opened the door when you did, I don't know if I'd have made it through. But I prayed, and God sent you."

Noah had never considered himself an answer to prayer. That would be a first.

"Oh, and what Butch said about me isn't true. I'm not a tease. I didn't do that. I wouldn't . . ." After she trailed off, she swallowed hard and ducked her head. "Maybe he was right about the last part."

What had Butch said at the end? Noah had been too busy watching Caroline's reaction. Butch's remark had been nasty, because she'd looked hurt. "I don't remember what he said."

"He said I throw myself at men."

Most women wouldn't have repeated that. One thing about Caroline—she was brutally honest. He wondered what it took to be so secure you could admit your faults like that.

"I guess I do," she admitted. "Or at least I used to."

Noah choked back a chuckle. Hadn't she just done it with him?

"You might be wondering what he meant by that. Or maybe you aren't, because Fred mentioned it too."

Give this girl a minute, and she'd tell you her whole life story. On the plus side, at least you'd always know where you stood with her and what was going through her mind. Not that Noah intended to have anything more to do with her.

"I made a fool of myself over—"

He cleared his throat, interrupting her. Later, she might regret spilling all this to a stranger. "I'm still trying to figure out why you were in the auction storehouse. Did you go there to meet Butch?"

After a sharp intake of breath, she exploded, "Absolutely not. I don't ever want to be around him. I know that sounds mean. And I should see people through God's eyes."

Something twisted in Noah's gut. How did you see people through God's eyes when they'd destroyed your life? He was tempted to ask Caroline that question. But they'd gotten far from what he'd asked. "If you weren't there to see Butch, what were you doing?"

She beamed up at him, and he forgot everything.

"I went back to sort out the puzzle pieces."

"I told you I'd do it."

"I know, but it was my fault. And guess what? I got the baby in the high chair done. It's so cute. At first, it was confusing because I couldn't find many edge pieces. Then I discovered it followed the shape of the high chair back and tray. I wonder why they didn't print pictures on the boxes, though. It would make it much easier."

"To print colors meant color separations and inking the press four times. They didn't have computerized printing back then, so it would have been very expensive."

"Oh, I didn't think about that. Why couldn't they do it when they printed the puzzles?"

"Hmm . . . I never thought of that. Maybe because they'd have to redo all the color plates to a different size."

"True. Anyway, I started the cat one. I didn't get far before Butch interrupted me."

"And you ran away?"

"*Jah*, I'm sorry."

"For running?"

Caroline giggled. A sweet sound that sent shivers through him.

"*Neh*, I'm glad I did that. I meant I'm sorry I didn't get the puzzles done."

How many times did he have to tell her she didn't have to do that? Evidently, once she got something into her head, she followed through no matter what. "It's no problem."

"Oh, and I'm also sorry about picking up pieces when

my fingers were so dirty. I hope I didn't ruin any of the pieces."

After she'd run into him, he hadn't been looking at her hands. He'd been too caught up gazing into her eyes. "No worries. I'm sure the puzzle pieces will be fine."

Her anxious expression relaxed. "That's good. I was so embarrassed when I went to wash my hands at the stand. I don't normally go around with dirt on my hands, but I'd just come from a volleyball tournament. I'd done a pancake to save the ball, and well, I got pretty muddy."

Noah's brows shot up. "A pancake?"

"That's when you dive and slide along the ground."

"I know what a pancake is." It had been several years since he'd played volleyball with his church youth group, but he hadn't forgotten the moves. He'd been trying to picture a girl as sweet and feminine as Caroline going after the ball.

She stared down at the ground and nibbled her lip. "Now you're probably thinking I'm—"

It bothered him that she appeared ashamed. "I'm thinking you must be brave."

Caroline shot him a surprised look. "Brave?"

Not the kind of courage he'd needed to get through the past three years, but still . . .

Noah forced himself to concentrate on the present. Getting tangled in the past caused too much pain and heartache.

While his thoughts wandered, Caroline's expression changed. He wanted to erase that skepticism. "You were brave going after the ball like that. So you're either fearless or very determined to win."

She laughed. "Definitely determined to win."

"I hope you were successful then."

"*Jah*, we won the championship."

Her eyes lit with a joy that called to his starving spirit. How long had it been since he'd seen such pure happiness on someone's face?

"And I bet your pancake saved the game." He shouldn't get sucked in like this, but he wanted to keep her beaming.

CHAPTER 4

Caroline couldn't help smiling, but she shouldn't be a show-off. "Actually, I just bumped the ball into the air, and Josh made the winning point."

"But he couldn't have done it without you."

"I suppose not." She needed to change the subject. Ever since they'd started walking, she'd been prattling about herself. Mostly out of nervousness.

Noah wouldn't know that, though. He probably thought she hogged every conversation. And he might be right.

She should pay more attention to him. "I heard you out there at the auction." No need to tell him she stood outside staring at him. "You're really good. If I'd been in the audience, I'd have lifted my number even if I didn't want what you were selling."

His curt *danke* made it clear he didn't appreciate her comment.

Had she embarrassed him? Or did he worry about *hochmut*? She hadn't meant to make him uncomfortable. What could she say to smooth things over?

"I'm sorry. You probably don't want to seem prideful, but after we talked about me and volleyball . . ." Caroline's words skidded to a stop. She'd almost admitted she liked his compliments.

They'd reached the employee entrance. "Here's where I go in. Thank you for walking me to the door. And for saving me from Butch."

Noah nodded. "Might be best if you stayed away from the auction."

Was that concern for her safety, or a message to keep away from him?

Not that she blamed him for wanting to avoid her after she'd upended his puzzles, gotten him in trouble with Fred, forced him to walk her around the building, and rambled on like a— Like a what? A chattering magpie. Heat flushed up her neck and splashed onto her cheeks. She turned so he couldn't see her blush. Blindly, she fumbled for the door handle, and her hand bumped his.

He'd been trying to open the door for her. Did he think she'd tried to grab his hand? Her face burned even hotter. "*Ach*, I'm sorry. I thought—" She yanked her arm back.

"No worries." In one smooth movement, he opened the door, acting cool and casual, while the tingles flowing up her arm flustered her.

She longed to flee into the market, but she couldn't be rude. For once, her usually talkative mouth failed her. She managed a gulped *danke* without even glancing in his direction.

His deep *you're welcome* shook her to her core.

She had to get away before she made a fool of herself. "See you tomorrow," she blurted out. But when she turned to flee, her brother stood just inside the doorway.

"Caroline? I was just coming to find you." Gideon frowned as he glanced past her to Noah.

It's not what you think. Caroline longed to defend herself, but that would only make the situation worse. Plus, she didn't want to explain why Noah had accompanied her while he stood there listening.

Gideon heaved a sigh. "It's Friday night. Nettie had to leave for the center. We needed you. Aidan stayed to help, but he's impatient to go out with his friends."

Poor Aidan. He usually shot out the door the minute the market closed. As an *Englisch* teen, he always had plans. And Gideon must be eager to get home to Fern and their newborn son. Nettie had been helping out at their stand this week so Fern could stay home with the baby, but Nettie and her husband always spent Friday and Saturday nights at the STAR center, helping ex-gang members turn their lives around.

"I'm sorry." Once again, Caroline had inconvenienced everyone with her impulsiveness. "I'll get everything cleaned up." She brushed past Noah, sidestepped around her brother, and ran down the aisle.

What must Noah think of her? She'd left piles of puzzle pieces for him to sort, and now he'd learned she'd stuck her family and friends with all the cleanup at the stand. He probably believed she shirked all her duties. Thank heavens she'd sworn off auctioneers!

Noah stood, holding the door open, staring after Caroline as she blew past him like a whirlwind. A whirlwind that lifted him in the air and twisted him around like a cyclone. Once she disappeared from sight, the tornado of emotions dropped him down hard, leaving him dazed and disoriented.

In a fog, he headed back to the auction storehouse, but Butch had already locked up. No chance of fixing the puzzles tonight. He'd have to do it tomorrow. Fred usually arrived early, so between then and the start of his shift, Noah would get them ready to sell. He only hoped Fred wouldn't notice they'd been missing from tonight's sale list.

Noah headed for the back road and began his long walk home, trying to prepare himself for another night alone. Somehow, after spending time with a girl as lively as Caroline, his solitary lifestyle left him feeling lonely rather than peaceful.

He'd trudged two miles, with five more to go, when an elegant car glided past him and pulled to a stop on the shoulder. Noah ignored the Bentley, but the passenger rolled down the window and called to him. The elderly *Englisch* woman appeared harmless, so he approached her.

"Noah, right?" The woman's chipper voice and smile belied her ancient, wrinkle-filled face.

His stomach clenched. How did she know his name? She was much too old to be a reporter. Who else in this Pennsylvania town might recognize him?

She laughed. "I didn't mean to make you nervous. I'm Mrs. Vandenberg, former owner of the farmer's market."

He'd heard stories about her—all good ones. Most people labeled her a saint.

"You're probably wondering how I identified you. Actually, I had the pleasure of watching you auction off several items earlier this evening. You're quite good at it, you know."

Caroline had told him the same thing, but Noah hadn't believed her. He didn't quite believe Mrs. Vandenberg either. He'd taken to auctioneering quickly, but plenty of others did as well or better than he did.

"Oh, that's right. Most Amish men worry about being prideful, but if God gives you certain gifts, you should appreciate them. I'm glad you're using yours."

Because he'd had plenty of practice, Noah managed to keep from wincing. But talk of God always started a slow burn deep in his gut.

"Forgiving others and getting right with God takes care of inner pain."

Noah stepped back. Was this woman a witch? Had she read his mind?

"Don't worry, I haven't uncovered all your secrets. God just gives me messages for people from time to time."

If God spoke to this woman, Noah wanted to get as far away from her as possible. He had no desire to receive any messages from above. He already carried enough guilt.

"You're not ready yet to totally embrace that message. Keep it in mind for the future."

Noah doubted it'd be much use later, but he kept silent. Surely, Mrs. Vandenberg hadn't stopped him to lecture him about God. A change of subject might be in order. "Can I help you with something?"

"You certainly will. But again, that's for the future. Right now, I stopped to offer you a ride home."

"I—I don't want to take you out of your way." He couldn't—wouldn't—accept a ride.

"It's not a problem. We came this way expecting to see you."

Why? Suspicions crowded to the surface. Noah had learned his lesson the hard way: Never trust a stranger. No

Englischers did favors like that unless they had a hidden motive. But he hadn't figured out her angle yet.

"It's just a simple ride home. No strings attached."

Once again, she seemed to have peeked into his brain, making Noah wary. He had a sudden vision of her kidnapping him. He stole a quick glance at the driver. The older man stared straight out the windshield, seemingly not interested in the conversation. Yet Noah had the distinct impression the man could repeat back every word.

Noah had honed his muscles over the past few years. He'd learned stealth and quickness. He could easily take both Mrs. Vandenberg and her driver. But he'd rather not get in their sleek car. "Thank you. I'm fine with walking. I can use the exercise."

"I insist." The steeliness underlying Mrs. Vandenberg's soft words took him by surprise.

Would he lose his job if he refused? He couldn't afford that.

The driver's side door opened, and the man stepped out. Noah tensed in case he had to fight for his freedom. But the fifty-something chauffer only opened the back door and, with a tilt of his head and a sweep of his hand, motioned for Noah to get in.

"You have nothing to fear." Mrs. Vandenberg's tone resembled one you might use to calm a wild animal caught in a trap.

Was that how she saw him? Or had she investigated him and discovered his secrets?

"The past no longer matters. Only the present counts. Isn't that so, Noah?"

He desperately wanted to believe that. But she'd spooked him again with her knowledge of what he'd been thinking.

"Just get in, and we can work everything out."

Now she was promising an impossibility. Noah couldn't leave the other man standing there with the door open, though. All his senses on alert, Noah slid onto the luxurious leather. He'd never been in such an expensive car. In fact, other than his ride from the station, Noah hadn't been in a car since . . .

He closed his mind to that thought as the chauffer eased the door shut, snaring Noah in a swanky prison.

That word sent his thoughts squirreling in circles. He had to escape. He couldn't let them drop him off at his place. "You live off this road, right?" The firmness of Mrs. Vandenberg's question hinted she already knew the answer.

Had she researched him? Noah squirmed. "If you could drop me at Yoder's Country Store, I'd appreciate it." That way, if she didn't actually have his address, he'd keep it private. "I, um, want to get a few groceries."

Caroline popped into his mind. She'd have eagerly given her address, along with telling Mrs. Vandenberg how much her family paid for the house, who they bought it from, and details about the family members who lived there. His lips quirked.

Without looking back at him, Mrs. Vandenberg bobbed her head up and down in a knowing nod. "Someday, you'll trust us more than you do at this moment. For now, Yoder's is a good solution."

What in the world did she mean by that? Not only did she read minds, she also spoke in riddles.

The car glided into Yoder's parking lot and eased to a stop. Noah reached for the door handle to jump out. He fumbled to figure out the release. Which button or lever did he push or pull, or did he need to wait for the driver to let him out?

"If you'd like a ride back and forth to work, I can arrange for someone who works at the market to pick you up," Mrs. Vandenberg said. "If you give me your schedule, the driver can pick you up at your door." He tried to keep a neutral expression, but the thought of anyone finding out where he lived bothered him.

As if sensing his reluctance, she amended her suggestion. "Or they could stop here at Yoder's if you prefer."

"Thanks, but I'll be fine." Noah hoped he didn't sound ungrateful. He preferred to keep to himself. He'd rather not ride with any coworkers.

During the past few years, his normal conversational skills had gone rusty. Besides, what would he talk about? Not much of interest happened at the auction, and he needed to keep his past hidden. If Fred discovered the truth about that, Noah would be fired.

Mrs. Vandenberg swiveled her head to study him. "Don't worry about your job. Everything will be fine sooner than you think."

Huh? Another confusing statement. This woman didn't know him. Even if she'd dug into his life, she wouldn't have the full picture. And no one could foretell the future.

Finally, Noah figured out the door latch, and with a deep sense of relief, stepped onto the asphalt parking lot, eager to get away from Mrs. Vandenberg's probing looks and predictions about his future. If she knew more about him, her certainty would evaporate. Although his life might appear normal on the surface, he doubted the painful emotions bubbling underneath could ever heal.

CHAPTER 5

Caroline scrubbed with a vengeance, determined to get everything cleaned quickly so Gideon could go home to Fern and the baby. And maybe if she stayed hard at work, her brother wouldn't have time to question her.

By the time Gideon returned to the stand, walking slowly as if deep in thought, she'd scrubbed the rotisserie, which he'd begun, and she'd started wiping down the glass display cases.

He mumbled to himself as he headed toward her, something he did when he was praying intently. Caroline had no doubt who he'd been lifting up to the Lord. She swallowed back the shame rising in her throat. She'd been a trial to her brother from the time she'd been old enough to walk. And he didn't know half the scrapes she'd gotten into when she hadn't been following him around.

When Gideon cleared his throat, Caroline steeled herself for a lecture. She deserved one for running off and leaving him here to do all the work alone. Instead, he surprised her.

"*Danke* for doing the rotisserie. That's the hardest job. And it looks great."

Caroline ducked her head at the unexpected praise. "You'd already done most of it."

As he headed for the sink filled with metal salad trays, she dropped her rag, intending to intercept him. "I'll get those." She hadn't meant to make him do her usual chores.

But the edge of her apron caught on the trigger of the spray bottle, knocking it to the floor with a crash. The lid flew off, and glass cleaner splashed counters on both sides of the aisle and puddled on the floor. She must not have screwed the lid on tightly enough when she refilled it.

Hissing came from between Gideon's lips, but he suppressed his sigh by pinching his lips together.

"I'm so sorry." Caroline's eyes stung. "I'll clean this up right away." Now she'd delayed their leaving even longer.

Her brother's face softened into compassion, and he nodded. "I'll get the dishes done."

His sympathy added to her guilt. She seemed destined to make everyone's life miserable today.

After wiping up the spill and mopping the floor, she refilled the spray bottle, tightened the lid twice as hard as usual, and finished shining the remaining refrigerated cases. By then, Gideon had washed most of the stack of dishes.

"I can do the rest," she offered as she put away the cleaner.

"Why don't you go out and hitch up the horse?" He seemed eager to get her out of the stand.

Not that she blamed him. She'd been more of a drawback than an asset. Not only to him but to Noah too.

Being outdoors and breathing in the cooler night air soothed Caroline's distress. *Lord, please help me to learn to slow down and avoid making so many mistakes.*

Although the parking lot had been empty when she exited, an elegant car pulled in as Caroline neared the shelter. A window glided down, and Mrs. Vandenberg called to her.

"I have someone I'm concerned about, Caroline, dear. Would you be willing to drive your own buggy tomorrow and take the back roads past Yoder's Country Store to pick this person up if you see them walking?"

"Of course. Who is it?"

Mrs. V acted cagey. "You'll know when you see them."

"Do I just stop everyone who's walking along the road to see if they need a ride?"

"Only if they're Amish." Mrs. Vandenberg's smile held a touch of mystery.

Why couldn't she just tell Caroline the person's name? Plenty of Amish people walked along that road to the market. Would she have to ask every single one of them?

Caroline bubbled with curiosity. "Why can't you tell me who it is?"

A sudden thought struck her. Maybe Mrs. V didn't want to say because it was someone Caroline didn't like, someone she'd rather avoid. The only name that came to mind was her tormentor from volleyball. The thought of having to pick him up made her sick.

"Is it a man or a woman?"

A twinkle in her eye, Mrs. Vandenberg pushed the button to roll up her window. "You'll find out."

"But why can't you answerrr?" Caroline practically wailed that. Then realizing she sounded like a petulant child, she shut her mouth. She wouldn't embarrass herself more by begging.

Mrs. Vandenberg's car pulled away, leaving Caroline

frustrated. Everyone always told her she needed to curb her curiosity. But it was so hard. Caroline wanted to know everything about everyone. *Mrs. Vandenberg must want to teach me a lesson.*

God often sent Mrs. V into people's lives to point out how they needed to change. *He might be trying to teach me patience.* A virtue Mamm stressed Caroline needed to learn. But she liked to get things done *now* and find out answers *now* and satisfy her curiosity *now*.

This time she had no choice but to wait.

By the time she'd hitched up the horse, Gideon had locked the employee entrance and crossed the parking lot. Without saying a word about how long it had taken her, he took the reins, and she slid into the passenger seat. They rode without speaking for the first mile, while Caroline nibbled at her lip, trying to decide what she should apologize for first.

Gideon startled her by breaking the silence. "Caroline, I know you're twenty and old enough to make your own decisions, but you're still my little sister and always will be. I care about what happens to you."

Her brother's words brought tears to her eyes. Although he was affectionate with his wife and baby son, he'd never expressed his feelings openly to Caroline before. They didn't do that in their family. And everyone frowned on Caroline for her outbursts of emotion, both positive and negative.

Not that she'd ever doubted her parents' love. Or Gideon's, for that matter. To them, love should be expressed through actions not words. But Caroline, whose deeds often ended in disaster and whose heart and lips overflowed with words, had always been out of sync with the rest of her family.

"I know you care, Gideon. And I'll try harder not to rush around and cause so many accidents."

He released a long, slow breath. "That would be helpful, but it's not what I meant. I'm more worried about the man you were with."

"Noah?"

"*Jah*, Noah. What do you know about him?"

"Nothing, except that he's an auctioneer." *And that he makes my heart patter and his touch sends tingles through me.* With effort, she stopped her tongue from spilling out those reactions.

"Another auctioneer?" Gideon didn't have to say any more. His tone implied it—*are you making a fool of yourself over another auctioneer?* Although her brother wouldn't have phrased it like that. He'd have found a nice way to express his concerns.

"I'm not falling for Noah." *Or chasing after him like I did with Zach. I learned my lesson.* "I caused an accident as I rushed through the auction storage building."

Her brother bit back a sigh, but he said nothing.

"I bumped into Noah." She changed directions before she shared her reaction to him with her brother. "I mean, I knocked two crates out of his hands and puzzle pieces spilled all over the floor. They were these old-fashioned wooden puzzles. Did you know that back in the early nineteen-hundreds puzzle pieces didn't have the little tabs?" Caroline stopped to draw in a breath.

"No, I didn't." Gideon scrunched his brows, reminding her she'd gotten off track.

"Anyway, I was late coming to our stand so I couldn't

stay and help Noah pick everything up, but I'd scrambled four puzzles."

Gideon's faint "*I see*" revealed he understood her predicament.

"Noah said not to worry about it, but I did. So I went back to the building while he was auctioning off an armoire, and I put together one of the puzzles. It was really hard at first until I realized it was shaped like a baby in a high chair and—"

Her brother's long-suffering puff of breath stopped her prattling.

"Right. I finished that one and began the second one, but I got interrupted and when Noah noticed I was nervous, he walked me to the employee entrance. That's all he did. He was only being polite."

"You, nervous?" Gideon's arched eyebrows indicated he didn't quite believe her story.

"Butch came in, and I didn't want to be around him so I hurried out of the building."

"Stay away from Butch," Gideon growled. "I've heard he's trouble."

"That whole family is trouble." Russell had gone to jail, and Fred seemed headed in that direction.

Gideon frowned. "We shouldn't be bad-mouthing others."

Caroline caught herself before she snapped back, *You started it.* She'd done pretty well about holding herself back in this conversation. No point in ruining that now.

"Anyway," she finished after a quick breath, "that's why I was with Noah and why I didn't help with cleanup. Oh, and you don't have to worry about me getting interested in another auctioneer."

*Because I already am interested, but I won't act on it.
I promise.*

Noah had woken up later than he'd planned on Saturday morning and had to rush to work. He needed to sort
those puzzle pieces before Fred found out they were missing from the lineup. Noah had jogged two of the seven
miles when a buggy pulled up beside him.

"Want a ride?" The sweet voice startled him.

He'd spent so much time trying to push thoughts of
Caroline from his mind. Now here she was beside him.
Accepting a ride from her would make it harder for him to
fight his attraction to her. Yet, even if he kept jogging, he'd
still be late.

Stay away from her, his inner voice warned. At the
same time, other thoughts plagued him. *Fred will be furious if you're not there on time. And if he finds out about
the puzzles not being sold yesterday . . .*

Caroline waited patiently while his internal battle
raged. Noah's difficulty in deciding might make her late
for work. He pushed aside his worries and climbed into her
buggy.

For a moment, her blinding smile left him speechless.
He turned his attention to the trees outside the window.
"*Danke* for the ride. I was worried about being late this
morning."

"I don't know how Mrs. Vandenberg does it." Caroline
laughed. "I guess she had a message from God about that.
Yesterday, she asked me to pick you up today."

Noah ignored Caroline's reference to God, but he had

to be sure he heard her correctly. "Mrs. Vandenberg said what?"

"She told me to drive past Yoder's this morning to give someone a ride. She didn't tell me who."

"And you just did what she said without questioning her?" Noah asked incredulously.

"*Jah*, I've found when she suggests things, she's right. I think she has a direct line to God."

Noah shook his head. He had to admit the elderly woman had an uncanny ability to read his mind. But her skill spooked him. Caroline seemed to trust Mrs. Vandenberg. Once again, he was reminded of Caroline's innocence and openness.

"You shouldn't just blindly trust people like Mrs. Vandenberg," he suggested in a gentle tone.

"Why not?" Caroline appeared puzzled.

"Because not everyone has your best interests at heart."

"True. It's good that we can always depend on God to take care of us. Nothing happens to us that's not His will for us."

Noah's hands clenched into fists, and he ground his teeth. He'd once been as sure of that as Caroline. Since then, he'd learned that bad things, cruel things, unfair things occurred, that people you loved and trusted could betray you, that you could sink to the depths of despair, that God didn't always answer prayers.

He didn't want to tear down her faith, so he kept his distress to himself and hoped they'd arrive at the market soon. He needed to get away from her. Not only was it dangerous for him to be around her, he might prove to be a stumbling block. Although he no longer believed the same things she did, he didn't want to tear down her beliefs. They were part of her sweetness and her appeal. Caroline's buggy arrived at the market as Fred unlocked the doors to the auction storeroom.

"Could you drop me here?" Noah asked as she approached the auction tent.

"I don't mind taking you to the door."

"Here would be best." Noah didn't want Fred to see him come in. He didn't start his shift today for another hour. He planned to sneak into the building while his boss got coffee and find a secluded spot to put together the puzzles.

At his insistence, Caroline pulled on the reins to halt her horse. She turned to Noah, guilt written across her face. "I'm so sorry about the puzzles. I'll try to stop by and help."

"*Neh*, don't do that." Fred would explode if she arrived. "I've already taken care of it." Noah's conscience twinged. He'd fudged the truth. But he'd have it all fixed in an hour, he hoped. He didn't want Caroline to fret. Or show up and cause trouble for both of them.

"I feel so bad."

Noah waved away her guilt. "It's no big deal. We often have to reorganize things or clean up after spills. That happens." He slid open the door and hopped out. "*Danke*, I really appreciate the ride." More than she'd ever know.

Her beautiful smile lit his day with sunshine. Even if he could never have a relationship with her, things were definitely looking up. Spending time with her and getting to work at exactly the right time lifted his spirits. Concealed in the shadows of the auction tent, he waited until his boss completed his rounds to be sure everything was in order. Noah had spent a lot of time learning to remain invisible in plain sight. That skill had kept him safe, and now it came in handy. As soon as Fred headed to the market for his daily coffee-and-doughnut run, Noah slipped into the storage building.

He went straight to the back shelves where he'd stored the crates, but a gaping hole greeted him. Usually, Fred just did a cursory check before unlocking the doors. Had he pulled the boxes because he'd noticed the jumbled pieces?

Wait. Caroline had said she'd put some of the puzzles together. Where would she have taken them?

His breath came a little easier when he spotted wooden pieces spread on the back worktable. She'd made a good choice. Full shelves surrounding the alcove hid the table from view. But as Noah entered the narrow space between shelves, he reassessed. Maybe it hadn't been such a wise place for her to work.

His fists clenched as he imagined Butch trapping her back here, blocking her only way out. How had she escaped? He must have come close to her, leaving an opening behind him. Had he touched her?

At the sight of the overturned chair, acid burned in Noah's mouth. Had she struggled to get away?

No wonder Caroline had been sprinting for the exit at full speed. If he hadn't opened the door when he did, what would Butch have done? Noah couldn't bear to think about it.

Why had she been so foolish to come in here alone? Anger steamed upward from his gut and seared through his chest. Typical Amish, believing that whatever happened was God's will. She assumed God would take care of her. Despite being Amish, Noah had learned the hard way that didn't always happen.

He shook off the dark memories, picked up the chair, and lowered himself into the seat Caroline had last occupied. His jaw clenched and muscles tense, he slid the words *The Cat* toward him. She'd touched these pieces before . . .

Noah slammed down the steel doors in his mind. He'd long ago learned to avoid unwanted thoughts and feelings. That was the only way to survive.

He raked pieces across the table toward him and built small piles of similar colors. Unlike the puzzle Caroline had done last night, this one had edges. He assembled those first, attaching them to the words she'd connected.

Mindless tasks like this allowed his mind to wander. Soon, unwanted thoughts seeped out from under the doors he'd locked to confine them. Bits about Caroline appeared first. And as fast as he tamped them down, more trickled in. Noah gave up. For some reason, that chattering girl had overtaken his defenses.

He tried not to remember the softness of her skin as he held her arms. That led to longings for closeness, for family, for connection . . .

Noah shook his head. No sense longing for an impossible future. A future he'd never have.

Caroline vowed to do her best to help today and not get distracted, although she doubted Noah really had sorted the puzzles. Something about the way he'd said it made her wonder. Unfortunately, if he hadn't, she wouldn't have a chance to help. Nettie and her family worked at the center today, and some of the former gang members they'd trained took over her husband's market stand. With Fern missing and Aidan darting between the fries and helping his dad with candy sales, she and Gideon had to handle everything.

Once the late-morning rush began, they were run off their feet trying to keep up with all the customers.

Gideon wiped his brow with the back of his arm after unloading cooked chickens from the spit. "Whew. We really need to hire some more help."

Sovilla, who normally helped her family run their pickle and pet food business, had offered to take over for Fern, making and selling baked goods. She had long lines and could use some help, but Caroline had all she could handle with the chicken and salad customers.

She dipped out quart containers of macaroni and potato salads, and handed them to an *Englisch* customer. After the woman paid, Caroline turned to her brother. "Anna Mary mentioned recently that she might need to get a job to help her family. I could ask her."

"Anna Mary, *hmm*." He loaded the spits with uncooked chickens and brushed them with barbecue sauce. "She'd be dependable. Why don't you see if she can come in on Tuesday? It'll be a slow day, so we can teach her what she needs to know."

Caroline wanted to cheer, but she kept it in check. She hoped working together in the stand wouldn't strain their relationship. Anna Mary would have even more time to scrutinize and criticize Caroline's behavior. The only good thing—besides having much-needed help—was that Caroline generally acted more demure at the market. So maybe Anna Mary would have fewer opportunities to disapprove.

After Caroline handed an *Englisch* man a chicken and his change, a crowd of twenty-something Amish boys jostled all the waiting customers out of the way and lined up along the counter, laughing. She sucked in a breath. She'd never seen Amish *youngie* act so rude.

Two of them elbowed the boy standing in front of her. "Go on. Ask her."

Caroline glanced behind her to see if they meant Sovilla, but she was busy packaging cinnamon rolls down at the bakery counter.

"I don't need any help," the middle guy said. "I'll ask when I'm good and ready."

He lazily leaned one elbow on the counter and set his chin on his fist. "Remember me, Caroline?"

She turned her attention to him. *Ach*, the volleyball player she'd embarrassed yesterday. What was he doing here? For once in her life, she found herself at a loss for words.

Gideon banged the door of the rotisserie shut and hurried to the counter. "Did you boys want something?" He glanced at the long line of impatient customers behind them.

One of the boys waggled his eyebrows. "Tim here does." He waved a hand toward his friend leaning on the counter.

"I sure do," Tim replied. "If Caroline here will give it to me." He flashed her a sharklike smile. "Whadda you say we go for a buggy ride after you finish work? Maybe we could play a little one-on-one volleyball."

He was asking her out in front of all of these customers? This had to be a joke. They were trying to get her back for embarrassing him at the game.

"Sorry. I have other plans."

"How 'bout Monday, then? The market's closed."

"I don't think—"

"Caroline," Gideon cut in, "why don't you take your friends elsewhere so our customers can order?"

"They're not my friends." She hadn't meant to sound so rude. "I mean, I only met them yesterday at the game and—"

"Not your friends?" Tim made a stabbing motion toward his heart. "When you came running after me yesterday, I thought you were interested."

Ooo, that liar. He made it sound as if she'd been chasing him.

Her brother shot her a *not-again* look.

"I didn't chase him, Gideon. It's not what you think."

"You mean you chase after all the boys like that? Now I'm hurt." Tim put on a wounded expression.

"I. Did. Not. Chase. Anyone." She enunciated each word. But as she said it, her conscience twinged. She'd just fibbed. She'd chased after the auctioneer. And her brother knew it.

"Sure looked like you did to me," one boy piped up.

"Me too," said another. "You raced across the field after Tim and, all breathless-like, asked if he'd forgive you."

"Only because . . ."

Gideon silenced her with a wave. "Just move everyone so I can wait on people."

"*Neh*." Tim kept his elbow planted on the counter. "Not until Caroline says *jah*."

"We have a business to run. Why don't you come back after closing? You can talk to Caroline then." Gideon sent apologetic glances to the other customers, but some of them slipped out of line and headed for other stands.

Caroline had to do something. They were missing out on sales, and it was all her fault. If she hadn't been so snippy yesterday, these boys wouldn't have come here today. They intended to pay her back, and they'd succeeded. But her family didn't deserve to lose money because of her.

"I'll go out and talk to them," she said miserably. She'd be leaving her brother alone to handle all the work. But letting the boys block everyone from getting to the counter was worse.

She hurried to the half-door exit at the other end of the stand, and after brushing past Sovilla, Caroline let the door bang shut behind her. The customers gathered at Sovilla's counter stared at Caroline as she headed past the crowded café tables, all the boys trailing in her wake.

To get away from the prying glances, she stopped in the empty space near a support beam under the stairs and then regretted it. Darker and more secluded, it hid her from view of the stand and most of the tables. But she'd not only isolated herself, she'd also backed herself into a corner without an escape route. The boys crowded around her, caging her in, suffocating her with their closeness.

Caroline shivered at the mocking intensity in their eyes. Surely, they wouldn't do anything to hurt her. Not with all the crowds milling around the market. And these were Amish boys. Not that they couldn't do mean things, but they wouldn't, would they?

She sent up a quick prayer for safety. Then she put on a nonchalant expression, one that didn't match her pounding heart and shaking hands. Could they tell she was frightened? What did they plan to do?

CHAPTER 6

Noah's stomach growled as he finished the third puzzle. He hadn't had time for breakfast this morning. He tossed all those pieces into the correct box and swept the remaining ones into the fourth box. Breathing a sigh of relief, he placed the last two puzzle boxes into the crate and slid it into the afternoon's lineup.

With half an hour until he had to be onstage, he had time for a quick meal. As soon as he entered the market, the smell of barbecuing chicken tempted him. That stand had long lines, though. Maybe he should find a less busy food counter.

Off to his right, movement in a dark recess under the stairs distracted him. He tensed, all his senses alert. He'd learned to fear shadowy threats, which could lead to sudden attacks. He snapped into defensive mode and assessed the danger.

A group of Amish boys, their backs to him, had surrounded someone and were closing in. Noah searched the center of the circle for the victim. He stopped in shock when he spotted the person they'd trapped.

Caroline?

A girl as pretty as Caroline was sure to attract many

would-be suitors. They'd flock around her like bees to honey. But from the tense lines on her face, she was afraid these bees might sting her.

She looked up and caught him staring at her. The fear in her eyes called to him. Were they harassing her? Noah couldn't stand seeing anyone bullied. And definitely not someone as sweet as Caroline. He strode in that direction determined to protect her.

As he neared, she backed away from the dark-haired one who pressed closer. "I can't go out with you because— because . . ." She seemed to be floundering for an answer. "Because I already have a boyfriend."

"Really?"

The boy's *I-don't-believe-you* smirk added flames to Noah's ire. No woman deserved to be treated that way.

"Why didn't your boyfriend come to the game? And does he know about the pancake?"

"He—he had to work." Caroline's flimsy excuse sounded fake even to Noah's ears.

"Does he work at the market? Maybe we can tell him what you're really like."

Caroline lifted her chin and sniffed. "He wouldn't be-lieve you."

Noah admired her attempt at bravery, but the boys only snickered.

The dark-haired one tossed his head. "When we get done with him, he'll know the truth." Desperation in her eyes, Caroline flung out her arm and pointed behind them. "There he is."

As they turned to look, she broke free of the circle and raced straight toward Noah, her eyes begging him not to give her away.

He froze. The last time he'd gotten caught up in someone

else's lie, he'd paid a terrible price. He'd vowed never to let that happen again. But what else could he do? She was dashing toward him, and he had to save her. Even if he put himself at risk.

"What's going on?" Noah's deep, authoritative tone stopped the boys in their tracks.

Caroline's heart swelled. He appeared so strong and fierce. His clenched fists made his biceps flex. Gratitude flooded through her that he hadn't called out her lie. She reached his side and whirled around to face her tormentors.

They appeared to be intimidated by Noah's muscular shoulders and chest. He towered over most of them. She'd picked the perfect person as a rescuer.

One of the smaller boys elbowed Caroline's nemesis. "Tell him, Tim."

"Tell me what?"

Tim backed up a step as Noah's voice cracked out like a whip.

With his friends crowding close for support, though, Tim adopted an attitude of bravado. "Bet your girl never told you about her volleyball pancake."

"She certainly did. Pretty impressive, huh? Especially for the last point in the game."

Tim blinked. So did Caroline. Noah remembered all that from her babbling? Her pulse sped up. He even sounded as if he admired her. She reminded herself they were role-playing.

Puffing up like a banty rooster, Tim straightened his shoulders, which were puny compared to Noah's. "So you don't mind that she plays volleyball like a boy."

Caroline's cheeks flushed hot. Both her *mamm* and Anna Mary always chided her for that.

"Mind?" Noah's stare lasered into Tim. "Why would I mind her winning?"

Although Noah's comeback discomfited Tim, it punctured Caroline's bubble of joy. Of course Noah didn't mind. He barely knew her and could care less.

"You're not bothered that she does shoulder rolls?" Tim sneered.

Humiliated, Caroline whispered, "I never did a shoulder roll." She didn't want Noah to believe she'd do a somersault in a dress.

Noah ignored that comment. "She won the championship, didn't she? Maybe it hurt your pride? Is that what this is about?"

With a snort, Tim threw back his head. "I can beat her with one hand tied behind my back."

Noah called Tim's bluff. "Then why didn't you?"

Tim zeroed in on Caroline. "I'll be back to schedule a one-on-one rematch to prove it."

Noah took a step forward, his presence menacing. "Stay away from Caroline, or you'll have me to answer to."

Caroline tattooed the word *hero* on her heart. But as much as she appreciated Noah protecting her, he'd humiliated Tim even more than she had. As arrogant as Tim was, he'd be determined to make her pay for that. And he was sneaky. He'd find a way to catch her alone.

His parting shot—"See you, Caroline"—accompanied by a slimy smile proved he intended to seek revenge.

He pivoted and strode off, still trying to maintain his tough-guy image, but most of his friends slinked off. Maybe they wouldn't accompany Tim next time. As soon as the boys were out of sight, Caroline turned. "Oh, Noah, *danke, danke, danke . . .*" She would have gushed out more *thank-you*s, but his lowering brow stopped her.

"I'm not sure I helped. I suspect that kid will be even more determined to come after you."

"I wouldn't be surprised," she agreed. "He doesn't like to be bested."

"That's obvious. Does he go after all his volleyball opponents like that?"

Caroline hung her head. "*Neh.* I insulted him after the game."

Noah listened intently as she described their run-in after the game. "I can see why that might have embarrassed him in front of his friends, but that doesn't excuse what he did today."

Her brother waved frantically from the stand to attract her attention.

"*Ach*, I forgot all about helping Gideon. Look at those lines."

"And I need to get over to the auction. With lines that long at most of the stands, I won't have time to wait for food."

"Did I keep you from getting lunch?" Caroline needed to get over to the stand, but she couldn't let Noah go hungry. Not after all he'd done for her. "If you come to the salad display case, I'll take your order now."

Noah shook his head. "Wouldn't be fair to all those people who've been waiting all this time. Thanks anyway. I need to go." He turned and hurried away.

Caroline called after him, "Noah?"

He glanced over his shoulder.

"*Danke* again."

With a brisk nod, he strode out the exit. Caroline stared after him as the door swung shut behind him. He'd come to her rescue twice now. She owed him a lot, but how could she ever repay him?

Hungry rumbles came from Noah's stomach. The tantalizing aroma of crisping chicken roasting on the spit wafted through the market door each time it opened. Maybe he should have grabbed a candy bar or whoopie pie to take the edge off. Too late now.

When he headed into the auction storehouse, Fred exploded, "About time you got here. You need to be onstage in less than ten minutes."

Rather than arguing that he'd arrived earlier, Noah only said mildly, "I'm ready."

"In that case, get out there and get started."

"You don't want me to take the mic from Abner."

"I most certainly do. Send him in here to help get things set up for the next lots we'll be auctioning off."

Noah didn't want to cut someone's time short. "But—"

Fred made a chopping motion with his hand to stop Noah. "You questioning my judgment?"

"Of course not. It's just—"

"Then get out there and do it." Fred's tone brooked no argument.

Although he'd rather not interrupt another auctioneer, Noah followed his boss's directive. He waited until Abner reached for the next item. Then Noah said in a low voice, hoping the mic wouldn't pick it up, "Hey, Abner, Fred wants you to go to the storeroom to help him."

"Right." Abner nodded. "I already planned to as soon as I finished here."

"I think he means right away."

Abner's hand stopped midair. "Now?"

"I'm afraid so."

Around them, audience members shifted in their chairs, eager for the bidding to restart. If they took too long to switch auctioneers, they'd lose some of the restless bidders.

Flicking off the mic so his words wouldn't broadcast around the tent, Abner shot Noah an incredulous glare. "You can't mean that. I still have ten minutes to go."

"Fred really did ask for you to come. You can ask him."

A mutinous expression on his face, Abner thrust the microphone in Noah's hand. "You better not be lying to me," Abner said as he stalked off.

Last night, Noah had angered Butch. Today, he'd upset Abner. Both times, it had been at Fred's orders. The last thing Noah wanted was to take someone else's rightful place, but he had no choice. And now with Abner gone, Noah couldn't lose the buyers. Some had already drifted toward the exit.

He turned on the mic and, skipping over some of the smaller items Abner had been about to offer, Noah waved toward one of the best pieces of furniture on display. "You don't want to miss this mahogany Chippendale highboy." He pointed out the pediment top, cabriole legs, the dovetail joints, brass hardware.

The people who'd been about to leave turned around and reentered the tent. Two of them began bidding, reinforcing Noah's idea that selling this piece would attract them back. The lively bidding also drew in passersby interested in the beautiful chest. And Noah kept bumping everyone's offers higher.

By the time the rivalry ended and the *Englisch* woman in the front row won, the highboy had set a record for auction furniture sales. Fred stood off to one side, a gloating smile on his lips. Beside him, Butch stood with clenched teeth, his face contorted by jealousy.

Noah's excitement nose-dived. He'd seen looks like that before. He'd need to watch his back. Both he and Caroline had people who wanted to get back at them. Noah had experience handling rivals.

But he worried about Caroline. She'd probably grown up sheltered in the Amish community. He'd need to keep an eye on her and find a way to protect her without her noticing.

To avoid being distracted, he shook off thoughts of Caroline and concentrated on the auction items. He loved the ease he felt onstage and the rapport he developed with each audience. For a short while, it helped him forget his loneliness.

Not that he wanted to get close to anyone ever again. He'd been too badly burned.

CHAPTER 7

Noah had been going for almost two hours straight. His throat parched, he reached for a water bottle while one of the younger helpers carried the Tiffany table lamp to its overjoyed buyer.

Next up—the puzzles. He bent to lift them from the crate. For some crazy reason, he didn't want to sell them. They brought back memories of Caroline. Caroline in his arms. Her soft skin. Her beautiful green eyes. Her joy and openness. Her free-flowing words. Her friendliness.

Those puzzles represented the first bond he'd had with someone since . . . He closed his mind to the pain, the betrayal.

How could he sell these?

His gut twisted. He had no choice. Unless one of the other men auctioned these off, Noah couldn't bid on them.

Impatient sighs rose from the people seated in front of him. The most important rule of selling was to keep the audience's attention. Reluctantly, he lifted the first two boxes, showed them, then displayed the next two, and started his patter. He'd sell them as a set. He might not get as much money that way, but at least the puzzles would all stay together.

To his left, a slight commotion attracted his attention. An elderly woman, her back to him, walked unsteadily into a row, attempting to get to an empty seat. Several people scooted over so she could have a chair close to the aisle. He dragged his focus back to the puzzles he'd been describing. Lifting the lid of the one Caroline had sorted, he held up a few of the wooden pieces—pieces she'd touched—to show their still-bright colors. He highlighted the way they fit together and then held up the original box covers, explaining their uniqueness. Tamping down the emotions swirling inside, he called for the first bid.

Offers started off slow. Perhaps his hesitancy to sell the puzzles affected the buyers. He had no right to damage sales for his own sentimental reasons. Banishing thoughts of Caroline from his mind, he tried to see the puzzles as just another auction item.

Soon, his newfound enthusiasm had paddles going up across the room. The price shot up, and several people fought to be the winning bidder. One by one, they dropped out until only one man remained.

Taking a deep breath, Noah began the phrase he dreaded, "Going . . . going . . ." Before he could say *gone*, a paddle waved frantically in the back of the crowd.

An elderly woman upped the final bid by one hundred dollars. Noah turned to the man and raised his eyebrows in question. When the man shook his head, Noah again ended the bid.

"Going . . . going . . ." He paused to see if anyone else would jump in. When no one did, he finished, ". . . gone.

Sold to number two hundred and thirty-seven." He pointed to the raised paddle and handed the boxes to the young boy who ran them back to the buyer.

Instead of starting on the next item, Noah waited until the puzzles had been delivered. Leaning heavily on her cane, the woman got shakily to her feet, her smile broad. She handed money and her paddle to the young man, who scooted off with the boxes after a few whispered instructions. Then she turned and winked at Noah.

Mrs. Vandenberg. The woman who'd picked him up yesterday. Why had an old woman like that paid so much for these puzzles?

Maybe they reminded her of her childhood. She must really care about them if she bid such an exorbitant amount. If they were that precious to her, she'd take good care of them. It eased Noah's reluctance to give them up. But he did hate losing them because of their connection to Caroline.

Speaking of Caroline, were his eyes playing tricks on him? All his concentrating on her must have conjured her up. Either that or Mrs. Vandenberg had just started a conversation with someone who looked remarkably like Caroline from the back.

The Caroline lookalike held up a finger and showed Mrs. Vandenberg something in her hand. The elderly lady smiled and nodded. Then the younger woman twirled around—a typical Caroline movement—and faced the stage.

Jah, definitely her. Her brilliant smile dazzled him, and he went numb. Forgetting he was in front of an audience, Noah returned her greeting with a sappy grin.

She held up a brown paper bag splotched with grease. After nodding toward it, she pointed to him. *For you*, she mouthed.

She'd brought him lunch? "Noah?" one of the boys who carried goods to customers stared at Noah with worried eyes. "You okay?"

"*Jah*, I'm fine." *I think. Or I will be if I can get my racing pulse under control.* He tried to tell himself the emotions coursing through him were gratitude and relief.

"Noah," an irritated voice snapped, "get off the stage. Abner, get up there."

For the first time ever, Noah eagerly relinquished the mic to another auctioneer. His stomach growled as he exited.

Hands on hips, Fred stood waiting, his face pinched into a scowl. Had his boss seen the interchange with Caroline?

"I thought I made it clear you were to stay away from that girl."

Noah swallowed hard. Fred definitely had noticed. "I, um . . . She's just bringing my lunch order."

"Since when does Hartzler's Barbecue deliver?"

"Since right now," a sweet voice answered behind him. "Noah didn't have time for lunch, so I brought it to him." Caroline appeared on the walkway outside the tent.

Fred spun around to glare at her. "He could have eaten before his shift if he'd gotten here on time."

"He got here earl—"

Behind Fred's back, Noah signaled her not to let his boss know. He didn't want to face questions about what he did earlier. And knowing Caroline, she'd probably natter on about him defending her from that punk and, even worse, explain he'd agreed—silently—to pretend to be her boyfriend. That would really get under Fred's skin.

Red spots bloomed high on Fred's cheekbones, and he narrowed his eyes. "I thought I warned you to stay away from the auction, Caroline Hartzler."

"You did what?" Mrs. Vandenberg tottered into view beside Caroline.

"I—I . . ." Fred gulped. "I don't want employees fraternizing. It's awkward when relationships go sour," he blustered. "And this girl here chased off one of my best employees. I won't let her do it again."

Mrs. Vandenberg thunked her cane down close to Fred's feet. He jumped back as if expecting her to whack him with it.

"First of all," she said, emphasizing each word, "Caroline had nothing to do with Zach leaving. That young man had some major problems because of his employment here. And he still does."

Caroline turned shocked eyes in Mrs. Vandenberg's direction. "You know where Zach is?"

"Of course. I keep track of all the employees. My father began this as a family business, and I intend to maintain his legacy, no matter how large the market gets."

Noah squirmed inside. That might explain how she'd known where he lived. What else had she found out about him?

"But that's not the issue here." She wobbled as she re-balanced herself on her cane, and Caroline reached out to steady her. "Thank you, dear." Mrs. Vandenberg beamed a tender smile in Caroline's direction, then caught Noah's eye. "Caroline's very thoughtful, isn't she?"

Of course she was. He'd had evidence of that. She'd

been determined to help him put those puzzles together. And she'd brought him a meal. The delicious aroma seeping from the bag in her hand made his mouth water.

But he still hadn't answered the question. How could he with Fred breathing down his neck?

Mrs. Vandenberg nudged Caroline. "Don't you have something for Noah?"

"What?" Caroline broke the gaze she'd fixed on him. "*Jah,* I brought your chicken dinner." She held out the paper sack. "I hope it's still warm enough."

Noah didn't care if the meal was ice-cold. Anything would taste good right now. Conscious of Fred scrutinizing their interaction, Noah reached for the bag, careful not to touch Caroline's fingers.

"How much do I owe you?"

Hurt flared in her eyes. "You don't owe me anything . . ." Noah winced, and Caroline's gaze flicked to Fred, who was observing them both like a hawk, and understanding dawned in her eyes. ". . . now. You can pay me after work."

"That after-work payment better not be what it sounds like." Fred glared from one to the other.

Caroline sucked in a sharp breath. Then she lifted her chin. "I don't know what you're thinking, but you don't have to worry. Noah won't give me any of your antiques."

"I don't think that's what he had in mind, Caroline." Mrs. Vandenberg trained a steady gaze on Fred until he lowered his eyes.

He shuffled. "Sorry." He didn't sound it, though.

Noah admired Caroline for challenging Fred. And Noah couldn't believe this feisty old lady had managed to put Fred in his place with only a look.

"And did I hear you forbidding these two to meet?" Mrs. Vandenberg demanded.

Fred shifted from one foot to the other. "Ever since Zach got run off, I don't let my employees date each other." He didn't mention Caroline's name this time, but he implied she was to blame.

"That's never been a rule in this market. If it had been, Gideon and Fern never would have married, nor would Stephen and Nettie, Sovilla and Isaac, Jeremiah and Keturah . . ."

"The last thing I need is your matchmaking interference." Then obviously rethinking his outburst, he added in a conciliatory tone, "Not that you don't do a good job of it, but I can't afford my auctioneers getting distracted. Did you see how Noah here flubbed his pitch when Caroline showed up? It's bad for business."

A furnace burned in the pit of Noah's stomach, spreading heat through his chest and to the tips of his ears. "I was watching to be sure Mrs. Vandenberg got her puzzles." He had done that, but he'd also gotten preoccupied with Caroline, so his defense wasn't totally honest.

Fred snorted. "Yeah, right. I'm not blind. She mouthed something to you. And you didn't even pick up the next auction item. Abner had to take the mic from you."

Noah couldn't deny that. But did Fred have to humiliate him?

It bothered Caroline that Fred made Noah so uncomfortable. And what Fred said wasn't true. Noah hadn't been looking at her, had he? She was pretty sure he hadn't.

He said he'd been watching Mrs. Vandenberg, and Caroline believed him. If anything, he might have been staring at the meal she'd brought. A meal that was getting cold while they talked.

"Noah needs to eat that lunch." She waved toward the bag in his hand, not caring that she'd interrupted Fred, whose mouth hung open ready to form his next words.

"He'll have to wait until after work. He's already used up his fifteen-minute break, so he needs to get back on-stage. If he can manage to keep his mind on his job, that is."

Fred's annoyance reminded Caroline she'd been hanging around here all this time, leaving Gideon alone with their customers. She'd promised her brother she wouldn't be long. "I have to go."

Fred flashed her a *good-riddance* look.

"Just a minute, dear." Mrs. Vandenberg laid a hand on Caroline's arm. "I need your help getting into the market when it's so busy. And don't worry, Gideon will be fine. I prayed the customers would wait for your return."

Fred sneered at the word *prayed*. But Caroline, who'd seen the effects of Mrs. Vandenberg's petitions to God, had no doubt Mrs. Vandenberg's requests to the Almighty would be answered. Her deep faith in the Lord had worked many miracles.

Noah held up the bag. "*Danke* for bringing this. I'll pay you after work."

"I wish you could eat it now." It might be lukewarm, but later the cold fries would be grainy and gummy.

"He'll eat it now, won't he, Fred?" Mrs. Vandenberg's question came across as a command. "Noah didn't get his break because we were talking. I don't want to be responsible for flouting the law by not letting him have his legally mandated time."

Fred's face twisted, but Mrs. Vandenberg had backed him into a corner. He shooed Noah toward the outdoor picnic tables. "Go, eat, and hurry up about it."

Not exactly gracious, but at least Noah would get to sit down and have a meal.

"*Danke* again." Noah lifted his bag in a playful salute. "Can't wait to eat it."

"It's nice to be taken care of sometimes," Mrs. Vandenberg remarked as he started off. "You don't always have to carry everyone else's burdens. Let others help you."

From the tightening of his shoulders, Caroline got the impression Mrs. Vandenberg's remark had hit a nerve. Her comments often did. She cared about everyone, but she did have a way of making people see the truth.

That skill, as well as her matchmaking, had given her quite a reputation. She'd matched all the couples she'd mentioned in the past few years, but Caroline had heard stories of Mrs. Vandenberg matching couples at the market since the mid-1950s.

Who did she plan to match next? It was always fun to watch her bring unlikely couples together. Maybe Caroline should ask Mrs. Vandenberg for dating advice. *Who would be a good match for me?* She wanted someone who loved her for herself, but who'd want to marry a determined, outspoken tomboy?

Caroline pushed those depressing thoughts away and took Mrs. V's arm to assist her.

"You know, dear, you should concentrate on your good points rather than dwelling on the negatives. And someday you might even come to realize the things you believe are negatives can be your greatest strengths."

Mrs. Vandenberg's comment startled Caroline. "How do you always know what I'm thinking?" After the words left her lips, she wished she'd thought before speaking. She hadn't meant to sound accusatory.

Luckily, she hadn't offended Mrs. Vandenberg. The

elderly woman only laughed. "With you, my dear, it's quite easy. All your feelings show on your face."

"They do?" Caroline cringed. Could everyone read what she was thinking all the time?

"And if your face doesn't tell the world what you're thinking, you're sure to say it aloud." Though Mrs. Vandenberg's words were pointed, her tone was gentle and kind.

Caroline already knew that was her worst fault. But it stung that Mrs. Vandenberg felt the need to call her on it.

Trying not to let her hurt show, Caroline steered Mrs. V through the crowds exiting the market but had to let go of her arm to open the door.

Evidently, Caroline hadn't done a good job of masking her feelings, because when Mrs. Vandenberg looked up to thank her, she studied Caroline's face for a moment, then reached out and patted her arm.

"Ah, Caroline, if you look at yourself through God's eyes, you'll realize honesty is a blessing rather than a curse."

Caroline had never thought of blurting things out as a blessing. But Mrs. V was right. Honesty was a good thing. Maybe her bluntness had a positive side.

"Being open and clear about your thoughts and feelings can be helpful. It lets others know where you stand. And it keeps you humble."

That was for sure and certain. Caroline's faults burst from her lips, even things she wished to keep hidden.

Mrs. Vandenberg tapped her cane on the threshold a few times before venturing forward. Her speech, though, showed no hesitation. "It can have drawbacks—as you've discovered. Tempering your speech can also be a virtue."

"I know." Caroline hung her head. She spent a lot of

time apologizing. And her family always warned her about taming her unruly tongue.

Mrs. V had put her finger on Caroline's biggest struggle. Another was getting distracted. And from the look on her brother's face as they approached the stand, he intended to lecture her about that right now.

CHAPTER 8

"Good afternoon, Gideon." Mrs. Vandenberg's cheery greeting wiped the irritation from his face.

Caroline breathed a sigh of relief. At least while Mrs. V stuck around, Gideon wouldn't scold her. Not that he ever did. But he had a way of making her feel extremely guilty. Even more guilty than she already did.

One other thing on her side was the fact that the stand wasn't too busy. Only a few customers stood in line. Quite unusual for a Saturday afternoon. They were always busy until closing. Caroline smiled to herself. She had no doubt who was responsible for this lull. Mrs. V and her direct line to God.

While Mrs. Vandenberg chatted with Gideon, Caroline hustled into the stand to wait on the customers. After she'd sent a Mennonite mother on her way with two barbecued chickens and several quarts of potato salad, she tuned in to her brother's conversation. Mrs. Vandenberg asked all the usual questions about Fern and the baby, the market expansion that had recently gotten underway, and Gideon's responsibilities at the market.

"You know, Gideon," she said, "it seems you could use more help here at the stand."

"That's for sure." He glanced around at the empty counter and drew his brows together in confusion. "Well, we normally could use several people. I'm not sure why it's so dead this afternoon."

Caroline put a hand over her mouth to hold back a giggle. She suspected business would return to normal as soon as Mrs. Vandenberg left.

The older woman caught Caroline's eye and smiled. "I'm sure it'll pick up soon. But I wanted to ask you about hiring a few people from the STAR center."

Gideon hesitated. "They'd need to be trained, wouldn't they?"

"Yes, but all the ones who've applied to work at the market are eager to learn. And those who've already been placed here have been working out well. Stephen and Nettie have already turned their business over to one of the STAR trainees to manage."

Caroline whispered a prayer that her brother would agree. It would take a huge burden from her shoulders if they had more workers. And it would free Gideon and Fern to spend more time together.

Her brother glanced at her, his eyes thoughtful. "If it were just me, I'd say *jah* in a second, but I have Caroline and Fern to think about."

"You don't trust the Lord to watch over them?"

Gideon's face scrunched up as if Mrs. Vandenberg's question had stung him. "I do, but . . ."

She shook her head. "Whenever you follow something with a *but*, you don't mean what you said before that."

His face grew even more pinched. Then he released

a long, drawn-out sigh. "You're right. The thought of gang members working with my sister and my wife . . ." Gideon's words trailed off under Mrs. Vandenberg's piercing gaze.

"I think you underestimate Caroline's abilities. She's quite capable of defending herself."

Gideon's eyebrows rose, and it bugged Caroline that he was acting so surprised. She longed to remind him she'd tagged along with him and their other older brothers. And even though she was five years younger than Gideon, she'd always managed to keep up with all of them and do whatever they were doing.

But a still, small voice inside reminded her that, here at the market, she'd proven herself to be flighty and unreliable.

Mrs. Vandenberg looked thoughtful. "One possibility would be to hire only females."

Gideon pursed his lips. "If they're young, I'd worry about their influence on Aidan."

"But they're trying to turn their lives around," Caroline burst out. "They wouldn't be a bad influence. And Aidan has been different ever since his false arrest. He's also changed a lot now that he's helping out at the center."

"Good points, Caroline." Mrs. Vandenberg beamed at her.

"I guess"—Gideon stroked his beard—"having children makes you more cautious."

"That's for sure." Caroline regretted saying it, even if it was true. Before he married Fern, her brother would have jumped at any chance to help others. "If Fern and I didn't work at the stand," she demanded, "would you do it?"

"Of course. I'd be happy to train as many workers as needed."

"I'm so glad to hear that, Gideon." Mrs. Vandenberg's smile stretched across her face, deepening the crinkles around her eyes. "I'll ask Stephen and Nettie to choose the best candidates for you."

Gideon held up a hand. "Wait a minute. I didn't mean . . ."

"Perhaps not." Her lips quirked. "But your heart answered for you. I'll take that as your true response. I'm sure God will bless you for it."

"But—but . . ."

Mrs. Vandenberg wagged a finger at him. "What did I say about that word? Don't go around negating your faith with all those *but*s." She turned and headed off, her cane clicking a joyful rhythm.

"What have I done?" Gideon ran a hand through his hair.

"Answered God's call?" Caroline's heart overflowed with gratitude toward Mrs. V. "Did you still want me to ask Anna Mary?"

Her brother didn't seem to hear her. "I didn't even get a chance to pray about it. Or to ask Fern."

Caroline could guess Fern's response. A wholehearted *jah*. Her sister-in-law loved to help others. "You think Fern would object?"

At her pointed reminder of his wife's generous spirit, Gideon shook his head. "*Neh*. She'd be the first to agree."

"Then what are you worried about?" When Gideon turned to her with a frown, Caroline wished she hadn't asked that question. She'd brought his attention back to her and her behavior.

Before he could launch into any complaints, a crowd lined up, and she and Gideon stayed too busy to talk the rest of the afternoon. Caroline breathed a sigh of relief.

Maybe if she helped handle this flood of people, he'd forget her earlier desertion.

Rushing from the rotisserie with another spit of barbecued chickens, Gideon wiped his brow. "Where were all these people hiding while we were talking to Mrs. Vandenberg?"

Caroline hid her secretive half smile. She knew the answer. Leave it to Mrs. Vandenberg. And God.

And Mrs. V had given Caroline several other valuable lessons today, both spoken and unspoken. But the one that made the most impact hadn't been addressed to Caroline. Like her brother, she'd been adding a lot of *but*s to her prayers, especially the ones about her future.

Noah savored every bite of the meal. He still couldn't believe Caroline had taken time from her busy day, with all those crowds gathered at the counter, to bring him a meal. And what a meal it was. Half a barbecued chicken, a large bag of fries, and small lidded containers of applesauce, potato salad, broccoli salad, macaroni salad. Even a chocolate cupcake packed carefully in a small bakery box.

Mrs. Vandenberg had been absolutely right about Caroline. She had a generous heart. If only he could date a woman like that. He wiped away the thought along with the pain it brought.

But Mrs. Vandenberg's parting comment still haunted him. Let others take care of him? Did she have any idea what something like that would cost him? He'd learned a lot in the past few years, and the most important lesson of all had been: *Never trust anyone, even those closest to you. You never know when they'll betray you.*

The only sure thing in life is that they would. And sometimes when you least expected it.

Noah stood abruptly, both to break off the dark thoughts and because he'd dawdled too long. Fred would be timing every second of this break, and Noah didn't want to give his boss anything else to grouse about. Crumpling the lunch bag and the trash inside, he jogged to the trash can and then back into place beside the stage with about ten seconds to spare.

As he debated whether or not to interrupt Abner, Fred hissed out a snakelike breath behind Noah's shoulder. "What are you waiting for? Get up there."

As Abner bent to pick up the next item, Noah reached out a hand for the mic. "Um, Abner, I think Fred wants you." Noah hoped his words were true.

With a hurt look, Abner handed over the microphone, and Noah jumped onto the stage, exuding energy and excitement. The delicious lunch had fueled him, and for the rest of the afternoon, he sold antique furniture, toys, and tools as if he were on fire, until the overhead PA system announced the auction would end in ten minutes. Auctioneers stopped selling shortly before closing so people could turn in their numbers and pay their bills.

Both Butch and Abner, who were sorting out and organizing items for next Tuesday's auction, looked up when Noah strode into the storage building.

"You did pretty good up there," Fred said grudgingly.

Abner's shoulders slumped. He'd been the head auctioneer for years, and he'd been the one who'd trained Noah. Abner had been generous with advice and tips. Now his pupil kept getting more time onstage than Abner did as the teacher. That had to be hard. Noah couldn't help feeling sorry for the older man.

Beside Abner, Butch gritted his teeth. He plainly disliked his father praising Noah. Unfortunately, now that Noah had arrived, Butch rarely got to sell. Once in a while, he'd fill in for breaks, but Butch craved being front and center. If he had his way, it'd be all day, every day the auction stayed open. Fred didn't leave much time for his compliment to sink in. "Too bad you don't do that all the time."

At his dad's comment, Butch broke into a grin. Shooting Noah a disgusted look that mirrored his son's usual expression, Fred tromped toward the exit. "I'll be over in my office if anyone needs me. When I get back, everything better be ready for Tuesday's auction."

After the door shut behind Fred, Butch took charge, ordering the two other men around. "Noah, bring that blanket chest here. We'll start with that. Then the Saratoga steamer trunk. Abner, you grab that."

Abner strained and grunted to lift the trunk. Noah rushed over to help. But when Butch lined up Windsor chairs, followed by a whole raft of furniture, Noah worried the lineup was too focused on their biggest pieces.

Should Noah correct Butch, or wait for his dad to do it? Fred wouldn't agree with these choices, and they'd have to stay later to rearrange the order. Noah hoped to get off in time to thank Caroline for the meal.

He cleared his throat. "Might be better to save some of the furniture for later in the day or Friday evening or Saturday when we get larger crowds."

Abner didn't back Noah up verbally, but he did nod.

Butch glowered at Noah. "You've only been working

here a short while. You think you know more than I do? Don't forget, I've grown up around this business."

Noah didn't dispute that, but he still tried to steer Butch in the right direction. "Your dad usually likes to auction smaller items between the furniture." That strategy kept everyone interested. "What about those milk glass eggs or a hooked rug after the blanket chest?"

"What don't you understand?" Butch snapped. "This is our auction house, and you'll do it my way or you're out."

Noah didn't know if Butch's influence stretched to the hiring and firing of employees, but he'd better not take that chance. Pressing his lips together to avoid a smart-aleck retort, Noah followed Butch's directions.

Fred popped his head in. "We took in more money than usual tonight, so good job, everyone." From his gloating expression, they'd brought in a pile of money. He didn't say it, but most of those sales were due to Noah. Abner had been bumped out of his normal slot and only sold when Noah went on break.

"That's great, Dad." Butch threw his shoulders back as if he'd been solely responsible for the profit.

"Hey, what's this?" Fred's gaze had fallen on the proposed lineup. "Whose idea was it to sell all this furniture early on a Tuesday morning? That's crazy. We have the smallest crowds then. Lots of stay-at-home moms and homemakers. They come for practical things or small decorative items."

"Noah was trying to show off his knowledge," Butch answered, pretending to sigh and throwing a quelling glance at Noah. The warning flashing in Butch's eyes made it clear he'd get Noah sacked for disagreeing. Abner shrugged and made a face behind Butch's back but didn't correct the misinformation.

"And you listened to him?" Fred's eyes bugged out. "Why would you take advice from someone who's only just started?"

"He's very insistent." Butch's words had an unattractive whine. "Noah refused to see things our way. He doesn't seem to be a team player."

"I've noticed that."

Fred's sarcastic comment cut into Noah. He'd done nothing but helpful things since he'd been here. He'd worked hard to understand the business, practiced his patter every chance he could, worked extra unpaid hours, and bumped Fred's profits by a lot, judging from his boss's triumphant look when he'd entered the storeroom.

Noah debated defending himself, but he'd risk angering Butch more. Would it be worth it? Most likely, Fred would believe his son in the end.

"Get this all rearranged. Abner, you've been here the longest. Take charge of the lineup." Fred turned to Noah. "And since this fiasco was your idea, Butch and Abner can leave once the list is written up. You can move everything you mistakenly chose back into place and set up the rest for Tuesday."

Just before Fred let the door close behind him, he barked, "And don't take too long. I don't want to be here for hours."

Neither did Noah. But it looked like he'd blown his chance to thank Caroline. Maybe it was better that way. He should stay as far away from her as he could. Perhaps Fred had done him a favor.

CHAPTER 9

After Gideon locked the market doors, he returned to the stand. Caroline had worked hard while he was gone. She had the rotisserie parts soaking in the sink, and all the salads and leftover chicken had been transferred to the refrigerator. On Saturday, they always did a deep cleaning of the refrigerated cases to kill germs and prevent stale odors from developing over the next two days until the market opened on Tuesday.

Caroline was scrubbing out the cases when her brother entered. She hoped her hard work would help to erase her missteps of the past two days and prove to Gideon how responsible she intended to be from now on. Maybe, just maybe, it might save her from a lecture. A lecture she had to admit was well-deserved.

Gideon smiled to see how far she'd gotten on the end-of-the-day chores. "*Danke*, Caroline." He started on the interior of the rotisserie.

If she'd planned better, she should have started at the other end of the salad counter. Instead, she'd begun to clean at the section closest to her brother.

"Listen, Caroline, we need to discuss you working in

the stand. If you're going to be part of the business, then you have to be here. You left me alone several times yesterday and today."

"I'm really sorry, Gid."

Her brother sighed. "I don't like to bring up the past, but we ran into this problem before."

He didn't mention her running off after the previous auctioneer—taking him baked goods, hurrying to meet him for lunch breaks, twisting his arm to get him to take her home.

She'd pushed all that from her mind and forgotten it long ago, but Fred had brought it up today. And then Mrs. Vandenberg mentioned she'd stayed in touch with Zach. That brought the past into the present. Caroline only hoped Zach had moved far away, like he'd planned. She never wanted to run into him ever again.

When Caroline didn't answer, Gideon continued. "So what was with the boys today? Who are they, and what did they want?"

She'd hoped he wouldn't ask that. What could she say? "I think they wanted to embarrass me." *Or intimidate me. Or pay me back.*

Her brother stopped cleaning and turned toward her. Although his eyes bored into her back, she didn't turn around. Instead, she hunched her shoulders and concentrated on wiping out the small crevices inside the glass case.

"Why would they want to do that?"

"Probably because I insulted one of them."

Gideon didn't say *Oh, Caroline*, but his long-suffering sigh made it clear. He knew her mouth often got her in trouble.

She might as well get it over with. His questions would

only make this a long, drawn-out process. Caroline spilled the whole story. Or most of it. Winning the volleyball game. Her snide comment. Her apology. Tim's friends teasing him. She left out the pancake and Tim's humiliating comment about the shoulder roll.

"I see." Gideon turned back to his work.

They worked in silence a few minutes before he asked, "Do you think they'll be back?"

Caroline nibbled her lip. "They might." Tim hadn't liked Noah putting him in his place. "I'm not sure they'll quit until they feel they've gotten me back."

"That doesn't sound like boys from the Amish community. You did ask for forgiveness, even if you hurt his pride by doing it. Have you tried apologizing again?"

"*Neh.*"

Although she usually rushed to ask for forgiveness—and she needed to do it countless times a day for running at the mouth—for some reason, she'd hardened herself against doing it in this case. Why was she so reluctant?

In the stillness of her heart, a spotlight shone on that unforgiveness. And God's searching light revealed her wounded pride, her shame, and most of all, her belief that she was undeserving.

Tim's nasty teasing along with his comments today questioning who'd want to date a girl like her had exposed those sore spots. She kept her personal pain hidden from the rest of the world. Somehow, he'd figured out how to hurt her in the meanest way possible.

Noah had soothed her wounds with his words, but he'd been playacting. He'd come to her rescue and said everything she'd dreamed her ideal man would say. But Noah hadn't been saying those things about her. He'd only been parrying Tim's insults.

If only his defense of her had been real. Caroline drifted off into a daydream where Noah repeated those statements while the two of them were alone together. Was it possible some man might feel that way about her someday?

"Hey, Caroline?" Gideon's voice shattered her fantasy. "Do you plan to scrub those cabinets or just sit there staring at them?"

Caroline was grateful her back was to him, so he couldn't see the slow burn that crept up her neck and face at his words. Mamm often warned Caroline about indulging in false hopes.

Keep your feet on the ground and your mind on the Lord. That will keep you from imagining things that aren't true.

Picking up the spray bottle, Caroline squirted the glass and rubbed vigorously. But she couldn't wipe away the wishing. If only someone like Noah could be a real boyfriend instead of just a pretend one.

Abner, eager to go home, made a rapid list of items while a smirking Butch watched Noah return all the furniture to its original places. Noah didn't mind toting heavy things. He'd built up his muscles over the past few years, so moving furniture substituted for lifting weights.

Besides, now that he couldn't thank Caroline, he didn't care how late he stayed. He had nothing to return home to on a Saturday evening. Nothing but loneliness.

After Abner handed over the list, he and Butch hightailed it out of there, leaving Noah with all the work. Noah would never have done that to them even if Fred had told him to, but Abner played poker on Saturday night, and no doubt Butch had a date. They'd been itching to leave as soon as the auction closed.

Noah rushed through the work so Fred wouldn't be annoyed when he returned. By the time Fred stuck his head in the door, Noah had replaced most of the items.

"How much longer will you be?" Fred demanded.

"Maybe twenty minutes? A half hour?"

"Try to hurry it up. I have things to do tonight."

Although they could cut the time in half if Fred helped, Noah refrained from pointing that out. He just kept hustling.

About ten minutes later, Fred glanced at his watch. "Forget the rest. You can come in early on Tuesday and finish. We have enough here for at least the first few hours. I gotta go."

Noah set down the box he was carrying and headed for the door.

"Next time," Fred warned, "don't try to show off until you know more about how auctions work. Let Abner take the lead."

Noah locked the words he longed to say behind closed lips. He should defend himself, but for some reason, he always went quiet when it came time to speak up. He'd paid for his reticence in the past. And because of it, he'd gotten stuck with extra work today. His early training in giving a man the shirt off his back or going the extra mile kept him silent, even in the face of injustice.

Strangely enough, though, he had no trouble standing up for others, like he had for Caroline today. He hoped he'd convinced those young men to stay away from her. It seemed she ended up in a lot of man trouble. He'd only known her two days, and already he'd rescued her twice.

Although in both cases, he had to admit, she seemed quite capable of handling things herself. He'd only come along after she'd extricated herself. But she'd depended on him to assist with her escapes.

What would a relationship with her be like? She'd keep things lively, that was for sure. And the last thing Noah wanted or needed was to have his life stirred up. After the last few years, all he longed for was peace and quiet. Even if his isolation often left him sad and lonely.

Caroline stood abruptly and moved to the sink to wash the rotisserie parts that had been soaking. Gideon might think she was trying to avoid his questions, but she only wanted a little time to indulge in her daydreams.

She'd rather remember Noah's spirited defense of her than recount the reasons why Tim disliked her. And even more, she wanted to ignore the nudges of her conscience. Would God really expect her to apologize to Tim again?

Caroline wasn't sure. She'd been taught it was her responsibility to make things right. But sometimes other people should do it first. After all, Tim had insulted her several times. But she didn't want to waste time thinking about him or about the other auctioneer.

Noah, with his serious eyes and perfect comebacks, was much more fun to picture. And he made a great hero for her fantasies. What would it be like to go out with him?

She and Noah were having a picnic by a stream, laughing and talking, when Gideon interrupted her.

"Caroline?" His voice had a sharp edge, indicating he'd called her name more than once.

"What?" The lovely image of time with Noah popped like the soap bubbles in the sink, and Caroline stood holding a dripping spit in midair.

"Were you planning to wash that or just hold it up all night?"

She plunged her hand into the water and scrubbed the metal hard. "I'll be done soon."

"I'd appreciate it. I'd really like to get home to Fern and the baby."

"I know." Caroline wished she hadn't delayed him again today.

"Why don't you give that to me and I'll dry it?" Gideon held out his hand for the long metal rod.

Caroline finished cleaning it, ran it under warm rinse water, and passed it to him. Then she rushed through the rest of the dishes.

"Did you get the cases done?" Gideon asked after he reassembled the rotisserie parts she'd washed.

"*Neh*. I only finished the one near the cash register."

He blew out an exasperated breath. "I'll do the ones on the other side. When you're finished here, can you get the rest of them on the left?"

Pushing all thoughts of Noah from her mind, Caroline tackled the section Gideon had assigned her, and they both finished at the same time.

Her brother rewarded her with a huge smile. "*Danke* for hurrying. I can't wait to get home."

"I know." She grinned back. "I'll go out and hitch up the horse while you lock up." Caroline dashed off before Gideon answered, and she had the horse ready by the time he'd turned out the lights and locked the employee door.

As they passed the auction house and storeroom, light seeped from around the doors. Was Noah still inside working?

Caroline turned her thoughts to other things. If she didn't, she'd get caught up in fanciful thoughts again. The last thing she needed was to fall for another auctioneer. Fred had already told her to stay away, and she should heed that warning. No point in getting herself tangled in another fiasco.

CHAPTER 10

On Sunday morning, Caroline carried Anna Mary's freshly washed apron out to their buggy as her parents got ready to leave for church. The house seemed lonelier now that her widowed sister-in-law, Nettie, had married Stephen Lapp. Nettie and her four children had moved into Stephen's large house with his five children. And Gideon and Fern had a place of their own.

As the youngest, Caroline was the only one of the family still at home. She missed having her nieces and nephews in the house. Before everyone moved, she'd often taken a few of the children to church in her buggy. She longed for their cheerful squabbling and cute antics.

To fill the silence, Caroline chatted with her parents most of the way to the Bontragers' house, telling them about the volleyball games, omitting the parts about Tim and the pancake. Then she discussed Gideon's plans to hire more workers.

"I'm going to ask Anna Mary if she can help." Caroline wriggled on the back seat. "I hope she can do it." It would be so much fun to work with her best friend . . . if Anna Mary didn't spend all her time reminding Caroline to curb her enthusiasm.

As they pulled in to the Bontragers' driveway, Mamm held up a hand. "I hope you talked yourself out on the way here and will spend more time listening rather than speaking." She softened her rebuke with a kind smile.

Once again, Caroline had monopolized the conversation. She'd only done it to keep the family engaged, but instead of asking questions that included her parents, she'd centered the whole conversation around herself. When would she learn?

Caroline determined to think of others first today. She'd act calm and ladylike to please Mamm. But the minute she hopped out of the buggy with her friend's apron, Anna Mary waved and beckoned. Caroline squealed and raced over. She couldn't wait to ask Anna Mary about working at the market.

Behind Caroline, Mamm let out a sigh. The critical voice inside Caroline warned her to slow down and walk instead of run, but the excitement fizzing inside kept her flying across the lawn.

Breathless, Caroline screeched to a stop in front of Anna Mary, and words tumbled out, "Gideon's thinking of hiring people to work at the stand and I asked him about you and he said *jah* and—"

Like Mamm, Anna Mary held up a hand. "Wait a minute. Catch your breath first. Then, why don't you start with *Hi, Anna Mary, wie geht's?*"

Only two minutes ago, Caroline had promised herself to be sedate, and she'd already broken her vow. She bowed her head and gulped in a deep breath. Then she repeated her friend's question. She tried not to shift impatiently while Anna Mary asked how she was.

"I'm fine, *danke*." *I would have been even better if you'd been as thrilled as I am about the job.* Caroline managed to keep that thought to herself.

Anna Mary delayed Caroline's question until they'd exchanged aprons and put them in their buggies. Caroline seethed as she rushed to close the distance between them.

"Now what did you want to tell me?" Anna Mary asked gently. "You spoke so fast I couldn't understand a word you said."

Again, another criticism dinged Caroline. And a little resentment flickered inside. Why couldn't other people be as joyful and excited as she was?

In the Bible, God said to make a joyful noise. Did He really mean for them to run around with flat expressions and never show how they felt? Wasn't that lying? Or did nobody but her buzz with emotion?

"Caroline?" Anna Mary waved a hand in front of Caroline's face. "I didn't mean to hurt your feelings."

"You didn't," Caroline said automatically. But that wasn't true. She corrected herself. "Well, you did, but you meant well."

Anna Mary winced, and Caroline rushed to apologize. "I'm sorry. I shouldn't have said that." *Even if it was the truth.*

"*Jah*, sometimes it's better to keep our feelings to ourselves."

Caroline wasn't so sure about that. She changed the subject. Speaking slowly, she told Anna Mary about Gideon's plan. "And he said I could ask you to work with us." Caroline squeezed her hands together. "I hope you can."

"Let me ask Mamm. There she is—talking to Lenore Raber."

A spring in her step, Anna Mary headed toward the

two women. Unlike Caroline, who would have interrupted the conversation with her news, Anna Mary stood quietly while her mother talked.

Impatience almost drove Caroline across the yard to demand an answer. Instead, she forced her fists down at her sides and held herself back. She made herself study Anna Mary as an example of how to approach conversations properly.

When Anna Mary's *mamm* finally turned and listened, she frowned, then followed that with a thoughtful expression. Caroline wished she were close enough to hear the response. As Anna Mary came skipping back, Caroline's spirits lifted.

"Mamm is worried it'll be too much for me to do, and I won't be around enough to help her. I promised to keep up with my usual housework and chores. Besides it'll really help out if I'm making money. So she said *jah*! I can start on Tuesday, if you'd like."

Instead of jumping up and down with glee, Caroline curbed her eagerness. She tried to follow Anna Mary's example. Struggling against impatience, Caroline spoke calmly, "I'm sure Gideon will be fine with that."

Anna Mary's brows drew together in puzzlement. "I thought you wanted me to work with you. You don't sound very happy."

Caroline clenched her hands together to refrain from giving her friend an exuberant hug. "I'm thrilled. I'm just trying to act like you and Mamm tell me I should."

Anna Mary burst out laughing. "You look like someone asked you to scrub the inside of an outhouse."

After all my hard work to keep my feelings in check, all I get is more criticism?

"Oh, Caroline, I didn't mean to make you feel bad."

Anna Mary put a hand on Caroline's arm. "I'm proud of you for trying. But, to tell the truth, I think I like it better when you jump up and down."

Now Caroline was totally confused. "That's what I wanted to do when you told me your *mamm* said *jah*."

"Maybe you could find a happy balance between your excitement and acting calmer." Anna Mary glanced toward the front door. "*Ach*, everyone's gone inside. We'd better hurry."

Caroline wrapped Anna Mary in a brief hug. "I'm so glad you'll be working with me." Then she stepped back. "Was that a good balance?"

Anna Mary smiled. "It was perfect. And I'm glad we'll get to spend more time together."

They both rushed across the lawn and hurried inside the house. The younger girls had already lined up ready to enter, so Caroline and Anna Mary took their places farther back. And they both walked into the women's side of the room filled with suppressed anticipation for the coming week.

Noah paced from one end of the RV to the other, pivoted, and headed back. He sympathized with caged animals. They endured this restless motion in a confined space every day of their lives. He only had to bear it all day on Sundays. A fitting punishment for avoiding church.

Most people around here would be at church now. And the Amish would have several more hours to go if they stayed for the meal. But after three years with no opportunity to go to an Amish service, he'd gotten out of the habit. Yet, he still adhered to his *daed*'s overly strict Sunday rules. Work, outdoor play, toys, and noise had all been forbidden. If it had been any other day of the week, Noah would have gone outside and found something in nature to keep himself busy—studying birds, identifying trees, fishing in the creek, or walking the trails. But not being allowed out of the house on Sunday as a child had ingrained that discipline in him.

It also served another purpose. It protected him from discovery. If other people saw him outside on Sunday rather than at church, they'd question him. And sooner or later, someone would notify the *g'may* about an absentee Amish man. The last thing he wanted was to call attention to himself and his non-attendance. So far, no one realized he lived here. Most of the campground residents stayed for a week or two and moved on. The older couple who ran the place smiled and waved in passing, but generally, they kept to themselves.

Noah had a book he could read, but he couldn't settle to it. Every time he tried, his eyes glazed over. And images danced in front of his eyes. Caroline's beautiful smile. Her constant chatter that washed over him like birdsong. If only he could be that carefree. That open and honest. That trusting.

If only he could be that free. Free to give away his heart.

Arghh. Why couldn't he get her out of his mind? He didn't want to leave this job. It represented the first stability he'd had in a long time. But if he couldn't find a way to get his feelings under control, he'd have to take off. And hope he could find a job somewhere, anywhere. As far from here—and her—as he could get.

* * *

Caroline had trouble concentrating on the sermons. For some reason, her mind kept straying to yesterday's encounter with Tim and to Noah's rescue. For the first time in her life, someone had stood up for her and made her feel like her personality was not only normal, but desirable. Noah might have been making it up, but he sounded convincing.

She wondered where he lived and what *g'may* he belonged to. Was this a church Sunday or an off-Sunday for him? Maybe if he went on a different Sunday, she could show up at one of his services. Even though she was forward, she wouldn't do it, but she enjoyed imagining his surprise when she showed up and sat in the women's section across from him.

Feeling guilty, Caroline squeezed her hands together in her lap and forced herself to tune into the final sermon. If Daed or Mamm asked her what she'd learned today, she'd need to have an answer.

The minister quoted Galatians 5:26. "'Let us not be desirous of vain glory, provoking one another, envying one another.'"

Caroline didn't need his explanation of vain glory to know her excessive pride in winning the volleyball game fit the definition. And that wasn't the only jab to her conscience. Hadn't she also provoked Tim? She'd railed against apologizing to him a second time. This verse exposed her conceitedness, her pride. And, added to that, her inability to forgive.

The minister went on to talk about humility and putting others' needs before your own. By the time the service ended, Caroline had been thoroughly convicted over her actions in the last few days—gloating over the volleyball win, angering Tim, talking over people without giving them a chance to get a word in . . . She'd even done that coming over here this morning with her parents.

Father, please forgive me, and help me to live more like Jesus.

As they headed for the kitchen after the final prayer, Caroline fell into step beside her friend.

To practice her vow to think more of others, Caroline smiled at Anna Mary. "*Danke* for letting me borrow your apron Friday. I don't know what I would have done without it."

Anna Mary giggled. "Worked in the stand with a dirt-streaked one?"

"*Jah*, I can imagine Gideon's face if I showed up like that." They both broke into peals of laughter.

"If you girls can't keep your mind on serving the food, I'm going to have to separate you," Mamm warned, but her teasing smile showed she was only joking.

Side by side, Caroline and Anna Mary carried platters out to the serving table. They quieted as they entered the room where the men were seated, but after they set down the food, they whispered together on the way back to the kitchen.

Anna Mary leaned in close. "Guess what? My cousin goes to church with that guy who got so upset with you at volleyball. His name is Tim."

Caroline didn't tell her friend she already knew his name. A little flash of pride flickered through her for not interrupting or taking over the conversation. She'd let Anna Mary talk.

Her friend continued. "He's been bragging about how he's going to beat you next time."

Caroline promptly forgot her prayer during the service. "We'll see about that."

"Maybe you shouldn't try to win this time," Anna Mary suggested.

"I should lose just to keep his pride from being hurt?"

Anna Mary's eyes opened wide at Caroline's vehemence. "What do you get out of beating him?"

Mouth hanging open, Caroline stopped pouring applesauce into a dish. She couldn't believe her friend had asked that question. But once again, Caroline had been brought around to face the sermon's truth. She snapped her mouth shut.

When Caroline didn't say anything for a few minutes, Anna Mary ventured a timid "I'm sorry. I didn't mean to hurt your feelings."

"You didn't. I'm thinking about the sermon and trying not to talk so much about myself." She sighed. "It's not easy."

Anna Mary chuckled. "I imagine it's not. At least not for you."

Caroline tried to tell herself Anna Mary hadn't meant her comment as a dig. She'd only been trying to be sympathetic, but it still stung. Did everyone think Caroline couldn't keep quiet?

Determined to prove them wrong, she held in the story of Tim coming to the market. At least that's what she told herself. But if she were honest, she didn't want to share that with Anna Mary because she'd have to admit Noah came to her rescue. Then she'd need to examine her feelings about him—something she wasn't ready to do.

CHAPTER 11

On Tuesday morning, Noah arrived at work early. The deserted parking lot greeted him. Even though he'd already walked the seven miles from home, he paced around the building to walk off some of his nervous energy. He had no idea how long he'd have to wait for Fred.

Once he'd organized all the auction items, he'd head over to the market. If the chicken barbecue stand wasn't too busy, he'd thank Caroline for the meal and offer her money. She'd indicated she didn't want him to pay, but he didn't like being beholden to people. Once you were in their debt, they believed you owed them favors.

Noah had to admit it hadn't been that way while he was growing up in the Amish community. Everyone helped each other without expecting to be repaid, but his brain had been rewired since then. Every kindness came with a price tag attached. Most likely, Caroline didn't believe that, but she had felt obligated to give him something in return for standing up for her. All he'd done was put a bully in his place. He would have done it for anyone.

He tried to ignore the taunting in his mind. *But you especially enjoyed playing the hero in front of her.* As much as he hated to admit it, that was true.

A loud roar alerted him to a rusty truck pulling into a parking space at the market. Martin, the maintenance man, had arrived.

"Hey, Noah!" Martin waved as he hopped out of his truck. "You're here early. Need to get into the building?"

"That'd be great if you could let me in." It would give Noah plenty of time to get everything organized before Fred arrived.

Martin loped over, fingered through the huge ring of keys hanging on a metal loop attached to his belt, and selected one. With rapid, practiced moves, he unlocked the door and pushed it open.

Noah couldn't help admiring his ability to keep all those keys straight. "Thanks for letting me in. How do you remember what key goes to which door?"

With a laugh, Martin tapped the side of his head. "I have a filing cabinet right here."

"Seems like there'd be a lot to store there."

"Sure is." Martin beamed. "Most people don't realize how much work this job is. Not just the physical work, but all the details I have to keep track of."

"Better you than me."

"True. You have your own talents, though. I've heard ya up onstage. You're good."

Compliments made Noah uncomfortable. "I'm learning. Abner's a good teacher."

"Yep, he is. One of the best." With a wave, Martin headed off. "Lots to do before the market opens."

Noah had plenty to take care of too. He'd almost lined up everything by the time Fred showed up.

The key clicked in the lock, and Fred swore.

"It's open," Noah called.

Fred yanked open the door. "Thought I forgot to lock up. How'd you get in here?"

"Martin let me in."

"He shouldn't have done that. I don't ever want you coming in this building unless I'm here."

Noah had assumed Fred would be glad the work was finished. Evidently not. Nothing Noah did seemed to please his boss. And although Noah's shift didn't start for another hour, Fred kept Noah busy the whole time. He had no chance to go over and thank Caroline.

Caroline waited impatiently for Anna Mary to arrive. It would be so much fun working with her best friend. She'd already promised herself not to chat too much. Anna Mary would have to learn the layout and routine, so Caroline was determined not to distract her.

She spent so much time watching for Anna Mary, Gideon had to remind her to pay attention to setting up the salads. Nettie had always done that, so Caroline was still getting used to handling that job as well as making them all by herself and keeping up with all her own responsibilities. She couldn't wait to share some of the chores with Anna Mary.

Her friend peeked her head around the corner of the café, and Caroline squealed, "You're here!" She rushed out of the stand to greet Anna Mary and almost smacked into Sovilla, pushing a dolly filled with baked goods.

"Oops." Caroline veered to the right to let Sovilla pass.

Sovilla stopped so suddenly two of the plastic containers slid forward. With reflexes honed by volleyball, Caroline stopped them from tumbling.

"*Danke* for being so quick." Sovilla wiped a hand across her brow. "That would have been a disaster."

"Sorry," Caroline apologized. "It was my fault for rushing. I'm excited because Anna Mary just got here. She'll be helping us in the stand."

"Great. We can use all the help we can get."

Caroline helped Sovilla maneuver the boxes into the baked goods stand, then rushed back to welcome Anna Mary. "I'm so glad you're here. Let me show you around."

Half an hour later, Anna Mary had helped Caroline set up trays with napkins and plastic silverware, make the last few salads, and prepackage some salad containers for the lunchtime rush.

Nick Green, the *Englischer* who ran the candy counter at the other end of the stand with his son Aidan, did his usual harassing. Anna Mary surprised Caroline by holding her own against Nick's teasing comments. Caroline beamed at her friend. Anna Mary would work out well.

Gideon appeared happy to see Anna Mary when he returned from a meeting about the expansion. "Mrs. Vandenberg wants to feed the construction crew who'll be starting work today. Can you prep twenty-five extra trays before we open?"

"I still need to set up the salad counter, but Anna Mary knows how to do it."

"That'll be a big help." Gideon sped through preparing chickens for the rotisserie, a job he usually didn't start until later in the morning. Once he had that done, he headed off to unlock the market doors.

Caroline groaned as the first person pushed through the side door. Not again. Would the volleyball group continue to bother her? Anna Mary's eyes filled with concern. "Are you all right?"

"Don't look now"—Caroline grabbed Anna Mary's arm—"but that Tim guy from volleyball just came in."

Of course, Anna Mary ignored Caroline's instruction and turned to stare straight at him. "You don't think he's coming here, do you?"

Caroline didn't just think it. She knew it. "I didn't get a chance to tell you after church, but he and his friends came to the market on Saturday to bug me."

"What did they do?" Anna Mary's shrill question carried.

"Shh. He'll hear you."

"Explain to me why you blab about everything on God's green earth, but you never said a word about this." Anna Mary's offended tone didn't match the wounded look in her eyes. "I even told you what my cousin said about Tim. You could have told me then."

After listening to the sermon, Caroline had been trying not to monopolize the conversation. But she had to admit she'd also been reluctant to tell Anna Mary about roping Noah into the conflict. Now Caroline regretted hurting her friend's feelings.

A small crowd hid Tim from view, but they didn't have much time before he reached the counter. She hoped he didn't push his way past customers like he had the last time.

"I'm going to duck back there." She waved a hand toward the prep area. "Maybe if he doesn't see me, he'll go away."

"I don't know how to wait on customers."

But Anna Mary's comment came too late. Caroline had already crouched low by the refrigerator. She prepped some trays on the lower shelf so she wouldn't be wasting time. Tim's voice carried. "Where's Caroline? I'm sure I saw her when I came through the door."

"She's, um, busy somewhere else."

"Another stand? Or did she run off to spend time with her boyfriend? I guess he works here in the market?"

Anna Mary sounded puzzled. "Boyfriend? What boyfriend?"

"Aren't you her friend?"

"*Jah*, her best friend."

"And you don't know her boyfriend?"

Ach, Anna Mary could undo all the work Caroline had done in pretending Noah was her boyfriend. She breezed over with trays in her hand and inserted herself in front of Anna Mary. "I don't appreciate you asking people about me."

"Just wondering if you were visiting your boyfriend. But I see you were hiding from me."

"What makes you think that?" Caroline's aggressive answer didn't quite cover her embarrassment.

"I just wanted to invite you and your boyfriend to the next tournament. We're organizing one for next Saturday evening after the market closes. Can you make it to the field by six?"

"I'm not sure. I may have other things to do that night."

"You don't want to miss this rematch." Tim included Anna Mary in his wide grin. "You're invited too, of course. Bring your whole team. Or if you'd like, you can play on my team." He waggled his eyebrows at Caroline.

Remembering the minister's sermon, Caroline tempered her response. "*Danke* for asking, but I should stick with my own group." Her lopsided smile probably revealed her true feelings. "If they want to go," she added.

Tim's mouth twisted. He almost appeared disappointed. "I have to get to work, but I wanted to invite you to a rematch. Be sure to bring your boyfriend. I'm curious if he'll still defend you after he actually watches you play."

"He'll be there." As soon as she said it, Caroline regretted it. She doubted Noah would want to attend a volleyball game with a bunch of *youngie*. She didn't know how old he was, but he seemed so much more mature than her buddy bunch. Hastily, she added, "If he doesn't have to work, that is."

Tim extended his gaze and invitation to Anna Mary. "You'll be there, won't you?"

She nodded. "My boyfriend is the best spiker on the team."

"He can stay home then." Tim flashed her a grin. "Just kidding. We can beat you easily."

Anna Mary huffed. "We'll see about that."

After Tim walked away, Anna Mary crossed her arms. The hurt look in her eyes cut Caroline to the core. "You're dating someone, and you didn't tell me?"

What should she say? If she told Anna Mary the truth about her pretend boyfriend, her friend might feel she needed to inform Tim. But if she didn't, Anna Mary might never forgive her.

Well, that wasn't true. If Caroline apologized, Anna Mary would feel obligated to forgive her.

A long line had started to form. "We can't talk now." Caroline motioned to the crowd with her chin. "I'll take orders and ring everyone up if you can put things on trays or in bags until Gideon gets back."

Her lips set in a mutinous line, Anna Mary did her best to fill the orders while Caroline called out instructions. "In the case at the far end. The left front. Great."

When Gideon returned to take orders, Caroline remained at the register until Anna Mary struggled to keep up. Then Caroline flew back and forth from making change to filling quart and pint containers with salad to helping Aidan with fries.

After the initial rush ended, Anna Mary blew out a breath. "I don't know how you keep up with all this."

"You'll get used to it, but if you want to take a break, go ahead and walk around the market. Get yourself a snack, unless you want something from here."

"The only thing I want is the truth. What is going on with you and your *boyfriend*?"

Gideon caught the last word and stared at Anna Mary. "Caroline has a boyfriend?"

She waved to silence Anna Mary and shook her head behind her brother's back.

Anna Mary looked about ready to cry. "I don't know what's going on here."

Gideon glanced around behind him to check with Caroline.

"It's nothing. Tim asked me out, and I—"

"Wait a minute. Tim asked you out, and you didn't tell me?" Anna Mary's eyes glistened with tears. "I told you the second Josh asked to take me home after the singing."

"You had to," Caroline pointed out. "You came to the singing with me."

"That's beside the point."

"Well, I turned Tim down. He didn't really want to date me. He just asked to make a fool of me. All the other guys were laughing. They knew it was a joke."

"But still . . ."

"Girls?" Gideon broke into their spat. "We have customers."

Anna Mary blinked hard and turned around to face the

counter. Caroline slid past her brother to get to the cash register. He stood as a buffer between them.

Caroline ached inside. This was not the way she'd envisioned Anna Mary's first day. They'd never had a disagreement like this before. Caroline didn't want this stupid charade to ruin her closest friendship.

When Gideon went to brush the chickens with barbecue sauce, she leaned over to Anna Mary. "I'm sorry I didn't say anything. I was too embarrassed to tell you about Tim mocking me."

Anna Mary's tightly pursed lips softened a little. "I understand. But you still should have told me."

"You're right."

Gideon moved between them again, cutting off conversation, but Caroline hoped she'd made a start at repairing her friendship. Working with someone who was upset at her would be rough. She had to win her friend back somehow. And she also had to ask Noah for another favor. Would he agree?

Noah wished he'd had a chance to thank Caroline. He wouldn't be free until lunch break, and their stand stayed so busy then, he'd never get a chance to talk to her.

Maybe he could write her a note. That would be easier than speaking to her. He waited until Fred went for his morning doughnut and coffee, then took a clean sheet of paper from the scrap pad they used.

It took Noah so long to compose his ideas he barely had time to scribble a quick note, fold it, and tape it shut. He started to print her name on it, but he wasn't sure if she spelled it *Carolyn* or *Caroline*. He'd only written *Caro—*

a cute nickname that suited her—but he couldn't leave it like that.

The doorknob rattled. Fred was back. Noah didn't want his boss to catch him with a letter to Caroline. Fred would be sure to think Noah was sending a love letter. He added *line* at the end of the name and slid the folded paper into his pocket as Fred, balancing a small cardboard box of doughnuts in one hand and coffee in the other, leaned his back against the door to push it open.

"Can't you see I have my hands full?" he groused. "The least you could do is come over and hold the door."

Noah dropped the pen and dashed over to help. He might have reacted faster if he hadn't been secreting the note. Now Fred would be in a foul mood for the rest of the morning. The boss didn't forgive slights.

All Noah's hard work and coming in early wouldn't erase his failure to jump to Fred's assistance. And Noah had probably blown his chance to go into the market for lunch or a break. No Mrs. Vandenberg would appear to stand up for him either.

With a sigh, Noah headed for the stage. A small crowd had already gathered, mostly Amish and Mennonite mothers surrounded by their children. A few *Englischers* strolled in carrying bidding paddles. Some, who obviously were tourists, stared wide-eyed around the auction tent while they whispered and pointed at the Amish families.

The note crinkled in Noah's pocket each time he reached for a new item to auction, making it hard to concentrate. He'd been selling less than an hour when Abner stepped in front of him, hand out for the microphone. Noah raised his eyebrows in question. He might not have his usual enthusiasm, but he'd still been making good money.

Was this Fred's way of punishing him for the coffee-and-doughnut incident?

Embarrassed and ashamed, Noah handed over the microphone. He hoped this wouldn't affect his job. *What if Fred decides to sideline me permanently?* They needed another auctioneer, so Noah probably wouldn't get fired. But he'd dislike being as useless as Butch.

Head down, Noah headed for the side exit.

"There you are. What's taking you so long?" Fred frowned at him. "You shouldn't keep Mrs. Vandenberg waiting."

Huh? What did Mrs. Vandenberg want with him?

Seeing the question in Noah's eyes, Fred snapped, "She wants you upstairs in the market office. Don't take too long. I'll be docking the time from your lunch break."

Noah nodded, but he resented losing his time off for a meeting he had no choice about attending. Perhaps he could hand the note to Caroline before he headed up the stairs.

As usual, customers packed the chicken barbecue counters. An auburn-haired woman stood in Caroline's usual place. Noah scanned the stand, but Caroline wasn't in sight. He didn't want to keep Mrs. Vandenberg waiting, and he might not get a chance to stop by here during lunch. If he even got a lunch break.

Caroline's brother hadn't been too happy to see Noah with Caroline the other evening, so maybe he could give the letter to the young woman. With her easy, relaxed smile and kind eyes, she appeared trustworthy. Noah wove through the crowd, heading in her direction.

"Excuse me," he repeated as he wriggled through the lines of customers, earning glares and reproaches. "I'm not ordering. Just delivering a message."

Sighs, huffs, scowls, and nasty comments slammed him as he pressed forward. Finally, he reached the counter, earning a shrill rebuke from the next person in line.

He held up his hands in a gesture of innocence. "I'm not jumping the line, and I won't be long." He dug into his pocket and pulled out the now-crumpled paper.

The auburn-haired girl who'd been filling a salad order gave him a strained smile. "I'm sorry, sir, but the line forms over there."

"I know." Noah lifted the note. "Could you just give this to Caroline?"

The young woman's eyes widened, and she studied Noah. "Who should I say it's from?"

Noah slid over so someone else could move up to the counter. "I have to go, but she'll know once she reads the note." Then he turned and rushed toward the stairs. He only hoped she could be trusted to give the letter to Caroline.

CHAPTER 12

Her arms full of boxes, Caroline speed-walked back to the stand. She couldn't believe they'd run out of plastic silverware packets. In all the chaos of having a new baby and being in charge of the market and overseeing the expansion, her brother must have forgotten to inventory supplies.

Nettie, who'd been a worrier before she met Stephen, had always predicted they'd run out whenever supplies dipped low. She kept Gideon aware of their needs. Caroline should have paid more attention. The evidence proving her self-absorption kept piling up.

Luckily, Kauffman's Fish Fry had plenty of silverware packets and fewer customers than Hartzler's. Caroline promised to restock their storeroom shelves on Thursday morning. The only good thing about making this run for supplies meant avoiding Anna Mary's upset face. Keeping up with the long lines of customers prevented them from speaking, but Anna Mary communicated her distress quite clearly.

As much as Caroline ached inside for the cracks marring their friendship, she was still mulling over how much to tell Anna Mary. Tim's comments meant she had to come up with some explanation to satisfy Anna Mary without revealing too much about Noah and the fake relationship.

Tim's challenge to a volleyball rematch added even more pressure. Caroline had committed to bringing her boyfriend. Because she didn't want to admit the truth to Tim, she'd backed herself into a corner. Now she needed to invite Noah, but how likely was he to agree to come?

Caroline pondered that as she entered the stand and restocked the utensils. Then she slipped past Anna Mary to a place beside Gideon.

Anna Mary stopped her. "Someone came by here for you while you were gone." Her tart tone made her disapproval clear.

"Oh, who was it?" Maybe one of the stand owners needed something.

"How would I know? You haven't introduced me to your new friends."

The clipped response was so unlike Anna Mary's usual attitude it cut Caroline deeply. Should she press for more information or just let it drop?

If the message were important, Anna Mary would say so. Her friend wouldn't leave anyone else's needs unmet. They waited on the next few customers in silence. Then when Gideon went to reload the rotisserie, Anna Mary reached into her pocket.

Caroline studied the crumpled and taped paper Anna Mary held up. "What's that?" She prayed it wasn't Anna Mary's resignation letter.

"Why don't you tell me?" Anna Mary's snippy reply made it clear she hadn't written the note. She held it just out of Caroline's reach.

Her name stood out in bold letters. Caroline didn't

recognize the printing. Wondering who it was from, she put out her hand, hoping Anna Mary would turn it over.

But Anna Mary still clutched the message. "Who is he? The guy who brought the love note?"

Caroline laughed. "If I ever get a love note, you'll be the first to know. I expect it's a reminder for one of the market's special events or something."

After Anna Mary reluctantly turned over the paper, she studied Caroline as she undid the tape. Caroline sucked in a breath. Noah had written her a note.

Anna Mary planted her hands on her hips. "Sure seems like a love note from your reaction."

As much as Caroline wished it were, it was only a simple thank-you and an offer to pay for the lunch she'd brought. If Anna Mary hadn't been scrutinizing Caroline's face, Caroline might have pressed the unromantic letter to her heart. Instead, she casually tucked it into her pocket.

"Well?" Anna Mary demanded.

"Sorry to disappoint you, but it's only a thank-you for delivering a chicken dinner on Saturday."

Jah, it was that, but to Caroline, it represented much, much more. Because Noah had reached out, she'd find it easier to approach him later about going to the volleyball game. Maybe she'd be able to wrangle a date—even a fake one—after all.

Noah had never been upstairs in the market, so he studied the various shops and doors to find the meeting he needed to attend. He passed a gift shop, a clothing boutique, and a pet accessory store showcasing rhinestone-studded collars, pottery bowls with paw prints, and a window display of coats and costumes for dogs.

At the end of the hall, a sturdy wooden door with a brass nameplate, BOARDROOM, looked promising. But it appeared so imposing Noah hesitated. What if he walked into someone else's meeting?

He headed down the opposite aisle of the building, but other than an office marked with Gideon's name, Noah found no other meeting rooms. He strode over to the door, gathered his courage, and knocked.

"Come in." Mrs. Vandenberg's voice assured him he'd come to the right place.

He entered to find people seated around a huge conference table. The room reminded him of an interrogation room, except the highly polished mahogany furniture gleamed, making the space imposing and elegant.

Mrs. Vandenberg beckoned Noah to a seat by her side. Confused about why she'd called him here, he walked stiff-legged and uncertain to the place she'd indicated. Then she introduced him to everyone at the table. He didn't catch all their names because he was too busy trying to figure out her purpose in having him meet men who appeared to be contractors and construction workers.

"So, Noah, what do you think?" she asked.

About what? Had he missed something important while his mind had been wandering?

"Would you be willing to join the crew working on the addition?"

She'd blindsided him. Was she offering this job because Fred planned to fire him? If so, Noah had better take it.

"You can work around the auctioneering," Mrs. Vandenberg assured him. "Jose will be happy for whatever hours you can put in."

An older man studied Noah, taking in his muscles. Then

he beamed. "Anytime you can work is fine. We need all the help we can get."

"I did tell him about your experience laying cement block," Mrs. Vandenberg added.

Noah's head snapped up. How had she found out about that? She must have done a thorough background check. If so, then she'd discovered the past he'd hoped to keep hidden. Dread unspooled inside him, twisting like a rattler about to strike. "It's been a while," he admitted, "but I haven't forgotten how to do it."

Jose stood. "We should get back to work." He turned to Noah. "If you want to start today after the auction closes, come on over for several hours. Or we'll look for you bright and early tomorrow."

"All right. Thank you." Noah sat there, stunned. He'd been hired. Just like that. No questions, no papers, no interview.

As the men filed out, Noah jumped to his feet. "I need to go too."

"Hang on a minute." Mrs. Vandenberg motioned for him to sit. "We have a few things to iron out."

He gulped. Fred hadn't asked for previous employment or references. But now Noah would face a reckoning over his past.

"Don't look so nervous. I believe in second chances."

At her kind and soothing tone, the fear and tension inside him shriveled. She'd found out the truth, but she planned to overlook it. If only he could tell her the whole story. Then she'd know he was trustworthy.

"I have a good sense of people, and I can tell you'll be reliable. So let's discuss your pay."

She named a figure that almost made Noah fall off his chair. "I can't take that much for laying block."

"I believe in paying people living wages. Construction is hard work. And I try to compensate everyone fairly."

"Please divide the money among the other workers. I don't deserve it."

"Too many of us don't know our own worth. God is the only one qualified to judge."

Noah could pinpoint exactly where that left him.

"You might be surprised at how precious and valuable you are to Him."

I doubt it. Maybe Mrs. Vandenberg hadn't delved as deeply into his background as he feared.

"That's the going rate for new, part-time workers. The others are paid more, and you'll get a raise after the probation period."

"I'm grateful for the job, but I don't want to put you out of business."

Mrs. Vandenberg chuckled. "I've run this business and many others for over fifty years, and I find the more I pay people, the better the job they do. And with top-notch workers, the more my businesses grow. High wages pay huge dividends."

Noah had never heard a business plan like hers before. Most employers tried to cut costs. She must know what she was doing. And with that much money coming in, he'd be able to buy a buggy and get a place of his own much sooner than he'd expected.

"Thank you." He started to stand, but she waved him back into his seat. "My lunch break will be over soon, and Fred—"

She cut him off. "This isn't your lunch break. Let's take

care of that right now." After rummaging around in a huge purse, she dug out a notepad, scribbled on it, and handed it to him. "Give that to Fred."

But would his boss believe the message came from Mrs. Vandenberg?

"Don't worry. He'll recognize my signature."

Had she read his mind again?

"You can also let him know I'll be down later to check in." She dropped the pad back into the depths of her purse. "I appreciate you taking on the construction job, but I have one more favor to ask."

After all she'd done for him, Noah would agree to whatever she asked.

"You probably haven't met Gideon's wife, Fern, yet, but her brother plans to move back to Lancaster. Originally, he'd been planning to come a few weeks ago, but he's helping out in a flooded area and doesn't expect to return for six months or so."

Noah nodded politely. He had no idea why she was telling him about strangers. At Mrs. Vandenberg's age, she probably rambled a lot. He wished she'd finish, though, so he could get back to the auction. Even with her signed note, Noah suspected Fred would make him pay for all this time off.

"Anyway," Mrs. Vandenberg continued, "I bought him a horse and buggy, but I don't want to have to worry about caring for the horse all that time. I wondered if you'd be willing to take on that duty. You're welcome to use the buggy, and I'd be happy to pay you for your time."

She wanted to pay him to use a horse and buggy for six months? Noah was tempted to call it a miracle. His *mamm* would have called it an answer to prayer.

"I'll cover the cost of feed and have it delivered."

Noah wanted to jump at this chance. Only one problem. "I don't have a barn or any place to keep a horse."

"Oh, that's no problem. The Yoders have several out-buildings and small barns on the land behind the store. I already checked with them. They're happy to rent out the small blue barn."

Noah couldn't believe it. That barn sat along the road to the RV park, making it a fifteen-minute walk from his place. "That would be perfect. I'll pay for the rental."

"Absolutely not. You'll be doing me a favor."

"And you'll be doing me one." He wouldn't have to walk seven miles to work every day now that he'd started the construction job. Well, every day but Sunday. "There's no need to pay me."

"We can settle that when the time comes. Is it all right if I have one of my people drop the horse and buggy off at the shelter behind the market today? Then you can drive it home after the construction work tonight."

Now Noah wouldn't have to walk along the narrow country roads in the dark. "I can't thank you enough."

"No, thank you." She flipped open a leather folder and made two checkmarks on the list under his name—construction job and horse care. Her other hand covered the rest of the list. What else did she have on there?

CHAPTER 13

Noah hustled downstairs clutching the note. He highly doubted it would defuse Fred's irritation. And Noah had no doubt Fred would think up some type of punishment. But no matter what his boss did, it couldn't deflate Noah's excitement.

Today, he'd be getting a horse and buggy. Today, he'd be starting a new job with a man who seemed to be a fair boss. And nobody had asked about referrals or background checks or applications. Today, he'd be making more money than he'd ever thought possible. Now he could start saving for his future.

The smell of barbecued chicken called to him. But he didn't have time to stop. *Jah*, Mrs. Vandenberg insisted he had to have a lunch break, but he'd wait until Fred gave him the time off. And to be on the safe side, he'd choose something other than chicken. The last thing he needed when his life seemed to be looking good was to get tangled up with a green-eyed blonde.

Still, he couldn't help glancing her way as he passed the stand. Her eyes widened when she looked in his direction, and she shot him a blinding smile. *Ach*, no! His joyful reaction to Mrs. Vandenberg's generosity had brightened his spirits so much, his grin stretched across his face. Caroline must have assumed he'd been smiling at her.

Now what? With all this excitement bubbling inside him, he couldn't wipe the happiness from his face. And so much for avoiding her. He'd walked right into that trap. He should have gone the long way around.

The girl beside Caroline studied him intently, her face creased in a frown. Then she sneaked a quick glance at Caroline. The auburn-haired girl's jaw tightened, and her eyes reflected sadness, but Caroline never noticed. She was too busy staring at him.

Her gaze fell to the paper in his hand, and her bright smile dimmed. Noah didn't have time to puzzle out her change in expression. He needed to get back to work. *Now.*

He forced himself to turn away and head for the exit. When he pulled open the door, he almost bumped into a red-faced Fred, who'd been reaching for the door handle.

"There you are. What took you so long? I saw you eyeing that girl at Hartzler's. Were you over there flirting with her when you should have been working?"

"No." Noah's firm answer startled Fred, and he took a step back.

Knowing he had the construction job gave Noah more courage to confront Fred's accusations. Noah held out the paper from Mrs. Vandenberg.

"What's this?" Fred frowned down at the note. "You're into forgery now?"

"That's from Mrs. Vandenberg, and she said to tell you she'd be stopping by later."

The crimson flush on Fred's face darkened to purple. "You asked her to check up on me?"

Rather than answering, Noah sidestepped away from the door to allow shoppers to enter. Fred had to slide over, too, if he wanted to keep glaring at Noah, which increased his boss's annoyance.

"Well, if you think you're going to get a break now after being gone all this time, think again. Get onstage and take over from Abner."

If Fred considered that payback, he underestimated how much Noah enjoyed auctioneering. With a spring in his step, Noah headed into the auction tent. He didn't care when he took his lunch break. For the first time in years, life seemed to be going his way.

After Noah had startled Caroline with his heart-stopping smile, her spirits plummeted at the paper in his hand. Another note? Perhaps he'd given them to other stand owners in the market. The letter in her own pocket lost some of its luster.

Beside her, Anna Mary stiffened. She'd seen the smiles Caroline and Noah had exchanged. To avoid questions, Caroline broke Noah's gaze to concentrate on the customers. Luckily, they stayed too busy for conversation until two.

By then, Anna Mary appeared ragged and drained.

"Why don't you take the first lunch break?" Caroline suggested. "Feel free to take anything you'd like and eat it back at the prep area."

Gideon seconded the idea and added, "You've done a great job so far, Anna Mary. We'll have another rush just before closing, but things are usually a little slower for about an hour."

Caroline sympathized with Anna Mary's exhaustion. "You'll get used to the hectic pace after a while."

"You can't take a break with me?"

Ordinarily, Caroline would never have resisted that plaintive request. She could have dropped everything to join her friend, only hopping up whenever Gideon got overwhelmed. But today Caroline had a plan for her own lunch break. A plan she couldn't share with Anna Mary or Gideon.

Anna Mary's reproachful look as she gathered a small meal and trudged back to the worktable cut into Caroline's heart. Abandoning her best friend on her first day here to pressure a man she barely knew to come to her volleyball game increased her guilt.

"Maybe I could stand back there with you," Caroline said, "and keep an eye on the counter at the same time."

"Never mind," Anna Mary mumbled. "I don't want to take you away from your work."

"If you're sure?" Now that Caroline had weighed the importance of her errand and her friend's needs, she couldn't put visiting Noah ahead of Anna Mary. "I do need to fill a few salad containers. Maybe we could talk at the same time."

With a shrug, Anna Mary turned. "You don't have to." Her tone made it sound like she was a burden.

"I want to." Caroline assessed the levels of the salad containers and slid open the refrigerated case to take one back with her. "I'm so glad you're here. You've been a big help."

That comment brought a fleeting smile to Anna Mary's lips but did nothing to erase the hurt in her eyes. To keep the conversation from turning to Noah, Caroline chatted the whole time about the salads, the business, and the upcoming volleyball game. She and Anna Mary divided up the list of friends to contact about Tim's challenge.

For once, Caroline blessed her own gift of gab. She

rarely let anyone get a word in edgewise, so she used that talent to avoid questions, ignoring Anna Mary's irritated sighs and her repeated attempts to interrupt.

After Anna Mary had finished her meal, Caroline asked, "Will you be all right here without me? I need to run an errand during my break. I promise not to be long."

Without waiting for an answer, Caroline rushed around gathering a takeout meal. She'd get a quick snack for herself when she returned, but right now, she wanted to visit Noah. And she hoped the chicken dinner might be an incentive for him to agree to her request.

Anna Mary eyed the bag in Caroline's hand. "You're not going to eat here?"

"This isn't for me. I'm just doing a quick delivery. Then I'll be back."

Caroline headed for the bakery counter and paid for a cupcake and two chocolate-chip cookies. Trying not to act too guilty, Caroline thanked Sovilla and waved cheerily to Anna Mary, whose eyes flashed with suspicion.

Caroline pushed open the door to the outside with determination that faltered when she spied Noah onstage. This had been a foolish idea. He'd probably already had lunch and who knew when he'd have a break? She should have thought this out better. Mesmerized by Noah's patter, she stood there, undecided.

She couldn't trust Fred or Butch to deliver a note and a meal. Abner stopped by the stand once in a while, but she didn't feel comfortable asking him to pass on the lunch.

"Quite talented, isn't he?" a cheerful voice asked. "And very handsome. He also has a good heart."

Caroline turned to find Mrs. Vandenberg hobbling toward her. "Do you need help?" Caroline extended her arm and avoided agreeing with the elderly woman's comments.

"You look like you're wavering. The Bible says, 'A double-minded man is unstable in all his ways.' That goes for women too."

Everyone always said Caroline's feelings were easy to read, but had her dilemma been that obvious? She needed to hide her emotions better. That might prove even harder than keeping secrets. She'd already found it out with Anna Mary. And part of her struggled with hiding what she was feeling. Wasn't it deceitful?

"Only God can answer that," Mrs. Vandenberg said gently.

Did she read my mind?

Mrs. Vandenberg waved to the edge of the stage where Fred stood watching Noah. "I need to talk to Fred. Can you help me over there?"

That was the last place Caroline wanted to go, but she couldn't desert Mrs. Vandenberg. "All right, but I need to get back to the stand." That would give her an excuse to make a quick exit once they reached Fred.

"But what about the meal?" Mrs. Vandenberg nodded to the large carry-out bag Caroline held.

"I, um, made a mistake." She'd hurry back to the stand and eat it all.

"Being kind to others is never a mistake."

Caroline's head whipped around to stare at Mrs. Vandenberg. Did she suspect who the bag was for?

"I'm sure he'll appreciate it. Auctioneers expend a lot of energy onstage." When Caroline grimaced, Mrs. Vandenberg patted her arm. "Don't worry. Your secret's safe with me."

Although she didn't add *for now*, Caroline sensed those words hanging in the air.

"Fred?" Mrs. Vandenberg's sharp call echoed around the tent.

Even Noah glanced over as Fred whirled to face her. Noah recovered rapidly and returned to his patter. Fred, on the other hand, twitched with nervousness.

"Did you get my note?"

"Er, yeah. Yeah, I did." He didn't meet her eyes.

"So you gave Noah his lunch break?"

"Well, I . . . Not yet," he admitted.

"I thought not." Mrs. Vandenberg shook her head as if disappointed.

"I didn't want to lose the momentum. He's going strong."

Then she brightened. "Actually, this might be perfect timing. Right, Caroline?"

Fred, who'd had his gaze glued to the ground near Mrs. Vandenberg's feet, raised his head and groaned. "Not again. I told Caroline I don't want her fraternizing with my employees."

"And I advised you not to interfere. What do you have against young love?"

At Mrs. Vandenberg's question, both Fred and Caroline gasped, but for different reasons. Caroline couldn't believe Mrs. V had said that. Caroline's relationship with Noah—if it could even be called that—had nothing to do with romance. Mrs. Vandenberg loved to matchmake. But this time, she was dead wrong.

Is she? Caroline's internal voice challenged. She quickly shut it down. But after Fred sent Abner to take over the mic and Noah loped toward them, Caroline's accelerating pulse made it clear she'd tipped into the danger zone.

* * *

As Noah coaxed bidders higher, Caroline distracted him. She stood to one side with another lunch bag, and he struggled to get back on track. But with his stomach growling, he couldn't help wondering if she'd brought the carry-out bag for him. If so, he hoped she didn't plan to make this a habit.

Although his thoughts and nerves jostled each other, he forced himself to focus on keeping the bidding going strong. But once he finished and Abner reached for the microphone, Noah had to face her. And Fred.

As he strode toward them, Noah hoped his thank-you note hadn't encouraged her. He'd have to find a way to discourage her nicely. Fred's ultimatum about not dating coworkers might help. But Mrs. Vandenberg had over-ridden Fred last week. And now she stood between Fred and Caroline. Noah feared he'd be railroaded into spending time with Caroline again.

"You can take your break now," Fred announced as Noah drew near.

"Thanks," Noah muttered, wishing he could brush past the others. But that wouldn't be polite. "Good afternoon, Mrs. Vandenberg, Caroline." When his gaze strayed from the elderly woman to the attractive blonde beside her, he nodded a greeting, hoping he appeared neutral.

As he started to walk past them, Mrs. Vandenberg balanced on her cane so she could reach out and touch his arm. "Just a minute, Noah. I believe Caroline has something to ask you."

Caroline's wide, startled eyes flew to Mrs. Vandenberg's face.

Had Mrs. Vandenberg unexpectedly exposed something

Caroline wanted to keep secret? For the first time since Noah had met her, Caroline seemed at a loss for words.

Mrs. Vandenberg nudged Caroline. "Why don't you two go over to the picnic tables so I can speak to Fred in private?"

Seemingly lost in a daze, Caroline headed in the direction Mrs. Vandenberg indicated.

In a voice too low for Caroline to hear, Mrs. Vandenberg whispered to Noah, "I hope you'll help her out. And don't worry about taking time off from the construction job. Jose knows you need personal time."

"I see." Noah wouldn't make any promises until he heard Caroline's request. He trailed behind her to the picnic tables.

Rather than turning around and talking to him the way she had every other time they'd been together, Caroline cruised ahead of him. When they reached the table, she sat opposite him and slid the bag across to him without looking at him.

"I'm probably too late with this. I'm sure you've already eaten, but I—"

He cut her off. "Actually, I haven't had lunch yet, so this is great. Let me pay you for it." He reached into his pocket for his wallet.

Caroline waved a hand to stop him. "*Neh*, wait."

"I can't accept two free meals. Your family has a business to run. They need to make money." *And I don't want you to get the wrong idea.* Making this a business deal would get rid of his half-formed wish that he could enjoy her company and—

She shook her head. "You can, um, pay for it in a different way." For a few moments, she stayed silent, biting her lip and staring down at the scarred wooden boards of the tabletop. "The lunch is kind of a bribe."

A bribe? Noah stopped rustling the flap of the paper bag. Maybe he'd better fold it down and pass the lunch back. Tempting as that chicken smelled, he'd never get mixed up with anything shady.

CHAPTER 14

When Caroline said *bribe*, Noah looked sick. She regretted her choice of words. "I mean, I want to ask you a favor."

Her correction didn't lessen the alarm in his eyes. He closed the bag and slid it in her direction.

She pushed it back. "You can keep it even if you don't agree with what I ask."

This was proving harder than she'd expected. Usually whatever she wanted to say just poured from her mouth, but she'd spent so much time today filtering everything, her sentences seemed to have gotten stuck.

Finally, she forced herself to start. "Tim—that guy you protected me from the other day—came back to the market today."

Noah straightened and his jaw clenched. "He did?"

Caroline's heart fluttered. He looked ready to go to battle on her behalf. "He, um, challenged me—"

"What? Where is he?" Noah slung a leg over the bench.

"Wait. He isn't here now. And I only meant he challenged me to a volleyball rematch."

"I see." Noah slid back into place. "And you accepted." The corners of his lips quirked.

"Of course. I'm sure I'll beat him again."

"So, there's no problem. And you'll have your team-mates to protect you, right?"

She nodded. "*Jah*, I'm not worried about that. It's just that Tim added something to the challenge."

"What? He wants you to play with one hand tied behind your back? I'm guessing that's the only way he can win."

Caroline giggled. "If he'd asked for that, I might have agreed. I'm pretty sure we can beat him, even if I play one-handed."

"You're that good, huh?"

"What?" It took a moment for his comment to register. Did he think she'd been bragging about her skills? "*Neh.* I meant my team's good enough even without me."

"But I bet you'd be in there spiking the ball with your one free hand."

She couldn't help smiling. "*Jah*, I'd be trying to do that for sure." Then she sobered. Caroline wished Tim had asked that. Because then she'd be the only one to suffer. And if she were defeated, she'd have herself to blame.

Instead, she had to depend on someone else . . . and put that person in an awkward position. All to prevent herself from being teased or humiliated. She had no right to ask Noah to reinforce her lie. A lie she'd only told to save face.

Caroline jumped to her feet. "I'm sorry. I shouldn't have come. Please eat the meal and enjoy it."

But as she stepped over the bench, Noah stopped her. "You came here to ask a favor. What is it?"

"It's not important." She turned to flee, praying she'd leave behind her embarrassment.

* * *

Noah hated to see her in such distress. "Do you want me to talk to this Tim? Ask him to stop bothering you?"

Caroline whirled around, her expression an odd mixture of shame and gratitude. "*Neh*, that's not necessary. It's just that—" She took a deep breath and then blurted, "Tim wants me to bring my boyfriend to the game."

Boyfriend? The word punched Noah in the gut.

"Except I don't have one, so Tim meant you. I guess he believed us the other day. And I came here to ask you to pretend again, but I realize it isn't right. I was letting my pride get in the way, but I deserve to be embarrassed."

Her sentences whizzed out like a train whooshing down the tracks at full speed. Noah tried to follow her reasoning, but she'd jumped from one subject to the next.

"Whoa, slow down. I'm trying to understand. Tim wants you to bring your boyfriend?"

The rest of her nattering was slowly sinking in. *Ach*, Tim believed Noah was Caroline's boyfriend after their pretense. But Noah didn't see how that connected to her embarrassment. Unless she was ashamed she didn't have a boyfriend?

Then it hit him. The lunch. A favor. Caroline wanted him to be that boyfriend. For a second, a long-buried desire flickered in his heart. But common sense doused that tiny flame. *No, a thousand times no.*

Across from him, Caroline, her head down, fidgeted from one foot to the other. "I—I shouldn't have bothered you. I need to get back." She pivoted on her heel and started to rush off.

"When and where is this game?" he called after her.

She spun around, her eyes filled with hope, and rattled off a location and a time on Saturday.

Noah heaved a relieved sigh. "I'll be working then."

Her eyebrows wrinkled in confusion. "It's after the market closes."

"I know, but I just started another job. I can't ask for time off already."

The disappointment on her face made him regret asking about the date and location. He'd gotten her hopes up, only to let her down.

"It's all right." She offered him a halfhearted smile. "I'll survive the teasing. It'll remind me to be humble."

But more than a loss of pride peeped out behind her words. Heartache showed on her expressive face. A heartache that had nothing to do with the upcoming volleyball game.

Before Noah could identify the reason for her hurt, she raced off.

Caroline wished she'd never come out here to talk to Noah. She'd made a huge mistake. Now all she wanted to do was get back to the stand. Staying busy with customers might help her forget her elation when he'd asked about the date and time. But it couldn't erase her crushing disappointment.

As she wriggled through the crowds to get back to work, Mrs. Vandenberg called to her. Caroline couldn't be rude. She waited to see what Mrs. V wanted.

Slightly out of breath, the elderly woman caught up to Caroline. "I'm so sorry you didn't get the answer you wanted, but you never know how things will work out."

"How do you know that? And how did you know I wanted to ask Noah a question?"

"With age comes wisdom."

Caroline hoped she'd be as wise as Mrs. V someday, but she had her doubts.

"Don't worry," Mrs. Vandenberg assured her, "you're on your way. Lean more on God than on yourself."

Warmth flushed Caroline's cheeks. "You always seem to know what I'm thinking."

"Most of the time I rely on heavenly help, but with you it's easy. You wear your emotions on your face."

Mrs. V kept pointing that out. With effort, Caroline wiped her feelings from her expression.

"Your face isn't the only thing that gives you away." Humor brimmed in Mrs. Vandenberg's eyes. "Earlier, I could tell you were excited because you leaned forward, balancing on your toes as if you were about to pounce."

"You make me sound like a tiger or something."

"Not exactly, dear. You just reveal your eagerness. But your eyes held some uncertainty. That led me to guess you planned to ask a question. The takeout bag gave me a clue to your intended target."

"Target? It sounds like I planned to attack him."

"Lunch was more like bait, wouldn't you say?"

Though it pained Caroline to admit it, Mrs. V was right. "I told Noah it was a bribe."

"I love how honest you are, Caroline. Most girls would have played it coy and tried to hide their real motive."

She winced. Maybe she shouldn't have admitted that to Noah. Or to Mrs. V.

"That wasn't a criticism, my dear, although I can see you took it as such."

"How did you know?"

"You went like this." Mrs. Vandenberg squinched up her eyes.

"Will I ever learn to hide my feelings?" Caroline cried

in despair. She'd worked so hard today to keep things from people, but it drained most of her energy.

"I think your candor is refreshing. And I'm positive your future husband will appreciate your honesty."

Husband? Caroline almost choked. She couldn't even get a boyfriend. Not even a pretend one. She doubted anyone would ever marry her. And even if someone did, he'd probably join her family and friends in criticizing her constant chatter.

"Most people don't say I'm honest. They call me blunt or impolite. Everyone's always telling me I talk too much."

"Perhaps they mean you don't give them a turn to speak. You might want to watch other people's movements for clues that they have something to say and then listen carefully."

Caroline hadn't done that for Anna Mary today. *Ach*, and here she'd been talking and leaving her friend to handle the afternoon rush hour on her first day. "I need to go. I'm late getting back. But I do appreciate your advice."

"You're quite welcome. And keep your chin up. You'll be surprised at how things will work out."

What did Mrs. V mean? Not let Tim know his taunts affected her? That would make things turn out well?

Caroline was so late already she didn't have time to ponder it. After a quick goodbye, she took off for the stand.

Gideon frowned as she banged through the half door. "I was expecting you back a while ago so I could get a lunch break. We can't leave Anna Mary here alone." He pulled chickens off the spit.

"I know, I know. I'm really sorry. It's just that I ran into

Mrs. Vandenberg outside, and you know how she likes to talk."

"She kept you all this time and ate the huge lunch you took with you?"

Caroline lowered her eyes. "*Neh*, that was for someone else."

"I see." Gideon nodded toward the long line and Anna Mary's panicky expression as she tried to take orders and count money. "We need to talk about this. After Zach, you promised me . . ."

But Caroline didn't hear the rest of his sentence. She dashed to Anna Mary's side and took the money the customer held out. "I can take care of payments, and I'll help with orders until Gideon gets all the chickens in the warmer."

Relief washed over Anna Mary's features. "I thought you'd never get here. What took so long?"

"I got stopped by someone who wanted to talk."

"And you listened?" Anna Mary's teasing tone had a sarcastic bite behind it.

Caroline didn't blame her. She'd ignored Anna Mary's pleading eyes all morning and cut her off every time she started to ask questions. But it dawned on Caroline that she had listened to Mrs. V. What had made the difference?

Noah licked the last of the chocolate icing from his fingertips, then wiped his hands on the napkin Caroline had put in the bag. He could get used to a lunch like this every day. But from now on, he'd pay for it. With his new job, he wouldn't have to scrimp and save. He'd even have a horse and buggy.

Near the stage, Fred motioned for Noah to get moving.

He hadn't had a full lunch break, but he didn't care. He'd rather work than sit around thinking about Caroline and feeling guilty about the sadness in her eyes when he told her he couldn't come to her game.

He had to admit, he'd like to see her play. If she put as much energy and passion into that as she did into talking, she'd be hard to beat. And the memory of Tim taunting her made his jaw clench. He'd enjoy seeing her beat those boys who'd surrounded her the other day.

Pushing all thoughts of her from his mind, he rose, tossed his trash into the nearest bin, and headed for the mic.

The afternoon bidding went well, and as he declared the final item of the day sold, Mrs. Vandenberg tottered into the back of the tent and waved to him.

While the audience dispersed, Noah headed her way. She greeted him with a huge smile.

"Your horse is waiting in the buggy shelter. I know I can trust you to take good care of Rosie."

"I'll do my best." He'd treat the borrowed horse as if she were his own. Noah thanked Mrs. Vandenberg several times. He still couldn't get over her generosity.

As much as he'd like to meet the horse and see the buggy, he wanted to make a good impression on his new boss, so he headed straight to the construction site.

"I'm glad I can count on you to look after both of my favorite girls," Mrs. Vandenberg called after him.

Both girls? What in the world did she mean by that?

The afternoon whizzed by in a blur of orders. Caroline barely had to time to talk, let alone breathe.

But as soon as Gideon left the stand to lock the market

doors, Anna Mary confronted Caroline. "I want answers and I want them now."

"About what?" She hoped she could avoid telling Anna Mary anything about Noah.

To get her friend's mind off the questioning, Caroline explained the cleanup procedure. "First, we need to transfer all the salads to the refrigerator. If you pass all the metal containers to me, I'll store them." Then feeling rather bossy, she asked, "After we finish the salads, would you rather scrub the rotisserie parts or spray clean the refrigerated cases?"

"I'll do whichever one you like least." Anna Mary picked up the large container of macaroni salad and slid it across the worktable.

With a relieved sigh, Caroline covered it and put it in the refrigerator. Maybe they'd stay too busy for Anna Mary to bring up Noah and Tim. But after Anna Mary carried the broccoli-bacon-raisin salad to the worktable, she waited until she caught Caroline's eyes. "So who's this Noah?"

Caroline glanced away and busied herself with covering the container. "Just someone I met at the market. Well, actually, I bumped into him when I was racing through the auction house the other day because I was late. I spilled some puzzles he was carrying for the auction."

"*Ach*, Caroline." Anna Mary shook her head. "You really need to learn to slow down."

"I know, I know. Anyway, I tried to help him pick up the pieces. That's how I got to know him."

"You could have told me this on Sunday after church."

Caroline tried to act casual. "Not much to tell."

"Then why does Tim think Noah's your boyfriend?"

Nibbling at her lip, Caroline debated how much to

confess. This decision not to reveal everything put her in a dilemma. How did closemouthed people handle all the information they didn't share? Picking and choosing facts seemed so dishonest.

Anna Mary put her hands on her hips. "Well?" When Caroline still didn't answer, Anna Mary's forehead creased in concern. "What is going on with you? I've never seen you at a loss for words."

"I—I, um . . ."

"Oh, no." Anna Mary groaned. "You don't have a crush on him, do you? Not like you did with that Zach."

Caroline couldn't answer that truthfully. She did kind of, sort of have a crush on Noah even if she'd never act on those feelings. Instead of answering, she deflected her friend's question. "I won't ever do anything like that again."

Yet, hadn't she already started? Twice now, she'd chased after Noah, bringing him meals. And she'd forced him to walk her to the employee entrance. Not to mention asking him to attend the volleyball game. Even though he couldn't make it.

"I hope you learned your lesson."

Anna Mary was still stuck on Zach, while Caroline had already focused on Noah. But her friend's remark jabbed Caroline in a sore spot. She bent and put the salad tray on the lowest shelf of the refrigerator so Anna Mary couldn't read the pain in her eyes. *Why does she have to remind me of my old humiliation?*

"I'm sorry." Anna Mary came around to the work prep area and set a hand on Caroline's shoulder. "I shouldn't have brought that up. Will you forgive me?"

The old Caroline would have forgiven immediately, jumped up, hugged her friend, and rejoiced they'd restored their friendship. This new, more hesitant Caroline stayed cautious and wary, afraid of getting hurt. But she couldn't leave Anna Mary hanging.

"There's nothing to forgive." Even that statement wasn't totally honest. Caroline rearranged containers on the bottom refrigerator shelves so she didn't have to face her friend.

"If you say so." The edginess in Anna Mary's tone made it clear she didn't believe Caroline. "I still want to know why Tim called Noah your boyfriend and why Noah dropped off a note and what the note said and—" She stopped suddenly when Gideon returned to the stand.

As she passed over the potato salad, Anna Mary turned sad, puppy-dog eyes to Caroline and kept her voice low so Gideon couldn't overhear. "There are a lot of things I want to know, but the most important question is why my best friend in all the world no longer wants to talk to me about anything in her life."

"Oh, Anna Mary, that's not true." Caroline wanted to discuss lots of things. Just not Noah.

CHAPTER 15

Noah wrapped up his final sale late Saturday afternoon, then helped with cleanup and organizing for next Tuesday's auction, which Abner supervised despite Butch's annoyance. As soon as Noah was free to go, he took a quick trip to the shelter to check on Rosie. He wished he'd brought an apple for her. Unfortunately, the market had already closed, so he couldn't get one.

Stroking Rosie's neck, Noah inhaled her horsey scent, so comforting, so familiar. After going such a long time without a horse or buggy, he could hardly believe he had transportation. And having Rosie to care for and talk to was helping to fill his lonely hours.

With a spring in his step, he headed for the construction site. Unlike Fred, Jose was easygoing and upbeat—the perfect boss. Noah also enjoyed the comradery among the other workers, who tried to include him, but mostly he kept to himself. Something he'd learned to do for protection. Keeping your head down and working hard had been the key to his survival.

Jose greeted Noah with a smile. "Hey, man, good to see you. You did a great job last night laying all that block."

Unused to praise, Noah rocked from foot to foot. "Glad you're happy with it."

"I am. Sorry I don't have any work for you today."

Noah had been here less than a week. Was Jose firing him already?

"Don't look so glum. Young guy like you should be going out and enjoying Saturday night with a pretty girl." Jose winked.

But Noah didn't have a pretty girl to be with, and he never would. Unless you counted Rosie. He planned to spend time getting to know his horse. But right now, he'd rather work than spend lonely hours in the rented barn or cramped inside the RV.

And why was Jose dismissing him? "Did I do something wrong?"

"Wrong? No, why?"

"Well, you don't have any work for me."

Jose laughed. "First time I ever met someone who didn't like having a day off. The supplier didn't deliver the load of cement blocks today like they shoulda. We'll have plenty of work on Monday once they arrive. Be here as early as you can."

Jose's reassurance calmed Noah's worries, but his boss's comment about a pretty girl reminded Noah of Caroline's request. He didn't want to encourage her, but he had to admit he'd like to watch her play volleyball. At the thought of her diving for the ball, his lips curved up. What would it hurt to drive by the field? The players would be busy with the game, so they'd be unlikely to notice him. He didn't have to stop, just mosey by at a slow clip for a quick glimpse.

* * *

Caroline had spent the rest of the work week doing her best to mend her relationship with Anna Mary. And following Mrs. V's advice, Caroline even practiced listening more. It surprised her that she could get as much joy from hearing others' ideas. And once they started talking, curiosity about what they might say kept her from interrupting. As they left for the volleyball game, Anna Mary tilted her head to one side. "You've been acting different."

"Is that good or bad?"

"I'm not sure. I like that I'm getting a chance to speak, but it feels weird. What's going on?"

"Mrs. Vandenberg lectured me about letting other people talk." Caroline didn't mention the part about watching for signals. And she didn't share that listening kept her from accidentally dwelling on the topic that was on her mind much too often—Noah. If only he didn't have to work today.

When they pulled into the field, Tim shouted, "There she is. Pancake Girl."

"Just ignore him," Anna Mary advised.

Caroline had already decided to do that until they started walking across the field.

With a sneer on his face, Tim called, "Where's your boyfriend?"

His jab hit her in a sore spot. "He had to work." She slung the answer back without thinking.

Anna Mary gasped and stopped walking. She clutched Caroline's arm and studied her face. "You have a boyfriend you haven't told me about? Is it Noah? Or were you lying?" Anna Mary looked equally upset about either choice.

Hanging her head, Caroline mumbled, "You know I don't have a boyfriend."

"Then why did you—"

"I shouldn't have done it. It's just that Tim gets me so upset."

"Caroline!" Anna Mary stared at Caroline in shock. "You never lie."

"Only because I always say everything I think." Caroline couldn't keep the sourness from her tone. And her answer didn't deflect her guilt.

"Hurry up," Tim called. "We're ready to play."

Caroline rushed toward them—both to get the game started and to avoid Anna Mary's censure.

Tim shot Caroline a mocking look as she took her place across the net from him. "Bet you didn't even invite that boyfriend of yours."

"I did too." She wished she'd kept her mouth shut when Anna Mary gasped. Although Caroline had told the truth, Anna Mary believed Caroline had told another lie.

Another piece of Mrs. V's advice flooded back. With a lift of her chin, Caroline faced Tim. She refused to let his taunts faze her any more today. And she vowed to keep her mouth shut throughout the whole game. No matter what.

As Rosie trotted along the country roads, a sense of relief crept over Noah for the first time in ages. He had transportation, two jobs, and his independence. Being able to make his own decisions meant the world to him. But until he could erase the inner scars, he'd never truly be free. When they neared the field, Noah edged Rosie onto the shoulder and slowed her to a walk. A car filled with laughing teens whizzed by, rattling the buggy's sides and sending Noah's stomach into a tightly clenched ball of nausea. They distracted him so much, he almost missed the turnoff. As he tugged on Rosie's reins, the *Englischers* screeched to a halt, backed up, and swerved onto the un- paved road Noah planned to use. He yanked Rosie to a halt to avoid getting hit.

Gravel sprayed from under the car tires, pelting Rosie and the buggy. Rosie shied into the field beside the road, but Noah's firm hand calmed her. He encouraged her to return to the roadway, staying a safe distance behind the car.

The boys hung their heads out the car window, calling out insults to the Amish girls as they passed. Noah longed to stop them, but the volleyball players, used to tourists and hecklers, continued their game uninterrupted.

When the *Englischers* got no reaction, the driver revved the engine and sped off. The racing motor attracted the attention of several *youngie* on the sidelines, who glanced in Noah's direction. He'd hoped to pass by unnoticed. At least Caroline hadn't looked his way. Nor had that Tim.

The two appeared locked in a fierce battle for the next point. Noah marveled at Caroline's skills. He couldn't help smiling, picturing her playing with one hand tied behind her back. He had no doubt she'd lead her team to victory.

One of Caroline's teammates lobbed a soft return in Tim's direction. He jumped, intercepted it, and slammed the ball down in a vicious spike right toward Caroline. She twisted sideways and batted the ball in the air with a closed fist. Then she ducked so the boy behind her could hit it. What amazing moves!

Tim's gloating expression shriveled to a scowl as the ball sailed over his head to the back row of players.

"Serves you right," Noah muttered as he drew Rosie to a stop. Nobody seemed to notice him, so he watched a few more points.

Each time, Caroline stunned him with her clever moves.

She twisted and twirled and dodged, always managing to be in the perfect position. Yet, she didn't hog the ball. Instead, she instinctively helped others play to their strengths. Most of the time, she set it up so someone else could make the point.

Tim, too, proved to be an excellent player, but he lacked Caroline's natural ease and grace. No matter what moves he made, she anticipated them. Each time, his face screwed up in frustration. And his eyes burned with a desire to get even.

Caroline needed to watch her step. Noah had seen that look before, and it worried him. While he could understand Tim's envy of Caroline's superior skills and his growing aggravation, it was clear Tim wasn't just playing a simple game of volleyball. He wanted more than a win. He wanted revenge.

As the next server stepped into place on the other side of the net, Caroline bounced on her toes, getting ready to fight back.

"Game point," someone on Tim's team yelled.

She rallied her team. "Don't let them get this point. We can take them."

The ball flew over the net, and Anna Mary batted at it and missed. Josh rushed up behind her and popped it high in the air. As the ball floated down toward her, Caroline waited for it to reach the right spot. Then she slammed it down right behind Tim.

She'd sent it to his team's weakest player, who missed. Tim whirled around but not fast enough to intercept it. The ball bounced at his feet. With a disgusted groan, he kicked the ball upward into his hands and pitched it over his head to Caroline's side of the net without turning around.

She caught it. And when he pivoted to face the net, she grinned. Then she tossed the ball to her server. "Two points and we win this game. We can do it." Twisting back around, she bit back a smile at Tim's blazing eyes and ferocious scowl.

He'd be determined to beat her. But she wouldn't let him win.

After she rotated to the next position, the ball whizzed back and forth over the net several times. Then a tall boy who'd never played on Tim's team before jumped up and spiked the ball. Anna Mary cowered back.

Caroline dove for the shot. A pancake would save it, but conscious of Tim's eyes on her, she lunged instead. She tipped the ball into the air only a few inches. Josh dove forward and managed to lob a high-arcing shot over the net.

"Way to go, Caroline!"

The loud, distant shout distracted her. Already off-balance, she teetered and splatted facedown into a muddy spot. Josh tripped over her and landed nearby. Anna Mary screamed and ran to them.

Tim was laughing so hard he muffed the easy return. The tall boy scrambled to hit it, but the ball caught the top of the net and dropped at his feet.

"Abe!" Sharp anger edged Tim's voice.

The tall boy shrugged. "Don't blame me. You messed up first."

Gritting his teeth, Tim kicked the ball under the net right where Caroline was struggling to her feet. The volleyball splashed into the small puddle, splattering more mud over her face and arms.

Ooo that Tim! Despite her team winning the game, he'd

managed to humiliate her. If she'd attempted the pancake, she might not have looked ladylike, but at least she'd have been graceful and avoided a muddy face. Instead, she'd appeared uncoordinated and made a fool of herself.

And even worse, she'd recognized that cheering voice. She couldn't turn around and face in that direction because not only had she totally and completely embarrassed herself, but now she was covered with mud, dirt, and grass stains from head to toe.

How long had Noah been watching?

CHAPTER 16

As Caroline scrambled onto her hands and knees, Anna Mary rushed over to help Josh. He ignored her outstretched hand, pushed himself to his feet, and then whirled to face Tim.

Red-faced, Josh glared at Tim. "I can't believe you did that."

"Did . . . what?" Tim's words shot out between snorts of laughter. "You two . . . did it . . . to yourselves."

"You didn't have to kick the ball at Caroline. That was just mean."

"It was . . . an accident."

That's a lie! You did it on purpose. But Caroline didn't say that aloud. She had no right to call anyone else a liar when she'd lied to Tim multiple times.

With pity on her face, Anna Mary stared down at Caroline, who was untangling her dirty dress and apron as she tried to get her footing. "Need any help?"

"I'll be fine." As fine as she could be after Tim's snickering and Noah watching her flop headfirst into a puddle.

She refused to turn around and let Noah see her filthy clothes and her face dripping with mud.

Tim stopped his mocking laughter long enough to call

out, "Thought you told me your boyfriend was working and couldn't make the game. Anyhow, he's taking off. You'd think he'd at least help you out of this mess. Bet he's disgusted."

Caroline drew in a shuddery breath. Thank heavens, Noah didn't plan to stay around. One less thing to worry about. She almost snapped back that he had to get to work, but stopped herself before the untruth slipped out.

From now on, she'd ignore Tim's taunts. They'd gotten her into too much trouble already. Let them sting, then brush them off. Without saying a word.

But she couldn't do the same with Anna Mary, whose eyes bounced back and forth from Caroline to the departing buggy.

Caroline's shoulders relaxed as the clip-clop of hooves receded in the distance. She turned for a final glimpse before Noah rounded a curve and disappeared. Her pulse sped up at the thought he'd come to see her. Had he taken off work to be here? Maybe . . .

She checked her fancies. After seeing her faceplant, would he want anything to do with her? Like all the boys in her youth group, he'd probably rather have someone feminine and sweet. He might only have stopped by because he felt obligated after she gave him two lunches. But all the logical thoughts in the world couldn't destroy the tiny niggling of hope.

Arms akimbo, Anna Mary crashed Caroline back to reality. "What was that all about?"

"I didn't mean to do it." Caroline brushed at her dress and only succeeded in smearing the dirt stains. "It was an accident. I'm sorry I tripped Josh."

"That's not what I'm talking about, and you know it."

"Then what?" Caroline suspected what Anna Mary

meant. But in case she'd guessed wrong, Caroline wasn't about to bring up Noah. Mrs. V's advice helped Caroline hold her tongue while she waited to hear Anna Mary's answer.

"That was Noah, wasn't it? What was he doing here, and why didn't you tell me he would be at our game?"

"I didn't know he was coming."

Eyes blazing, Anna Mary shot back, "So he just *happened* to show up?"

"Well . . ." Caroline couldn't lie. "I did mention it to him."

"Oh, really. And when did you have that conversation?"

Before Caroline could confess the whole story, Tim sidled over to them with a smarmy grin. "Even though your boyfriend didn't stay long, he got to see your best move ever." With a snigger, he motioned to her mud-stained dress and face.

Though her cheeks warmed, Caroline lifted her chin. Anna Mary's side-eye helped restrain Caroline's impulse to clap back, and with effort, she stayed silent.

"Invite him to stay for the whole game next time to watch you get beaten."

Once again, Caroline managed to hold her tongue. When she didn't answer, Tim sauntered off, his disappointment evident, leaving her to face an irate Anna Mary.

Planting her hands on her hips, Anna Mary blocked Caroline's escape. "I want the whole truth. And I want it now."

"There's nothing to tell." The lie burned inside her. Why was she keeping all this to herself? As Caroline wrestled with her reluctance, movement in the nearby trees distracted her.

Josh, Anna Mary's boyfriend, stood in the shadow of a

huge oak. Rachel Glick stared up at him adoringly. From Josh's smile, he seemed to be basking in her attention.

"Anna Mary," Caroline warned, "Josh is over there."

"He'll wait. You're not leaving until I hear everything about you and this Noah."

"You don't understand. Josh is with—" Caroline stopped herself before she said *the youth group's worst flirt*. "He's with Rachel Glick."

"What?" Anna Mary stared at Caroline, confused. "You're trying to distract me. Josh wouldn't . . ."

Caroline's serious expression stopped Anna Mary's protest. "Turn around slowly. They're in the trees behind you."

Anna Mary shifted her position until she faced the spot Caroline had indicated. Josh noticed both of them. As Anna Mary stalked toward him, he shot her a smile tinged with guilt.

Caroline followed her.

Rachel's greeting dripped with innocence. "I was just telling Josh what a great job he did in the game. Those two spikes were awesome. If it weren't for him, we'd never have won."

Her lips pinched into a thin line, Anna Mary studied Rachel for a moment. "What about Caroline? She set up both of those shots for him. Maybe you can thank *her*," Anna Mary added sarcastically and waved Rachel toward Caroline.

Josh blinked as if he'd been slapped. Anna Mary had just discounted his winning points. Caroline wished she could fade into the background.

"And if you don't mind"—Anna Mary elbowed her way closer to Josh—"I'd like some time with Josh *alone*."

Her sharp tone didn't faze Rachel. "Of course. I'm sure you couldn't wait to rush over here as soon as we finished to let him know what a great player he is." With a self-satisfied smile, she waved to all of them and headed off.

"What did she want?" Anna Mary demanded.

Josh shrugged. "To tell me good game, I guess."

"Why didn't she do that on the volleyball court?"

"I'll see you both later." Caroline melted away as Anna Mary's voice rose. No point in waiting around. The two of them would settle their argument, and Anna Mary would ride home with Josh the way she usually did. But Caroline's conscience troubled her. She'd never seen Anna Mary so annoyed. Over the past week, her friend had become increasingly short-tempered. Caroline blamed herself. Being closemouthed and hiding secrets had hurt Anna Mary, and now she seemed to be taking it out on Josh. All of this was so out of character for her.

Luckily, Josh was easygoing. He'd calm Anna Mary down. And maybe it was time for Caroline to confess everything. Not that she had much to admit. The fake boyfriend request and two chicken dinners. Oh, and the invitation to the game. The only thing she wanted to keep to herself was her growing attraction to Noah.

She couldn't believe he'd actually come. And he'd cheered for her. If only he'd been there for one of her triumphs rather than her worst fumble. Still, taking time from his workday to stop by the game had to mean something, didn't it?

Longing and regret swirled inside Noah as he pulled away. As much as he wanted to see Caroline play, he never should have come. That had been a poor decision. And even more, he should have stayed quiet. He'd startled her and made her lose her balance.

Better to get out of here now before he did more to cause her harm. He hadn't intended to say anything, but her self-sacrificing save had stirred him. He'd been amazed. Not only had she avoided a smackdown by Tim, but she'd managed to bump the ball into the air while twisting away. He'd been so excited she'd evaded Tim's nasty move he'd yelled without thinking.

He'd managed to stop himself from dashing across the field when Tim kicked the ball toward her face. One of her teammates had jumped to her rescue and yelled at Tim. Noah wished he could have confronted Tim too. Who would do that to a girl sprawled on the ground? Especially a girl as sweet and kind as Caroline?

Noah had been right about Tim's vengeance. Anyone who got that worked up about losing a volleyball game needed to be watched. Like a snake in the grass, you never knew when he might strike.

If only I had the right to defend her . . .

CHAPTER 17

Anna Mary dragged herself into the stand on Tuesday with red eyes and slumped shoulders. Because they'd had an off-Sunday, Caroline hadn't seen her friend since the volleyball game. Although Caroline should be chopping cabbage for the coleslaw, she stopped, knife in midair. The salad could wait. She needed to find out what was wrong. "What's the matter? Are you all right?"

"Why should you care?" Anna Mary's despondent answer shocked Caroline.

"Because we're friends." At least they used to be. That hadn't changed for Caroline, but Anna Mary's skeptical look reminded Caroline how often in the past week she'd shut her friend out. And Caroline had promised herself to be more open from now on. "Friends don't leave friends stranded at a volleyball field," Anna Mary mumbled.

"What? I thought you'd go home with Josh."

"You thought wrong."

Anna Mary's words, edged with bitterness, tugged at Caroline's heart. Gently, she asked, "What happened?"

Head drooping, Anna Mary picked up a stack of trays and methodically set each one with a napkin and plastic silverware packet. For a minute, Caroline thought her friend didn't plan to answer.

When Anna Mary finally responded, she choked back tears. "I suppose some of it was my fault for getting jealous. Josh stormed off. I'm sure he thought you were still around and would take me home."

"I'm so sorry." Caroline reached out and hugged Anna Mary. "I never would have left if I'd known."

"I know you wouldn't. I don't blame you." Anna Mary backed away from Caroline's embrace. "We'd better get to work. It's almost time for the market to open."

But Caroline wanted to hear the whole story. "I'll shred cabbage while I listen."

Anna Mary's lips twisted into an ironic smile. She didn't say, *You, listen?* But her expression gave her away.

"I promise to stay quiet." Forgetting she held a knife, Caroline placed her hand on her heart. At Anna Mary's quick indrawn breath, Caroline lowered the sharp steel blade to the cutting board.

In a slow, robotic way, Anna Mary filled tray after tray without speaking. Caroline longed to break the silence with chatter, but she forced herself to wait.

Finally, Anna Mary said so low Caroline could barely hear her, "Josh accused me of not trusting him. I should have told him I did, but I pointed out he and Rachel had hidden in the trees."

A soft *ach* escaped from Caroline's lips before she caught herself.

"Things got worse from there." Anna Mary nibbled at her lip for a moment before continuing. "I—I saw him with Rachel before the singing at Yoder's a few weeks ago. I never said anything, but Rachel had her hand on Josh's arm and—"

"Rachel does that with a lot of people. It's just her way."

"You don't understand. Maybe if you were dating someone, you'd know how I feel."

Caroline sucked in a breath. How could Anna Mary be so cruel? She knew how much it pained Caroline that no one wanted to court her.

Anna Mary's gaze flew to the hurt expression Caroline couldn't hide. Dropping the tray she held, Anna Mary rushed over to Caroline and hugged her. "I'm so sorry."

Caroline stood stiff in the embrace. But when Anna Mary begged for forgiveness, Caroline thawed and returned the hug. "I'm sorry you think Rachel has come between you and Josh, but you have nothing to worry about."

"Maybe I do. Rachel's so pretty and lively. I'm dull and plain."

"That's not true. Besides, if Josh preferred Rachel, he'd be taking her home after the singings instead of you."

"I guess." Anna Mary sniffled. "Maybe he will now that we've fought."

"I doubt it."

Gideon interrupted them. "I'm going to unlock the doors now. Are you two ready?" He eyed the empty salad cases and frowned.

"*Ach*, I'm so sorry." Anna Mary appeared close to tears.

"It's not your fault," Caroline hastened to reassure her.

Gideon flicked an *I'm-disappointed-in-you* look at Caroline. "Anna Mary, I'm counting on you to tell my sister to stop gabbing and get to work." His tone was teasing, but the glance he threw at Caroline was stern.

"She wasn't—"

Anna Mary never got to finish because Gideon held up a hand and rushed off.

"Get it done before I get back," he called over his shoulder.

"I didn't mean to mess everything up. Or to get you in trouble."

Hoping to stop her friend's tears threatening to fall, Caroline hugged Anna Mary again. "It's all right. You needed to talk. And don't worry about Gideon. He never stays upset for long. Let's get these salads set out before it gets busy." After they hustled to fill the display case, Caroline returned to preparing the coleslaw. "We don't get many customers this early in the day, so I'll finish this container if you don't mind standing at the counter."

Anna Mary drew in a shaky breath and blinked until she'd stopped the welling tears.

"Will you be all right?" Caroline didn't want to ask someone else to do her job, but she wanted Anna Mary to feel comfortable. "You can work back here if you like, and I'll go out front."

"I'll be fine." Anna Mary squared her shoulders and headed for the counter as people streamed into the market.

Most of them lined up at the far end of the counter for baked goods. That gave Caroline an idea. She walked down the back aisle behind the refrigerator to Nick's candy stand. A few children stared with longing at the colorful jars filled with all kinds of candy—rows and rows of fire-balls, bubble gum, peppermints, licorice, hard candy . . .

"Psst, Nick," she whispered, "can you do me a favor?" She held out some money.

Nick waggled his eyebrows and pressed a hand to his heart. "Oh, Caroline, I thought you'd never ask. But I'm worth more than a few dollars."

Caroline rolled her eyes. Nick, the older *Englisch* man

who ran the candy stand, thought he was God's gift to women. If he looked in the mirror once in a while, he'd see his balding head and extra-large paunch. She shook her head. God wouldn't want her to be judgmental.

"In God's eyes, you're priceless, Nick."

His eyes narrowed. "You're not going to start preaching at me, are you?"

"Not right now. I'm in a hurry." Caroline hid her smile at his relief. "Could you ask Sovilla to take a cinnamon roll to Anna Mary? I don't want her to know it's from me."

"Why not? You two have a fight or somethin'? I thought you were best buds."

"We are. She's just feeling sad today. I'm trying to cheer her up."

"That's thoughtful of you."

The way Nick said it, though, made it sound as if Caroline never thought of anyone but herself. And maybe he was right. She needed to work on that.

As she headed back to the prep area, a deep voice called, "Hey, where's Car-o-line?" The familiar emphasis on her name grated on her nerves. Was Tim going to keep annoying her? She stopped moving and stayed behind the refrigerator.

"I don't know." Anna Mary sounded confused. "She was right here a minute ago."

"Bet she saw me and ran. I think she's scared of me."

Caroline clapped a hand over her mouth to prevent herself from responding, *I am not!* Just because she was hiding from him didn't mean he frightened her. She was only back here because . . . well, because she didn't want to interact with him. That wasn't the same as fearing him. Or was it?

"Hi, Anna Mary," a soft male voice said.

"Hey, Abe." Anna Mary's response sounded enamored.

Caroline's curiosity got the better of her, and she peeked out to see what was going on between Anna Mary and this Abe. Who was he? And how did Anna Mary know him?

To her surprise, Abe turned out to be the tall, thin guy from Tim's volleyball team. He and Anna Mary were staring at each other as if nobody else existed. Caroline had never seen Anna Mary look at Josh that way.

Caroline shifted to get a better view and then regretted it. Her movement caught Tim's attention.

"Oh, there you are, Caroline. Were you hiding from me?"

"Of course not. I'm fixing coleslaw." Well, she had been. But now that she was nowhere near the shredded cabbage, Tim was sure to think she'd lied to him.

She opened the refrigerator door. "I need to add carrots." She bent to get into the vegetable drawer both to get away from the intensity of Tim's gaze and to finish her job.

After taking an extra long time to take out the carrots, giving her some time to compose herself, she stood and pretended to be totally absorbed in grating carrots into the mixing bowl. But she kept sneaking peeks at Abe's and Anna Mary's interactions. They seemed to be talking quietly to each other.

Tim, meanwhile, had fixed his attention on Caroline, following her every move. His intense focus unnerved her. She scraped her finger on the grater instead of the carrot. She bit the inside of her lip to keep from crying out. She grabbed a paper towel and wrapped the finger.

"Hurt yourself?" Tim almost sounded concerned.

But Caroline knew him well enough to know he'd follow it up with a jab. So she ignored him and concentrated on shredding the carrot. Oddly enough, he didn't say a word.

She got out the dressing she'd made earlier and stirred the vegetables to thoroughly coat them. Then she dumped the coleslaw from the mixing bowl into the metal container. She should take the container out front, but she hesitated. "You'd better come over here," Tim called to her. "I have something important to tell you."

Caroline tossed her head. "I'm not interested."

"You will be. It's a warning about your boyfriend."

Anna Mary's head snapped around at the word *boyfriend*. Caroline should clarify she didn't have a boyfriend, but she couldn't bring herself to deny it. She'd open herself up to more of Tim's ridicule. Instead, she pretended disinterest. "I don't want to hear gossip."

"You need to know this. And I don't think you want me to blast this so everybody hears."

What could Tim possibly know about Noah? He was probably making it up. But if he spread false stories around the market, he could damage Noah's reputation. Caroline didn't want to give in to Tim's bribe.

Gideon returned to the stand and gave her a pointed look. She still hadn't put the coleslaw in the case, and two customers stood behind Tim.

Her brother headed to the counter. "Excuse me." He directed his words to Tim and Abe. "We have people to wait on."

Anna Mary blushed and mumbled *sorry*, while a red-faced Abe stepped to the side to let the line forming behind him reach the counter. Tim didn't move.

"This won't take long. I came to tell Caroline her boyfriend just got out of jail."

"Boyfriend?" Gideon turned to her with a stunned expression.

Anna Mary, her eyes wide with shock, turned. "Jail?"

Caroline gulped. But she didn't have time to explain to her brother. She had to stop Tim from repeating those horrible things. People might overhear and believe him. Tim's attempts at trying to annoy her had gone too far.

Grabbing the salad container, she charged over to the counter and glared at him. "Stop spreading lies! You have no proof." She slammed the metal container into the refrigerated case.

At the loud clang, Tim jumped. But Caroline's triumph fizzled as a self-satisfied smile slid across his face. "I do have proof. Well, at least my cousin Abe does." Tim elbowed the tall boy beside him. "Tell her, Abe."

After glancing around at the people at the counter and Anna Mary's distressed face, Abe shuffled his feet. "Not now, Tim."

But Tim ignored him. "Abe's from New York State, and he recognized your boyfriend from the Fort Plain newspapers a few years back."

Newspapers? That didn't sound good. Rather than spouting that, Caroline pinched her lips together and followed Mrs. Vandenberg's advice to listen.

"I can tell from your face you didn't know," Tim gloated.

She had to learn to school her expressions if she didn't want everyone to read her feelings. How did people keep their feelings from showing?

"Tim," Abe protested, "not now. Not here." He sent an apologetic glance to Anna Mary.

"Caroline needs to know her boyfriend killed a man." Tim's announcement carried, and curious shoppers stopped to listen.

"You take that back. That's not true."

"Tim," Abe protested. With apologetic glances at Anna Mary and Caroline, he clamped a hand on Tim's elbow and steered him away, but Tim couldn't resist shooting one final triumphant smile at Caroline.

CHAPTER 18

After a worried glance at Caroline, Gideon leaned over the counter to wait on one of their regular customers who'd been trapped behind Tim. "How can I help you, Mrs. Anderson?"

Her face creased into anxious lines, Mrs. Anderson didn't respond to Gideon. Instead, she focused on Caroline and asked in a shaky voice, "You're dating a murderer?"

"*Neh*, Noah would never kill anyone." She should deny she was dating anyone, but Caroline had to combat Tim's vicious rumor.

"Why would the young man say something like that then?"

Because he's cruel, and he wants to get even with me. Caroline struggled to control her temper and refrained from saying that aloud. "I plan to find out. But it's not true."

"I hope you're right, dear." Mrs. Anderson's puckered brow revealed she was still troubled.

"Can I help you with something?" Gideon asked again.

Mrs. Anderson blinked. "Oh, yes. Can you have this order ready at closing today?" She slid a list across the counter along with three twenties. "We're having company for dinner tonight. I'll pay now, but my husband will pick up the food on his way home from work."

Gideon handed the paper to Caroline. "Pin this up so we don't forget, would you?" He took the cash and made change, a job that should have been Caroline's. Still trembling with anger at Tim's falsehoods and cruelty, Caroline clipped the list to the ticket holder. Then she headed back to wait on other customers.

"Caroline," Anna Mary whispered, desperation in her tone, "I don't think Abe would lie."

How long had Anna Mary talked to Abe? Ten minutes maybe? "You can't tell that from one conversation."

"It wasn't only one conversation."

"What?" Caroline skidded to a stop.

"Tim and Abe drove me home from the volleyball field after Josh left me. I invited them in for lemonade." When Caroline raised her eyebrows, Anna Mary defended herself. "They were hot and sweaty after the game, and they'd gone far out of their way to drop me off."

"You asked Tim into your house after the way he treated me?"

"He's all right once you get to know him. And Abe . . ." Anna Mary stared dreamily into the distance. "I've never met anyone so nice."

"Even Josh?"

Anna Mary lowered her eyes and refused to meet Caroline's probing gaze. "I was upset with him that day."

"I see."

Gideon cleared his throat. "Do you two plan to wait on anyone today?" The stiffness of her brother's shoulders and the tightness of his jaw told Caroline she was in for the lecture of her life as soon as the customers had gone.

Caroline took her place at the cash register to handle the orders with Gideon, while Anna Mary dipped out salads and Aidan started the fries. People would soon be coming for early lunches.

As Anna Mary scurried past Caroline, she whispered, "I think Tim likes you."

If they didn't have a line at the counter, Caroline might have burst out laughing. "He has a funny way of showing it." Perhaps Anna Mary's starry-eyed view of Abe colored her opinion of Tim. That had to be the explanation for her crazy suggestion.

"I'm not kidding." Anna Mary came across deadly serious. "He talked about you a lot."

Probably to think up more ways to torture her. No way was he interested in her. He'd made that clear every time they met. And as far as she was concerned, she wanted nothing to do with Tim. Everything he'd said earlier today totally eliminated him from consideration. And that wasn't even counting all the mean things he'd done at the volleyball games.

After all the customers had been waited on, they had a rare break. Gideon tensed the way he did when he was reining in his temper. When he approached Caroline, Anna Mary shrank back, watching both of them, as if expecting an explosion.

"I want an explanation, and I want it now. What's this about you having a boyfriend?"

"I don't," Caroline squeaked out. Conscious of Anna Mary staring at her, Caroline squirmed inside. This hadn't been the way she'd intended to explain her situation with

Noah to her best friend. Or her brother. But she might as well get it over with. Yet, despite her usual talkativeness, she was reluctant to put everything into words.

"Caroline." The sharpness of Gideon's tone warned her he was getting impatient.

She opened her mouth, and the story gushed out. Bumping into Noah. Spilling the puzzle pieces. Tim's teasing. Pretending to have a boyfriend. Noah's rescue.

When she stumbled to a halt, she added, "It's not true, of course. Noah saw I was desperate and didn't contradict me calling him my boyfriend. But it was pretend." She had to be honest. "I lied."

Gideon examined her with a steely gaze. "That's the same Noah who walked you to the employee entrance the other day?"

She'd forgotten that part of the story. "*Jah*. Like I told you, he protected me from Butch."

"You didn't tell me anything about that," Anna Mary accused. "And if he's not your boyfriend, why did you take him the chicken dinners? Why did he give you a note? Why did he come to the volleyball game?"

Now it was Gideon's turn to look upset. He didn't say anything, but he studied Caroline closely as he waited for her answer.

"The first dinner was an apology for spilling the puzzle pieces."

Both of them had skeptical looks. Seeing it through their eyes, Caroline could understand they might think that was excessive. Maybe it had been. In their view, a simple *I'm sorry* would have been sufficient. Mamm always said Caroline overdid things. But if this gift of a meal bothered them, wait until they heard her next reason.

She stared down at the floor so she wouldn't have to watch their reactions. "The second dinner was a bribe."

Anna Mary sucked in a breath.

Before Anna Mary or Gideon could say anything, Caroline continued. "When I gave Noah that dinner, I asked him to come to the volleyball game."

"You did what?" Anna Mary sounded incredulous.

Caroline didn't repeat it. Instead, she forced herself to continue. As long as she'd started confessing, she needed to be completely honest. "I asked Noah because I didn't want Tim to know I couldn't get a boyfriend."

Although admitting that shamed her, it also released some of the guilt connected to all her lies and half-truths.

"You can get a boyfriend, Caroline." Her brother's insistence rang hollow. "But you have to stop chasing men who aren't interested."

His long-suffering sigh bothered her conscience. She'd promised Gideon she wouldn't go after anyone following the Zach incident. She disliked Gideon calling it *chasing*. It frustrated her that her acts of generosity or kindness could be so misinterpreted. But she'd scared Zach off by her exuberance and her gifts and . . .

She yanked her mind away from her past foolishness. Right now, she needed to calm her brother's fears. "I promise I won't bother Noah again, but I need to tell him about Tim's lies. I'll do it now before we get busy."

Without waiting for Gideon's approval, Caroline dashed out of the stand and toward the side doors. He called after her, but she ignored him and sprinted to the auction tent. She had to warn Noah that several stand owners and quite a few customers had overheard Tim's announcement.

She'd let him know she'd do whatever she could to fight the rumors.

Noah wasn't onstage at the auction, nor was he sitting at the picnic tables outside. She scanned the crowds but didn't see him. He must be in the storage building. She headed over there, but with her hand on the doorknob, she hesitated.

What if she opened the door and ran into Fred? He'd threatened to call the cops if he caught her in there again. Not that she was afraid of him or the police, but what if Noah had something bad in his past and she got him in trouble?

Noah crossed the parking lot after carrying an antique desk to an *Englischer*'s car. Normally, he didn't get asked to tote furniture to people's vehicles, but Fred had insisted Noah assist this special customer. By *special*, Fred meant a big spender.

A light breeze ruffled Noah's hair peeking out from under his straw hat, and he smiled at this chance to stretch his legs and enjoy the sunshine. A young Amish woman, holding a baby in one arm and balancing two heavy paper bags in her other, walked past him. A bawling toddler clung to her dress.

Fred would have a fit that Noah hadn't hurried right back, but he had to help.

"Can I get those bags for you?" Without waiting for an answer, he hurried over and lifted the groceries from her arms.

She'd been about to protest, but the strain lines around her mouth eased when he lightened her burden. "*Danke.*"

She looked down at her son. "We're almost at the van, Andrew. Not much farther." To Noah, she said, "He wants me to carry him."

"I can do that." He reached down and scooped the bawling boy into his other arm.

The boy stopped midcry and stared at Noah, then glanced around fearfully for his mother.

"It's all right," Noah soothed. "Your *mamm* is right beside us."

"Tell the nice man *danke* for carrying you, Andrew," she told her son.

Andrew ducked his head. "*Danke*," he said in a tiny, shy voice.

"Here's the van," she said as they approached a blue nine-passenger van with assorted car seats. "*Danke* for your help."

An *Englisch* woman sat in the driver's seat reading a novel. "You can pop the bags in the back," she told Noah. Then she turned to the Amish *mamm*, who was strapping the baby into one of the car seats. "Is your sister done, Miriam?"

"*Neh.* She has a few more things to get yet." Miriam finished buckling the baby and started untangling the belts of a larger car seat. "I can take Andrew now."

Noah moved closer, planning to put Andrew in the seat, but the small boy wriggled in Noah's arms.

"Do it myself," Andrew insisted.

Bending down, Noah set Andrew gently on the ground, and Miriam smiled her thanks over her shoulder as she untwisted the last strap. Noah rounded the back of the van to set the groceries inside. He'd put one bag in the back when Miriam screeched.

"*Neh*, Andrew! Come back!"

Noah dumped the second bag and spotted Andrew, who was squealing and chasing a tiny gray kitten.

"Come back," Miriam shouted as he darted between parked cars.

Noah charged after the little boy, running on an angle, hoping to head him off before he reached the busy main driveway. A teen in a jacked-up truck with music blaring raced down the row.

"No! Stop!!" Noah shouted and waved at the oncoming truck. "Andrew, wait!" But neither the teen nor Andrew heard him over the racket. The kitten shot across the row and under a nearby car. Andrew darted after it. Noah dove for the boy's suspenders. Caught them in one hand. Dragged him back just before the truck bumper clipped him.

Wide-eyed, the teen slammed on his brakes. His tires smoked and squealed on the asphalt. The vehicle fish-tailed. His face a mask of terror, the teen twisted the wheel.

Snatching Andrew into his arms, Noah jumped back.

The truck spun away from them and rocked to a stop.

Noah exhaled a long, deep breath, his heart hammering painfully against his ribs. Miriam caught up to them, her eyes filled with tears.

"*Danke, danke, danke!*" She gulped in a ragged breath. "I thought . . ."

Noah hugged Andrew close. The little boy could have been killed or badly hurt. "I'm sorry. I shouldn't have set him down until you were ready to put him in the van."

"It's not your fault. You saved him."

Andrew started to wail.

Alarmed, Noah checked him out. The truck hadn't hit

Andrew, but Noah had pulled hard on the suspenders. "Did I hurt you?"

The small boy shook his head. "Kitty gone."

Miriam's relief switched to a stern expression. "You are not to chase kitties or run away from me again. You know better than to do that in a parking lot."

CHAPTER 19

At the shouts, screeching, and squealing tires, Caroline let go of the storeroom doorknob and raced toward the parking lot, praying nobody had gotten hurt. She stopped short at the sight of Noah with a small boy in his arms.

Her heart revved up. Noah looked so appealing as he bent his head to examine the child. The concern etched into Noah's brow showed how much he cared. What a wonderful father he'd be.

Deep longing surged through her. If only she could find someone like him to share her future. She'd been so busy focusing on Noah, it took her a while to recognize the boy. Andrew Raber went to her church. So did his mother, Miriam, who was gazing at Noah with gratitude.

Without thinking, Caroline rushed across the parking lot. But she stayed out of Noah's line of vision.

A blue pickup sat sideways blocking the row. Skid marks extended far beyond its back tires. Aidan hopped out of the truck.

"I'm sorry, man. I didn't see the kid." Aidan wiped his forehead. "The little boy's okay, isn't he?"

Noah gave Andrew a quick hug. "He's fine."

Aidan nodded at Noah. "Thanks to your quick thinking." He turned to Miriam. "Hey, I didn't mean to hurt your boy. It's my friend's truck, and I've never driven it before. It kinda got away from me."

"It's all right. He wasn't hurt." Miriam held out her arms for Andrew.

Noah leaned over so Miriam could take her son, but Andrew clung to Noah's neck. "I want my kitty."

"You'll have to ask your *mamm*." Noah looked at her, one eyebrow quirked. "I can get the cat if you want."

Miriam shook her head. "We can't take someone else's kitten."

"I'm pretty sure it's a stray. A few of us on the construction crew take turns feeding her."

Caroline's heart expanded until it hurt. Noah was so kind and generous. Caring for Andrew, feeding a stray cat. No way would he kill someone. Tim must have lied.

When Miriam agreed, Noah handed Andrew to her and went after the kitten. He crouched by a car tire and spoke softly to the tiny kitten before lifting it carefully. At first, it hissed and clawed him, but after stroking it for a while, he soothed it. Then, cradling it close to his chest, he returned to Miriam.

She'd strapped Andrew into the van, and after getting her permission, Noah leaned into the van to put the kitten on Andrew's lap. At Andrew's rapturous *danke*, Noah's face softened, and he instructed the little boy on how to hold and pet a cat.

Until now, Caroline had watched silently, afraid to break the bond between Andrew and Noah. And Noah hadn't noticed her standing in a different row of parked cars. But once he emerged from the van and rushed toward the auction tent, she hurried to join him.

"Noah?" She hoped he'd slow down enough to talk to her, but he broke into a jog. Had he not heard her? Or was he trying to get away?

Caroline started to dash after him but stopped. She'd promised Gideon she wouldn't chase anyone again. She hadn't meant like this, but if anyone who knew her saw her running after Noah . . .

When he neared the storeroom, Noah slowed. Caroline picked up her pace to reach him before he went inside. She didn't want to take a chance of Fred overhearing.

"Noah?" she called.

He turned, and fleeting expressions crossed his face. Emotions she couldn't identify.

"I don't have time to talk, Caroline. I'm already late getting back."

"Because you helped Miriam and Andrew and rescued a kitten."

"How do you know that?"

Normally, Caroline would have answered readily, but her new, more cautious self hesitated. She didn't want him to think she'd been spying on him, even though she had. She waved vaguely in the direction of the truck Aidan was maneuvering slowly out of the parking lot. "I was over there."

"I see." At least he didn't ask what she was doing in the middle of the parking lot. "Well, nice to see you. I have to go." He started for the storehouse door.

"Wait," she begged. "I have something important to tell you. Tim came to the market."

Fists tight at his side, Noah bit out, "Again? Did he bother you?"

Caroline shook her head, then reconsidered. "Well, he

did, but only because he said some terrible things about you."

Noah waved a hand dismissively. "I couldn't care less what he says about me."

"Even if he says you killed a man?"

A wave of darkness closed over Noah. The old man hadn't died, but it had been close. And a few local papers had misreported his death. Someone from Fort Plain must have passed that news on to Tim. What else had they told him?

Breathless, Caroline babbled on. "I didn't believe Tim. I don't think anyone who is kind enough to help Miriam and risk their life to save Andrew and who cares for little kittens could be a killer."

Once again, Noah marveled at her innocence. She'd never been exposed to real evil, to the underbelly of society. Amish life here in Lancaster had kept her insulated from the cruelties he'd endured. The worst she'd faced had been Tim's taunts and insults. Noah wished he could protect her even from those.

"Tim also said you were in jail." Behind them, the storeroom door banged open, just as Caroline said, "He lied, didn't he? You weren't in jail, were you?"

She gazed up at him so trustingly, so sure he'd deny her question. He'd give anything not to disillusion her. But he had to tell the truth. He lowered his eyes so he didn't see that hopeful look on her face disappear. "*Jah*, it's true."

"You went to jail?" Her surprised exclamation broadcast his secret to everyone around them.

Behind him, someone gasped. "You did?"

Noah's stomach plummeted. Fred. The last person he wanted to know about his past.

Fred circled around to confront Noah, a disgusted look on his face. "Answer the question."

Swallowing hard, Noah forced out a *jah*.

Caroline uttered a soft cry. The tiny sound twisted Noah's gut. It pained him more than Fred's fury. He'd lost any chance of her friendship. And of keeping his job.

Noah had seen Fred seething and crimson-faced before, but now veins throbbed in the boss's temples, and his eyes bugged out. "You lied to me."

Neh, Noah hadn't. Fred hadn't even interviewed him or asked about his past. The day Noah showed up to apply for the job, Fred had been shorthanded. He'd ordered Noah to set up for the auction and said they'd talk later. But they never had. Straightening his spine, Noah pointed out, "You didn't ask me anything—"

Fred jabbed a finger at Noah. "Don't you dare blame it on me. You should have told me that right away. I wouldn't have hired you. I don't want an ex-con working here. You're fired."

"But . . ."

"No *if*s, *and*s, or *but*s about it. Get out of here before I call the cops and report you."

For what? Noah wanted to ask, but that would only rile his boss more. *Neh*, not his boss. His *former* boss. The words filled him with sickness. He'd lost this job. Would he lose his position with Jose too?

Caroline stood there, shell-shocked. She'd come out here to protect Noah from gossip. Instead, she'd caused him to lose his job. Sick inside, she fought back tears as he walked away. She couldn't run after him, beg his forgiveness. Not with Fred watching.

"Well, you've managed to get rid of another of my good auctioneers."

She whirled to face him, temper flaring. "You didn't have to fire him. You should have given him a chance to explain."

"Explain? How do you explain going to jail?"

His derisive look added fuel to the flames blazing inside her. "You don't even know what happened," she blasted to Fred. She had no idea about Noah's past, but something inside her refused to believe Noah would ever hurt someone, let alone kill them.

All Noah's actions flashed through her mind. She'd never seen him lose his temper, not even with Fred. And the way he'd saved Andrew . . . Noah could have been hit by the truck, but he'd been willing to risk his life for a child. No killer would do that. And he'd never answered that question. He'd never admitted to murdering anyone.

Another thought struck her. If Anna Mary's farfetched idea about Tim was right, maybe he lied to get Caroline to break up with Noah. Tim had no idea the boyfriend story was fake. As hard as she found it to believe Tim might be interested in her, that possibility gave her renewed hope he'd embellished the gossip. After all, Abe had pulled Tim away. Perhaps Abe hadn't wanted to be part of a made-up story.

Caroline had to get back inside. The early lunchtime rush had already begun, and Gideon would be furious with her for leaving the way she did. But no matter what it took, Caroline was determined to find out the truth.

* * *

Shoulders slumped, Noah strode across the parking lot to the shelter. Right now, he was grateful for Mrs. Vandenberg's gift of transportation. He had a way to escape. At least for the moment. Once she discovered his past, he'd have to return the horse and buggy.

No way could he stay around here. He had to go farther away. But how could he ever outrun the stories from his past? He'd carry them wherever he went.

He'd paid the RV rental until the end of the month. That'd give Mrs. Vandenberg time to find someone else to care for the horse. And his auction paycheck came out then, but would Noah get what he was owed? Knowing Fred, he'd find a way to dock Noah's pay. And no doubt, he'd spread the rumors about Noah's jailtime far and wide.

As much as Noah enjoyed working on the construction crew, once Jose found out he'd hired an ex-con, he'd have to let Noah go. It might be best to confess to Jose before the gossip reached him. Would Jose also try to withhold Noah's pay?

Noah wanted to tell Jose now and get it over with, but he couldn't do it when the market was open. If Noah stayed on the market grounds, Fred might cause a ruckus.

And Noah couldn't chance running into Caroline. He hadn't looked at her when he'd admitted his past, but he couldn't bear to have her ignore him or look at him with disgust.

He'd cautioned himself over and over not to get involved with her. Yet, despite his wariness, he'd fallen for her. And fallen hard. If he'd followed his inner warnings, he'd still have his job, his sanity, and a whole heart. Now when he took off, he'd leave a major piece of himself behind.

Heavyhearted, Caroline trudged back to the stand. Why hadn't she kept her mouth shut? Noah's past was none of her business, yet she'd forced him to reveal something he wanted to keep secret. She'd just learned powerful lessons about not prying into other people's business, not spreading gossip, and not keeping her mouth shut. If only she could remember them the next time she grew curious or planned to broadcast news she'd heard.

What hurt her most was the damage she'd done to Noah. She had no idea how to make things right. She couldn't get his job back for him. He'd mentioned another job. Would he have enough hours there to meet his expenses? She couldn't bear to think of leaving him with money troubles too.

"Where have you been?" Gideon demanded when she slipped into the stand.

"There was an accident in the parking lot. Aidan lost control of a friend's truck and almost hit Miriam Raber's Andrew."

Anna Mary clapped a hand over her mouth and sucked in a breath.

"Are they all right?" Her brother looked horrified.

"*Jah*, they're fine." Her conscience jabbed her for misleading them by not mentioning Noah, which was where she'd spent the most time.

Gideon returned to waiting on customers, and they

stayed busy the rest of the day. Too busy for talk or for questioning.

But after closing, Anna Mary came close and whispered, "Did you talk to Noah?"

Caroline had been hoping to skip that topic. She couldn't lie, though. "He admitted he went to prison."

Anna Mary gasped. "Is it safe to have a murderer working here?"

"You don't have to worry. He won't be around. Fred fired him." Caroline couldn't keep the bitterness out of her voice. "And it's all my fault." Once she admitted that, the rest of the story tumbled out—from seeing the near-accident to confronting Noah, and Fred's reaction to overhearing her question.

"I can see why you feel bad about what happened, but we're all much safer without him here." Anna Mary's expression darkened. "Unless he shoots up the market to retaliate."

Caroline's irritation went from simmering to full boil. "Noah isn't like that. You should have seen how gentle he was with Andrew and with the kitten."

"That doesn't mean anything. In the newspapers, neighbors of killers often say the person was quiet and seemed nice."

What papers was Anna Mary reading? Certainly not the *Budget* or *Die Botschaft*.

"We'd better get more done before Gideon comes back from locking up. We can talk later." Or not. Caroline had already decided to keep her thoughts and information about Noah private. Holding in information, though, made her want to explode. And her thoughts whirled. She had to find a way to apologize to Noah. But she had no idea how to get in touch with him. She didn't know where he lived or what *g'may* he belonged to.

Several times, she caught Anna Mary examining her closely. Each time, Caroline pointed out another chore that needed to be done to escape her friend's scrutiny. Once they finished all the cleaning, Caroline had no excuses to avoid Anna Mary's questions.

Anna Mary gathered her things. "I need to get home, but . . ." She hesitated, as if unsure she should speak. Then her words came out in a rush. "I know it's not my business, but you're my best friend and I don't want to see you hurt. When you set your mind to something—or someone— nobody can discourage you or get you to see reason. We saw that with Zach. I can tell you're upset about what happened, but I'm glad Noah won't be working here any- more."

Caroline prayed for strength to hold her tongue and grace to hear Anna Mary's criticism. Her friend's state- ment rang of truth—Caroline often made up her mind about things and rejected others' advice. She did things her own way and acted headstrong.

Although she understood Anna Mary's concern, this time her friend hadn't gotten to know Noah the way Car- oline had. Something inside her refused to believe he had killed a man. If he had, it must have been an accident. She had to find out the true story.

CHAPTER 20

Noah ran a hand down Rosie's neck, and she nosed him to get the apple he'd tucked in his pocket. He'd brought a treat to give her between his two jobs today. Now he'd lost one of them. Would the other soon follow?

He had to get out of the parking lot before Fred discovered him still here. Noah had no doubt Fred would call the police to get rid of a criminal. In fact, knowing his boss, Noah wouldn't put it past Fred to make up a crime. He could easily accuse Noah of stealing things from the auction.

At least Fred hadn't overheard Caroline saying Noah had killed a man. He didn't even want to imagine how Fred would react to that. Right now, though, it would be in Noah's best interest to get off market property as rapidly as possible.

Still, he didn't want to rush Rosie. He drew out the apple and held it on his palm. As Rosie snuffled his hand, an ache started in Noah's gut and spread until it filled his chest and constricted his throat.

"I'm going to miss you." He choked the words out

before the lump in his throat completely blocked off his words.

He'd miss a lot of other things too. The peace and seclusion of the campground. The joy of auctioning items and watching smiles blossom on buyers' faces when they won. The neutral expressions on people's faces as they walked by him because nobody knew about his past.

He'd lost that privacy now. Soon the rumors would fly around the market, and everyone would look at him askance the way they had in Fort Plain. If they branded him a murderer, they'd fear him and skitter away. He'd have no future here.

Once again, he'd be on the run, searching for a place to start over again. He had no idea where he'd go. He only knew it would be far from Fort Plain and even farther from Lancaster. That knowledge added to the deep pain inside. When he'd listed all the things he'd miss, he hadn't focused on his greatest heartbreak. Leaving Caroline.

She represented everything he admired in a woman— generous, caring, strong, capable, courageous, and most of all, completely honest and transparent. Until now, he'd never met any woman who'd touched his heart and soul in this way. Even though he'd cautioned himself he'd be making another major mistake in his life, he'd been drawn to her like a hummingbird to a beautiful flower. When he left the area, he'd be ripping his heart in half. Why had he let himself get entangled with a woman, especially an Amish woman, when they could have no future together?

During his years in jail, he'd learned to erect a concrete wall to seal off his emotions. He tried to do that now, but tiny tendrils of plants snaked through, crumbling his defenses, cracking the solid block, like flowers poking through sidewalks. If he had to label those buds, he'd call them hope and love. And only one person—one special woman—had planted those seeds. A woman he'd never see again. A woman he'd never allow himself to see again.

He toyed with going over to the construction site but decided to wait until the market closed and the parking lot cleared out. He hadn't paid much attention to what time most people left. There'd been a few scattered cars and buggies when he'd headed off to see Caroline on Saturday. Maybe he'd be safe waiting an hour or two after closing.

While Fred and Butch usually locked up around four thirty on Tuesdays, Caroline's brother closed the market after everyone else left, so they'd be one of the last stand owners to depart. If Noah waited until six, he'd miss most people. But it would make him late for work. Still, he didn't want to chance running into anyone, especially Caroline. An Amish couple with several children headed toward the shelter carrying bags, signaling to Noah he needed to go.

After hitching up the buggy, he gave the horse one last pat. "Come on, Rosie. We'd better get out of here." With a heavy, weary heart, he pulled out of the parking lot.

He had several hours to kill before he returned so he wound along backcountry roads, enjoying the light scent of honeysuckle on the air, the patchwork quilts of green fields, the farmland dotted with cows, the blue of mountains in the distance, the scattered canopies of oaks and maples overhead filled with twittering birds. He'd miss all this. But most of all, he'd miss a sweet blonde with green eyes.

* * *

Instead of dropping Caroline off at home the way he usually did, Gideon pulled into their parents' driveway. She glanced over at him in surprise. Her brother always rushed home to Fern and the baby. For him to stop, something must be very wrong.

"What are you doing?"

"Going in to talk to Daed." Gideon hopped out and tied up his horse.

"About what."

His face grim, Gideon didn't answer.

Two thoughts ran through Caroline's mind. One, business troubles. Or two, Noah.

She'd start with her first question. "Are we doing all right at the stand? Making enough money and everything?"

Gideon turned startled eyes to her. "Why wouldn't we be?" The set of his jaw warned her not to ask the second question.

Maybe she could eavesdrop. If Gideon told Daed about Noah, she wanted to make sure to give her own opinion about his character.

But her *daed* and brother closeted themselves in the small office off the living room and spoke too softly to be overheard. When they emerged, they both wore concerned expressions.

"*Danke* for letting me know, *sohn*." Daed set a hand on Gideon's shoulder. "I'll check into it." From the worried glance Daed sent her way, Caroline surmised they'd talked about Noah.

Determined to do something to salvage his reputation, Caroline waited until they sat around the supper table. After the silent prayer, she broke into her usual chatter. She started with details about Anna Mary's spat with Josh and the concern that the two of them might break up.

"It's early days yet." Mamm blew on a spoonful of chicken corn soup to cool it. "If God intends for them to be together, He'll work it out. If not, they'll each find someone better." She beamed at Daed.

He chuckled. "When I was seventeen, the girl I liked started going out with my best friend. My heartbreak lasted six whole months until I met your mother. Then I saw God had a much better plan for my life. Disappointment often is the pathway to greater blessings."

Caroline loved her parents' stories about being young. This one, though, twisted a knife into a soft, vulnerable spot in her heart. It had been years rather than months since she'd fallen for Zach. Recently, she'd recovered from that disaster. Except now the man she'd secretly been hoping might heal her heartbreak had been accused of not only being a criminal but also a murderer.

Something deep inside her rebelled at that last label. Noah didn't deserve to be condemned until he'd told the whole story. And even then, they should forgive him and let him begin his life afresh. As much as her community believed in letting others make a new start, Caroline was clear-eyed enough to know many in their church loved to gossip and air dirty laundry. The smears Tim had broadcast would make the rounds, tarring Noah's character. She had to do her part to counteract them.

"Guess what else happened at the market today." She launched into an account of Andrew Raber's almost-accident, making sure to highlight Noah's part as rescuer. Then she reinforced his gentleness and caring. "He crawled under a car to get the kitten for Andrew and even gave Andrew tips for caring for it. Wasn't that sweet?"

Her mouth full, Mamm smiled and nodded, but Daed's lips pressed into a thin line. That proved he and Gideon had discussed Noah. It made Caroline even more determined than ever to prove Noah deserved to tell his side of things. Until she heard it from him, she'd never believe he'd hurt anyone.

That led to a major problem. How could she hear Noah's story if she had no idea where to find him?

Feeling guilty about being so late, Noah pulled Rosie into the shelter and loped across the deserted market parking lot to the construction site. During his drive, he'd decided he had to tell the truth about his past. He'd probably get fired on the spot, but he didn't want to deceive Jose.

Rather than getting right to work the way he usually did, Noah headed for the ladder where Jose was inspecting some recent work.

"Lookin' good," he called before climbing down. "Keep going like that."

As soon as his feet hit the ground, Noah called his boss's name. Jose turned around and broke into a wide grin.

"Thought you weren't coming today. I was kicking myself for suggesting you find a pretty girl. I just hoped you hadn't found another job. We can really use you."

Any other day, those words would have lifted Noah's spirits. Today, they only plunged him more deeply into gloom.

Jose peered closely at Noah. "You okay? You don't look so good. Go home if you're sick."

Noah would be going home soon. First, though, he needed to say what he'd come here to confess. "Jose, I really like working here, but there's something you should know about me. I was in jail for three years in New York before I moved to Lancaster."

His expression calm and unperturbed, Jose nodded. "So you're with that gang program Mrs. Vandenberg started, huh?"

What? "I don't know anything about that."

"Oh, sorry. My mistake. Mrs. Vandenberg runs some programs in the inner city to keep kids out of gangs. And you know Gideon—the one who runs the market for her? His sister-in-law Nettie is in charge of this center where they train former gang members. Some of them work here and at the market. I think Gideon's planning on hiring some at his stand."

Noah's mouth hung open, and he snapped it shut. So many things swirled through his mind, he could only stand there staring numbly at Jose. Mrs. Vandenberg rehabilitated gang members? That shaky little old lady? Wasn't she frightened?

Next, Noah's thoughts zigzagged to Gideon. He'd be hiring gang members? What about Caroline? She needed to be protected. Gideon couldn't risk her life like that. Noah had been around gang members in jail, and they could be some of the hardest, cruelest men. He cringed thinking of any of those men near sweet, kind Caroline.

"Thanks for being honest." Jose interrupted Noah's fears. "I admire you for being up-front with me."

With effort, Noah pulled his attention from Caroline being attacked to his cheerful boss. Jose didn't plan to fire him? Had he indicated some of the crew used to belong to gangs? Or had Noah imagined that?

When he got no response, Jóse clapped Noah on the shoulder. "Just so you know. I never judge a man on his past. I only go by his present actions. And you've proved you're trustworthy."

"Even after showing up late?" Noah couldn't believe it.

"We already agreed you'd work whatever hours you can. When you're here, you put in more work every hour than most of my men. I'll take whatever time you can give me."

That was it? He still had his job? Noah struggled to process Jose's reaction. After spending the afternoon expecting to lose his position, Noah still couldn't believe his good fortune.

"I'm glad you're willing to let me stay on."

"Why wouldn't I be?" Jose looked even more puzzled than Noah felt.

"I don't know." Noah shuffled his feet in the loose dirt, setting up clouds of dust. He forced himself to hold still. "I just thought maybe with my past . . ." He struggled to force words past the lump in his throat.

"Like I said, we only look at what you're doing now. God forgives our past, so to my mind, it doesn't count."

At the reminder of God and religion, the blockage in Noah's throat grew tighter. He'd been raised to believe that God forgives as you forgive others. Since Noah had a tangled ball of unforgiveness lodged inside, God had become a sore spot in Noah's life. Still, he had to say something after Jose's kindness.

"*Danke.* I'm really grateful for this job." Even more so now that he'd been fired from the auction.

"And I'm grateful to have you whenever you're able to come." Jose beamed at him. "Now instead of us both grinning at each other like maniacs, how 'bout you get over there and lay some block?"

"I'm on it." Noah hustled over to the spot where he'd left off yesterday. He still found it hard to believe he'd kept this job. He wished he could ask to work on market days too, but he didn't want to run into Fred. Or Caroline.

Noah would miss this job when he left the area at the end of the month. And, of course, he'd tear his heart in half by leaving Caroline, even if it was for the best.

CHAPTER 21

Caroline helped Mamm with housework the next day, rushing through the chores as fast as she could. When they finished, she called to her mother, "I'm going out for a while, but I'll be back for supper." She rushed outside before Mamm could question her.

But Mamm called to her from the back door. "I'd like your help with the cooking and baking. It's our turn to take a meal to the bishop's house. And I'll need you to make our supper while I drop it off."

Swallowing back a sigh, Caroline returned to the kitchen. Usually, she'd be glad of the chance to help the bishop's wife, who'd recently had a baby, but today, Caroline was eager to find Noah. She banged around the kitchen, trying to pull together all the ingredients as quickly as she could.

"*Dochder*, it's not like you to be this impatient to visit Anna Mary. You saw her yesterday at the market, and you'll see her tomorrow morning. What is it that can't wait?"

"I'm sorry." Caroline always did everything fast, but she never slammed cupboard doors or thumped ingredients onto the counter like this. She slowed her movements and hoped her apology and changed behavior would distract Mamm from her question.

They worked silently, and Mamm didn't press for an answer. Inside, Caroline's natural honesty warred with her desire to keep her errand secret. Mamm had assumed Caroline planned to visit Anna Mary. Caroline's conscience pushed her to be honest. What if she told the truth, though, and Mamm forbade her to see Noah?

Mamm had been upset over the situation with Zach. She might assume Caroline would act the same way with Noah. Caroline didn't want to take a chance of being told she couldn't go to see him.

"You're so quiet, *dochder*. Is something wrong?"

Jah, something was very wrong. She'd gotten Noah fired. She'd ruined someone's life.

"Did you and Anna Mary have a fight?"

Mamm had given Caroline the opening she needed. Words gushed out of her as she explained about Anna Mary's fight with Josh. "So she's upset with me for leaving her stranded at the field."

"*Ach*, that's a shame. Don't fret about it. When she's had time to think it over, she'll realize you're a true friend and that you didn't leave her on purpose."

Caroline hoped Mamm was right. But the friendship with Anna Mary had hit other ruts. The biggest one happened to be Noah. Also, if Anna Mary became friends with Tim and Abe, it would drive a wedge between Caroline and her best friend.

Time trickled by, each minute seeming more like an hour, until at last, the meal had been prepared and delivered to the bishop's wife, and they'd finished their own supper. Breathing a sigh of relief, Caroline dried the last dish and placed it in the cupboard. Finally, she was free to go. Once she hitched up the horse and started down the driveway, she realized she had no idea where Noah lived. Her only clue came from that time she'd offered him a ride. He'd been walking along that wooded stretch of road beyond Yoder's Country Store. If he lived nearby, he might shop for groceries there. The Yoder girls loved to find out all about their customers. One of them might be able to direct her to Noah's place. When Caroline pulled into Yoder's, only a few cars and buggies were scattered around the parking lot. *Good.* Maybe someone would have time to talk to her. Before approaching Jenna Yoder at the baked goods counter, Caroline checked the aisles to be sure Noah wasn't in the store.

Then she headed for the nearly deserted bakery section and studied the cookies. "Hi, Jenna, could I have half-dozen peanut butter cookies?"

Jenna pulled out a white bag and slid six cookies into it. "I guess you miss Fern's cookies. When will she be back at the farmer's market?"

"In another week or two, I think." Now to bring up Noah. Caroline took the bag and, keeping her tone casual, asked, "Do you know Noah Riehl?"

"He comes in from time to time."

"I need to get in touch with him. It's urgent. Would you happen to know his address?"

"*Neh.* All I know is that he rents our blue barn out back for his horse."

That was odd. If he had a horse, why did he walk to work? "So he must live nearby?"

"I guess. Most people wouldn't want to be too far away from their horse and buggy."

"Did he give his address when he rented the barn?" Caroline asked that loudly enough that Jenna's *mamm*, Mary, who was packaging up day-old doughnuts in the back, could hear.

Through thick lenses sliding down her nose, Mary peered at her. "Oh, it's Caroline Hartzler. And what would you be needing Noah for?"

"I, um, have to give him a message."

"From you or someone else?" Mary slid her glasses up her nose and studied Caroline.

Too late Caroline realized what a gossip Mary was. She'd be sure to tell everyone who stopped by the store that Caroline had been inquiring about visiting Noah. "I just need to tell him something. It won't take long." Was that the truth?

"And it couldn't wait until tomorrow morning?"

Caroline squirmed under Mary's and Jenna's inquisitive stares. "Not really." Caroline wouldn't see him tomorrow or the next day or the next . . . At that thought, her spirits plunged even lower.

"I hope, dear, this isn't a case like—" Mary shrugged. "You know what I mean."

Caroline certainly did. And *neh*, this was nothing like that. Or was it? She hoped her guilt didn't show on her face.

But Mary had gone back to counting doughnuts into bags. "Too bad you didn't come in this morning. You might have caught him at the barn. He left around seven. I don't know when he'll be back. Some nights he gets in pretty late. Long after we're in bed."

What was he doing out so late? Caroline wouldn't ask the question burning on her tongue. And she couldn't catch him tonight if he came back late. She'd be adding to the gossip, but she had to find him. "So did he give an address to rent your barn?"

"*Neh*, a lady rented it for him."

"A lady?" Caroline could have bitten off her tongue. She sounded as if she were jealous. But as soon as Mary said those words, Caroline's hopes nosedived. Maybe Noah had a girlfriend or fiancée. Perhaps he stayed out late courting her.

"The lady's an *Englischer*," Jenna said slyly. "Don't worry. She's really old."

"You looked quite worried." Mary laughed. "That *Englischer* who owns the farmer's market paid for the barn."

"Mrs. Vandenberg?"

"*Jah*, that's the one."

She rented the barn for Noah? Couldn't he afford it? Would Mrs. Vandenberg know where he lived? Caroline could ask her, but with Mrs. V being able to read everyone's mind, she'd guess Caroline's hidden feelings. It would be better not to bring up the subject. Besides, Caroline was determined to find Noah today, and she didn't have much time. Her parents would expect her home before they went to bed.

Plus, as she'd told Noah, she liked to win. When she set out to do something, nothing could stop her. She'd ask at all the houses around here until she found him.

"Did you ever notice which way he went home?" Caroline directed her question to Jenna.

Although Jenna acted as if she were trying to remember, her cheeks pinkened. "I think he may have turned left out of the parking lot." She glanced over her shoulder at her *mamm*. "Does that sound right?"

"I'm not sure."

Caroline didn't need Mary's confirmation. Jenna's blush proved she'd paid attention to more than the direction Noah traveled.

Only one problem with that information—the whole area to the left was wooded. No farms, no houses stood between Yoder's and the spot where Noah had been walking the other day. Had Jenna purposely misdirected her?

Noah had arrived at the construction site early that morning and worked through his lunch break. Other than taking care of Rosie, he'd laid block nonstop. He wanted to prove himself to be a valuable employee, so Jose wouldn't regret keeping him on.

Jose had rewarded Noah with smiles and calling out *good job* as he passed during the day. Noah reached the last block. He laid it as carefully as he had the others, then went looking for his boss.

"Any more block to lay?" he asked Jose.

Jose squinted at the level he'd set on a section of wall Noah had completed earlier. "This looks great." Jose lifted the level and turned to Noah. "You're out of block already?"

Noah nodded.

"Guess I'm gonna have to order more pallets at a time. I'm not used to my workers getting so much done in a day."

"Anything else I can do?"

"Naw. Go on home. You deserve a rest. We'll have more block delivered before you arrive tomorrow afternoon."

Noah debated about telling Jose he'd be willing to work all day Thursday, but the need to avoid Fred and Caroline stopped him. "I may not make it here until around six."

"Like I said before, whenever you can get here is fine."

If only he could work his market hours over the next few days. He'd only have a few hours on the construction site tomorrow, Friday, and Saturday. He could use the money to fund his move. But if Fred saw Noah, he might interfere with Noah's employment here or call the cops on him. Then Noah would lose those hours as well. Better to stay away from his ex-boss. With a wave to Jose and a few of the crew, Noah left the construction site. Once again, he meandered down back roads, taking his time going back to the RV. Tomorrow would be his hardest day so far. When he got up, he'd have nowhere to go and nothing to do until he left for the construction site in the early evening.

When he reached his turnoff, he pulled into Yoder's Country Store to grab a quick snack.

"Hey, Noah." One of the Yoder daughters waved at him. For some reason, he could never keep their names straight. They all looked so much alike with their strawberry blond hair, freckled noses, and wide smiles.

He gave her a businesslike smile. She ignored his standoffishness and came hurrying over. Noah groaned inside. When the store wasn't busy, like now, one girl in particular loved to chatter. This must be the one.

He wasn't in the mood for conversation and pretended he didn't see her approaching. He grabbed the nearest bag of chips and handed the cashier his money, preparing to bolt as soon as he received his change.

"Wait, Noah, I have something to tell you."

Since she'd called him by name, Noah couldn't ignore her and slip out. He took his change and turned to her.

"Guess what?" Breathless, her cheeks a mottled red that made her freckles more prominent, she waited for him to respond.

He shrugged. Why did people ask questions that had no possible answer?

"Someone came in here about thirty minutes ago asking about you."

Noah's stomach curdled. Fred, coming to cause trouble? A reporter who'd heard Tim telling about Noah's past? No matter who was looking for him, it'd be trouble. Maybe he'd need to leave before the end of the month.

"You don't look very happy about it." Her eyes held a hopeful look. "I guess it's a good thing I told her I didn't know your address."

Her? Caroline came to mind first. His heart skipped a beat. Then reason took over. She wouldn't be looking for him. Only one other person might have come to reclaim the horse and buggy because the real owner had arrived. Or worse yet, she'd heard about him being in jail and had come to fire him from the construction crew.

"Mrs. Vandenberg?"

The redhead giggled. "*Neh*, she was much younger. Do you know Caroline Hartzler? She works at the chicken stand in the farmer's market, and she said she had an urgent message for you."

An urgent message? What would Caroline have to tell him? Maybe Mrs. Vandenberg had sent her.

The Yoder girl picked up on his hesitation. "If you don't want to see her, I can let her know." She sounded quite eager to do that.

"*Danke*, but I'd better find out what she wanted." Perhaps he could check with Mrs. Vandenberg first. He'd rather not see Caroline again. It would be too painful. Thank goodness she hadn't found out his address.

CHAPTER 22

Caroline drove up and down the road twice from Yoder's to the spot where she'd seen Noah that day. The only place to turn was a rutted dirt road right beside the market. It led back to the Yoders' barns, and beyond that, a weathered wooden sign pointed to a campground. Caroline had never traveled back here before. Perhaps a few houses might be tucked along this road. She turned into the lane and stopped at the blue barn, hoping Noah's horse would be there. Caroline peered through the small window in the door, but the stall was empty.

She continued down the winding road until she came to the campground, its entrance almost hidden from view by overgrown bushes and drooping trees. A barely legible sign stood outside a small log building. At the top, it said OFFICE with an arrow to the right. Below that, faded printing indicated a CAMP STORE to the left.

Caroline tied her horse to a sapling. Several people sitting around a campfire in the center of a group of tents whispered and pointed. Caroline turned away before they pulled out cameras. She should have realized she'd be walking into a tourist area. Most people who lived on these back roads were either Amish or used to the Amish, but a campground would host travelers from other places. She was a novelty.

Keeping her back to the group, she rushed up the stairs and knocked on the screen door.

"It's open," a man yelled. "Come on in."

Caroline hurried inside, and the door sprang shut behind her with such a loud bang she jumped.

The man at the desk stared at her in amusement. "You comin' camping?"

She shook her head. Standing here, she realized how foolish she'd been expecting this trail to lead to Noah. Since she was already here, though, she might as well ask.

She'd seen a few trailers scattered back in the woods. The RVs in the rows behind the tents probably belonged to visitors, but the trailers might be permanent housing. Did Noah live in one of them? "Do you have any year-round residents?"

"We do." The man swiveled in his chair and nodded at the property map pinned up behind him.

Caroline went straight to the point. "Do you rent to any Amish?"

He rotated to face her. "Of course. You want to rent a place?"

"*Neh*. I mean *no*. I'm looking for someone and wondered if you might have seen him. He's Amish."

"You from law enforcement?" His half smile revealed he was teasing.

She shook her head. "I just want to find a friend. I wondered if he's staying at the campground."

"Sorry, I can't tell you that. I respect people's privacy.

Unless you're here with a search warrant or on official police business, I won't reveal anything about our guests."

"I see." Caroline turned to leave. Other than knocking on the doors of every trailer and RV in the park, she had no way of finding out if Noah lived here. Unless some of the residents had seen him and would help her.

"A word of advice," the man said as Caroline reached the door. "If he didn't give you his address, he didn't want to be found. Might be best to leave him alone."

Caroline shriveled inside. Did she look like a desperate ex-girlfriend or wife chasing a man who'd left her? "It's not like that."

"You going after him for child support? You should get a government worker to come after him."

"Child support? Of course not." There wouldn't be any need to do that in the Amish community.

"Then take my advice and don't bug him. The poor man probably wants his peace and quiet."

Maybe Noah did want to avoid people. He'd sort of hinted at that when he thought she might be chasing him. Yet he showed up for her volleyball game. Did that mean anything?

Caroline eased the screen door shut behind her instead of letting it bang. Even though the campground manager had made her sound like a man-hunter, she wouldn't be rude.

The group of tenters, roasting hot dogs or marshmallows over the fire, looked up when she exited. A few elbowed their neighbors and pointed. Caroline headed toward them.

"She's coming over here," one of them whispered loudly enough for her to hear.

"Have any of you seen an Amish man at the campground? He's about six feet tall and—"

"Sure did," said a blond woman with flowers tattooed up and down each arm. "He your boyfriend?"

Caroline ignored the question. "Do you know where I can find him?"

The blonde waved a hand toward the hill behind her. "I saw him somewhere over there."

The man next to her, sporting a skull and crossbones tattooed on his forehead, nodded. "He cuts through those trees sometimes. Not sure which place he belongs to."

Well, that narrowed things down a little. "*Danke.* I mean, thank you."

In a stage whisper, the blonde said to the other campers, "She jest said some of them Pennsylvania Dutch words."

An older man laughed. "You'll hear plenty more tomorrow when we go to the market and auction."

"I can't wait. I gotta text my BFF to tell her I talked to a real, live Amish person."

Caroline hoped the group wouldn't recognize her if they toured the market tomorrow. The last thing she needed was a group of tattooed tourists swarming the counter to say they recognized her. How would she explain that to her brother?

Noah pulled the buggy into the barn and unhitched Rosie. Then he washed her legs, brushed her, and picked her hooves. Staying and spending more time with his horse sounded appealing, but suppose the Yoder girl had told Caroline about him using this barn and she stopped by the barn to check for him? He'd be safer in the RV. He took the shortcut through the woods to avoid Caroline spotting him if she were anywhere around. As he rounded the RV, smoke drifted his way from a campfire near the park entrance. Sizzling hot dogs made his stomach rumble. He'd skipped his lunch break, and he hadn't had supper. If only he'd picked up something more substantial to eat when he'd stopped at Yoder's.

Noah slipped into the RV without attracting any notice. His time in jail had taught him how to do that. He sat on the couch with the bag of chips. That would have to do for tonight. As he reached for his second handful, someone knocked on the door. Noah froze with his hand in the bag.

No one had ever come to the RV. He paid his rent on the first of the month in cash, and next month's rent wasn't due yet, so it wouldn't be the campground owner. Noah considered scrunching down so the person outside couldn't see him if they peeked in the window. Then he could wait for them to leave. But he wasn't a coward.

Noah strode to the door and cracked it partway open. He came face-to-face with Caroline. She looked as startled as he felt. She stood there, gazing up at him in wonder. His pulse ricocheted at her beauty. Her sweetness. Her smile.

Before he could stop himself, he was drowning in gentle green pools of concern and caring. A deep longing swept over him for an eternal connection. For home, family, and love.

Neh! his rational mind screamed in warning. Alarm

bells clanged, drawing him back from the brink. What was he thinking?

"Caroline?" Her name came out too husky, too emotional. Standing before him was everything he ever dreamed of . . . and everything he could never have. "What are you doing here?"

She stared up at him, dazed and starry-eyed. Had she read the message in his eyes? He lowered his lids to erase any traces of yearning for an impossibility. He'd spent years perfecting his poker face—neutral, void, emotionless.

With great effort, Noah exerted control over his feelings and his features. When their gazes met again, he'd adopted the icy demeanor he'd used in prison.

Caroline blinked as if stunned by the change. Tears welled in her eyes.

Please don't cry. He couldn't maintain his outer toughness if she did. And he needed that resistance to ward off his attraction to her when all he wanted to do was enfold her in his arms.

"Noah?"

Her voice, shaky and vulnerable, unlike her usual confident chattering, stabbed him. How could he be so cruel? But if he let down his guard, he'd do and say things he'd regret.

"I came to say I'm sorry. Everyone tells me I talk too much, and they're right. But this is the first time I've ever done something this terrible. I didn't mean to make you lose your job."

Noah held up a hand to stop her confession. "It's not your fault. If Fred had done a proper interview, he'd have found out. I expected my past to catch up to me sometime."

Not this soon. But getting the auctioneer's job had been too good to last.

Caroline's guilt flowed into more apologies, and she brushed aside all his reassurances. Then she stopped him cold. "I don't believe you killed a man. You didn't, did you?"

When she looked up at him so innocently, so trustingly, the hard outer shell he'd built around his heart shattered. She believed in him. Nobody, not even his parents, had given him the benefit of the doubt. Caroline had only known him a short while, but she'd seen deep into his soul and recognized his real character.

If he lied, she'd go away crushed. And he'd be able to keep his secret. As much as he wanted to do that, her honesty called for the truth. "The man didn't die."

She breathed out a long sigh of relief and met his eyes with such joy shining on her face that his chest constricted. She not only believed him, she cared about him. His love-starved soul drew in every drop of her sympathy and compassion.

Caroline tilted her head like an inquisitive little bird. So charming. So endearing. "What happened?"

No one had ever asked him that question. He'd bottled up the truth for so long he wasn't sure he could share it. The heaviness that weighed on him had been his alone. It would be a relief to tell the whole story.

Caroline would listen and understand. And maybe, just maybe, he could pull the thorn from the wound and release the festering poison. Even if she told people around here, it wouldn't matter. He'd be gone at the end of the month.

"It's a long story. Maybe you'd better come in."

He started to open the door wider, then thought the better of it. Although he hadn't been baptized, she had. She shouldn't be inside alone with him. "Wait." He held up a hand to stop her.

Caroline stood on the small concrete pad outside Noah's RV, her head reeling. The unguarded look of attraction in his eyes when he first saw her had set her heart thrumming.

She'd been right about him not killing a man. Except he'd only said the man hadn't died. Did that mean he tried to kill someone? She couldn't accept that. And his eyes had softened when she'd asked what happened, as if he appreciated her interest. He even invited her in, but then changed his mind.

She tried not to let her disappointment show. Perhaps she'd pushed too far and he needed to back off. He'd headed into the RV. She should turn to go, but she couldn't bring herself to leave.

The door opened, and Noah emerged carrying two canvas folding chairs. He set them on the patio under the blue striped awning.

Through the trees, the sun went down in a blaze of glory, streaking the sky with orchid, peach, and rose. Caroline's heart burst with colored sparklers at its beauty. And at the two chairs in Noah's hands. He wanted to talk to her, be with her.

After he'd opened both chairs and they'd each settled into one, he glanced at the nearest RV. Maybe he was checking to see if his neighbors were home or if he'd be overheard.

Then he asked, "How did you find me?"

Heat raced up Caroline's neck and set her cheeks aflame. She didn't want him to know she'd been stalking him.

"Caroline?" he said it gently, nonjudgmentally.

"I remembered that day you were walking on the road, so I thought I'd ask at Yoder's."

"They sent you here?" Noah sounded alarmed.

"*Neh*, they don't know where you live. Jenna said you turned left out of the parking lot, so I did that. There aren't any houses between Yoder's and where you were on the road that day, so I drove down the back road to the campground and asked at the office."

Disappointment crossed Noah's face. "The owner told you where I lived?"

"He said he only gives out that information to the police." Caroline hung her head. "I asked the campers if they'd seen you. They pointed me in this direction. Then I knocked on doors till I found you."

Noah shook his head. "Persistent, as always." The corners of his lips lifted. He didn't seem angry, just amused.

Caroline shifted in her seat, impatient to get Noah talking about himself. And she promised herself she'd follow Mrs. Vandenberg's advice about listening without interrupting. Right now, though, she needed another skill she'd never practiced—getting someone else to start a conversation.

She plunged right in. "Enough about me. It's your turn to talk."

Noah's eyes grew sad and distant, and Caroline regretted pushing him. She should have waited until he was ready to speak.

After a long, tense silence, Noah cleared his throat several times, a pained expression on his face. "I've never told anyone else this story."

"Not even your family?" Caroline couldn't believe

anyone could keep information like this from their parents or siblings.

"My brother knows what happened, but he's never shared this with anyone." Noah's lips twisted. "And he never will."

She regretted bringing up something so hurtful. She intertwined her fingers in prayer position and locked her lips into a tight line to prevent herself from breaking her vow to listen.

CHAPTER 23

If Noah hadn't been so overwhelmed, he might have smiled at the prim way Caroline had folded her hands in her lap and pressed her mouth shut to hold back any of her usual chattiness and questions.

Instead, he strained to pull the words from the depths where he'd buried them. He'd planned to go to his grave without ever telling a soul.

"About four years ago, my younger brother, Benji, went wild during *Rumschpringa*—buying a truck, going out drinking, and getting in trouble with the law."

A small *ach* escaped Caroline's lips, but her compassionate expression encouraged him to continue.

"I never rode with him in the truck because I didn't want to encourage his disobedience to our parents. But that afternoon, I was worried about his plans with some friends that evening. I hoped to prevent him from getting into trouble by asking him to drive me to work, figuring he wouldn't get back in time to join them." Noah groaned and lowered his head into his hands. "That led to the biggest mistake of my life."

Down, down, down he went, sucked into the quicksand of the past.

He screamed for Benji to slow the truck down as his sixteen-year-old brother rounded a curve at breakneck speed. Noah never would have gotten in the truck if he'd known Benji was drunk—AGAIN! But now it was too late. Noah clutched the door handle so tightly his palms cramped.

"Benji was driving about thirty miles over the speed limit. A flash of white and silver appeared ahead of us on the road. I'll never know if Benji planned to pass the car or if the glare of the setting sun blinded him, but he didn't ease off the gas pedal even though I shouted at him to brake."

Caroline's eyes widened, and she pressed a hand against her lips.

Noah squeezed his eyes shut trying to erase the images unspooling in his brain. The same sickness that had overcome him that day roiled in him now, and the metallic taste of fear stung his mouth. His words came out hoarse and gravelly. "Benji plowed into the slow-moving car, smashing it into the guardrail at the side of the road. Instead of pulling over, he revved the engine and sped away."

Noah tumbled back through time into the terror and desperation.

Craning his head, Noah tried to check on the driver in the crumpled car. But weaving back and forth, Benji crested a hill, and Noah couldn't see what had happened behind them.

Noah ordered, "Pull over. That man might be hurt." He prayed the old man hadn't been killed.

Benji ignored Noah's commands and flew along the road even faster.

God, please stop Benji, and help that man. Please don't let him die.

"Pull over right now," Noah insisted, *"or I'll . . ."* He *didn't know what would make his brother stop.* "Or I'll tell Daed where you hide your truck." *Their strict father would never tolerate his son having a vehicle. He'd have it towed away.*

Benji slammed on the brakes, fishtailed off the road and onto the shoulder. The truck's bed stuck out into the road. Noah wanted to tell him to straighten it. The last thing they needed was another accident. But he didn't trust his brother to steer the truck safely off the road.

His brother narrowed his eyes and slurred out, "You . . . ca—can't."

"I will." *Noah regretted not doing it earlier. He could have saved that poor driver from being hurt. But right now, all Noah cared about was getting back to the scene of the accident.*

"I—I can't . . . a-a . . . ford 'nother one."

Which would be a huge blessing. "If you don't get out and let me drive, I'll tell Daed, the bishop, and Hannah," *he said through gritted teeth. In fact, he'd tell Daed anyway. Noah regretted not doing it sooner. Benji shouldn't be allowed on the road.*

"Nooo," *Benji moaned.* "Not Hannah."

"Get out. We have to go back to the scene of the accident."

"Noah?" Caroline called his name softly, and he broke the grip of the haunting memories. At least for now. Many nights, they returned to torment his dreams.

He tried to get back on track, to recount the story instead of reliving it. "Benji finally pulled over far from the accident. I had no license and had never driven a truck, but we needed to get back to the scene of the accident to assist that driver. I figured I'd do a better job of steering than my brother."

Glassy-eyed, Benji stumbled his way around the truck while Noah slid into the driver's seat.

"Tell me how this works." Noah was desperate to get the truck moving. He prayed someone had stopped to help the man, but Benji never should have left.

Benji garbled an explanation of the brake and gas pedals and the gear shift. Gripping the wheel, Noah silently willed his brother to talk faster.

In the distance, sirens wailed. Noah relaxed a little. The EMTs in the ambulance would care for the man, but he and Benji still needed to get back there.

One siren whirred louder, and a police car roared up the incline and slammed on its brakes. Lights flashing, the officers pulled to a stop behind the truck.

Benji gripped Noah's arm. "Don—don't . . . shay . . . I wasss drivin'."

Before Noah could respond, an officer stood outside the window. "Driver's license and vehicle registration." He held out his hand. "You left the scene of an accident."

"I don't have a license, but . . ." Noah hesitated, weighing Benji's request. With his brother's driving record—two speeding tickets and losing his license for six months for underage drunk driving—Benji might go to jail.

Before Noah could decide what to do, Benji broke in. Stuttering and in almost incoherent speech, he laid the blame on Noah. Too stunned to defend himself, Noah sat

*there tongue-tied and shocked as his brother claimed to be
the one who'd convinced Noah to return to the scene of the
accident. When had Benji become such a practiced liar?*

To this day, every time Noah remembered that memory,
his gut tightened. That afternoon, his vocal cords froze. He
kept waiting for Benji to change his story, to tell the truth.
But it never happened.

Caroline reached out and set a hand on Noah's arm.
"You don't have to tell me everything. I didn't mean to
upset you like this."

Noah shook his head. Now that he'd started, he wanted
to finish. Maybe telling the whole sordid story would finally get rid of the nightmares.

"An ambulance arrived and took the man, who was in
his early eighties, to the hospital. We learned later that he
almost died. Two newspapers reported his death, but he
pulled through."

Caroline sucked in a breath.

"The man eventually recovered, but I never did. Because I was in the driver's seat, the police thought I was
driving. Benji lied and insisted I was. So the police arrested me."

"What?" Caroline had forced herself to stay silent all
this time, but she shrieked that question. "Couldn't you tell
them the truth?"

Noah gripped the chair arms and bowed his head. "My
brother had citations for drunk driving. If the cops had
arrested him instead of me, he'd have been jailed for seven
years or maybe longer, depending on what they charged
him with."

"He deserved it." Caroline wanted to right this wrong.
"What about you? Is that why you went to jail?"

"*Jah.* I ended up with three years. Because I had a clean record, they gave me a much lighter sentence. The whole Amish community rallied around me, and multiple *Englisch* neighbors vouched for my character, so the judge went easy on me."

"Except you hadn't committed a crime." Fury filled Caroline at the injustice. "Why didn't you tell the truth? What about your parents? Didn't they stand up for you? Force your brother to tell the police what really happened?"

Noah's shoulders slumped, and his head sank even lower. "They believed Benji's lies. At the time, that hurt worse than the criminal punishment."

"I can't believe this." Caroline leaped to her feet, almost overturning the lightweight canvas chair. "You should have told them. They should have known you well enough to know you hadn't done it. Even I figured that out, and I hardly know you."

"I thought they'd realize . . . But they never did. Even after I was released, my father wanted nothing more to do with me. He assumed I'd led Benji down the rebellious path and that I'd put the truck in Benji's name. I guess that's the way Benji explained away his truck purchase."

Caroline struggled to rein in her temper as she returned to her chair. She wanted to give his parents—and that brother of his—a piece of her mind. Noah had endured three years in jail to protect his brother. Then to be turned away by his own family. So unfair!

"After I got out, I no longer fit into the community, so I moved on." Noah glossed over the worst, most painful three years of his life and the terrible hurt that followed after his release. As innocent as she was, Caroline would never understand the cruelty and depravity he'd witnessed and been subjected to during those years in prison. Yet, none of that cut as deeply as his *daed* basically disowning him.

He'd been Amish all his life, and he still kept the dress and customs because they felt familiar, but during his years behind bars, his heart had hardened against God and against those who'd condemned him. Now that he was out, Noah had no intention of getting baptized. He had nothing to hold him in Fort Plain. Even the girl he'd been courting had gotten engaged to someone else while he'd been locked up. It had been time to move on. He'd left those memories behind to find someplace where no one knew his past and he could start over fresh. Now that, too, had been destroyed.

Noah had been so submerged in his old memories, Caroline's squeeze on his arm startled him. He'd barely registered her comforting touch earlier, but now her fingers burned through his shirtsleeve, setting all his nerve endings zinging.

Danger, his brain screamed. *Don't fall for her. You can't possibly have a future with her.*

But the warning had come much too late. And how could he resist the magnetic pull of her tear-filled eyes? He wanted to entwine his fingers with hers, to pull her close, to press his mouth to her full, generous lips.

The talkative Caroline had intrigued him, but this quiet, thoughtful side of her drew even more admiration. She had depths most people would miss if they never sat with her in silence. She'd listened quietly to everything he'd shared and had empathized with every word. He could never express his gratitude for what she'd done for him. Believing in him when no one else had meant the world to him. The tenderness of her touch and the understanding in her eyes reached a place deep in his heart and soul. A dark place he'd thought would never heal.

His gaze lighted on her fingers, so beautiful and feminine. Caroline noted his look, and pink blossomed on her cheeks.

She ducked her head. "I'm sorry." She hastily removed her hand, leaving a cold, empty spot in place of the warmth and comfort. "And I'm so sorry for what you went through."

At her genuine empathy, a lump rose in his throat. He wished he could say everything that filled his heart to overflowing.

"This was all so unfair. You didn't deserve to suffer like this. And you certainly shouldn't have lost your job over it."

Noah couldn't bring himself to tell her it didn't matter because the time had come for him to move on. Once rumors took hold in a community, his reputation would be so damaged, he'd never be able to stay.

Caroline sat forward, eagerness in every line of her body. "I'll tell Mrs. Vandenberg. I'm sure she'll see that Fred gives you the job back."

"*Neh.*" That's the last thing he wanted. "If Fred's forced to rehire me, he'll do everything in his power to make my life miserable."

Caroline's excitement deflated. He hadn't meant to discourage her. Not after she'd been so kind. And she only wanted to help, to champion his cause.

His lips quirked. She'd joined his team, and she always

won her matches. He pictured her getting in winning shots as she defended him.

"What's so funny?" she demanded.

"I was picturing you playing volleyball."

Her rosy cheeks blossomed into crimson. "You mean my fall?"

Noah shook his head. "Not at all. And that was a great save. Although I was hoping to see a pancake."

"Oh, you." She batted at his arm. "How can you be thinking about volleyball at a time like this?"

He turned serious. "I was comparing your determination to win to the way you want to make things right for me." His voice grew husky. "It's like you're on my team, fighting for the winning point."

"*Ach*, Noah." She sounded close to tears.

It had been so long since he'd had anyone on his side. "I can't tell you what that means to me." If only he could find a way to pay her back for this gift she'd given him.

Her eyes, burning with ardor, met his, and he was lost. The world around him disappeared. All of him, every fiber of his being, focused on this beautiful, bright light in his life. A light he never wanted to extinguish.

CHAPTER 24

Caroline's heart sang. Her dreams had come true. Noah was gazing into her eyes the way she'd always longed for a man to do. And what a man. So honorable, so self-sacrificing. More than anything, she wanted to lean over and lay her head against his chest and feel his arms around her.

For so long, she'd thought she'd never find someone who could love her for herself. Noah had proved her wrong. And all the love she'd stored up, as she wished and hoped for the future, she wanted to share with him.

As dusk faded into star-spangled darkness, the fire glowed farther down the hill, and a yellow glow lit some windows of the RVs and trailers scattered around the woods. Caroline could stay here all night, basking in the beauty of nature and the warmth of Noah's gratitude. For the first time in her life, she relaxed into silence.

Neither of them needed to say a word. Unspoken words and deep feelings passed between them as birds chirped and frogs croaked in a distant pond. All the sounds of nature wrapped her in a newfound bliss.

Noah's abrupt movement shattered her dreamlike state.

He stood and motioned to the starry sky. "It's getting late. Your parents must be wondering where you are. You should get home."

Her parents? Were they still up waiting for her to come home? She'd never stayed out this late before.

"I'm sorry. I didn't mean to keep you." Caroline pushed herself to her feet while clinging to the cottony cloud of contentment.

He laughed. "I think it was the other way around. I'm the one who kept you here."

"I didn't mind." *Not at all.* She'd love to sit here with him until dawn.

"Where did you park? I'll walk you to your buggy."

For a moment, Caroline couldn't remember. She forced her mind from the mist of romance to mundane things like horses and driving home. If Noah hadn't mentioned her buggy, she might have floated home.

Heading down the hill to the office, her arm brushed his several times, setting her nerves afire. She drew in a breath of fresh night air, hoping he couldn't hear the thumping of her heart. She'd never dared hope for something this wonderful, this special.

Driving home with twinkling pinpricks of light overhead, Caroline's soul overflowed with hymns of praise. God had answered her prayers.

As Caroline drove off, Noah kicked himself. What had he done? He'd let her softness and acceptance lull him into sharing one of his darkest secrets. After promising himself he'd never tell anyone, he'd spilled the whole story.

How had Caroline found a way under his defenses? She'd flipped his life upside down in so many ways.

Now, armed with all he'd told her, she might confide in others, lighting a spark that would spread like wildfire. In the Amish community, as he'd found to his sorrow, gossip flowed faster than rainwater gushing from a roof, and often the victim ended up drowning in half-truths and speculation.

If Noah intended to head off to Ohio at the end of the month, it might not matter. Except Tim's cousin lived in Fort Plain. What if he brought the rumors home with him? Would people believe the cousin's tales? More worrisome, would the news damage his brother's reputation? Since the accident, Benji had turned his life around. If the truth came out, could his brother be prosecuted?

Noah should have sworn Caroline to secrecy. She wouldn't take an oath, but if she gave her word, he could trust her. But would it be fair to ask an open, talkative woman like Caroline to hide the truth from others? She had no secrets of her own. All her inner thoughts and emotions revealed themselves in her words and on her face.

She might not mean to give away the memories he'd confided, but they could easily slip out. Caroline hadn't spent years developing a filter as a safeguard and practicing hiding the truth. And it wouldn't be fair to ask her to do that.

Other concerns about Caroline clouded his mind. What had she read in his eyes and body language? He'd tried to conceal his real feelings whenever he spent time around her, but tonight, she'd caught him by surprise. He'd never expected to open the door and see her.

And after opening up to her, he'd felt such a deep

connection between them, he lowered the wall he'd erected around his heart. Now all he wanted was to pursue a relationship with her. It had taken every ounce of his self-control to keep himself from reaching out and touching her.

Noah sat outside mulling over all the possibilities. As the campfire at the bottom of the hill died out, he'd come no closer to a decision.

When Caroline got home, she slipped into the house, glad to see her parents had gone to bed. She hugged every precious memory to her as she drifted off into sweet dreams of the future and woke the next morning filled with joy.

With all the excitement bubbling inside her, ordinarily, she never could have remained quiet on the ride into work, but her brother talked the whole way to the market. Fern would be coming back next week, and Gideon was thrilled he'd have his wife back with him every day. He'd missed her so much, and they'd decided she'd try bringing the baby with her to the stand.

"I'll help," Caroline offered, eager to spend time with her nephew.

For the first time that day, Gideon frowned. "Fern and I would appreciate that . . . if you pay attention to customers."

Her brother knew how much Caroline loved holding babies, but she'd do her best not to let it distract her from the job. "I'll—" She'd been about to say she'd promise, but Scripture said, "Let your *yea* be *yea*, and your *nay*, *nay*." Knowing how caught up she got when she took care of little ones, Caroline couldn't make a promise she might break. "I'll try," she replied instead.

Her brother's long-suffering sigh leaked a little happiness from her day. She wished she weren't such a trial for him. And when Anna Mary arrived with a morose expression, Caroline tamped down her joy even more.

"Mamm's not doing well," she whispered as they prepared the salads. "I probably should have stayed at home."

Those words were a code for her mother's low times. Her *mamm* had been widowed twice. Anna Mary had been nine when her *daed* died. Her *mamm* remarried and had several more children. After the recent death of her husband, Anna Mary's *mamm* had fallen into a deep depression. Some days she struggled to care for the little ones.

"Sarah's almost ten. She'll do a *gut* job taking care of the little ones."

"*Jah*, but she can't handle Mamm." Anna Mary blinked back tears.

Caroline gave Anna Mary a quick hug in passing. "I wish I could do more for you."

Anna Mary managed a wan smile. "You've helped a lot. This job will pay for things we need. That might take away some of Mamm's worries."

"If I can do anything else, please let me know."

"Being my friend and letting me talk about my problems"—Anna Mary's lips curled up—"when I can get a word in edgewise, that is, means a lot."

"I'm trying to be better at that."

Anna Mary picked up the container of garden salad Caroline had finished mixing. "I noticed. You have been listening more."

And Caroline had been working on paying attention

to other people's signals. Before Mrs. V's advice, Caroline probably would have blurted out last night's events without noticing Anna Mary's distress.

"I'm glad I have you." Anna Mary's chin trembled. "You and Josh are the only two people I've told about Mamm. But Josh hasn't stopped by all week. I worry he's spending time with Rachel."

"I hope not. Maybe it's a busy time for his family business."

"I suppose." Anna Mary didn't sound convinced.

Knowing Josh hadn't been around to support her friend, Caroline was doubly glad she hadn't mentioned Noah. Hearing Caroline's good news would have added to Anna Mary's pain.

The minute Gideon opened the doors, a steady flow of customers flooded their business. Gideon kept busy with chickens, Aidan ran from fries to assisting his dad in the candy stand, and Caroline juggled orders, making change, and refilling salads. They barely had time to snatch a mouthful of lunch, but Caroline insisted Anna Mary take her full lunch break. Her friend needed some peace amidst all the chaos in her life.

In the midafternoon, Jose, who headed up the construction for the market addition, stopped by and asked to talk to Gideon after he locked up. "I have some concerns about a new employee."

Gideon agreed to meet him. "Hope it doesn't take long," he said after Jose left.

Caroline did too. She'd been trying to decide if she should stop by Noah's place tonight. With the market closing at seven, it would be pretty late till Gideon dropped her at home and she hitched up her buggy and drove to the campground. Also, she didn't want to seem too forward, but Noah most likely didn't know where she lived. Maybe she could just drop by with a few leftovers from the market and let him know her address—in case he wanted to come calling.

Close to closing time, Caroline was dying to confide in someone when Mrs. Vandenberg showed up at the counter.

"You're sparkling today, dear. It's like you're lit from within. Good news, eh?"

After checking to be sure Anna Mary couldn't overhear, Caroline beamed. "*Jah!*"

"Anything to do with a certain young auctioneer?"

Caroline wouldn't call him young. He must be around twenty-five or so, but she supposed he'd seem young to Mrs. V. And the word *auctioneer* hit Caroline hard. Her happiness flatlined at the memory of Noah getting fired.

"Could I talk to you for a moment?" Caroline sighed at the long lines. Gideon would never let her leave the stand. Not on a Thursday evening. And she didn't want to ask Mrs. Vandenberg to pray about crowd control.

Mrs. V followed Caroline's gaze. "Maybe we should wait until closing."

"I don't want to keep you."

"I suspect I'll be needed after closing. The Lord gave me a nudge to come over here. I'm waiting to see what He needs me to do."

Caroline wanted to reply, *He wants you to get Noah's job back*, but she couldn't broadcast Noah's private business to strangers. "I'll see you then."

She sent up a prayer of thanksgiving. God had brought Mrs. Vandenberg here at exactly the right time. It meant missing a visit to Noah tonight, but she could see him tomorrow after the market closed. With Mrs. V's assistance, she might have great news for him too.

Her conscience twinged. Noah had asked her not to talk to Mrs. Vandenberg about his job. She'd forgotten his request in her eagerness to help him. How would she get around that?

She mulled that over until closing time, but still hadn't settled on the right approach. *Lord, please help me to find a way to let Mrs. Vandenberg know without breaking my word to Noah.*

"Let's hurry with the cleanup tonight," Gideon said as he went to lock up.

Caroline had already planned to speed through her tasks so she wouldn't keep Mrs. Vandenberg waiting. And Anna Mary was eager to get home to her Mamm. By the time Gideon returned, the rotisserie parts were soaking, and they'd emptied the refrigerator cases and cleaned the first set.

Her brother's eyebrows rose. "Wow, wish you had this energy every night."

Caroline always did, but she often invested that energy in talking or planning or worrying. Tonight, she couldn't wait to get done. And Anna Mary hadn't been in the mood to chat.

They all finished in record time. Anna Mary hurried away, leaving Gideon to do a final walkthrough while Caroline counted the money and put it in the deposit bag.

As soon as they emerged from the employee entrance, Jose rushed up to Gideon. "I prepared a list of employee hours to submit to the accountant for paychecks, and I got this message back." He held out a paper.

Curious, Caroline read the note her brother held. *No information on file for Noah Riehl. Please send documentation.*

Gideon tilted his head to one side. "This doesn't make sense. He's been working as an auctioneer. I assume he's been getting paid."

Mrs. Vandenberg's Bentley glided close to the group. Her driver opened the door and came around to help her get out.

She waved him away. "I can do it myself."

Keeping an arm out ready to assist her, he waited patiently as she scooched her legs around, set her cane on the ground, and propped herself up on shaky legs.

"So what's going on?" Despite asking the question, she acted unsurprised at the answer. "Hmm . . . I suspected as much. Gideon, please call Fred. He should be in the auction office now. I believe he'll have the explanation."

Gideon followed her instructions, and when he called into the building and asked for Fred, a loud, angry diatribe exploded.

"Never interrupt me when I'm tallying up the day's receipts. Now I'll have to start all over again."

"Mrs. Vandenberg sent me." Gideon's calm tone pointed up Fred's rudeness.

"M-Mrs. Vandenberg?" Fred's response sounded shaky. "Why didn't you say so? Is she out there?"

"I certainly am," she called out tartly.

Fred rushed from the building. "I'm sorry to keep you waiting." He bobbed his head in a little bow.

"No, you're not," she snapped back. "But it doesn't matter. You're here now. Jose has a question for you."

"Who's Jose?"

Mrs. Vandenberg waved toward Jose. "The head contractor on the addition. I'm sure you've seen him around."

"Maybe," Fred muttered. "So, what's the question?"

Jose took the paper Gideon had handed Mrs. Vandenberg when she arrived. "I need contact information for Noah Riehl."

"Sorry I can't help you with that. I fired him."

"You what?" Mrs. Vandenberg looked shocked.

"That's what I wanted to talk to you about," Caroline whispered, hoping nobody would overhear.

She hadn't spoken softly enough, though, because Fred glared at her. "You stay out of this, Caroline Hartzler. You already caused me to lose one good auctioneer."

Fred's comment poked at Caroline's sore spot. She already blamed herself for getting Noah fired, but being reminded of her past failure sparked her temper. She wouldn't address the situation with Zach. Still, this was her chance to stand up for Noah. "You don't know the whole story."

Mrs. Vandenberg laid a hand on Caroline's arm. "And I'm not sure you do either, my dear. Calm down. We'll have time for your defense of Noah later. Right now, we need to figure out why the accounting department has no records for him." She directed a *you're-going-to-tell-us-the-whole-truth-and-nothing-but-the-truth* look at Fred.

He stammered out an incoherent explanation about possible mixed-up records.

She lasered him with an incisive stare. "Only the truth, Fred. You can tell us now, or my lawyers will question you in court. I know you're close to your brother, but I'm sure you don't want to share a cell with him."

"I—It's not like that. I didn't do nothing illegal."

Mrs. Vandenberg's raised eyebrows showed she didn't believe him. Neither did Caroline. She wouldn't put it past Fred to do something outside the law.

A defiant look on his face, Fred blustered, "He worked as an independent contractor, so I paid him cash."

"You paid him under the table, you mean?" Mrs. Vandenberg drove straight to the heart of the matter. "We don't have any independent contractors working here. And I suppose you planned to give him a 1099."

Fred appeared uncertain. "Of course, of course."

"I see." Leaning heavily on her cane, Mrs. Vandenberg tried to rummage through her huge purse.

Caroline leaned over. "Can I help you find something?"

"That would be wonderful. My notepad and pen."

Marveling at all the compartments and pockets inside the purse, Caroline located a tablet with a pen attached and handed it to Mrs. Vandenberg, who flipped it open and made some notations.

"First of all, how much did you pay Noah per hour?"

Fred focused on his shuffling feet. "We didn't do an hourly wage. I just paid by the day."

"Exactly how much?"

"Fifty a day."

Fire flashed in Mrs. Vandenberg's eyes. "For eight hours a day? That's less than minimum wage."

"Well, he didn't always work a full eight hours," Fred said defensively.

"What about Fridays, when the market's open from eight A.M. to seven P.M.?"

"He didn't usually come in until noon or so."

"That's not true," Caroline burst out. "He was here in the mornings and in the evenings."

Fred sneered. "Figures you'd be keeping track of his hours."

"That's not the issue here." Mrs. Vandenberg appeared to be on the verge of exploding.

Caroline had never seen Mrs. V so infuriated. The tiny, elderly woman could be a dynamo, but Caroline would never want to be caught in the whirlwind of her fury. Evidently, Fred agreed.

In an obsequious tone, he tried to soothe her. "I did tell him I'd pay extra for overtime." He shot Caroline a *so-there* look and lifted his nose.

"Telling him and paying him are two different things. Did you actually give him the extra cash?"

Fred shifted from foot to foot. "Um, not yet. But I plan to."

"You'll be giving him more than a little extra. I sent out a notice awhile back announcing a major increase for all my workers. I expect you to pay him all his back wages, and you can take it from your own paycheck."

"But that's not fair," Fred whined, and his forehead broke out in a sweat.

"Neither is paying someone below minimum wage. I want this taken care of immediately." Wiping the sweat dripping down his face with the back of his hand, Fred gave her a phony smile. "I'd be glad to, but I have no idea how to contact him. No phone, no address."

"I know where he lives."

Everyone turned to gawk at Caroline—Jose surprised, Fred furious, and Gideon shocked. Mrs. Vandenberg had a knowing smile. Caroline wished she'd kept her big mouth shut.

"Perfect." Mrs. Vandenberg's eyes twinkled. "But Noah may solve the problem for us shortly."

Caroline gave her a puzzled glance. Mrs. V often knew things before they happened, but what did she mean by that?

CHAPTER 25

Noah headed to the market around six thirty. Most people cleared out quickly on Thursday nights, so he hoped the parking lot would be empty by the time he arrived.

But when he went to pull Rosie into the shelter, two horses waited patiently inside. One belonged to one of the builders. But the other was Gideon's. Noah's stomach knotted. That meant Caroline must still be here too. He'd been hoping to avoid her until he'd figured out what to do.

He couldn't pull back out because they might see him if they came out the employee entrance. Perhaps he could slip behind the auction house and make it to the construction site without being spotted. They'd see his horse, but he doubted they'd recognize it.

As he crossed the parking lot, Mrs. Vandenberg called out, "Noah, why don't you join us?"

She and Caroline stood in a group with Gideon, Jose, and Fred. The knots in his stomach twisted tighter. Jose in a conversation with Fred spelled trouble. Was he about to lose his construction job too? He trudged over to join them.

Mrs. Vandenberg greeted him with a friendly smile.

"First of all, Fred has something to give you." She turned to Fred. "Go get your checkbook while I call the accountant."

When she had the accountant on the line, she handed Noah her phone and told him to go somewhere private to give his contact and tax information. "Then bring the phone back here so I can talk to the accountant."

Until that point, Noah had avoided looking at Caroline. In fact, he'd kept his head down so he wouldn't have to meet Fred's eyes or see Jose's disappointment. But after he moved into the shadow of the deserted auction tent, he chanced a quick peek, only to find her gazing at him with such love his heart flipped over.

"Hello? Hello?" a voice squawked from the phone in his hand.

Noah flashed her a quick smile before turning his back. He answered all the questions, but he felt guilty about it. He probably should tell the man he planned to quit next week. Right now, though, the pressure of facing Fred and Caroline occupied his full attention.

After he finished, he explained to the accountant that Mrs. Vandenberg wanted to speak to him, and he jogged over to give her the phone. He kept his eyes fixed on the cracked asphalt near his feet as she named a huge sum, told the accountant to back the taxes out, and asked for the final net figure.

Jose gave her a questioning glance, and she nodded. "Oh, and please process the hours Jose sent over and issue the paycheck now that you have all the info verified." A few minutes later, she smiled at Jose. "It's taken care of."

"I'd better get back to the construction site." Jose faced Noah. "You come on over whenever you're finished here. I got plenty more block for you."

"I can come now." Noah started to follow Jose, but Mrs. Vandenberg held up a hand to stop him.

"Jose, I'd like to talk to you." Gideon caught up with Jose and walked with him to the construction site.

Red-faced and puffing, Fred returned to the circle, a checkbook and pen in his hand.

"Perfect timing." Mrs. Vandenberg hung up the phone and named an amount. "You can deduct what you already paid from that. I'll verify the amount with Noah."

Fred's eyes bulged out. "You've got to be kidding me. I can't pay that."

"It's your choice. Either that or court."

"But—but that's not fair."

"It wasn't fair what you did. I'm hoping it'll teach you a lesson. What do you think you'd have to pay in fines and lawyer's fees if I accuse you of embezzlement?"

"I didn't embezzle you."

"Anything that's done to hurt my employees is done to me. Don't forget, I still have the agreement you signed after what you did to Zach. We could add charges for that."

At Zach's name, Caroline gasped. "What did you do to him?"

"He didn't tell you?" Mrs. Vandenberg appeared surprised.

"Tell me what?" Caroline sounded close to tears.

Noah wished he could comfort her, but he didn't have that right. And he certainly couldn't do it in front of all these people.

Mrs. Vandenberg beckoned to Fred. "Explain to Caroline."

Fred busied himself with writing the check. When Mrs. Vandenberg prodded him a second time, he sighed heavily and mumbled, "I paid him under the table, but he didn't know he'd owe taxes. The IRS came after him."

"He had to get a different job to pay the taxes and fines. We lost a good employee because of it."

"I thought . . ." Caroline swallowed hard. "I thought he wanted to get away from me."

"Fred Evans," Mrs. Vandenberg thundered, "did you tell Caroline that Zach left because of her?"

"Not exactly." He didn't meet her eyes.

"*Jah*, he did. He blamed me for losing his best auctioneer. Until Noah, that is." Caroline turned her blinding smile in his direction.

Noah's heart ached with love for her, but it could never be. He lowered his eyes to avoid giving away his feelings.

"I don't believe it." Mrs. Vandenberg patted Caroline's arm. "I'm so sorry you believed that. I didn't find out about it until fairly recently. Once I did, I made sure we repaid Zach all that we owed him. I wish he'd come back, but he'll never work for Fred again."

Zach? Wasn't that the auctioneer Caroline had been accused of chasing? Maybe learning the truth about this Zach was a blessing. Caroline would go back to him, and Noah could leave in peace, knowing she had someone to love and care for her. And unlike him, someone worthy of marrying her. Why did that solution make him ache so much inside?

Caroline's thoughts swirled crazily. All this time, she assumed Zach had run away because she'd chased him. Fred had kept that lie going every time he saw her. But if it wasn't true, what did that mean? Maybe Zach had cared about her after all.

Not that she wanted to go back to him. Not now that she'd met Noah. But it lifted a huge burden from her. She thought she'd driven off the only man who'd seemed to be interested. Knowing it wasn't true calmed her fears about scaring off Noah by being too forward.

Noah seemed to like her, and he didn't mind her talkativeness, her outspokenness, her forwardness, her persistence, her drive to win at volleyball. She'd never felt the need to change herself to make him love her. Maybe *love* was too strong a word, but he definitely seemed attracted. Perhaps given time . . .

She glanced over shyly, hoping to catch his eye, but his attention stayed fixed on the ground. If only she hadn't mentioned he was the best auctioneer. He'd done the same thing when she'd complimented him before. He was so modest.

"Well, Fred, I think you owe Caroline and Noah both apologies." Mrs. Vandenberg pinned Fred with a pointed stare until he muttered something that sounded like *sorry*. "And turn over that check. And I'd better not find out it bounced."

From the ruddiness that suffused his face, Fred might have been planning to give Noah an uncashable check. With a snarl, he thrust the small rectangle at Noah. "Here."

Noah stared at it as if it were a snake about to bite his hand. "What's this?"

"Take it," Mrs. Vandenberg encouraged. "That's what Fred owes you for the hours you've worked here so far."

Gingerly, Noah pinched the edge of the check between his thumb and forefinger as if touching Fred might poison him. Caroline didn't blame him. The man had been cruel.

When he glanced at the amount, Noah sucked in a breath. "This can't be right."

"It isn't," Fred said under his breath.

Mrs. Vandenberg frowned at Fred to silence him. Then she faced Noah. "That's how much Fred should have been paying you. As I told you before, I've made it my mission to pay all my employees a living wage."

Noah stared down at the small piece of paper in his strong, tanned hands. Hands Caroline longed to hold. He appeared stunned. And filled with wonder. If only he'd lift his head and give her that same look.

Knowing Zach hadn't run away from her gave Caroline more courage to be bold. It freed her to be honest about her feelings without worrying about scaring Noah off.

He cleared his throat. "I don't know what to say."

"Say *yes*—I mean *jah*—to coming back to work at the auction tomorrow. We—"

Fred cut off Mrs. Vandenberg with a loud yelp. "What the—?"

"Watch your mouth, Fred. I'm old enough to be your mother or more likely your grandmother, and I have no qualms about washing your mouth out with soap."

"But—but—"

"Caroline can tell you my theory about *but*. For right now, though, I'm waiting for this young man to tell me *jah*."

Before Noah could answer, Fred erupted, "If he comes back here, I quit."

Mrs. Vandenberg gave him a sweet smile. "What a wonderful idea. Thank you, Fred. That solves a lot of problems. Please send Abner out when you go in to collect your belongings."

"I didn't mean—" Fred stood there flabbergasted.

"You should never say what you don't mean," Mrs.

Vandenberg advised. "I think Abner will do a wonderful job as supervisor."

Caroline covered her mouth to keep from laughing at Fred's expression. Mrs. Vandenberg had done it again. She had quite a knack for turning conversations and situations her way.

Fred stalked off.

Good riddance, Caroline wanted to call after him, but as she'd been practicing lately, she held her tongue.

Noah blinked as he tried to take it all in. What had just happened here? He held a check in his hands for a huge amount. With his pay from Jose, he'd have more than enough to start over in Ohio.

But Mrs. Vandenberg hadn't finished. "So, Noah, what do you say? Would you be willing to come back to work under Abner? I don't want to leave him without any backup auctioneers."

"I—I don't know." He couldn't tell everyone he planned to leave at the end of the month.

Noah suspected Butch would leave with his dad. Abner couldn't run the auction alone. The man had taught Noah his job. The least Noah could do was help out for a few weeks, even if it meant staying here and facing the gossip.

He doubted if Mrs. Vandenberg would want him to stay once she'd heard the rumors. Caroline had been listening avidly. Was she hoping he'd say *jah*?

Gideon returned from the construction site and motioned to Caroline. "We should go."

Caroline's eyes reflected her disappointment.

"Could she stay here a few minutes?" Mrs. Vandenberg

asked Gideon. "We have something we need to discuss. It won't take long. I know you're eager to get home to Fern and the baby."

"I'll go hitch up the horse. Please hurry, Caroline."

"So, Noah, what do you think?" Mrs. Vandenberg focused on him.

He needed to tell her the truth. "You probably won't want me once you know the truth. Fred fired me because he heard I'd been in prison."

"I know about that. And I don't believe you should have been there."

Noah's trust in Caroline deflated. She'd promised not to tell. He'd known her sweetness was too good to be true. People always betrayed him.

Caroline whirled toward her. "How do you know that?"

"It's just my intuition. But I've found it's generally right."

He stared at Caroline. "You didn't tell her?"

Hurt filled her eyes. "I told you I wouldn't tell anyone."

"I know you did." Why hadn't he given her the benefit of the doubt?

"Sometimes when people have been betrayed by those they love, they find it hard to believe others won't do the same."

Mrs. Vandenberg's nugget of wisdom hit Noah hard.

"That's true. I haven't trusted anyone since . . . then." He made himself meet Caroline's eyes. "I'm so sorry, Caroline. I know you're honest and trustworthy."

Her wide, generous smile showed she forgave him, even though he didn't deserve it. And his gaze stayed locked on hers. He wanted to stay like this forever, but reason warned him to break the connection. Yet, he seemed powerless to stop the magnetic pull.

Caroline forgave Noah the minute his eyes expressed regret. She didn't blame him. If her family had turned against her like that, she'd be as wary as Noah. And he hardly knew her. She'd prove to him he could trust her.

She tried to send that message and so much more. He seemed to be sending her the same signals. Caroline basked in the wonder of finding a man she connected with on such a deep level. Whenever she spent time around him, she fell for him more and more.

Mrs. Vandenberg cleared her throat. "I love watching you two lovebirds, but I've been standing for a while, and I'm feeling shaky. Noah, you should get to work while it's still light."

When Noah broke their contact, Caroline ached inside. She wanted to be with him all day, every day.

"I'll see you," he said, and jogged toward the construction site.

Caroline enjoyed the sight until he disappeared around the back of the partially constructed block walls. Then she sighed.

Mrs. Vandenberg studied Caroline with shrewd eyes. "Things are progressing well, eh? At least from your point of view."

What did she mean by that? Was that a hint that Noah didn't care for her the way she cared for him? "You don't think he likes me?"

"Oh, he likes you well enough. That's not the problem. It'll be quite a while before he's ready to commit."

"I can wait." Caroline had already decided she needed

to give Noah time to trust her. She also wished she could get his family to admit the truth and ask for forgiveness. His parents needed to hear his brother admit the truth. She had no idea if that was possible.

"It's possible, dear."

Caroline didn't even blink. She'd gotten so used to Mrs. Vandenberg answering her silent questions. "You think so? I don't know how it could happen. If it were up to me, I'd go to Fort Plain and force them to face facts."

"You know, that might not be a bad idea. Someone outside the family who knows the truth and has Noah's best interests at heart might be able to convince them."

"If only I could. For now, I'll pray they'll find out."

"I have a better solution. Prayer works wonders, but adding deeds can speed along miracles. Why not go to Fort Plain?"

Questions crowded Caroline's mind and spilled from her lips. "How would I get there? A trip would take too long. How could I leave Gideon alone at the stand? Anna Mary doesn't know enough yet. And even if I could find a driver, how would I pay for it? Where would I stay?"

Mrs. Vandenberg held up a hand. "Wait. Put the questions in order, and then ask them one by one." She ticked them off on her fingers. "One, you'd get there in my car. No need to pay. I'll take care of lodging. Is it a church Sunday?"

When Caroline nodded, Mrs. Vandenberg pursed her lips. "What if we plan to go next weekend? We could leave on Saturday after the market closes and return on Monday. No need for you to miss any market days."

Caroline struggled to make sense of Mrs. Vandenberg's plans. Was she serious? Or just giving Caroline examples of answers to her questions?

"So shall we ask your parents?"

"You really mean it?"

"Life is too short to waste time on hypotheticals. I strongly believe that you should always confirm your inspiration with immediate action."

That must be how Mrs. Vandenberg accomplished so much. Caroline liked to act quickly after getting ideas, but her parents often warned her not to be so impulsive. She had always put herself down for moving ahead without thinking. She'd thought her way was wrong. Maybe she was more like Mrs. Vandenberg.

"One caveat: be sure your ideas are sound before plunging ahead. Although, I must admit, making mistakes can be a great learning experience."

"I've had plenty of those," Caroline admitted.

"Well, dear, the more you learn, the wiser you become."

If only that were true. Caroline wasn't sure she'd benefited from all her mistakes—other than to learn not to repeat them. Still, it was comforting to think she might be gaining something from them.

Gideon pulled around the market. "Sorry it took me so long. Martin and I had some business to discuss."

"Actually," Mrs. Vandenberg said, "it was perfect timing." She added in a quiet voice to Caroline, "Ask your parents, and I'll stop by the market sometime next week for an answer."

Excitement bubbled inside of Caroline. She couldn't believe she'd be going on a trip. And doing something to help Noah. At least she hoped it would.

But she'd never gone away on her own like this. What if her parents wouldn't give her permission?

CHAPTER 26

Gideon stayed silent on the way home as if brooding over something. Caroline hugged her plans close. Any other time, she'd babble out loud all she'd learned about Zach and Noah. And she'd be too thrilled to keep quiet about the upcoming trip. Tonight, however, she wanted to keep all the magic to herself.

When they got to the house, Gideon didn't drop her off out front. He drove into the driveway and tied the horse to the hitching post near the walkway to the front door.

She stared at him in surprise. "I thought you wanted to get home."

His face grim, Gideon said tersely, "I need to talk to Daed." He hesitated. "And you."

Fear gripped her. She'd never seen her brother so serious. He headed to the front porch so fast she had to sprint to keep up.

Daed must have heard the buggy because he was waiting for them by the front door. If anything, he appeared even more distressed than Gideon. "Come into the office both of you."

He ushered them into the small, closet-sized area off the living room where he used to do the accounts when he ran the market stand. He gestured to several piles of paper on the desk. "Colter did some computer research for me today, and I made several phone calls."

Caroline wondered what Daed needed their *Englisch* neighbor boy to find out. Colter had printed out quite a lot of information. And what did it have to do with her and with Daed's and Gideon's worried expressions?

"You were right to be concerned," Daed told Gideon. "I contacted the police department and got public records sent to Colter's email. He found quite a few articles online, and I called his family."

The police? She couldn't stay quiet any longer. "What's going on?" She had an inkling of what this might be about, but she couldn't believe her *daed* would go to this much trouble.

Her father ignored her question. "We were wrong about one thing. He didn't kill anyone. Almost did, but the man didn't die."

That confirmed Caroline's suspicion. "You investigated Noah? Why?"

"Your brother was anxious about your safety." Daed studied her with troubled eyes. "And it seems as if he was right."

"No, he's not." She had to stand up for Noah.

"Before you defend him, read all the things I've printed out."

Caroline didn't have to. She knew the truth. "Noah told me his brother was driving that day." Frantically, she recounted Noah's side of the story. She needed to get them to believe in his innocence.

Gideon shot her a questioning look. "When did you have time to have such an in-depth conversation with him?"

Caroline hung her head. "I went to visit him. I didn't believe he'd killed a man."

Her father sucked in a sharp breath. "You went to his house?"

"It's not a house. He lives in an RV."

His eyebrows shot up. "You visited him in an RV?" Daed's voice rose in alarm.

"I didn't go inside. We sat on the patio."

At Gideon's horrified expression, she said defensively, "There were plenty of people around. A whole group of campers was sitting outside." She had a twinge of guilt for not mentioning most of them weren't facing the RV.

"I'm sorry, Daed." Gideon's downcast eyes showed he blamed himself. "I had no idea. I should have been paying more attention."

"It's not your fault Caroline chose to break her promise." With a sorrowful face, Daed turned toward her. "*Dochder*, what do you have to say for yourself?"

"I'm not chasing Noah. I just needed to find out the truth." But deep inside, her conscience nudged her. That hadn't been the only reason she'd gone to Noah's.

"My other concern," Gideon told their *daed*, "is that he's working on the construction site. I talked to Jose about it, and he said Mrs. Vandenberg insisted on hiring Noah."

"See," Caroline crowed, "Mrs. Vandenberg knows he's innocent. She even told me so." Her triumph was short-lived.

"Mrs. Vandenberg is a trusting soul. She's helping gang members turn their lives around," Gideon countered.

"Noah's past isn't our main concern." Daed pinned Caroline with a stern gaze. "We're worried about your behavior. We've gone through this before and—"

Caroline cut him off. "Mrs. Vandenberg said Zach didn't leave because of me. Fred did something illegal with Zach's pay."

Daed held up a hand. "Even if you weren't the cause of Zach leaving, you must admit your behavior back then was unseemly. And you seem to be repeating it by going to Noah's place."

Gideon still looked guilty.

Their father continued. "Caroline, I don't want you hanging around with someone who's spent time in prison and who's—"

"What about forgiveness?" she cried.

"According to the bishop and Noah's *daed*, Noah refused to confess to either of them, both before and after he went to jail." Daed's lips pinched together in a forbidding line.

"That's because he's innocent. He couldn't lie and say he did it."

Daed met Gideon's eyes, and a worried look passed between them.

Gideon said gently, "I know you want to believe him."

"I don't just want to believe him. I do believe him. He's telling the truth."

"If that's so, why does his family refuse to have anything to do with him? They'd be proud of his sacrifice."

"Benji lied to his parents and blamed Noah."

Daed sighed heavily. "I can see you're not ready to face the truth. I want you to read all these articles and notes from my interviews. Then pray about it."

Gideon stared at her sorrowfully. "Fern and I will both be praying too."

Daed nodded. "For now, you need to understand we want to protect you. To do that, I want you to promise me you'll stop chasing Noah and that you'll never, ever spend time with him alone."

Caroline's heart railed against those rules, but she needed to obey her father. "I promise."

"I know how strong the pull of attraction can be at your age, but it's important to be sure you're being drawn in the direction God wants you to go. He has the right future partner in mind for you. You don't want to spoil it by falling for the wrong person."

Caroline longed to protest. *What if he isn't the wrong one?*

Noah spent the rest of the evening laying block and trying to get Caroline out of his mind. Why couldn't he do it? Why couldn't he keep his eyes off her?

He had to stay away from her. She was much too good for him. He couldn't bring her down to his level. Her strong belief in God, the way she lived her faith, her openness and honesty intrigued and attracted him. But not enough for him to forgive Benji. And until he could do that . . .

When Jose called it a night, Noah was surprised to discover how much block he'd laid. He hadn't paid conscious attention to his work. Guiltily, he grabbed a level to recheck his work. He waited until the bubble settled in place. *Gut.* The part of his mind supervising his work must have done everything right. That was a relief.

On his way to get his horse and buggy, Noah noticed a light under the storehouse door. Fred and Butch had roared out of the parking lot hours earlier. Maybe they'd forgotten to turn off the lights.

Noah doubted they'd leave the building unlocked unless

Fred was too upset to think straight. Noah walked over and twisted the knob. To his surprise, the door opened. Maybe his boss had done it on purpose out of anger. Noah stepped inside to reach the light switch.

"Who's there?" a voice called from the back corner.

"Abner, is that you? It's Noah. I thought someone left the lights on."

Abner popped out from one of the aisles. "Do you have time to talk now?"

Noah didn't have anywhere else to go. "Sure. By the way, I'm happy for you. You deserve this job."

"You heard about it already, huh?"

"I was outside with Mrs. Vandenberg when Fred got fired."

"I wish I hadn't gotten my position this way. Now I gotta watch my back all the time."

"Why?"

"Fred'll find some way to stab me for taking his job."

"More than likely he'll come after me. I'm the one who made him lose his job." Noah recounted the scene from earlier. "I guess I should have said Fred fired himself."

Abner snickered. "Sounds like it. That Mrs. V is really something."

"She certainly is." Noah had plenty of experience with that. "She ever read your mind?"

"Yup. Plenty of times. She claims God gives her what she calls *nudges*."

Noah had seen some of those nudges firsthand.

"She's the one what turned me into a God-fearing man. She got me going to church on Sundays. Boy, was my wife ever happy. Best thing that happened in our marriage."

I hope Mrs. Vandenberg doesn't have plans like that for me.

Abner laughed. "She knows how to help people before they even know they need help. And she's got quite a reputation for restoring long-term marriages like mine and for matching young couples."

Noah swallowed hard. She had good taste. He liked the woman she seemed to have in mind for him. Caroline would be the perfect match. Too bad he wasn't the right man for her.

Caroline carried the DEWALT light to her bedroom along with the stack of papers Daed had handed her. She didn't need to read them because she already knew the truth. Nothing they said would change her mind.

She'd told Daed she'd read them, and she would. She wanted to see what Noah had endured. The first thing that jumped out at her was Noah's mug shot splashed on the front page of several of the newspapers. It was bad enough to have your picture appear in the paper, but to have these articles and headlines accompanying it must have been humiliating.

"Drunk Amish Man Kills Senior Citizen" one misleading banner read. The sensationalized story underneath had multiple pictures of the crushed car and the bottom half of a stretcher being put in an ambulance. The story said two drunk Amish brothers without drivers' licenses had smashed a car into the guardrail with their truck. They also showed a picture of a dazed Noah being handcuffed. Benji stood nearby, looking out of it.

Sickened, Caroline read story after story until she'd finished every word. Then she turned to her *daed*'s notes from his phone conversations. Two hours later, she got up and paced the floor, hoping she wouldn't wake her parents.

Furious at the injustice of it all, she walked back and forth, trying to understand how Benji could have let his brother take his punishment. Poor Noah. This was so unfair.

Both Noah's *daed* and the bishop railed against Noah for refusing to confess. Dad had made detailed notes on their conversations. Even after knowing Noah his whole life, it never occurred to them to ask for his side of the story. If they had, would he have told them?

She had to do something to set the record straight. Caroline prayed this trip with Mrs. V might start the healing process between Noah and his family. And if all went well, they'd be able to squash the false rumors about him—beginning with her own family.

Daed believed Noah had caused the accident and remained unrepentant. If she found proof, he'd have to change his mind. Meanwhile, though, she held out little hope he'd agree to a trip to Fort Plain.

CHAPTER 27

Caroline forced herself to stay away from Noah for a whole week. It had been torture, but if she wanted her parents to give her permission to go to New York with Mrs. Vandenberg, she needed Daed and Gideon to see she had no plans to chase Noah.

That wasn't entirely true. If Daed hadn't issued that warning and she hadn't promised to obey it, she'd probably have spent her midday break outside, watching the auction.

Her hard work had paid off. Tonight, when Gideon had dropped her off, he'd mentioned it to Daed. Then, while she and Mamm washed the dishes, Caroline confided about Mrs. Vandenberg's invitation.

"That's wonderful." Mamm beamed as she handed the final pot to Caroline to dry. "When Mrs. Vandenberg takes an interest in someone, good things happen. Look at Gideon and Fern. And Nettie and Stephen."

Jah, they'd been blessed by Mrs. Vandenberg finding them the perfect partners. She'd also hired them for good positions. Gideon now managed the market, and Nettie and Stephen ran the training center for gang members. Those jobs had been a great fit for each of them.

Caroline didn't much care about getting a different job. She enjoyed working at her family's stand, but she couldn't help hoping Mrs. Vandenberg might do some matchmaking. Caroline had a certain person in mind already. She hoped this trip would be more than a chance to help Noah heal his relationship with his family. Maybe, just maybe, it might be the start of a new relationship for him. A relationship with her.

"You're looking starry-eyed," Mamm observed. Caroline bent down to put the pot in the stove drawer. Had Mamm guessed her secret? Trying to keep her voice from revealing her giddiness, Caroline said, "I've never been to New York. I'm so excited!"

"Don't get your hopes too high until you've talked to your father. He hasn't agreed."

Whirling around, Caroline begged, "You'll help to convince him, won't you?"

"I can try," Mamm promised. "But you know your *daed*. He has a mind of his own. Let's go see what he says."

Please, please, God, let him say jah.

Mamm put an arm around Caroline's shoulders and accompanied her to the living room. "Ezekiel, your *dochder* has a question for you. I hope you'll agree."

Daed set his book in his lap and peered at both of them over the rims of his reading glasses. "I must say, Caroline, your brother has been very impressed with how hard you've worked this week. He also mentioned you'd been taking your breaks in the stand. I trust that means you took our talk last week to heart."

Caroline swallowed hard. She hadn't really done that because she still believed wholeheartedly in Noah's innocence. But she had tried hard at one thing. "I've been staying away from Noah the way you asked."

"*Gut, gut.* I'm glad to hear it." Daed turned his attention from her to Mamm. "So what was this question?"

Mamm prodded Caroline lightly. "Go on and ask your *daed.*"

After whispering another brief prayer, Caroline drew in a long breath and tried not to sound too eager. "Mrs. Vandenberg would like me to go with her to New York State on Saturday after the market closes. We'll come back on Monday."

"New York State? What brought this up? Why would she take you there?" Then his eyes narrowed. "Where in New York?"

"Fort Plain." Caroline's voice squeaked.

"Hmm . . . I thought so." Daed studied her. "Why is she interested in going there?"

"We both think Noah's innocent. We want to talk to Benji to find out the truth."

Daed frowned. "I've talked to everyone involved. This is a fool's errand."

"You didn't talk to Benji." The words burst from Caroline's lips before she could stop them. Now she'd done it. Daed didn't take kindly to disrespect. "I'm sorry. I didn't mean to talk back, I only meant—"

He shook his head. "*Dochder*, you must learn to curb that tongue of yours."

Caroline hung her head. "I know." Controlling her mouth was a never-ending battle. She and her unruly tongue had just destroyed her chance to go on the trip.

Her father stroked his beard. "I suppose it's only right to hear Benji's side of the story before we make a final judgment."

Jah, it is! This time Caroline didn't say it.

"And I don't like to disappoint Mrs. Vandenberg. She's

done so much for our family and for this area." Daed seemed to be thinking out loud. "I'm sure it would help her to have someone younger for company."

"I love helping her."

"You have a *gut* heart, *dochder*. Once you learn to tame your impulsive nature, you could do a lot to help others."

Mrs. Vandenberg had said quick action can be a good thing. Normally, Caroline would have shared that, but right now, the trip hung in the balance. She didn't want to tip it the wrong way.

"I'm inclined to let you go."

"*Danke, danke, danke!!!*"

"Caroline." Mamm set a hand on Caroline's shoulder.

Daed sighed. "I'd feel better about this if you had a bit more control over your emotions and your words."

Caroline tamped down the desire to dance around. She was going to New York. Joy filled her. She couldn't wait to clear Noah's name. For the moment, though, she needed to convince Daed he hadn't made a mistake.

Putting on a sober expression, she said in a quiet voice, "I'll do my best to act the way you want me to."

"That's a start. More importantly, I want you to ask yourself if you're behaving as the good Lord wants you to."

She nodded. "I promise to do that." She asked herself that question a lot. The only problem was she asked it after she'd done things she regretted. The key was to ask beforehand.

Now that he'd returned to the auction, Noah worried about finding ways to avoid Caroline. He timed his arrivals at the horse shelter after her normal starting time. He still hadn't figured out what he'd do if she stopped by with lunch or to talk. He spent most of his time thinking up creative ways to dodge her.

Working with Abner proved to be a major relief compared to Fred's dictatorial style. Abner asked for Noah's opinion on the lineup, shared mic time equally, and insisted on Noah taking all of his allotted breaks. Noah took all of them inside the storage building. He doubted Caroline would come inside even though Fred was gone.

By the following week, Noah tried to decide if he'd been exceptionally lucky or if she hadn't sought him out. He should have been thankful, but part of him was disappointed. He missed her terribly. So much so, he even considered peeking in the market or buying a barbecued chicken dinner just to see her.

Would her eyes light up? Would she smile at him? Maybe she'd even wait on him.

He curbed his impulses on Tuesday and Thursday, telling himself it was for the best. She needed to move on to someone else, someone more suited to her, someone with an unblemished past. Zach, perhaps.

Noah held out until Friday's lunch break. Then curiosity got the better of him. It couldn't hurt to walk in there casually and get a meal. Maybe he could buy food at another stand and just walk past Hartzler's Chicken Barbecue on his way back to the auction. She'd probably be too busy to notice him, but he'd at least get a glimpse of her from afar.

When Abner came for the microphone at lunchtime, Noah handed it over eagerly. He'd stroll past her stand to order fish and chips at the far end of the market. His stomach tight with anticipation, Noah joined the crowds pushing into the market. The door opened, he went through, and stopped. Several people bumped into him from behind, then impatiently elbowed their way around him.

Caroline, as lovely as always, stood directly in his line of sight. It was clear she'd never notice him. Tim and his tall teammate from volleyball stood at the counter. Caroline's friend's gaze was fixed on the tall boy, and he seemed as enamored with her as she was with him. But Caroline was bantering with Tim. She tossed her head in such an appealing way, Noah's heart stuttered. Except she hadn't done it to him.

That attractive move hadn't been lost on Tim. He'd not only seen it; he reacted much the way Noah had. Noah changed his earlier assessment of Tim. *Jah*, he was dangerous. And he was out to get Caroline. Just not the way Noah had originally thought. And from her cheeky smile, it appeared Caroline was falling for Tim's teasing.

Sick to his stomach, Noah spun around and banged out the door. He'd been a fool. Butch had considered Caroline a flirt, and she'd even admitted it to Noah. That didn't seem to fit Caroline's personality, especially not with her honesty.

Maybe it was a signal she'd moved on. And so should he.

At lunchtime on Friday, Anna Mary had filled a lunch tray, and Caroline had rung it up. But when she'd lifted her head to greet the next customer, she came face-to-face with Tim.

Ach, not again!

As usual, he'd elbowed aside other customers. "Here's something you need to read." He waved a paper in front of her.

"It's too hard to see," Caroline said dismissively. "Plus, you're blocking our customers from getting to the counter."

Tim ignored her suggestion to move. "This is too important to miss."

Caroline longed to tell him to stuff it in the nearest trash can because she wasn't interested in anything he thought she should read. But mindful of the line behind him, she refrained. Daed would have been glad.

He stuck the paper under her nose. "Just read the headline."

"Drunk Amish Man Kills Senior Citizen" jumped out at her.

"I already read that. My *daed* printed it out."

"So he was worried about you too?"

Too? Who else was worried about her? Tim? Despite Anna Mary's comment, that seemed too farfetched to be true. Maybe Abe. He seemed like a genuinely nice person who'd want to help others.

"It doesn't matter what that article said. Noah is innocent."

"Innocent? Did you read the whole thing?"

"Jah, I did. They got so many facts wrong." She pointed to the headline. "The man didn't die. And they claimed Noah was drunk, but he wasn't."

Tim snatched another paper from Abe's hand. "How 'bout this one then? It says the man was taken to the hospital in critical condition."

"That's correct. They're only wrong about Noah being the driver."

Tim shook his head in disgust. "Stand by your man, huh? Even if he's a jailbird."

"He's not." Caroline swallowed back the anger welling up in her. She didn't need to get into an argument with someone who loved to bug her. Tim got great joy from getting her upset. She shouldn't give him that satisfaction.

When she didn't answer, Tim's expression turned pouty. "Now that you know the truth, you're not going out with him, right?"

Ouch. Caroline winced. Leave it to Tim to hit her where it hurt. She wasn't allowed to be around Noah at the moment. She hoped to clear that up soon.

"If you're lonely, I'd be happy to cheer you up."

"How?" Caroline snapped. "By insulting me?"

"Aww, Caroline, I've only been teasing. I admire you from afar."

She shot him a skeptical look.

"From far, far away." He snickered. When she didn't laugh, he put on sad, puppy dog eyes. "That was a joke. Get it."

She got it all right. He was making fun of her again. And trying to embarrass her. Tossing her head, she returned her attention to the cash register. "I have work to do. I know my brother would like you to move far, far away from the counter, so our customers can order. And I would too."

Tim pressed a hand to his heart. "You hurt me."

Caroline couldn't resist one last dig. "And that wasn't a joke." She turned to flounce off and bumped into Anna Mary, who was carrying a refilled container of macaroni salad. Caroline grabbed for the edge and righted the container before it spilled.

"Good catch," Tim called. "Maybe we should play baseball together sometime."

Caroline ground her teeth together to keep from saying something she'd regret.

Anna Mary kept her voice low so the two boys couldn't hear her. "Why are you making things up to defend Noah?"

"I'm not. He told me the truth about the accident."

"Really?" Hurt flared in Anna Mary's eyes. "And when did you have time to talk to him?"

"I saw him last week with Mrs. Vandenberg and . . ." Maybe it would be better not to tell Anna Mary about going to Noah's RV. Before she could decide, Tim called out to them.

"What are you two girls whispering about? How handsome we are?" He gestured toward himself and Abe.

"You wish."

Anna Mary gasped. "Caroline, how could you?"

But Tim didn't act offended. "*Jah,* I sure do wish."

Caroline whispered, "He has a big head. Somebody needs to put him in his place."

"That's between him and God." Anna Mary shoved the macaroni salad into place and swished around Caroline, her annoyance clear. Her eyes on Abe, Anna Mary apologized. "I'm sure Caroline didn't mean it. She was just teasing."

Oh, no, I wasn't. Caroline kept that to herself.

"Hey, Caro-line," Tim called. "You gonna apologize too?" When she ignored him, he shrugged. "Guess I won't invite you to another volleyball match tomorrow then."

"That's all right. I have more important plans," she said airily.

Tim sneered. "A date with your ex-con boyfriend?"

"*Neh,* a trip to New York. And now if you don't mind, we have customers who'd like to order."

"I do mind, but just to show you how thoughtful I am—" He stepped aside with a flourish. Then he caught Anna Mary's attention. "The rest of your team want to play?"

Anna Mary's eyes flicked to Abe, who smiled broadly. "We'll be there, with or without Caroline."

"I hope it's with." Tim shot Caroline a cheeky smile. "I love how she dives into mud puddles." Abe elbowed Tim and frowned, but Tim kept going. "Without her, your team will get creamed."

With a wave, he left. Abe, as usual, trailed behind as he watched Anna Mary over his shoulder until they went out the door.

"I wish you wouldn't lie like that to Tim."

"I didn't tell any lies today."

"*Ooo*, Caroline. You fibbed about going to New York."

"*Neh*, I didn't. Mrs. Vandenberg is taking me after work tomorrow. We'll be back on Monday."

As she passed to fill a tray, Anna Mary whispered, "You're so lucky. Are you going to the city to shop or do something else?"

"We're going to New York State. Fort Plain." Caroline rang up the *Englischer* Gideon had waited on.

Anna Mary wrinkled her brow. "Fort Plain? Abe's from there. You plan to visit the Amish community?"

"*Jah*." Caroline debated how much to tell her friend, but they stayed too busy to talk.

As they cleaned up after closing, Anna Mary brought it up. "Why does Mrs. Vandenberg want to see the Amish in Fort Plain, and why is she taking you along? You don't know anyone there, do you?"

Not exactly, but she intended to get to know someone. Her friend stared at her, waiting for answers. "She thinks Noah is innocent, and I'm positive he is. We're going to get proof."

"The police would have that. What can you do that they can't?"

"Talk to the person who was really responsible for the accident." And pray he'd cooperate. If Benji refused to tell the truth or made up a different story, she'd have no way to clear Noah. Without proof, Daed would forbid her to see him. Caroline imagined the bleak picture of a future of never spending time with Noah again.

"Are you all right?" Anna Mary sounded alarmed. "You look really sad." She patted Caroline's arm. "I don't think Noah's worth all this trouble. But you do have another possibility for dating."

Caroline gazed at her blankly.

"Tim." When Caroline rolled her eyes, Anna Mary insisted, "That's what Abe says."

"Abe?"

Anna Mary's secretive smile hinted at some special insider knowledge. "*Jah*, I ran into him at the grocery store last night, and we talked for a while. He says Tim has a crush on you."

Caroline groaned to herself. Just what she needed. She pushed it out of her mind because all she could think of was Noah. And the trip to New York. If all went well, she'd have someone much, much better to date.

CHAPTER 28

As the Bentley cruised toward Noah's former home on Sunday afternoon, the rolling hills and trees and fields of the Fort Plain countryside reminded Caroline of Lancaster. They passed white Amish farmhouses with unpainted barns, some with children playing and buggies in the yards. Many buggies were open, like in the pictures on the yellow road signs. Brown buggies and bonnets seemed the most popular, but Caroline pointed out several heart-shaped *kapps* like hers.

Mrs. Vandenberg nodded. "When Pennsylvania farmland became scarce and higher priced, some Lancaster-area Amish moved up here to buy less expensive farmland. So did the Byler Amish from the Wilmington area. They're the largest group in this Mohawk Valley area. We'll also see Swartzentruber and Andy Weaver Amish."

"How do you know all that?" Caroline marveled at Mrs. Vandenberg's knowledge of people and places.

"I always read before I travel somewhere."

Caroline preferred to be surprised, but Mrs. V would be prepared for what she'd encounter. Maybe Caroline should try to be more like Mrs. Vandenberg.

"You know, Caroline, we all experience life differently. It's good to learn from others, but you also need to appreciate your own approach to life. God gave you a unique personality. Don't suppress it by forcing yourself to fit into someone else's mold."

As usual, Mrs. Vandenberg had guessed what Caroline was thinking. And had given her valuable advice.

"We're almost there," the driver said. "Maybe five minutes or so." He laughed as a buggy pulled onto the road in front of them. "Or maybe not."

The three young children in the back seat peeped shyly over their shoulders. Caroline had gotten used to *Englischers* staring at her, but this was a new experience. She waved, and the two youngest giggled and waved back. Then they turned around and faced front.

About ten minutes later, Caroline stood outside the Riehls' front door, the fluttering in her stomach crescendoing into waves of panic. "What if Benji isn't here?" Daed had confirmed with the bishop that today was an off-Sunday, but Benji could have gone visiting.

"Relax." Mrs. Vandenberg's face remained serene. "We both prayed about it."

Despite the prayers, more worries surfaced. What would she say to Benji? Could she convince him to tell the truth? What if he refused to admit what he'd done?

An Amish boy about her age opened the door. This had to be Benji. Nervousness clawed at Caroline's insides. Her whole future with Noah depended on this conversation.

The resemblance between Benji and Noah was striking. But Noah was taller, more muscular, and much more handsome. Even more importantly, Noah had a firmer jaw, along with a strength of character that showed in his face.

Whereas Noah had a clear-eyed, honest gaze, wariness filled Benji's eyes. Behind that, Caroline detected a deepseated fear.

Maybe Mrs. Vandenberg's sense of people is rubbing off on me.

That thought gave Caroline the courage to begin the conversation. "Is there somewhere we could talk in private?" She doubted Benji would confess to wrongdoing in front of his parents. Not after he'd deceived them all these years.

"You must want my parents. I'll go get them. What should I say this is about?"

Caroline refused to let him distract her from what she'd come here to do. "You're Benji, right?"

He took a step backward. "*J-jah*. Who are you?"

"I'm Caroline Hartzler, and this is Mrs. Vandenberg. We came from Lancaster, Pennsylvania, to talk to you."

Although he tried to put on a brave front, his free hand shook. His other hand gripping the knob tightened, and he appeared ready to shut the door.

"Wait." Caroline stuck a foot in the gap. "If you don't want to talk to us, maybe we can speak with your parents."

Now his legs joined the trembling. "They're resting. And if you're the people who called from Pennsylvania last week, you upset my *daed*. Leave him alone. What do you want?"

"To talk to you." Caroline kept her words firm. "And I don't think you want us to do it here at the door."

"Who is it, Benji?" a girl called from the living room behind him.

"It's all right, Hannah. I'll be right there." The quaver in his voice made it clear things were not fine.

Hannah must have picked up on his distress because she came up behind him. "Do you have company? Aren't you going to let them in?"

"*Neh*, the three of us are going to sit, um, out here." He indicated the rocking chairs lined up on the porch. "We won't be long, Hannah."

After a quick glance at Caroline, jealousy flashed in Hannah's eyes. "I'll bring lemonade for everyone."

"You don't have to." Benji's desperate gaze flicked from his visitors to the front door. He pulled three rocking chairs into a close group. "Please keep your voices low. I don't want my parents disturbed."

And you don't want them to hear the truth. Caroline managed to keep that comment to herself.

The door banged open, and Hannah emerged with a tray holding a pitcher and four glasses. "Where's my chair?" She eyed Caroline's chair so near Benji's.

Caroline didn't want Hannah to consider her competition for Benji, so she scooted her chair over. "You can sit here." She jumped up and added another rocker near Hannah's, but she angled it so she could look into Benji's eyes. Ignoring his irritated look, Hannah smiled at everyone as she distributed the lemonade. Then she sank into the chair beside him.

He went on the offensive. "I don't know why you've come all this way. My father's still not over those phone calls. You had no right to stir up trouble after all these years."

This time, Caroline couldn't hold back. "I have every right." She checked herself. *Neh*, she didn't. She didn't have a relationship with Noah. But she did care about him. "I want to clear Noah's name."

Benji's face drained of color. "Are you dating my brother?" he asked hoarsely.

"Not yet." That, too, qualified as a half-truth. Even if she exposed Benji's guilt, she had no guarantee Noah would ask her out.

He leaned toward her aggressively. "Then what gives you the right to upend our lives?"

"Benji." At Hannah's low warning, most of the fight drained out of him, and he slumped back in the chair.

"I have every right to know." Mrs. Vandenberg's crisp, strong assertion got his attention, and he sat up straighter. "I'm his employer," she said.

His "I see" came out a bit garbled.

"And Caroline is too modest. She has every right to know if her future husband's innocent."

Caroline stared at her open-mouthed. She'd never heard Mrs. Vandenberg tell a fib or exaggerate before.

"Don't act so surprised, my dear. I'm sure Benji understands that true love demands complete honesty."

A sickly expression crossed Benji's ghostly pale face. He sneaked a sideways glance at Hannah.

Future husband? True love? Caroline couldn't believe Mrs. Vandenberg's comments. How had she gotten that out of Caroline's secret crush on Noah? Caroline had to admit she'd fantasized. Though never around Mrs. V.

Neither Benji's nor Caroline's reactions fazed Mrs. Vandenberg. "We shouldn't take up too much of your time. Caroline, dear, why don't you ask your question so we can go?"

Still recovering from her disbelief, Caroline struggled to focus. *Noah*, she reminded herself. *Clear Noah.*

Rutsching forward in her seat, she planted her feet on the ground to keep the rocker from moving. She needed firm footing for this.

Whispering a quick prayer, she dropped her bombshell and waited for the fallout. "Who was driving the truck when it hit the old man's car?"

Benji stared at her in horror. His mouth opened and closed, but no sound came out.

Hannah nudged him. "Tell them the truth, Benji."

His head whipped around, and he stared at her, shock etched into every line on his face.

"Was Noah really driving?" Hannah asked. "I always wondered about that."

"You doubted me all this time?" Benji's question came out flat and almost unemotional, but deep hurt quivered in its undertones.

Hannah held his eyes with a clear-eyed gaze. "I know you, Benji. And I know your brother. At least I did. I grew up around you both. Anyone who spent that much time around the two of you should have figured out the truth."

"You never said anything."

"What could I say? Your parents accepted your story. They were desperate to believe the best of their baby. They wanted to save you."

Caroline choked back the angry tirade boiling in her gut, threatening to erupt from her lips. Other people had figured out the truth but stayed silent.

Benji sat there, flummoxed. Hannah set a hand on his arm. But her tenderness didn't seem to penetrate his distress.

"You should tell your parents," she said softly. "They might be glad to stop living a lie."

Benji glared at her. "You don't know what you're talking about."

"I think deep down you know I'm right." Hannah stared into his eyes until he lowered his gaze.

Caroline had her answer, but she wanted to hear it directly from Benji. He needed to admit it aloud. She waited while Hannah comforted and cajoled Benji, but they couldn't stay here all day. After all, it didn't seem fair for him to be coddled while his brother had endured time behind bars.

Finally, Caroline interrupted. "You haven't answered my question, Benji."

"You already have your answer." His words sounded sullen, but his expression was defeated.

"I don't want to guess. I want to hear it directly from you."

He hung his head. "I was driving, and I hit the car. Noah took the blame for the accident."

"He offered to do that?" Caroline wanted Benji to face all the facts.

"I'm not sure," Benji mumbled. "I was drunk."

Caroline wasn't about to let him get away with that excuse. "You were so drunk you lied to the police and blamed the accident on Noah?" That had been pretty conniving.

"All right, all right. I panicked because my license had been revoked. I lied and blamed Noah. I begged him not to tell, and he didn't."

She squeezed her eyes shut. All Benji had needed to do that day was tell the truth. Instead, he'd condemned his brother to three years behind bars. And Noah's spoiled brother acted as if it had been no big deal.

Tamping down her rage, she directed her words like bullets, hoping they'd hit Benji's heart. "I don't know what lies you tell people in this town or what they believe about Noah. I'll leave you to sort that out. But you do owe it to your brother to set the record straight in Lancaster so he doesn't live under a cloud of gossip."

Mrs. Vandenberg chimed in. "And your parents should be aware of their son's sacrifice and bravery."

Unlike Caroline, who might have been tempted to add they should also know their other son was a coward, Mrs. Vandenberg's arrow hit the target. How did she do that? Without saying a word, she'd condemned Benji and left him squirming.

"I'll, um, think about it," he stammered.

"Don't just think. Act."

Mrs. Vandenberg's crisp commands encouraged Caroline to press for a commitment. "When will you come to Lancaster to tell people the truth?"

"I don't have any way to get there," he whined.

"Not a problem." Mrs. Vandenberg waved her well-manicured hand toward the Bentley out front. "My driver will pick you up and return you home any day and time you'd prefer."

Benji hunched back like a rat cornered by a barn cat. "My schedule at the factory is, um, variable, so I don't always, um, know what days I'll be working."

Hannah sat forward. "You'll have off—"

He cut her short. "I might be able to do it when I take my vacation. I, um, can't say for certain. I may have other plans."

"The only plans you have for your next vacation is to do what is right." Mrs. Vandenberg leaned on her cane and pushed herself to her feet. "Let's set the dates now so there's no dillydallying."

"But—"

"I don't believe in *but*s. What day and time?"

As if he were a mule resisting the plow, Benji dragged out the process by waffling on his vacation days.

Hannah chirped, "Why don't you do it on the first two days you have off? We can plan our trip with your parents for another time. This is more important."

Benji's jaw clenched, and his eyes burned with frustration. "I don't think—"

"That's not a good excuse for making mistakes." Mrs. Vandenberg breezed past Benji's attempt to protest. "It always pays to think before speaking or acting. Now, Hannah, what dates are those?"

Hannah pressed her lips into an adorable apologetic pout. "It's for the best, Benji. This will be good preparation for next year's baptismal classes." She beamed at Caroline, then gave Mrs. Vandenberg the dates.

"You're both welcome to stay at my house," Caroline offered. "That is, if you plan to come along," she said to Hannah.

"I'd like to," Hannah said shyly.

Benji's lips thinned into a mutinous line.

Hannah sent a sympathetic glance his way. "It'll all work out for the best. You'll see, Benji."

It certainly would. Maybe not for Benji, but for Noah and Caroline. Three weeks was a long time to wait, but after that, Noah would have proof of his innocence. Meanwhile, Caroline would spread the truth far and wide.

CHAPTER 29

All Caroline wanted to do was head home so she could tell Noah, but Mrs. Vandenberg wanted to stay until Monday. They spent most of the morning stopping at small roadside stands and finally got on the road in the early afternoon.

The closer they got to Lancaster, the faster Caroline's brain raced. She couldn't wait to let Noah know. Except this wasn't something she could tell him in public. And Daed had said she wasn't allowed to be alone with him. Caroline had never defied her *daed*. Not deliberately. *Jah*, she sometimes ignored his advice to be calm, slow down, stop talking so much. That was only because, in the excitement of the moment, she forgot. But to disobey a direct order?

She couldn't pray about it. The Bible instructed her to honor her parents. She couldn't ask God to let her break one of the Ten Commandments.

How could she possibly let Noah know about his brother's confession and his upcoming visit? As they turned off the highway at the Lancaster exit, Mrs. Vandenberg turned to Caroline. "I know it's a bit late, but I think we should inform Noah about Benji so he's prepared for the visit."

"*Danke!*" Her parents might worry if they got home late, but this way, she wouldn't go against Daed's rules. And she wouldn't have to wait until tomorrow at the market to find a way to tell him without anyone overhearing and without being alone with him.

Mrs. Vandenberg laughed. "I guessed this stop would make you happy." She directed the driver to Yoder's Country Store. "When we get there, you can tell him where to go."

Caroline sat forward on the seat, watching every turn. The short drive seemed to take forever. At last, they turned down the road to the campground.

When they pulled in, some of the same tenters had gathered around the firepit. They stared wide-eyed as the Bentley drove past. When they caught sight of Caroline, they pointed and yelled.

"What's an Amish girl doing in that car?"

"Maybe they're shooting a TV show or a movie."

Some of them stood to get a better look. A few whistled and cheered.

"Oh, dear," Mrs. Vandenberg said in dismay. "I hope they won't disturb your talk with Noah."

"You'll be coming with me, won't you?" Caroline's anxiety spiked. She didn't want to disobey.

"I'm a little tired from the trip, so I'll chaperone from the car. I'm sure the two of you would rather talk privately. I can close my eyes if you two want me to."

"*Ach*, no. We don't do things like that." Not that she hadn't wanted to. Remembering her wishes from last time, her face burned.

The Bentley wove up the hill and pulled into a spot between Noah's RV and the one next door. Caroline relaxed. Mrs. V would have a good view of the concrete pad. As Caroline got out, though, she tensed. Suppose Noah didn't want company?

She straightened her spine. He'd want to hear this. Once she got to the door, she hesitated. Took a deep breath. Forced herself to knock.

When Noah opened the door, her breath whooshed out. He towered over her, so strong and handsome and desirable. She forgot why she'd come.

Noah froze. Caroline stood on his patio, her green eyes a lovely contrast to her pretty rose-colored dress. Behind her, the final blaze of the setting sun haloed her *kapp* and caused her blond hair to shimmer like gold. Speechless, he took in the gorgeous picture.

Then alarm bells rang. What was he going to do? He couldn't have her coming to his place and catching him off guard like this. Sooner or later, she'd wear down his defenses, and he'd make a huge mistake. He'd already made a terrible one by falling for her in the first place.

"Caroline." Her name came out too tender. He hardened his voice. "You shouldn't be here."

"I had to come. I have the best news. Mrs. Vandenberg agreed I should talk to you right away, so she's parked over there." She pointed to the right.

When a car engine had purred outside the RV, Noah had ignored it, assuming it belonged to his neighbor. Instead, Mrs. Vandenberg's Bentley sat in the neighbor's parking space. The idling motor comforted Noah. They must not plan to stay long.

"I'll get the chairs." He hurried inside, then stopped and took a few deep, calming breaths to slow his racing heart. Not that it did much good.

The minute he set the chairs outside, Caroline sat down and galloped through her idea to get Benji to confess, leaving Noah feeling as if he'd been trampled by a runaway horse.

He couldn't believe it. She and Mrs. Vandenberg had decided to go to Fort Plain and confront his brother. Part of him admired her for considering something so courageous and for caring enough to set the record straight. But those inquiries might roll downhill like an ever-expanding snowball and turn into an avalanche. He didn't have the heart to tell her that when her smile radiated pride and joy.

"Anyway, I wanted to clear up the rumors about you. I thought it might help you if your brother told the truth about what he did."

Neh, it would not. It would only open old wounds, cause trouble for Benji, and—

But Caroline jumped ahead. "So, Mrs. Vandenberg and I went to Fort Plain."

"You what?" He thought she'd meant they were planning to go. He'd intended to discourage her gently.

She repeated it more calmly, but he'd heard the words the first time.

"I confronted Benji, and he eventually admitted he'd been driving. So Benji's going to come down here in a few weeks. I told him he could stay at my house because I didn't know how much room you had. I'm sure my parents won't mind."

Caroline kept talking over his attempts to interrupt, to protest. She had no idea what she'd done.

"Benji agreed to go to your church and confess he'd framed you. With the way everyone gossips, the real story will spread around the market in no time. So if you tell me your *g'may*, I'll let Benji know."

"Wait!" Noah practically shouted. "I told you I didn't want you to tell anyone."

"*Neh*, you said not to tell Mrs. Vandenberg, and I didn't."

Noah couldn't believe this. Of the worst things he could imagine outside of spending time behind bars, it would be seeing Benji again, having to relive all that pain. His dread pushed him into fury.

He tried not to blast her, but he had to make it clear she'd trespassed over a boundary he never wanted crossed. "Caroline, I know you were trying to help, but when I asked you to keep the story secret, it was because I didn't want anyone interfering in my life."

"I wasn't trying to interfere. I only wanted to make things better. It's not fair that everyone blames you for something you didn't do." Her lower lip trembled.

Her quivering mouth added to his distress. He hadn't meant to criticize her. "I don't want to see my brother. Ever."

Seeing Benji meant Noah would have to deal with his pent-up resentment. As hard as he'd tried to forget all that had happened, he still wasn't ready to confront his past. Facing his brother would rip off the patches Noah had haphazardly glued over the holes in his heart. He'd barely begun to heal, to pull himself together, to move on.

"But Noah, it'll give him a chance to make amends."

"He had plenty of time to do that. He could have done

it when they arrested me. He could have done it when they booked me. He could have done it during the trial. He could have done it before they slammed the prison door shut and locked me in."

"*Ach*, Noah."

Caroline reached for his arm, but he moved it out of her reach. He didn't want to get distracted by her softness, her femininity. He needed to make his point clear.

"My brother also had a chance to apologize and ask for forgiveness when I got out of jail and went home. He could have told my parents he'd lied so my father wouldn't slam the door in my face."

Tears trickled down Caroline's face. Was it because he'd rejected her touch or because she empathized with his pain?

All he wanted to do was reach out and comfort her, but if he did, he'd be lost. The slam of the cell door in his mind gave him the strength to harden his resolve. It tore him up inside, but he was used to dealing with loss and isolation.

He looked out at the trees so he didn't have to watch her expressive face when he disillusioned her. "I agreed to help Abner train several new auctioneers from Mrs. Vandenberg's STAR center next week. My lease here is up at the end of the month, so I gave my notice. I plan to move out then. I won't be here in three weeks when Benji arrives."

"Where are you going?"

Noah made the mistake of glancing over at her and almost gave in to the pleading in her eyes. He'd been considering Ohio, but he didn't know for sure. Even if he had decided, he shouldn't tell her. The last thing he needed was her coming after him or bringing his brother back into his life.

Her eyes shining with tears, Caroline threatened, "Wherever you go, I'm going to follow you."

"I'm not worth it. Plenty of guys would be eager to date and marry a woman like you who's beautiful inside and out." *Like Tim, for example.* Noah didn't want to say that. She deserved a better match. "You need someone who'll share your faith, someone who'll be whole and pure, not damaged goods."

"You aren't damaged goods. You have the purest heart I know. How many other men would suffer through three years of jail to protect their brother and let everyone believe lies about them?"

"You're making me out to be a saint. That's one thing I'm not. Find a nice guy in your church and settle down with him. Forget you ever met me."

"I can't, Noah."

Tears streamed down Caroline's cheeks, and he clenched the chair arms until his hands ached so he wouldn't reach out. "Why not?"

"Because I care for you. *Neh*, more than that. I've fallen for you."

Noah stood and turned his back to her. Everything he'd ever dreamed of and wanted in a woman sat an arm's length away telling him what he'd always longed to hear, but he had no right to say he'd fallen for her too.

At his uncomfortable expression, his abrupt rejection, Caroline regretted baring her soul. If only she'd kept that truth bottled up inside. He obviously didn't feel the same way.

From the way he'd looked at her earlier, she'd assumed he shared her feelings. How could she have been so mistaken? She'd done the same thing with Zach, and he'd turned away too. She should have learned her lesson.

Gathering the little dignity she had left, Caroline pushed herself to her feet and started to walk away. "I promise never to bother you again."

"*Ach*, Caroline." The words sounded torn from Noah's throat. "I can't bear hurting you like this. You haven't done anything wrong. It's not your fault I'm not a suitable partner."

She couldn't stand the pain in his voice. "To me you are. And you always will be."

She should have kept her mouth shut, but her heart answered before her head had a chance to caution her. And every word was true. There'd never be anyone else but Noah for her.

He pivoted to face her. "You don't understand." He had to be as honest with her as she'd been with him. "I've fallen for you, and fallen hard. If things were different, I'd ask to court you."

She whirled around to face him, her eyes filled with wonder and hope. Hope he had to dash.

"The truth is, I never joined the church and never will. So there's no future for us."

Caroline squeezed her eyes shut and brushed at her damp cheeks. Noah wanted to cradle her face in his hands, to pull her into his arms, to dry her tears, to beg her to keep loving him. But he couldn't be selfish. He couldn't ask her to give up her faith. He couldn't hold her back from the future she deserved. He cared too much for her. The only thing he could do was let her go. "I wish you all the best." She'd never know what it cost him to watch the woman he cared about more than life itself walk away forever.

Caroline barely nodded as she headed to the Bentley. Just before she reached it, she turned. "I still intend to clear your reputation. And I'll be praying for you."

He wanted to tell her not to bother, but he didn't want to add to her hurt, so he stayed silent. He'd considered staying in the area for a few weeks after he gave up the RV to be sure the trainees could handle their jobs. Now that he knew Benji would be coming, he definitely needed to leave before his brother arrived.

Noah wished he could take off today. He wanted to go as far from here as he could. But no matter where he ran, he'd leave the largest part of himself behind. He'd never get away from this heartbreak.

CHAPTER 30

Mrs. Vandenberg took one look at Caroline's face. "Don't despair. He's not ready yet. You'll have to give him time."

Caroline climbed into the back seat, her whole body drooping. "I don't have time. He's leaving at the end of the month."

"We'll have to work fast then." Mrs. Vandenberg's upbeat response grated against Caroline's raw emotions.

She shook her head. "*Neh*, it's impossible."

"Nothing's impossible for God."

As much as Caroline believed that, this time it didn't apply. "We can't be together. Noah's not with the church. I can't date or marry him unless he's baptized."

"I see. But you must admit, even that isn't a problem for God."

Mrs. Vandenberg spoke the truth, but Noah had sounded unmoving. "He said he'd never have anything to do with the church."

"God may have other plans for him, my dear. Trust Him."

Caroline intended to, and she planned to pray that God

would work a miracle in Noah's life. But her heart ached that she wouldn't be around to see it.

When Gideon opened the market on Tuesday morning, Tim and Abe rushed through the door first. Caroline groaned. Tim was the last person she wanted to see after her world had fallen apart.

"I don't have much time because I need to get to work, but I have some great news for you, Caro-line." Out of breath from jogging over, Tim rushed out his sentence all in one breath. She wished for customers. Long lines of customers. But other than the bakery at the other end, their stand was rarely busy until around ten.

Caroline had to get away. "I need to help Fern. Why don't you talk to Anna Mary?"

Fern had come back to the baked goods counter last week, but Sovilla had helped her. This week Fern was on her own. She'd brought the baby with her, and he'd started fussing. Caroline thanked God for the distraction and rushed down to pick him up.

She cradled him close, inhaling his sweet baby scent. Her eyes stung as a deep ache welled inside, filling her with longing. She'd never have a child of her own. The only man she'd ever truly loved refused to join the church, and he was upset at her for talking to his brother. And he was leaving at the end of the month and refused to tell her where he planned to go.

"You give up on your ex-con boyfriend yet?" Tim called out.

Ouch. Caroline winced. Leave it to Tim to rip open her fresh wound. She tried not to let her misery show.

"Hmm . . . looks like things aren't going so well. Just

remember, you always have me. I'll even let you play on my winning team."

"Your team isn't the—"

Tim held up a hand. "I'll save you from telling a falsehood. As of Saturday, we're the champs. Right, Abe?"

After a quick apologetic look at Anna Mary, Abe said, "Well, we did win the game, but I don't know if it counts as the championship."

"Caroline here didn't say anything about a championship. She just said she wanted to play on the winning team. So now she has to play for us."

"I'm not interested. I have more important things to do."

"More important than spending time with *me*?" Tim acted offended. Or maybe he really was.

"What do you think?" she challenged.

With a sorrowful, defeated glance that appeared to be fake, Tim stepped back from the counter, and customers surged forward.

After they were out of earshot, Anna Mary said, "I told you he liked you." She tore her gaze from Abe's retreating back with a reluctant sigh. "Abe's heading back to New York soon." She didn't say she'd miss him, but from the way she moped around, Caroline got the message.

It looked like they'd be moping together. The only difference was that Anna Mary still had Josh. Caroline could never, ever love anyone but Noah.

When Noah arrived on Tuesday, Abner called to him. "Hey, Mrs. Vandenberg wants you to go to her office first thing this morning."

Mrs. Vandenberg? "Did she say what she wanted?"

"I think she wants to tell you herself."

Noah was reluctant to face her. He suspected she wanted to talk about last night. Caroline probably told her what he'd said. Mrs. Vandenberg had convinced Abner to go to church. Noah hoped she didn't plan to push him to go back to his faith.

That possibility made him reluctant to go and see her. "You need help getting this stuff carried out first."

Abner picked up an armload of items. "Go on. It won't take long. Besides, we have two guys coming in from the center to get trained today. They can set stuff up."

With no excuse to avoid it, Noah headed for the market. He pulled open the door and had to gulp for air. Caroline stood behind the counter, holding a baby. He ducked into the shadows near the steps so she wouldn't see him.

At the sight of her with a little one, his chest constricted until he couldn't breathe. If only he were worthy of loving her. If only she were holding their child. If only . . . He had to stop torturing himself. Noah tore his gaze away, and for the first time, noticed the two boys standing at the counter, both with lovesick expressions. One stared at Anna Mary, the other at Caroline.

Noah's stomach turned over at the one mooning over Caroline. That Tim from volleyball again. Did he come to see her every day? Caroline had seemed to be flirting with Tim the last time Noah had come into the market. Today, she must be showcasing what a good mother she'd be.

As she gazed down at the blanket-wrapped bundle in her arms with tenderness, Noah ached to hold her, to protect her, to cherish her, and to care for the little one she held. But he had no right. Last night, she'd told him she'd fallen for him, and he'd sent her away.

He clenched his fists at his sides. She was much too good for him. But she was also too good for Tim. She deserved someone better than that immature, competitive *dummkopf*. Noah wished he could run Tim off. But he had no right.

Then Tim's loud voice rang around the market, and people turned to look. "You give up on your ex-con boyfriend yet?"

Shame washed over Noah. Caroline was being mocked because of him. He'd damaged her reputation. And Tim had broadcast that around the market. As much as Noah wanted to teach Tim a lesson and confront him about his treatment of Caroline, comments from an *ex-con* wouldn't carry any weight. And it would only make things worse for Caroline if he showed up.

With a heavy heart, Noah tuned out the rest of their conversation. Now that Caroline knew the truth, would she correct Tim or let the rumors stand?

Staying in the shadows where he couldn't be seen, Noah headed upstairs to Mrs. Vandenberg's conference room, his steps slow and discouraged.

She greeted him with a brilliant smile. "Just the person I've been waiting to see."

Her cheerfulness took him aback. He'd been expecting a lecture for crushing Caroline's feelings. Or a stern reprimand about returning to the church. Instead, she appeared ready to celebrate.

His subdued *good morning* didn't match her upbeat demeanor.

She motioned for him to sit beside her at the conference

table. "Relationships can be painful at times. Forgiveness is the only remedy I know to heal those wounds."

That puzzled Noah. Caroline had been hurt, not him. Then it dawned on him. She must mean Benji.

"Anger at others is a punishment we inflict on ourselves. Sadly, we carry the pain rather than the other person."

Noah couldn't deny that. He'd endured a lot of anguish, while his brother had gotten off scot-free.

"Just something for you to ponder. Someday your heart will be ready. That isn't why I asked you up here today."

She always managed to get in zingers. How did she know his deepest hurt?

Mrs. Vandenberg opened a folder and pulled out a set of stapled papers. "I talked to Abner earlier, and he could use some help. Nettie and Stephen have recommended two of their former gang members who've successfully completed their program."

"*Jah*, he said they'd be coming in this morning. It'll be good to have more people." Especially since he didn't plan to stay long.

She slid the papers toward him. "Abner and I both would like you to train them. I've decided to make you training supervisor."

The contract had his name on it with a list of duties and a salary that took his breath away. It would be tempting to accept this, and he'd already agreed to help train new auctioneers. But he couldn't stay around. Mrs. Vandenberg looked so thrilled to offer him the position, he disliked turning her down. "I'm sorry. I've given up my rental, so I won't be around long enough to take the job. Thank you for thinking of me."

"If you need a place, I have an empty apartment that could use a few repairs. Free rent in exchange for some fixes."

"I did offer to help Abner for another week. I'd be happy to work on your place until I leave."

"Only a week? Abner could use assistance longer than that."

"I could stay ten days or so." As long as he was gone before Benji showed up.

Remaining around here with the possibility of seeing Caroline and Tim together would be unbearable. Noah would like to help Mrs. Vandenberg, though, after all she'd done for him.

"I'll take whatever time I can get." She pulled a tablet from her purse, jotted down an address, and handed it to him. Then she dug into her purse and pulled out a large key ring. After flipping through a dozen or more keys, she removed one and gave it to him. "Feel free to move in whenever you'd like."

He'd stop by tonight after work to see what needed to be done. It would be nice to have something to fill his lonely Sunday and evening hours. Keeping busy might also take his mind off the pain of losing Caroline.

"Oh, you'll also need this." She opened her wallet and pulled out a business credit card for a home improvement store. "I'll call and let them know you're an authorized user."

"You don't have to do that." He had two decent-sized checks he could use.

"Save your money. You might be needing it."

With the way she read minds, maybe she also saw futures. He wanted to ask her what she could tell him about his. When he looked ahead, all he could see was bleakness.

He'd given up three years of his life and his reputation for his brother. Now he'd given up his chance at a dream job for Caroline's reputation. That wasn't all he was sacrificing. He was leaving behind the woman he now realized he loved more than life itself. He'd do everything and anything for her future happiness.

For him, though, the only path forward seemed to be loneliness and heartbreak as he started over yet again in a new place.

The rest of the day, Caroline tried to push Tim's comments from her mind. Last week, he'd said things that indicated an interest in her. Several times today he'd appeared to be attracted to her, but she assumed he'd been trying to tease her. Suppose he'd been serious? Anna Mary seemed to think he was.

Was that what her future held without Noah in it? Would she have to accept attentions from an immature volleyball player? No one else had ever shown an interest in her. No one but Noah.

Dear Lord, please, please, please bring someone better into my life.

She stopped herself before adding, *Please make it Noah*. She couldn't ask the Lord for a husband who wasn't with the church. But she'd never find someone else she loved the way she did Noah.

She thought of him often and uplifted him in prayer many times since she and Mrs. Vandenberg had pulled away from his RV. Even if she and Noah had no future, she still wanted him to return to the Lord.

CHAPTER 31

Mrs. Vandenberg showed up at closing. "Caroline, do you have a minute?"

"It's fine," Anna Mary assured her. "I'll start the cleaning."

As much as Caroline disliked sticking her friend with the work, she owed Mrs. Vandenberg a lot. She slipped out of the stand and went to join the elderly lady at a café table.

"This won't take long." Mrs. Vandenberg looked more discouraged than Caroline had ever seen her. "I offered Noah a supervisory position training the new workers from the center. I hoped it would encourage him to stay here longer, but he turned it down. He's determined to leave before Benji comes."

Caroline lowered her head into her hands. All the hoping and praying she'd done—all for naught. "If he goes, he might never make up with his brother. That would be so sad."

"I agree. One of my assistants checked with his supervisor at the plant. Benji does four days on, three days off, which means he doesn't work this coming Sunday, Monday, and Tuesday. I could send my driver to get Benji."

"Will Noah still be here? He's moving out of his RV this weekend. He'll probably do that on Saturday so he won't have to work on Sunday." But if he wasn't with the church, would he still keep the rules?

"I offered him an apartment that needs work. He agreed to fix it for me, but he says he'll only stay ten days. We need to get Benji here now."

"This past weekend was off-Sunday for him, so he couldn't leave until Monday."

"If the driver stays over Sunday night, they can leave early Monday morning. I was hoping you could check with Hannah and invite them both to stay with you. I imagine you'll need to check with your parents first." She passed Caroline a piece of paper with two phone numbers on it—one for Hannah's family's bakery business and one for Benji's *daed*'s construction company.

"We have plenty of empty bedrooms." Now that Nettie and her four children had moved out, the upstairs seemed empty and lonely. "I'm sure my parents will agree once they know the whole story."

Last night, Caroline had gotten home after they'd gone to bed. She couldn't wait to tell them the truth tonight at dinner.

"Give me a call when you know for sure, and then we can get everything set up." Mrs. Vandenberg jotted her number on the paper too.

Caroline didn't mind calling Hannah, but she dreaded calling Benji. He'd been reluctant to come and tried to put it off. How likely was he to cooperate with their latest plans?

She jumped up. She'd left Anna Mary with all the work. "I'll talk to Mamm and Daed tonight, then give Hannah a call. I hope she'll be able to come."

"I do too. She's a good influence on Benji. He needs a truth-teller in his life."

Did Mrs. Vandenberg plan to start long-distance match-making on the Fort Plain couple? *I hope she's more successful with them than she was with Noah and me.*

Noah enjoyed training the new auctioneers. Both were quick learners and determined to succeed. He wasn't sure how their usual audience would take the hefty, barrel-chested guy with tattoos up and down his arms. With the exception of Fred, most of the auctioneers had always been Amish or Mennonite. But Roberto, with a broad smile to offset his rough voice, proved skilled at reading a crowd.

Noah complimented Roberto on it after he had his first solo twenty-minute trial.

The ex-gang member threw back his head and belly laughed. "You think I didn't need to read the crowd when people was out to stab me in the back? Or they might put a bullet in me?"

"I know what you mean."

Roberto threw back his head and bellowed. "You? Don't tell me you were in a gang too."

Noah shook his head. He didn't mention his time in prison. But he'd been around plenty of gang members as well as murderers and abusers with anger-management problems. He'd learned to anticipate other prisoners' actions. Like Roberto, Noah had depended on sensing every little movement. Maybe that's what helped him pick up auctioneering so quickly. He stayed alert to the tiniest shift, the twitch of a bidding paddle. So did Roberto. He'd be a good auctioneer.

The one nice thing about training the men was that Noah had to pay attention to every detail of their practice. On his breaks, he did what he could to assist Abner with planning and setup. That kept his thoughts from straying to Caroline.

Once he went to the construction site, he worked by rote and replayed every second of last night's encounter, wishing he'd done things differently. Still, he couldn't have changed the outcome. Not being baptized, he'd never be able to date or marry her. He only wished he could get her out of his mind.

Roberto had tattoos all over his body that revealed his past. Noah had a beautiful, sweet blonde with fetching green eyes tattooed on his heart forever.

On Thursday, Caroline longed to go outside during her break to watch Noah onstage, but she forced herself to stay inside. No point in torturing herself over something that could never be.

Anna Mary brushed past Caroline with a quart of potato salad for a customer. She took one look at Caroline's face and stopped. "What's wrong? I thought you'd be all bubbly after your trip." Her forehead wrinkled with concern. "I didn't ask on Tuesday . . . Did you find out Noah isn't innocent?"

"*Neh*, we got proof he is." Caroline gestured to the container in Anna Mary's hands. "You'd better give that to Mrs. Walsh. She looks impatient."

"*Ach!*" Anna Mary scurried over to the counter. "Anything else?"

Mrs. Walsh shook her head, and Caroline rang her up. They talked in bits and pieces as they waited on the people lined up for lunch trays and takeout. Caroline told Anna Mary a little about the sights and added a few details on the meeting with Benji.

"Mrs. Vandenberg's going to get him on Monday. I hope Noah will agree to see him."

"Why wouldn't he?"

"Would you want to see the person responsible for putting you in jail? The person responsible for your parents kicking you out of the house?" Caroline's voice rose.

Anna Mary shushed her. "I can see your point. But what about forgiveness?"

"I'm not sure Noah's at that point yet."

"But how can he go to church and live with unforgiveness in his heart?"

Now came the part Caroline had been dreading. "He's not with the church."

"*Ach*, Caroline! I hope you haven't fallen for him."

Caroline couldn't respond to that. Instead, she deflected, "I'm praying for him, but he's moving away soon."

"Is that what has you so down?"

She turned away to hide her sorrow and pretended to be adding up the items on the tray Gideon had just filled. But she had to start over because she hadn't been paying close attention.

When Caroline turned back to ring up Anna Mary's customer, her friend leaned over and whispered, "It's good you haven't known him long, so he'll be easy to forget."

Caroline bit her lip. With all the feelings roiling inside her, she had no comeback. She couldn't put any of it in words. But in the depths of her soul, she was convinced no matter what happened from now on, she'd never, ever forget Noah.

* * *

After they prayed at supper that evening, Daed turned to Caroline. "You've been looking glum this week. Did the trip not go well, *dochder*?" He lifted a forkful of chicken-rice casserole to his lips.

Mindful she'd need to ask her parents about having company next week, Caroline chose her words carefully. First, she described the area, the buggies with tan tops and brown bottoms, the differences in the dresses and *kapps*.

"At several of the roadside stands, the girls had *kapps* like ours. Mrs. Vandenberg said Lancaster Amish moved there for the farmland."

Daed nodded. "That's true. When you were younger, several of Deacon Raber's brothers and their families moved to New York State."

"Mrs. Vandenberg knew so much about the Amish living up there. She said she researches places before she travels to them."

"A wise idea." Mamm buttered a roll.

Daed set down his fork and studied Caroline. "You haven't mentioned the main reason for your trip. It's not like you to talk about little details. You usually jump into the important parts first. I'm guessing that means you didn't get the proof you were hoping to find?" He gave her a sympathetic look.

"*Neh*, that's not true." She didn't want Daed to figure out the true reason for her sadness, so she plunged into a rapid account of meeting Benji.

"And his neighbor Hannah was there. I think she's his girlfriend. But they couldn't really be dating since they're not with the church yet. But maybe they don't follow the same *Ordnung* we do."

Daed cleared his throat—a signal Caroline had gotten off track and was rambling.

"Well, Benji didn't want to admit he'd been driving the truck, but Hannah pushed him to tell the truth. He finally said he was drunk and he'd lost his license and he was the one who hit the car and nearly killed the man and—"

"Slow down, *dochder*. Take a breath." Daed's eyes were troubled. "So Noah took Benji's punishment?"

"*Jah*. Benji tried to say Noah volunteered, but after I questioned him—"

Mamm exhaled a long breath that vibrated with concern and a touch of judgment. "I hope you weren't pushy."

Caroline almost breathed out a long, irritated sigh of her own, but stopped herself. If she wanted to ask about having company, she'd better not be disrespectful. Besides, she should be honest.

She poked a piece of chicken with her fork. "I probably was. But Benji was acting like he deserved Noah's protection and that Noah did it willingly. I knew it wasn't true, so I pressed him . . ." She trailed off when both of her parents appeared troubled.

"Well, he was wrong, even lying. And I didn't want him to get away with it. Even Hannah tried to make him tell the truth."

Her parents both shook their heads, their eyes sorrowful.

"I know, I know. I shouldn't judge him. But it isn't fair for Noah to be punished for something his brother did. And for Noah to have people making up terrible stories about him when he didn't do anything wrong."

Her *daed* set his fork down on his plate. "I'm sorry I believed those rumors. I owe Noah an apology."

"So does Benji. And that's why I invited him and Hannah

to come to Lancaster. I think he needs to set the record straight."

"That makes sense." Daed nodded his approval. "Benji should clear Noah's name. And I'll do my best to stop the gossip whenever I hear it."

"*Danke*, Daed. But there's one other thing you can do. And Mamm too." Caroline sent pleading looks to both of them.

"Of course. I'm sure we'd both be happy to do what we can."

"That's *gut* because I told Mrs. Vandenberg that Hannah and Benji can stay here when they come to Lancaster. Mrs. Vandenberg will pick them up on Monday morning and take them back on Tuesday, so I hope that's all right." Caroline rushed her words out all in one long sentence without stopping for breath. She didn't want to give her parents a chance to object.

Her mother blew out a long, exasperated breath. Mamm seemed to be communicating in sighs and breaths tonight. But her message came through loud and clear. Caroline should have asked permission first before inviting company.

"I'm sorry, Mamm. It just came out when I was talking and then I couldn't take it back and uninvite them, could I?" She turned pleading eyes to her mother.

"We have plenty of room and are always glad to have company, but Caroline, I do wish you'd learn to think before you speak."

"I've been trying, Mamm. Sometimes I just get carried away."

Caroline had been holding back a lot of things lately. Maybe it wasn't always because she thought the better of it. Sometimes she'd used it to conceal things she didn't want to share with others.

"So it's all right for them to stay here?" she asked eagerly.

After both her parents nodded, she jumped up. "I'll go call them now and let them know."

"Let us finish our supper first," Mamm said.

Caroline wriggled until they'd cleared their plates. "I'll come back and do the dishes all by myself after I talk to Hannah. Please, Mamm."

Mamm laughed. "I suppose if I don't let you get this call over with, I'll probably have broken dishes to clean up."

Caroline hurried out to the phone shanty. Because Hannah had so much influence on Benji's decisions, Caroline had decided to call her family business first. After getting ahold of Hannah, Caroline told her about Mrs. Vandenberg's change of plans.

"I agree Benji needs to talk to Noah before he moves away. I'm not sure if I can make it Monday. I work in our family's bakery business, and that's one of our busy days because we can't bake on Sunday. I'll see if one of my married sisters can take my place for two days."

"I hope you can come." Caroline needed Hannah to prod Benji to do the right thing.

"Me too. I really like you, Caroline. And maybe some-day we'll be sisters-in-law."

Caroline sucked in a breath. If only . . . The dream exploded before her eyes. Hannah might marry Benji, but who would Noah marry?

"Are you there?" Hannah sounded alarmed. "I didn't mean to upset you."

Say something, Caroline. "I, um, really like you too.

And I hope we can be good friends. Would you want to be pen pals?"

"That would be fun. We can get to know each other before we become family."

Another dart hit Caroline's fragile emotions. She tried to compose herself. *Change the subject.* "First, we need to get the Riehl family back together. Do you think Benji will come?"

"If I have anything to say about it, he will." Hannah laughed.

"I planned to call him in about an hour, and . . ."

"You want me to go over there and soften him up?"

"That would be great."

"Don't worry. I'll get him ready for your call. But first I need to check with my sisters. Then I can let you know if I'm coming."

Please, Lord, help all these plans to work out. Then Caroline worried she was trying to direct God to do her will. Maybe the Lord had other plans, so she added, *if it's Your will.*

One hour later, after finishing the dishes, Caroline made the call she dreaded. When a man answered the phone, she asked for Benji.

"Who is this?" he demanded. "Benji is with Hannah." He sounded as if he suspected her of trying to break up the couple.

Caroline thought fast. "Oh, if Hannah's there, could I talk to her instead please?" She'd rather do that anyway, and it would ease Noah's *daed*'s concerns.

"Hannah," he called, "some girl is on our business phone for you."

A few seconds later, Hannah answered. She whispered, "Benji doesn't want to do it, but I think I've convinced him. And I can come too. I can't really talk now, but I'll see you on Monday."

The phone went dead.

Caroline called Mrs. Vandenberg and relayed the message. She was as thrilled as Caroline.

"Let's keep praying all will go well, and God will heal the relationship between the two brothers. That's the first step. Once that's done, we can move on to the next phase."

What in the world was Mrs. V talking about? What was phase two?

Before Caroline could ask, another line beeped, and Mrs. Vandenberg needed to answer it.

"Keep the faith, Caroline," Mrs. V said before she hung up.

For the rest of the week, Caroline continued to pray that God's will would be done and that Noah would accept Benji's apology and the brothers' relationship would be restored. She clung to the promise that "whatsoever ye shall ask in my name, that will I do . . ."

CHAPTER 32

When Benji and Hannah arrived at the market on Monday around noon, the van Mrs. Vandenberg had sent to collect Caroline pulled in. The four of them met outside at one of the picnic tables near the auction tent.

Hannah hurried over and hugged Caroline. "Benji's not in a good mood," she confided. "He didn't like getting up before five on his day off."

Caroline tried to control her irritation. She wanted to blast Benji for being so self-centered. Instead, she told Hannah, "I'm so glad you're here."

"Me too." Hannah's generous and genuine smile eased some of Caroline's tension. She'd spent most of the morning worrying about whether or not Benji would show up. Now that he'd arrived, her concerns changed to his attitude.

"I can't believe I have to give up two of my days off to come here," he whined.

Hannah set a hand on his arm. "We'll have fun tomorrow. Mrs. Vandenberg's driver is taking us to Hershey Park."

Benji brightened a little.

But his grumpiness bothered Caroline. "Your brother

spent three *years* in jail for you, and you can't even spend an hour or two to correct your lies?"

To his credit, Benji appeared a little guilty.

Hannah smiled at Caroline and Mrs. Vandenberg. She seemed to be trying to soften the impact of Benji's sulking. "I think he's nervous about seeing Noah."

"I am not," Benji growled.

If he didn't change his behavior, Caroline doubted his apology would sound sincere. Noah would see it as forced rather than voluntary. She wanted Benji to feel his responsibility for his brother's pain. Owning the destruction he'd caused might make Benji more willing to ask for forgiveness.

"Aren't you sorry for what you put your brother through?"

For a minute, Benji looked as if he planned to discount it. Then he swallowed hard. "*Jah.*" He didn't meet Caroline's eyes.

That made her feel a little better. At least he had some shame for his actions. If that came out during his talk with Noah, it might make his apology more believable.

"You should keep some of that guilt front and center when you ask for Noah's forgiveness." Mrs. Vandenberg's crisp, no-nonsense voice sliced into the conversation.

Once again, she'd made Benji squirm. Good for her. Caroline cheered silently for Mrs. Vandenberg's precise stab at Benji's conscience.

After a glance at her watch, Mrs. Vandenberg picked up her cell phone. "It's almost time for Noah's break. I warned Jose that we might keep Noah longer than usual."

She dialed. "We're ready for Noah now, Jose. Can you send him to the picnic table closest to the auction tent?"

Jose's voice came over the line. "Will do."

Caroline's stomach crimped into a tight knot. How would Noah react to seeing all of them?

Dear Lord, if it is Your will, please help Noah and Benji to reconnect. Help Noah to move beyond the pain.

A few minutes later, Noah reached the auction tent. "You wanted to see me?" he said to Mrs. Vandenberg who stood blocking his view.

"I did." She stepped to one side and gestured toward the picnic table.

He stopped dead. "Hannah? What are you doing here?"

"Hi, Noah. I'm here with— " She leaned forward so Benji was more visible.

Noah froze, and his eyes turned into hard, dark marbles. Then his gaze darted to the opposite side of the table.

"I can't believe you did this." Noah directed his fury at Caroline. He pivoted on his heel and stalked off.

"Noah, wait." Caroline ran after him. He walked so fast she couldn't keep up and talk at the same time.

When he neared the construction site, he slowed. "I told you I didn't want to see my brother ever again. I said I wouldn't be here if he came in three weeks. I thought you'd drop it."

In a tear-clogged voice, Caroline choked out, "You know I'm persistent, and I never give up."

Noah made an odd sound—a cross between a snicker and a sob. Then he turned. "Caroline, that's one of the things—of many—that I love about you. But can't you understand?"

Her heart fluttered at those compliments, but she ached at the misery on his face.

"I sacrificed more than three years of my life and my reputation for my brother. I paid for something I didn't do. I will not spend another minute in his company or listen to a sham apology."

"I don't think it's fake." Caroline hoped she wasn't fibbing. "He really does feel bad about what he did."

"So bad that he came chasing after me just now to make it right?" He waved at the empty parking lot behind her.

The rawness of Noah's pain pierced Caroline. He was right. Benji should have charged after Noah begging to be forgiven. "I'm so sorry."

Noah clutched his suspenders and closed his eyes. "I know you are. And you'll never know what that means to me. Or how much I value your belief in me before you even knew the whole story."

His voice deepened and grew huskier. "If I could have one wish, I'd wish we could be together forever and ever. But it's impossible."

Caroline's eyes burned. That was her wish too.

"But I'm begging you, please stay away from me. Resisting you is one of the hardest things I've ever had to do. I'm only human, and you're asking me to do something that takes more strength than I have."

A tidal wave of love swept over Caroline, but it crashed onto the shore and slid back into the ocean, leaving her drained and empty. The one man she wanted to be with was walking out of her life forever.

"I love you, Noah Riehl," she said in a broken voice. "And I always will." Then she turned and fled across the parking lot. Away from the picnic table. And away from him.

Noah couldn't go back into work with his gut twisted into knots and his emotions so tangled he couldn't think straight. Being around his horse might provide comfort, but Caroline had gone to the right, which blocked his way to the shelter. And if he went to the left, he'd pass the picnic table. He had no choice. Neither direction was safe.

He'd never been a coward. If his brother wanted to apologize, then let him. Noah had endured much worse. Then Benji could walk away feeling vindicated. And Noah could go on with his life. If that was even possible without Caroline.

Noah marched across the parking lot.

"Noah?" Mrs. Vandenberg appeared beside the auction tent.

"I'm coming back," he assured her.

She beamed at him. "I had a feeling you would. You've been through so much in your life, I was sure you'd have the courage to face this. I'm praying Caroline will join us too."

Part of Noah longed for that, but his sensible side hoped he didn't have to face her again.

Mrs. Vandenberg kept talking, but he didn't hear most of what she said until she mentioned Caroline's name again. "After all, this was all Caroline's idea. She even invited Benji and Hannah to stay at her place until tomorrow evening, hoping you'd both make up and spend time together."

It sickened Noah to think of Benji at Caroline's house. Noah had never visited her, and now he never would. Once again, Benji would have pleasures Noah missed out on.

Sensing his distress, Mrs. Vandenberg patted his arm. "Don't worry. We'll all find a way through this, and everything will work out in the end."

Noah wished he had her certainty, but he could see no way this could possibly work out.

"With God's help, of course," she added.

His jaw tightened. Why did she have to add that? The word *God* made him want to run the other way. But he'd come this far. He'd stick it out.

As they rounded the tent, a movement nearby drew his attention. Caroline, her eyes sparkling with tears, stood in the shadows on the other side of the tent. As soon as she saw him, she stopped and started to back up.

Don't go, he wanted to beg, but the words caught in his throat.

Caroline hadn't expected to see Noah approaching the picnic table. Finding him here threw her off balance. He wouldn't want her around. She needed to leave. But before she could escape, Mrs. Vandenberg beckoned to her.

"Caroline, I hoped you'd come back. Please sit down. I think God would like all of us here. We'll be witnesses to an important rebirth."

As much as she trusted Mrs. Vandenberg's predictions, Caroline was certain Mrs. Vandenberg would be wrong this time. Noah had forcefully rejected God, so it was highly unlikely they'd see his rebirth. She doubted he'd be swayed by Benji's apology.

Still, she prayed Noah would listen with an open heart. And even more so, that Benji would be genuinely repentant. Although she believed God answered prayer, she had doubts about the petitions she'd just lifted to Him.

"Let's all sit down and start over," Mrs. Vandenberg advised. She brought a loving, peacemaking energy to the table. Her faith and serenity poured over them like a soothing balm. "Perhaps we should start with prayer."

Everyone bowed their heads. Everyone but Noah.

Caroline peeked through her lashes to find him sitting stiff and uncomfortable, staring off into the distance.

Please, Lord, touch his heart.

Then she closed her eyes and joined in Mrs. Vandenberg's petition for all of them to open their hearts to God's love and guidance. When they lifted their heads, Hannah and Mrs. Vandenberg's faces glowed. Some of the tension and selfish lines had disappeared from Benji's face. Only Noah sat stoic and untouched.

"Well, Benji," Mrs. Vandenberg said, "I believe you have something to say to your brother."

Benji drew circles on the wooden planks of the tabletop. "Um, Noah, I'm sorry I lied and got you in trouble."

In trouble? Caroline bit the inside of her lip to avoid interrupting. Benji made it sound like Noah had gotten a tongue lashing from one of his parents. Didn't Benji realize how serious this was?

It's not your place to judge, a still, small voice chided Caroline. Maybe Benji had trouble finding the right words. As long as his heart was in the right place, that was most important.

Benji stumbled through various excuses. "I shouldn't have been drinking. It made me make foolish mistakes. I never should have been driving in that state. That was the only reason I made up that story. I was afraid of getting arrested again."

Hannah elbowed Benji. "You're apologizing, not explaining why you did it."

"Uh, sorry."

"That's a good start, Benji," Hannah encouraged. "Sorry for what?"

"Um, that we were in an accident. That the old man got hurt. That I didn't slow down when Noah told me to."

"You're apologizing to Noah," she whispered. She'd evidently meant only for Benji to hear her, but her words carried.

"Right. Sorry, Noah. I didn't know you'd go to jail."

Noah shot his brother a disbelieving stare. "Not even when the jury convicted me? You and Mamm and Daed were in the courtroom that day."

"I thought maybe with so many people standing up for you and saying you were a fine, upstanding member of the community, they'd change their minds." Benji sounded almost jealous of the praise his brother had received.

"And when the judge passed the sentence?" Noah's eyes bored into Benji.

Benji broke their gaze and stared down at the tabletop. "I'm sorry," he said lamely.

"How sorry are you really, Benji?" Noah pressed him. "Have you told Mamm and Daed?"

Benji lowered his eyes and scratched at the back of his neck. "Um, not yet."

"I see." Noah paused a beat. "If you were truly sorry, you'd tell them and clear my name."

"It'll upset them too much."

Caroline gritted her teeth over Benji's sniveling. One excuse after another. He was so self-centered.

She'd miscalculated by bringing him here. Everything he said was driving Noah further and further away.

Benji squirmed under Noah's intense stare. "Daed had a heart attack six months ago. If I tell him, he might have another one. You wouldn't want him to die, would you?"

Pain flickered in Noah's eyes. How hard it must be to be cut off from your family and not know when they had health emergencies. Would anyone tell Noah if his *daed* died? Caroline could never bear to be estranged from her parents like that. How had Noah survived that after life behind bars?

Noah's jaw tightened as if he'd steeled himself against hurt and loss. "What about the community? Are you willing to tell them the truth? And the people in town?"

Benji's eyes filled with fear. "If I do that, they might arrest me and put me in jail."

"Could be. It's a chance you'd have to take."

"But if I go to prison too, it would mean all your time in jail was a waste."

What an excuse! Caroline ground her teeth together.

Before she could say anything, Mrs. Vandenberg cut in. "So, basically, you're saying you're sorry it happened as long as you don't have to pay any penalties."

Benji's head snapped up.

"In my view, people who aren't willing to face the consequences are cowards." Mrs. Vandenberg's steely gaze penetrated the thin armor of bravado Benji had erected.

"I'm not a coward."

"Then prove it," Caroline challenged.

Mrs. Vandenberg held up a hand. "He'll prove it when he genuinely feels remorse. Perhaps if he realizes some of what Noah suffered on his behalf, he'll reach that point." She turned to Noah. "Why don't you tell Benji about life in jail?"

Noah buried his head in his hands. "*Neh*. Talking about it will bring it back. I never want to revisit that terrible time."

But Mrs. Vandenberg kept nudging until Noah, his voice muffled, revealed a little of the darkness he'd endured. He didn't look up or make eye contact, and he told the chilling details in a monotone, as if they'd happened to someone else.

Caroline's eyes overflowed with tears at all Noah had been through. Although she didn't agree with his unbelief, she could understand how he'd lost his faith after going through it.

Even Benji seemed affected. He hung his head, and when Noah finished, he offered a tentative *I'm sorry*. It sounded a bit more sincere than his previous ones, but still left a lot to be desired.

Noah lifted his head, his eyes haunted, and rose from the bench. "When you've cleared up all the lies about me, I might believe you mean it. Until then, I'm out of here."

With one last glance at Caroline, a glance that held all the love a man could give a woman mixed with the greatest pain he'd ever bear, he straightened and headed for the construction site. She longed to run after him, to beg him to reconsider, to ask him to stay with her—even though it was impossible. As he walked away—his final goodbye—Caroline's heart shattered into a million pieces. Pieces that could never be put together again.

CHAPTER 33

After Noah walked away from the picnic table, they all sat there in stunned silence. Caroline and Hannah had tears in their eyes from Noah's depiction of the hardships he'd faced. And he'd only glossed over a few of them.

Caroline ached for the agony he'd endured. So many deep-seated hurts and injustices he blamed on God—and on his brother, the real culprit. Rather than turning to the Lord for comfort, Noah had turned against the only One who could help and heal him.

Lord, please show him the way back to the faith. I'm willing to sacrifice anything in my life to see Noah turn his life over to You.

She'd endure all the loneliness and emptiness of losing Noah and much, much more if it meant he'd return to God. Even if she never saw Noah again, Caroline wanted him to be happy. And the only way to reach that happiness was through the Lord.

Overhead, the clouds darkened, and the thick density of the air threatened a storm brewing. The weighty pressure of the atmosphere matched the heaviness in her soul.

Benji shifted on the bench across from her, obviously

restless and irritated. Beside him, Hannah rubbed her forehead.

"Well, that didn't work. He didn't accept my apology. And he didn't say he forgave me."

"I wonder why." Sarcasm tinged Hannah's remark.

"Me too." Benji seemed oblivious to the part he'd played. "I wish we hadn't come all this way for nothing."

Caroline was about to blast him, when Hannah jumped up from the bench. "Benjamin Riehl, this is all your fault. And if you don't make it right, I'll never speak to you again." Hannah's voice cracked louder than the far distant thunder.

"You don't mean that."

"I most certainly do." Hannah stalked over to the car without him.

"What do you expect me to do?"

"Pray about it, and follow your conscience."

"But—"

Hannah flung the Bentley door wide without even waiting for the driver to open it. She slid across the seat and plastered herself up against the far door. "Hey, Caroline, why don't you come and sit next to me?"

The driver opened the front passenger door for Mrs. Vandenberg. Then he stood uncertainly by the back door. "We do have a third seat back here we can open."

Hannah looked over her shoulder. "That's a good idea. Benji can sit back there." She patted the spot near the opposite window. "Here you go, Caroline."

Benji stared at Hannah, his eyes welling with hurt.

Caroline tried to make peace. "There's plenty of room for all three of us." But Hannah didn't back down. "It'll be fun for Benji to ride back there."

"If you're sure?" The driver lifted a questioning eyebrow.

"I'm positive."

He fixed the third seat. Benji climbed in and sat staring at the back of Hannah's head with sad eyes.

Caroline would have given in, but Hannah whispered, "Help me stay strong."

Not sure how things would go once they reached her house if Benji and Hannah were fighting, Caroline tried to get a conversation going. After getting only a few lackluster responses, she gave up. Even Mrs. Vandenberg seemed disinclined to talk.

Normally, Caroline would have filled the silence with chatter, but Noah's leaving weighed too heavily on her.

"You don't look so good," Jose observed as Noah returned. "Maybe you should take the rest of the day off." Noah had never gone home sick in the middle of the day. He'd always worked through any illnesses. And you didn't get out of prison work detail unless you were hospitalized. He wasn't sick now, unless heartsickness counted.

"I'm serious, man," Jose said. "We don't have much more block to lay. You can finish up tomorrow."

Noah debated. He had repairs to do at Mrs. Vandenberg's apartment. Maybe he could work on those and be alone with his thoughts. He had a lot of things to come to terms with—like where to move to next, how to find a job where his past wouldn't be an issue, and how to survive without Caroline in his life.

"If you're all right with it," he told his boss, "I'll head off now and be back tomorrow."

"I'm fine with that. You've already done a full day's work." Jose waved toward the parking lot. "Go on. Get outta here. And if you need tomorrow off, stay home."

Taking more time off wouldn't help. Noah preferred working to brooding. He'd be living with this pain the rest of his life. Might as well get used to it.

At the apartment, he assessed the repairs—holes bashed in the walls, broken faucets and light fixtures, crooked cabinet doors hanging by one hinge, and water stains on the floor. He surmised the previous tenants had either unruly children or wild parties. They'd left a few pieces of battered furniture behind—a rickety table, a couch with a missing leg, and two wooden chairs with broken slats. He made notes, took measurements, jotted a shopping list, and headed for the home improvement store.

When he exited, lightning streaked the sky in the distance. Loaded down with gallons of paint and spackling compound, tools, and other supplies, he returned to the apartment. He made it inside before the heavens opened, pouring down a deluge. From time to time, thunder rumbled around him. The lights flashed on and off. If they went out completely, he had only a small travel flashlight in his duffel bag. He took it out and set it nearby.

Noah threw himself into the work with a vengeance— patching holes and sanding like a madman, scraping away at his inner rage, his pent-up frustration, his deep-seated loss, his buried misery. With each spot he completed, he released some of the pain tying him to the past.

He worked until the wee hours of the morning. As he applied a primer coat of white to cover all the sanded spots on the finished walls, a verse from childhood scrolled through his mind: *though your sins be as scarlet, they shall be as white as snow* . . . Painting the walls made them fresh and pristine. If only he could clear away all his mistakes and failings and start anew. In church, he'd been taught how to do that by asking for forgiveness and turning his life over to the Lord, but too much old garbage burbled up. Garbage he wasn't ready to release.

And he had too much anger toward God. *Why, God, why did You make me go through so much anguish? Don't You care? I tried to be good and live for You. Why did You punish me so harshly? I didn't deserve it.*

And now this supposedly all-loving God had added another burden to Noah's load with the loss of Caroline. How could he ever trust a God who let him suffer like this?

As Mrs. Vandenberg's car pulled into the driveway, Mamm and Daed stepped out on the porch to greet her and welcome their guests.

"I'm Elizabeth, and this Ezekiel. You must be Hannah and Benjamin." Mamm turned toward the Bentley. "You and your driver are both welcome to stay for supper, Liesl. It's nothing fancy, but we're happy to share."

"Not tonight, I'm afraid. I have a meeting at the STAR center. Nettie, Stephen, and I will be selecting some workers for the barbecue stand."

"How wonderful. They could use more help." Daed stepped over to the car to collect the overnight bags. "I want to thank you for taking Caroline to Fort Plain," he said as Mrs. Vandenberg started to roll up her window.

"It was a pleasure. I hope we can do it again."

Daed hid his dismay by bending to pick up the luggage, but Caroline caught his expression. She waved goodbye as the Bentley pulled away, and then moved close to him as Mamm beckoned a sullen Benji and irritated Hannah inside to show them to their rooms.

"Why don't you want me to go on another trip with Mrs. Vandenberg?" Caroline asked Daed, keeping her voice low so nobody overheard.

"You noticed that?" Daed turned to her with love in his eyes. "I missed you while you were away. The house seemed too quiet without you."

She stared at him in astonishment. "You and Mamm always say I talk too much."

Daed's eyes twinkled. "Sometimes you don't realize what something means to you until it's gone."

Caroline's heart warmed, but his unexpected compliment couldn't ease her deep sense of loss. She, too, had discovered how much *someone* meant to her now that he was gone.

To keep from revealing her heartache, she hurried after Mamm. Daed puffed up the stairs to the third floor, where Mamm had put Benji, and set his duffel bag on the desk chair.

Mamm waved to the two large windows. "Our boys preferred this room because they had a view of the fields and the roads, so they could see who was coming from both directions."

Caroline had always loved this view too. In the distance, blue hills peeked up from the horizon. Today, though, even beauty seemed bittersweet. As if sensing her mood, dark clouds massed over the hazy peaks. Thunder growled in the distance. A storm might be coming their way.

"*Danke*." Benji unzipped his duffel bag.

Hannah moved beside him, her annoyance evident, and whispered, "Why didn't you carry up your own bag?"

Benji stared at her in surprise. "Caroline's *daed* said he'd do it."

Crossing her arms, Hannah shook her head. "You're younger and stronger." She flashed a quick look at Caroline's *daed* to see if he'd heard.

If he had, he didn't let on. Still holding Hannah's suitcase, he gazed out the window, enjoying the view.

"Go get my bag," she muttered.

"What's gotten into you, Hannah? You're so critical today."

To defuse the fight, Mamm moved to the doorway. "Hannah, would you like to see your room?"

"Yes, Elizabeth." From the side of her mouth, she said quietly, "My suitcase, Benji."

"Oh, all right." Benji took Hannah's suitcase, and they all trooped down to the second floor.

"You can have a choice." Mamm opened a door at the far end of the hall. "This was my daughter-in-law Nettie's room. Or you could stay with Caroline. She has two beds."

"Caroline, would that be all right with you?"

"Of course. I'd like to have you."

"That's settled then." With a relieved smile, Mamm motioned for Benji to follow her and put the suitcase in Caroline's room.

A short while later, they all sat at the table for prayer. Once everyone had taken a few bites of meat loaf and brown butter noodles, Daed focused on the company.

"Benjamin, I understand you have something to tell us."

He squirmed in his chair. "I go by *Benji*."

Daed's "I see" encouraged Benji to continue.

Getting Benji to tell the truth was like pulling taffy. You had to keep going and going long after you got tired. Luckily, Daed had developed patience from years of raising children. He needed every bit of it.

Hannah poked and prodded to keep Benji from straying off on tangents. And finally, most of the story emerged. Benji didn't mention being drunk when the police pulled him over.

Caroline was tempted to mention it, but she didn't want to irritate Benji in case he clammed up. Hannah didn't seem to worry about annoying him. Caroline wondered what had happened to change Hannah from the sweet, supportive friend she'd been in New York. Instead of babying and protecting Benji, she seemed determined to make him grow up and accept responsibility. Caroline agreed he needed to do that, so she silently cheered for Hannah.

Once the dinner dishes had been washed, the three *youngie* went out on the porch. Hannah invited Caroline to sit beside her on the swing, leaving Benji to sit alone on the wicker love seat.

They talked for a while, then Hannah asked, "Caroline, would you mind if I talked to Benji alone?"

Caroline went into the living room, curled up on the couch, and picked up a book, but she had trouble reading because her thoughts kept straying to Noah. She didn't mean to eavesdrop, but Mamm had opened the windows to let in the breeze. The wind, growing in intensity as the storm neared, carried in snatches of the conversation.

Hannah berated Benji for not appreciating the sacrifice Noah had made. "Did you hear what he went through? He did it for you. Noah could have told the truth that day, and you would have been in that jail. And you'd still be in there. They would have given you seven years. I looked it up."

"*Jah*, it's good he didn't call me out."

"How would you have done behind bars, Benji?"

Benji's voice took on a swagger. "I'd never have let any of those gangs bully me or beat me up or—"

"And how would you have stopped them?"

"I'd—" Benji hesitated. Reality must be sinking in.

"So if six guys held you down and punched you and stole from you, you think you'd win?"

"*Neh*, probably not. But I'd report it."

"Then those gangs would be out to get you. They'd ambush you when no guards were around." When Benji stayed silent, Hannah pressed him. "That's not even the point. Noah took your punishment. Punishment you deserved. It should have been you in jail, not him. If someone did that for me, I'd be so grateful, I'd do whatever I could for them."

"What can I do for Noah? I can't take his place."

"You can confess to your parents and tell the church here and at home."

"You can't mean that. What will everyone think?"

"That you're honest. And brave to set the record straight."

The rain that had been threatening earlier broke overhead, and Caroline couldn't hear Benji's answer. It had been a long, tough day. She went to the front door. "Hannah, I'm going to bed because I have to get up early tomorrow for work. Come in whenever you're finished."

Hannah leaped to her feet. "I'm done now. I'll come with you."

"But Hannah . . ." Benji reached out a hand to restrain her, but she evaded him.

"Good night, Benji. I hope you'll think about what I said." Hannah took Caroline's arm. "*Danke* for having us here, Caroline."

When they were out of earshot of Benji, Hannah's shoulders slumped. "It's so hard to be firm with him. He needs to see the truth of what he did and how it affected Noah. We only heard a snippet of what Noah went through."

"I know." Caroline couldn't bear to think about all Noah had endured.

CHAPTER 34

At about three in the morning, Noah spread his sleeping bag on the couch and sat on it to rest. He didn't intend to sleep. He'd only rest his eyes a minute, then he'd get more work done.

Suddenly, he was trapped in a dark, narrow space. He couldn't get out. Wherever he turned, bars slammed down in front of him. They closed in on him. A jail cell. The space grew smaller and smaller. Bars pressed against his chest and back, crushing him. He tried to fling his arms out to stop them, but more bars squeezed his arms against his sides. He couldn't move. He couldn't breathe. He tried to claw the bars apart to free himself, but they kept squashing him and squashing him.

Noah woke, disoriented and gasping for breath. Shadows pressed in on him in that claustrophobic space. Nothing looked familiar. Terror clutched at his chest. His heart banged against his ribs. Lightning slashed through the sky. Thunder banged like gunshots and reverberated around him. The sudden flashes lit patched and plastered walls. Noah forced himself to inhale deeply. The familiar smell of fresh paint anchored him as he pulled himself back to reality. Mrs. Vandenberg's apartment.

Slipping in and out of nightmares, he tossed and turned as the storm raged. At first, jail scenes haunted him. All the details he'd recounted earlier, and many more he'd repressed, whorled through his head, leaving him dizzy and disoriented and tense with fear.

Each time he woke, he stretched and groaned. Every muscle in his body ached from sleeping on the lumpy couch. Lack of sleep left him foggy-headed.

He got up, felt his way around the apartment, and flicked on two lights. Maybe they'd drive away the awful dreams. But he was too edgy to relax.

His encounter with his brother reeled through his mind, spliced with scenes of Caroline he rapidly cut out and discarded. His brother's selfishness, his self-centeredness stood out. His sense of entitlement—Benji acted as if people should sacrifice for him, as if people were put on earth to do his bidding. Noah sat there cataloging all of his brother's failings. His blindness to his faults. His willfulness. His disregard for others' feelings.

All the old pain bubbled up, and this time, when Noah drifted off, a different prison awaited him. Trapped inside his brother's mind, Noah couldn't be sure where his feelings ended and his brother's began. Even worse, he was doomed to exist in this small, cramped space forever.

Noah jolted awake. Rain lashed the windows while remnants of the dream left him slogging through jumbled emotions. Being inside his brother's head had been frightening, not only because of the smallness and the constriction, but because of the connection and familiarity.

Fleeting fragments of the dream revealed how Noah's behavior mirrored Benji's—the whining and feeling like a victim, acting like a martyr. Noah had gone through unfairness and hardships that few people in the Amish community had dealt with, but many others had survived terrible tragedies—fires, floods, life-threatening illnesses, deaths of loved ones. Why had he set himself apart from others when he was so much like them?

Why hadn't he been more like Job in the Bible? Job had been innocent, yet God allowed him to be tested. When Job lost everything, he never complained. Benji's whining and grumbling annoyed Noah, but hadn't Noah been doing the same himself? And while Noah didn't pout and complain outwardly the way Benji did, he certainly did inside. He'd created a long list of grievances against God as well as against others, including his parents and his brother.

And Benji's sense of entitlement—acting as if other people owed him favors and that they should do his bidding—Noah had done the same. He'd expected God to clear away all obstacles in his life. To meet his needs and fulfill his desires. To reward him for doing something for his brother.

Why do I believe I deserve special treatment?

Most of Noah's tangled emotions traced back to *hochmut*. He'd been proud of being a hero, of suffering for others. Noah had expected Benji to honor him and shower him with praise. After all, Noah had given up three years of his life and his reputation to help his brother.

Outside, a huge clap of thunder followed a jagged flash of lightning. The building shook, and lights flickered off, plunging Noah into complete darkness. But in that blackness, Noah's inner light shone brilliantly, illuminating the shadows and revealing deeper truths.

Suddenly, everything in his life fell into perspective. How did his own sacrifice compare with Christ's? *The Son of God gave up His life. For me. And how have I reacted? With the same ingratitude Benji has shown toward me.*

Noah had been railing at his brother's lack of thankfulness, when Noah himself had been ungrateful for Christ's huge life-changing sacrifice. Shame filled him at his arrogance.

As the rain beat down on the roof and slid down the windows like cleansing tears, Noah wrestled with old hurt, anger, resentment, and sins for hours. When he finally asked for forgiveness and surrendered his life to God, the cleansing flood of Divine love washed away the bitterness and resentment Noah had carried since the accident.

Emotionally drained and exhausted, he lay back on the lumpy couch and fell into the first peaceful sleep he'd had in years. Hours later, he woke with a start. Late-afternoon sunshine poured through the windows and onto his face. Although his body felt battered and sore, his soul felt exhilarated. He'd gotten right with God. Now he needed to make peace with his brother. But would he be too late? Benji may have already gone home.

The dreary weather on Tuesday morning matched Caroline's mood. The pouring rain had canceled Hannah and Benji's trip to Hershey Park, so Benji looked as grumpy as Caroline felt. His lips twisted into a pout, but Hannah shot him a quelling look.

"You have more important things to do today," she said in a crisp, no-nonsense way.

"Like what?" Benji didn't sound thrilled.

"Maybe we can start by going in to work with Caroline and spreading the truth about your brother around the market. That way, you can fix some of the damage you've done."

When Benji started to protest, she cut him off. "It's the least you can do after what Noah did for you."

Soon after they arrived at the market, Mrs. Vandenberg showed up. Despite the heavy rain and lightning, she was in good spirits. "It'll clear up this afternoon before you head back to New York," she told Benji and Hannah.

Then she turned to Caroline. "You, my dear, will be seeing a different kind of sunshine today."

Caroline couldn't figure out the puzzling remark, but Mrs. Vandenberg had already moved on to other things.

"So what are you two planning to do this morning?" She directed her question to Hannah.

"We'll help Caroline if she needs it, but mainly Benji plans to talk to the stand owners to clear up the rumors about Noah."

"Ah, Benji, it's good to know you're doing the right thing. It would be even better if you put your heart and soul into it. Why don't you pray about your attitude? Has it ever occurred to you that your selfish actions ruined your brother's life?"

"That's exactly what I've been trying to tell him, Mrs. Vandenberg," Hannah said. "Maybe he'll listen to you."

"Even more important, he needs to listen to his conscience." She shot Benji a penetrating look that made him squirm.

"Before you get started, let me show you my conference room upstairs. I'll leave it unlocked. It's a good place to do some soul-searching. Perhaps, young man," she said sternly, "you could reflect on how your life would be different if Noah hadn't taken your punishment. It might make you more grateful."

Hannah directed a pointed look at Benji. "Maybe you could spend some time up there before we start talking to people."

Mrs. Vandenberg nodded. "A wise plan. Oh, and there's a phone in there. It's connected to my charity, so feel free to use it for any long-distance calls you'd like to make."

Benji frowned. "That's all right. We'll be headed home today, so we won't need your phone."

Mrs. Vandenberg tilted her head to one side. "There's no telling what use you'll make of it if you spend some time in prayer."

Caroline hoped at least one of those calls would be to Noah's parents.

Anna Mary dragged in, her clothing soaked, her sneakers squishing.

"Oh, dear, you need to come with me too," Mrs. Vandenberg said to Anna Mary. "We'll get you dried off in no time."

"I couldn't find an umbrella this morning." Anna Mary looked close to tears, and Caroline worried it meant her *mamm* wasn't doing well.

They all tromped off with Mrs. Vandenberg, leaving Caroline alone to get everything set up in the stand. She didn't expect many customers when it was storming like this, but she wanted to be ready for those who braved this weather.

When Anna Mary returned, dry and a bit more cheerful, she said, "Mrs. Vandenberg formally introduced me to Benji and Hannah. She said they're from Fort Plain. Do you know what they're doing here?"

"Benji is Noah's brother, and he's come to clear up

the rumors about his brother. Hannah is his friend and neighbor."

"I see. Having them here must mean you're still interested in Noah?" Anna Mary sent Caroline a concerned look.

Caroline would always be interested in Noah, but they had no future together.

The driver was waiting for Hannah and Benji when Caroline drove them home from the market. As Mrs. Vandenberg had predicted, the sun had broken through the clouds. And Caroline's heart was a bit lighter.

Benji had followed Mrs. Vandenberg's advice, and he'd done some soul-searching. He seemed more appreciative of Noah's sacrifice, and he and Hannah had stopped at every stand to meet the owners and to correct gossip about Noah.

But the thing that thrilled Caroline the most was Benji's decision to call his parents and tell them the truth. Both his *mamm* and his *daed* wanted to ask Noah's forgiveness.

Hannah's eyes shone as she recounted the story. "His parents have decided Benji will face some major consequences for lying. It won't be easy, but I can already see some changes in him."

"I'm so glad." Caroline tried not to let her own sorrow color Hannah's good news. "I hope you can come for another visit. I've enjoyed having you."

"Once we're both married to Benji and Noah, we'll spend a lot of holidays together." Hannah sounded overjoyed at that prospect. Caroline didn't have the heart to tell Hannah one of those dreams wouldn't come true.

Benji hurried inside to get their bags without being asked, impressing both Caroline and Hannah. He seemed to be a fast learner. A buggy pulled into the driveway behind them. Noah. Caroline's pulse quickened into double time. Had Noah come to say goodbye to his brother? That was promising.

Mindful that Noah would rather not see her, Caroline hurried into the house. But she didn't want to miss Benji and Noah's meeting. She stationed herself by the window and whispered a prayer they'd make peace.

CHAPTER 35

As Noah tied up his horse, Benji banged out the front door carrying a suitcase and a duffel bag. When he noticed the buggy, he slowed his pace and asked warily, "Noah?"

Noah wanted to get this out while it was still raw and real, before his instinct to bottle up his emotions took over. But Benji said something at the same time, rushing out words, and the two of them talked over each other.

Noah stopped speaking and held up a hand. "You first."

Benji's voice trembled. "I'm sorry for everything you went through. Hannah and Mrs. Vandenberg told me I didn't appreciate what you did for me, and they were right." His words gushed out. "I never should have blamed you for the accident. You could have called out my lie, but you didn't."

Only because Noah had been too blindsided and hurt. And during the trial, he'd waited for Benji to step up and take responsibility.

His brother hung his head. "I came to Lancaster to say I was sorry, but I messed it up yesterday. Will you forgive me for everything I did?"

Noah had given up expecting a sincere apology, but today, Benji truly sounded contrite.

"*Jah*, I will . . . if you forgive me."

His brother stared at him in surprise. "For what?"

Drawing on his new inner strength, Noah admitted, "For resenting you." *For wishing you'd never been born. For wishing bad things would happen to you.* He didn't want to admit how deeply rooted his bitterness had been, but he had to be honest. "I spent the past few years wishing for revenge."

After swallowing hard, Benji tried to get out words, but nothing came. Then he croaked, "I would have done the same."

For the first time, Benji had acknowledged putting himself in Noah's place. That admission lanced old pockets of poison stored in Noah's memories. It might take time for Noah to fully come to terms with everything he'd gone through, but with God's grace, those festering wounds had begun to drain.

Benji stepped forward and gave Noah an awkward hug. "Nothing to forgive. I'm the one who needed to be forgiven." Embarrassed, he let his hands drop to his sides.

Hannah called to him. "Benji, tell Noah what you did today."

Overwhelmed by emotion, Noah wanted to back away and lighten the situation. "I guess you didn't get to Hershey Park."

"*Neh*, we didn't." Disappointment flared in Benji's eyes. "We went to the market with Caroline and visited all the stands. Anyone who'd heard about you, we corrected the rumors. Hope that'll help."

"You did what?" Although he appreciated Benji wanting to clear things up, Noah's face burned imagining all

those people, many he'd never met, talking about him
and learning about his past. He felt exposed.

Noah wanted to blast his brother for invading his privacy. But Benji had meant it for good. And a picture of
Caroline flashed through Noah's mind. He loved her honesty, her ability to admit her faults. If he wanted to be more
like her, here was his chance. He hadn't stepped out and
opened himself up to others' scrutiny; Benji had done it for
him. Maybe Noah needed this nudge to be more open.

"That's not all he did, Noah," Hannah called.

Inside, Noah cringed. He wasn't sure he wanted to hear
anything else his brother had done.

Benji ducked his head and shuffled his feet. "I called
Mamm and Daed and told them the truth. Mamm was
shocked and angry at me."

Hearing his brother's words, Noah could barely breathe.
All these years, he'd held in the pain of being estranged
from his parents. He'd pushed it down, tried to forget it,
but nothing could ever totally erase that agony.

"Daed said he'd always suspected it, but when you
didn't deny it, he had to believe you were guilty."

Noah's emotions boiled like water simmering, with
bubbles rising to the surface, then popping. He'd buried
his anger at his parents for believing Benji's lies. He'd
suppressed his bitterness, resentment, and deep-seated
hurt toward them along with his jealousy of Benji. His
brother had a close relationship with their parents while
Noah had been rejected and cut off. He tried to tune in to
what his brother was saying.

"Daed and Mamm want to come down here to ask your
forgiveness. Mamm said to tell you she never stopped
loving you. Daed harrumphed, which I think meant he
agreed. He's never been very open with his feelings."

So many emotions Noah still had to deal with. At least he didn't have to do it alone. Now he could pray for help. He'd also like to have Caroline's support, but would she have anything to do with him after he'd hurt her so deeply?

Teary-eyed, Caroline watched Noah and Benji say goodbye. She was glad the two brothers had reunited. She hoped Benji's apology had brought peace and closure to Noah. That had been her goal in visiting Benji, and she'd accomplished her mission.

Well, if she were honest, Mrs. Vandenberg and God played the main roles in this reunion. Caroline had only planted the seed that went on to bear fruit.

Caroline had said her goodbyes earlier and made plans for Hannah and Benji to visit again, so she stayed inside to give the two brothers time together. And to stay away from Noah as he'd requested.

After he and Benji said their final goodbyes, Noah stood on the front sidewalk until the car disappeared from sight. His face reflected fleeting emotions—pain, resignation, wistfulness.

She debated about going out to talk to him, but he'd made it clear being around her was too painful. And with Noah not wanting anything to do with the church, she had no hope for a future relationship. As much as it hurt, they'd both be better off if she stayed inside and tried to forget him.

To her surprise, Daed opened the front door and called out, "Noah, can I talk to you a minute?"

What did Daed have to say to Noah? Caroline's curiosity drew her to the open doorway. She stood so she'd be hidden from Noah's sight, but she could still hear their conversation.

"I'm Caroline's *daed*, Ezekiel." He held out his hand, and Noah shook it.

Noah appeared as puzzled as Caroline felt. "Nice to meet you." Although he looked wary and unenthusiastic.

Daed plunged into the conversation. "When I heard the rumors about you, I believed them. But my *dochder* insisted they couldn't be true. She was determined to prove your innocence. And now she has."

Caroline wished she'd explained to Daed about Noah not joining the church. She hoped her father wouldn't say anything about her feelings for Noah or Mamm's hope that Caroline would settle down soon.

Her *daed* kept talking. "I'm sorry I listened to gossip and didn't believe the best of you."

Caroline choked up. As grateful as she was that Dacd wanted to apologize to Noah, she feared Noah might suspect she'd put her *daed* up to it.

Stunned, Noah tried to take in his second apology of the day. This time from Caroline's *daed*.

"Will you forgive me?" Ezekiel asked.

Noah didn't hesitate. "Of course." Although he was grateful for Ezekiel's willingness to make things right, Noah longed to make things right with Caroline. She was hovering in the living room nearby, eavesdropping on the conversation.

He smiled to himself. Typical Caroline—always curious, always sticking her nose in other people's business. That trait he'd once feared had become precious to him. She never did it to start gossip or hurt others. Like Mrs.

Vandenberg, Caroline had a gift for meddling in people's lives, but only to help them. If Caroline hadn't interfered in his life, he might never have healed his relationship with Benji and his parents or returned to the Lord.

And he'd returned her kindness by pushing her away. He'd told her he didn't want to be around her, and she'd honored his wishes. The way she'd scurried into the house to avoid him when he'd pulled into the driveway earlier had gutted him. What had he done? Had he permanently damaged his relationship with the woman he loved with all his heart? He needed to ask her forgiveness.

Since the accident, Noah had shut down, becoming closemouthed and determined not to share personal things. But he needed to send Caroline the message that he'd changed.

Gathering his courage, Noah announced at a volume loud enough for her to hear, "Ezekiel, I appreciate all you've done to reunite me with my brother. I needed his forgiveness as much as he needed mine. I also needed God's forgiveness. I turned my life over to Him today and plan to take baptismal classes."

"That's wonderful." Ezekiel responded enthusiastically, but he appeared a bit surprised at Noah's declarations.

"The reason I'm telling you this is because"—Noah raised his voice even more—"after I join the church, I'd like to court your *dochder*."

A bemused smile crossed Ezekiel's face, but Caroline squealed and raced out the door. Exactly the reaction Noah had hoped for.

"Did you mean that?" she demanded.

"I certainly did."

Ezekiel faded into the background and slipped into the house as Caroline's sparkling eyes met Noah's.

"*Ach*, Noah. I can't believe this. I'm so happy, I'm speechless."

"Not for long, I hope. I want to hear you talk for the rest of my life."

"Really, truly? Everyone always tells me to be quiet."

"I don't ever want you to be silent. Every word you speak is precious to me. As precious as you are."

Caroline stood on the sidewalk, gazing into Noah's eyes. Eyes that overflowed with love. She'd prayed God would send her a husband who would accept her the way the Lord had made her. He'd answered that prayer in the most wonderful way possible.

"I never thought anyone would love me when I'm so . . . so—"

"Perfect? Adorable? Generous? Caring? Honest? Open?"

"Noah, you'll make me prideful."

"How about determined? Persistent?" His eyes twinkled.

She giggled. "Oh, you. *Jah*, I am that. My parents would call me stubborn."

His expression turned serious. "If you hadn't been determined and persistent, I'd never have found the Lord. I'd be going through my life lonely and isolated. I'd never have connected with my brother or my parents."

Caroline's heart expanded as she recognized God had given her unique gifts she could use to help people. She'd always put herself down and grumbled about not being like others.

She had to be honest. "Before I met you, I never thought I'd ever have a boyfriend. Mamm and Anna Mary kept giving me advice on how to change myself so I could get a date."

"I'm so glad they didn't succeed."

For the first time in years, Caroline could truly say, "Me too."

She still had a lot of improving to do, but now she thanked God for the way He'd made her and for the man He'd brought into her life.

She and Noah fit together like the pieces of the puzzles she'd upended the day she'd first run into him. Even her rushing everywhere had worked out for good. She'd never have met Noah if she hadn't been hurrying.

Caroline sent up a prayer of thanksgiving. God had brought her the perfect match. And she prayed they'd have many, many years for piecing together the puzzles of life.

EPILOGUE

Eighteen months later . . .

Noah hummed a song from the *Ausbund* as he headed home from work. Could his heart be any fuller? After he'd fixed up Mrs. Vandenberg's apartment, she'd let him rent it. Leave it to her to trick him into moving to an apartment in Caroline's *g'may*, so he and Caroline could attend church and singings together. For a woman in her nineties, Mrs. Vandenberg did an amazing job of planning each detail of her matchmaking. And Noah appreciated her thoughtfulness.

Today, though, he wouldn't be stopping at home. He'd only be driving past his place on the way to the volleyball field. His heart quickened to a pace faster than his horse's hooves at the thought of spending time with Caroline. They did as many group activities together as they could, but until his baptism tomorrow, they couldn't date. She'd offered to pick up several teammates and take them to the field, while Noah stayed later at the market to help Abner with paperwork, accounting, and setting up for Tuesday's auction. Since he'd accepted Mrs. Vandenberg's job offer at the auction, Noah had extra responsibilities, especially on Saturdays, so Caroline and he should arrive at the field around the same time. He flicked the reins to get Rosie to pick up her pace. He didn't want to miss one precious second of time with Caroline.

When Noah pulled into the field, his spirits sank. She hadn't arrived yet. He'd been so busy searching for her buggy, he hadn't noticed the occupants in the buggy beside him until an annoying voice penetrated his disappointment.

"Why so glum? Did you and Caroline break up?" Tim looked hopeful.

"Absolutely not."

Tim snickered as he exited his buggy. "Guess you can't really break up if you're not dating."

But Noah and Caroline had made a promise. And she'd stayed true to that promise.

Even though he shouldn't take a dig at Tim, Noah wanted to wipe the smug smile off Tim's face. "Don't worry, after tomorrow, we'll be dating for real."

Tim's face screwed up in disgust. "I can't believe she's stuck with you all this time."

Neither could Noah. Every day, he thanked the Lord for the most wonderful gift a man could ever have. His heart overflowing with gratitude for his special blessing, Noah couldn't make a sarcastic reply. After all, if the situation were reversed and Caroline had chosen someone else, Noah would have been devastated.

He slid out of the driver's seat and clapped Tim on the shoulder. "Don't worry. You'll find the perfect girl for you."

Tim made a face. "*Jah*, sure. You got the best girl in the area."

Noah couldn't argue with that. He'd gotten the best girl

in the state. And in the country. And in the whole world. At least in his estimation. And that girl had just pulled into the lot. Holding the reins in one hand, she waved wildly with the other. One of the many things he loved about her—her exuberance. She always acted thrilled to see him, unlike some girls who only smiled shyly at their boyfriends, then quickly lowered their eyes. Caroline never put on an act or left him in any doubt about her commitment.

Tim clutched at his heart dramatically. "*Ach*, look how excited she is to see me."

One of his friends tugged at his arm. "Come on, Tim, stop trying to break them up."

Noah chuckled to himself. Nobody—especially not Tim—would ever break them up. And if anyone watching had any doubts, they'd only have to watch Caroline tie up her horse and rush toward Noah.

"You made it!" Caroline's exclamation sounded as if they hadn't seen each other a few hours ago at the market.

His heart swelled. "I missed you too."

When she smiled up at him, he lost track of his surroundings. No one existed except the woman whose green eyes held him under her spell. He might have remained there the rest of the day if Anna Mary and the other girls who'd come in Caroline's buggy hadn't caught up with them.

"Do you two plan to play volleyball? Or are you going to stare at each other while the rest of us play?"

Anna Mary's teasing brought Noah back to earth with a sudden thump. "Do you want to join them?" he asked Caroline.

"Not really," she whispered. "I'd rather stay here with you."

Noah loved her honesty. He still found it hard to believe

that a woman as wonderful as Caroline had fallen for him. "I'd prefer to be with you, too, but maybe we should help our team. They need you."

"You're right." She giggled. "I meant about helping the team, not about them needing me."

"Admit it. You're the best player on the team."

"You've made our team undefeated. Tim's been trying to get out of second place for as long as you've been on the team."

Tim's losing streak also extended to his choice of girlfriend. Noah had to feel sorry for the guy. But maybe Tim would have better luck after Noah married Caroline.

"Only one more day." Caroline gave an excited bounce on her toes.

Noah couldn't wait. Tomorrow he'd be baptized, something he'd been looking forward to ever since he'd surrendered his life to God. He wanted to make that commitment public. And he'd also be free to make another public commitment—to the woman he loved.

When Noah smiled down at her so tenderly, Caroline could barely breathe. Her insides fluttered with delight. In one more day, he'd be with the church, and they could date. She still pinched herself. She'd despaired of ever finding a husband, yet the Lord had answered her prayers with a man who not only loved her exactly the way God had made her, but He'd also given her a man of faith who was everything she'd ever dreamed of and much, much more.

A shrill sound pierced the air, and they both jumped.

"What was that?" Caroline's pulse, which had already been galloping, took off like a runaway horse.

Noah's lips thinned. "Don't turn around, but Tim has a whistle. Let's pretend we didn't hear him."

Caroline grinned. "We're good at pretending, aren't we? After all, we might not be together if you hadn't agreed to be my pretend boyfriend."

"And soon to be your real one." He waved a hand as if to gallantly suggest she go ahead of him toward the volleyball court.

She turned and moved in the direction he'd indicated, a secret smile tugging at her lips. Things had definitely changed from that long-ago day when she'd begged him with her eyes not to give her away to Tim. They'd been through a lot since then, but it had only drawn them closer.

"It's about time," Tim called as they strolled across the field. "Everyone's been waiting for you to start the game."

"I'm surprised you didn't start without us." Caroline couldn't help her sassy tone.

Noah chuckled. "Are you trying to annoy him?"

"*Jah.*" Still, she had tempered her comments. She'd almost added, *so you could win for a change.* This past year and a half, she'd worked hard to follow Mrs. V's advice, and she'd made major improvements. But her snappy and sometimes too-honest replies often escaped before she could stop them. Noah told her he liked that about her, so she'd decided not to change too much. But she did try to be more aware of other people's feelings.

They took their places in the lineup. With Noah beside her, Caroline struggled to keep her mind on the volleyball game. "If you two don't stop staring into each other's eyes," Tim said sarcastically, "you're going to lose."

With one last longing glance at Noah, Caroline faced forward to concentrate on the server on the opposite side of the net. As she waited for the ball, she flexed her knees and readied her feet to spring in any direction.

When the ball sailed over the net, Caroline leaped into the air to spike it. Their opponents fumbled her return, and her team was off to a good start. That tiny triumph, which gave them the serve, paled in comparison to Noah's admiring glance and whispered, "Well done."

Despite the crisp fall air, by the final serve of the third set, Caroline's forehead was damp. She'd been jumping and twisting and bending to keep the ball in the air or to get it over the net. Together with Noah, they'd made some amazing saves. He anticipated her every move and was ready for each ball she set up.

But Tim was on fire today and determined to punish her. His team had squeaked by to win the second set after a tie. Now they were fighting to keep Caroline's team from making the final point. The ball flew toward Anna Mary, and she returned a soft lob straight to Tim. With a wicked grin, he spiked it to Caroline's left.

No way would she lose this point. Caroline dove, and this time, knowing Noah would defend her, she didn't care what Tim said about her pancake. She slid along the ground and tipped the ball in Noah's direction, setting him up for a spike. He drove the ball down hard on the opposite side of the net. Two players dove for it, collided, and missed.

"We did it!" Caroline started to scramble to her feet.

"*Neh*, you did it." Noah held out a hand to help her up. Unlike Anna Mary, he didn't frown at her dust-covered apron. Instead, he stared into her eyes with admiration—and love.

Caroline longed to throw her arms around his neck and hug him, but she restrained herself. Someday she'd be able to do that—in private and after they married. But one step at a time. Tomorrow, one of her dreams would come true—seeing Noah join the church—and then they could begin courting. She smiled to herself about the surprise she'd planned for him tomorrow. Caroline only hoped he'd like it.

As Noah filed into church the next morning with the other baptismal applicants, he kept his eyes lowered and his focus on the Lord. If anyone had told him two years ago he'd be making this solemn vow to join the church, he'd never have believed it. Yet despite his past rebellion, he had no doubts about this decision. His heart and life belonged to God. Today, he'd publicly prove his whole-hearted commitment to the Lord.

As the congregation sang, he and the others from the baptismal class followed the bishop into another room, where he reminded them they were making a promise for life.

"If anyone is uncertain about this decision," he continued, his gaze boring into each one of them, "now is the time to reconsider and turn back."

Noah met the bishop's eyes with assurance. He had no intention of turning back. After they returned to their seats at the front of the congregation to listen to the sermon about Philip and the Ethiopian, Noah's soul burned with the same zeal.

The bishop asked as the Ethiopian had, "'What doth hinder me to be baptized?'" When the bishop echoed Philip's answer, "'If thou believest with all thine heart, thou mayest,'" Noah's heart echoed the words.

Along with the bishop, Noah silently repeated the

Ethiopian's reply. *I believe that Jesus Christ is the Son of God*. Then Noah knelt with the other applicants and answered *jah* to the questions the bishop asked. As water trickled through the bishop's cupped hands onto Noah's head, he prayed he'd always remain faithful to God's will.

Not until after the bishop greeted Noah as a brother with a holy kiss did Noah lift his eyes to the men's section. He searched the benches for Caroline's father to thank him for all his encouragement in the faith over the past eighteen months. Ezekiel's eyes shone with happiness, but then Noah's gaze flicked to the men seated beside Ezekiel— Daed and Benji.

How? What were they doing here? Noah couldn't believe it. Although he'd forgiven his brother and now had a good relationship with his parents and Benji, they'd never said a word about coming.

Daed's eyes brimmed with pride. As members of the congregation gathered around to welcome the new members, Daed and Benji slipped through the crowd.

"I never thought I'd see this day." Daed clapped Noah on the shoulder. "The Lord is good. I can't believe two of my *sohns* are now with the church."

Benji gave Noah a swift, fierce hug. "I owe you for that. If you hadn't taken my place, I'd still be in jail. Instead, Hannah and I are planning to get married."

"That's wonderful." Noah was happy for his brother. Hannah would be a settling influence on Benji. But right now, all Noah wanted to do was turn and connect with the woman he loved.

Caroline's heart swelled with joy as Noah knelt before the church. Memories of her own baptism and the peace that descended lifted Caroline's spirit to heavenly realms. And today, the man she loved had just made the same commitment.

When Noah lifted his head to look at the men in the congregation, the slight jerk of his head revealed he'd seen his father and brother. She'd wanted to surprise him, so she hadn't mentioned his family had arrived yesterday.

Her eyes stung with tears as Benji embraced Noah. They'd been through some rough times as they worked through their relationship and Noah released all the pent-up hurt and grief, but after Benji had truly come to see the depths of Noah's sacrifice, it had humbled him, and he'd genuinely sought forgiveness. That had helped to heal the relationship.

Caroline blurted out to Hannah, "I'm so happy I can hardly contain it." She sneaked a peek at Noah's back and wished she could run over and throw her arms around him the way Benji had. Her cheeks heated. What a thought to have in church!

Noah must have sensed her attention because he turned and beamed at her, his eyes expressing all his love and tenderness. She returned the sentiments.

Hannah giggled. "I guess you two will be courting now."

Reluctantly, Caroline broke Noah's gaze. "We will. And you and Benji are dating?" Caroline asked it as a question, but she'd already guessed the answer.

"*Ach*, Caroline, it's so wonderful. I've loved Benji all my life. We grew up next door to each other, but I doubted he'd ever join the church. I worried about Noah too."

"So did I," Caroline admitted. "I never dreamed . . ." Her voice trailed off as she drifted back into the past. She'd despaired of finding love and of Noah returning to the faith. Now both of those dreams had come true.

And later that afternoon, another dream came true. Noah stopped by the house after church to spend time with her and his family. And when it was time for the singing, she rode in Noah's buggy.

She clasped her hands together and declared rapturously, "I've been waiting for this day forever."

"Me too." The longing in Noah's eyes echoed the desires of her heart.

They both struggled to keep their minds on the board games the youth group played when they sat across from each other. And later, Anna Mary elbowed Caroline in the ribs whenever she sang too enthusiastically or got so caught up in Noah's smiles, she forgot to pay attention to the words.

That night as they drove home under the stars, Noah stopped the buggy in a secluded lane and turned to her. "Caroline, I feel like I've been waiting forever to be alone with you."

"It's been so hard. But now the waiting's over. I wish we could get married right away." She clapped a hand over her mouth. Why had she blurted out her private thoughts? And on their first date?

Noah laughed. "Are you proposing to me?"

"*Ach*, Noah, don't tease. I'm so embarrassed."

"Why would you be embarrassed? Do you know how that makes me feel?"

When she didn't look up or answer, he reached out and put a gentle finger under her chin to make her meet his eyes. Eyes that were shining with love and joy.

"I'm in love with you, and I love your honesty. I've been agonizing over how soon I could ask you to marry me. My heart wanted to do it tonight, but I told myself it was too soon. So I pushed down my desire."

"Really?" She searched his face to be sure he was telling her the truth. After he reassured her that he meant every word, she didn't hesitate to spill her other longing. "I always wanted to have a spring wedding."

He shot her a teasing grin. "I don't know if I can wait that long."

Neither could she.

The next seven months rushed by. Caroline's parents gave her and Noah their house, and Noah helped Caroline's brothers build a *daadi haus* on Gideon's property. Caroline wanted to be near her parents, and Noah had no desire to move back to Fort Plain. Lancaster had become home. For the first time in years, he had friends. But most importantly, the woman he loved preferred to live here.

Hannah had come with his family for the wedding. She and Anna Mary would be Caroline's attendants, while Benji and Josh had agreed to be Noah's. Yesterday, the wedding wagon had arrived, and they'd all worked together to prepare the house. Smells of delicious foods cooking surrounded them as Noah, Caroline's older brothers, and her father set up the benches and prepared tables in the basement. Noah detoured by the kitchen whenever he could to catch a glimpse of his bride-to-be as she bounced from task to task, her animated face lighting up the room.

"*Danke*, Lord," he whispered each time he passed.

And now, seated beside her in front of the congregation, Noah prayed he'd be a worthy husband as he listened to the Scripture reading and sermons. The reminders of God's design for marriage and stories of biblical marriages through the ages reminded him of the sacredness of the vows he'd take today.

Lord, please help me to always show the depth of Your love to Caroline every day throughout our married life.

And then it was time to step forward. After the congregation surrounded him and Caroline to support them, the bishop began the vows. Noah made each promise with reverence, and he delighted in Caroline's steadfast *jah*s.

When the bishop came to the final question, he paused and met their eyes. "Do you both promise together that you will with love, forbearance, and patience live with each other, and not part from each other until God will separate you in death?"

Caroline's enthusiastic *jah* joined Noah's fervent one. During the final prayer and as he clasped her soft hands in his own, his spirit soared with gratitude at this gift from God.

And when he glanced over at his bride, she radiated joy. He basked in her smile. A smile that wrapped him in love and bliss. A smile that assured him she'd meant every vow.

Tears sprang to Caroline's eyes at the love in Noah's tone as he promised to love her forever. The first touch of Noah's strong hand on hers sent shivers of delight through her. She still couldn't believe she could now call Noah her husband.

As they sat in the *eck* for the wedding meal, Noah caressed her hand, hidden by the tablecloth. Reluctantly, she let go to eat, but tucked her hand back into his between bites.

Hannah leaned over and whispered, "You're glowing with happiness. I hope I'll be as radiant on my wedding day."

"You will be," Caroline assured her.

"I can't wait until we're sisters-in-law." Hannah peeked around Caroline and Noah to catch Benji's eye and give him a secretive smile.

"It won't be long."

"Six more months," Hannah moaned. Then she brightened. "I hope Benji will look as thrilled as Noah does."

Caroline turned shining eyes toward her husband. Sure enough, Hannah was right. Her husband—she didn't think she'd ever get tired of saying that word—appeared ecstatic. His expression mirrored the feelings bubbling in her heart and soul.

Soon after they'd finished dessert, a chair scraped back from a nearby table, and Mrs. Vandenberg rose shakily to her feet.

Noah jumped up. "I should help her up the steps and out to the car."

"I'll go with you." Caroline stood too. "I want to thank her for her part in the most wonderful day in my life."

He planned to do the same. "I don't know how I can ever thank her enough for all she's done, but I at least want to try."

Mrs. Vandenberg beamed at them as they approached. "I was hoping I could convince you to come out to the car with me. God answered that prayer, didn't He?"

A deep sense of gratitude washed over Noah. "He's answered so many of our prayers."

"And He'll keep on answering them." Mrs. Vandenberg patted the arm Noah extended to help her. "Just keep your eyes on Him."

"I intend to." Noah couldn't live his life without God's help.

After they reached her Bentley, parked in the shade of a grove of trees, the driver set down his book, jumped out, and opened the back door. Mrs. Vandenberg reached into the car and pulled out a package wrapped in sparkly silver paper.

"I know I should have dropped this off at the house before the wedding," she said, "but I wanted to watch you two open it."

Caroline burst out with the words in Noah's heart. "We should be giving you a gift instead of you giving us one."

"You've already given me the best present of all." When they both looked at her with puzzlement, Mrs. Vandenberg laughed. "It filled me with joy watching you two fall in love and marry. That's a precious gift."

Noah's heart, already overflowing with love for his beautiful wife, expanded until his chest ached. He could barely get words out. "We're the ones who received that gift."

"We all did." Mrs. Vandenberg's eyes twinkled as she handed over the box. "I wanted to give you something meaningful. I'm sure you'll understand when you open it."

Something shifted and rattled inside the package as Noah took it, and he hoped it hadn't broken. He'd hate to see Mrs. Vandenberg's disappointment.

"I'll hold it, so you can take off the paper," Noah said to Caroline.

Her eyes shining, she slid her pretty, graceful fingers under the edge of the wrapping paper, slowly and carefully lifting the edges to reveal a deep cardboard gift box. Caroline lifted the lid and sucked in a breath. "*Ach, ach, ach!*"

She lifted her head and, eyes brimming with joy and wonder, she whirled around to hug Mrs. Vandenberg. "How did you know? When did you get this?"

The elderly woman teetered under Caroline's exuberance, and Noah shifted the carton to one hip so he could reach out and support both women.

His throat constricted by emotion and his heart filled with thanksgiving, he tried to choke out a thank-you. "I can't believe you did this. I longed to buy these that day at the auction."

"I could tell they meant a lot to you, and God nudged me to bid on them."

Caroline released Mrs. Vandenberg from the embrace and stepped back, but Noah kept an arm under the elderly lady's elbow to steady her.

"But—but how? How did you know they were so special to us?" She reached into the carton and pulled out the top cardboard box. The wooden puzzle pieces inside clunked together. "This one's the baby in the high chair."

"Very fitting, don't you think?" Mrs. Vandenberg's face, lit with joy, mirrored Caroline's expression.

A sudden picture of Caroline holding the baby that day in the market flashed into Noah's mind. That day, he'd thought he'd never have a wife or a family. He swallowed hard at the sight of the beautiful woman beside him. The woman he'd just married. The woman who'd be starting a family with him. The woman who'd be spending the rest of her life with him.

And Mrs. Vandenberg's gift would always remind them that no matter how jumbled their lives became, they had Someone who'd help them reassemble the pieces. They just needed to keep their eyes on Him. Noah met his wife's eyes, and her expression, so filled with wonder and delight, started an ache deep inside him. He longed to reach out, enfold her in his arms, and hug her the way she'd hugged Mrs. Vandenberg.

Good thing his hands were full. It wouldn't do to express that yearning in public.

"*Ach*, Mrs. V, you couldn't have given us a more meaningful gift. Noah and I met when I crashed into him and spilled these puzzle pieces."

"I know, dear." Mrs. Vandenberg's knowing smile revealed she had inside information. And Noah had no doubt about the source.

"Banging into you"—Caroline smiled up at Noah—"must have been part of God's plan."

Back then, he never would have agreed, but now, he knew for sure and certain God's hand had been leading both of them. Overcome with tenderness, he smiled down at her. When their eyes met, the sparks flying between them heated his whole body. He barely heard Mrs. Vandenberg's goodbye.

Before she closed the car door, she said with a chuckle, "We pulled the Bentley next to these trees for a reason, Noah."

As her driver pulled away, Noah smiled. Leave it to Mrs. Vandenberg to ensure the perfect setup. Then he did what he'd been longing to do ever since he first met Caroline that day almost two years ago. He set the box on the ground, took his wife's hand, and led her into the privacy of the grove. Wrapping his arms around her, he drew her close and touched his lips to hers gently, reverently. As they shared their first tender kiss, Caroline's fervent response melted the prison bars that had long confined his heart, setting his spirit free. Free to love her. Now and forever.

Visit our website at
KensingtonBooks.com
to sign up for our newsletters, read
more from your favorite authors, see
books by series, view reading group
guides, and more!

BOOK | | CLUB
BETWEEN THE CHAPTERS

Become a Part of Our
Between the Chapters Book Club
Community and Join the Conversation

Betweenthechapters.net